D0893687

Other books by Janice Kulyk Keefer

The Paris-Napoli Express

White of the Lesser Angels

Transfigurations

*Under Eastern Eyes: A Critical Reading of
Canadian Maritime Fiction*

Constellations

Reading Mavis Gallant

Travelling Ladies

Rest Harrow

THE GREEN LIBRARY

THE GREEN LIBRARY

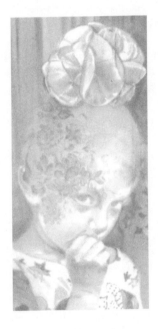

JANICE KULYK KEEFER

HarperCollins*PublishersLtd*

First Edition

Canadian Cataloguing in Publication Data

Keefer, Janice Kulyk, 1953-
The green library

ISBN 0-00-224370-9

I. Title.

PS8571.E435G74 1996   C813'.54   C95-933315-0
PR9199.3.K4115G74 1996

96 97 98 99 ❖ HC 10 9 8 7 6 5 4 3 2 1

Printed and bound in the United States

For Anna and Irene

Thanks to Ed Carson and Janet Turnbull Irving for their support and savvy; to Iris Tupholme, Becky Vogan and Marie Campbell for so attentively seeing this book through production; to Lydia Palij and Maryna Bondarenko for guiding me to and through Kiev; to Irene and Nigel Guilford for providing a perfect writer's retreat; to my parents, Joseph and Natalie Kulyk, for their generosity; to Irene Guilford, Anna Simon, Myrna Kostash, and Connie and Leon Rooke for their astute comments on various stages of this manuscript; to Natalka Husar for the haunting power of her images.

And, as always, to Michael.

A dignified funeral and a marked grave express our will to preserve the identity of a person. We erect a stone on which we carve a name and a few numbers, but in fact we are trying to maintain the shape of a former life, a single unrepeatable story. When compassion and the commandment that life should be lived in dignity have been lost, where awareness of the past is lost, there are no stories, there are only cries of horror.

Ivan Klima, "The Painter's Story," *My Golden Trades*

KIEV, NOVEMBER 1993

*Y*ou ask me to tell you what I know of her. I know that she loved one place above all others, here. The Green Library. She named it years ago, in a poem that's vanished like the place itself. A place like no other, even in this city of parks and gardens and long, long avenues of chestnut trees. On fine days, on warm, summer evenings when the light seemed to last almost forever, people would come to that enormous room built of leaves and grass, with no roof but the sky. Bringing the books they loved, the ones that held them fast between their hands and wouldn't let them go. Reading their own stories in the lives of others, stories rising like birds into "the green tongues of the trees."

The scraps I remember of her poems, that I know or guess about her life. Paper torn into pieces smaller than a fingernail, to be safe, to leave nothing behind that could harm the living. She died, and for a long time I thought all trace of her had vanished. But I have learned that the dead travel in our blood, crossing seas and years to show themselves in those they've never seen: in the shape of an eye, a way of touching a face.

I have often wondered who will hear what I have to tell, who *will make room to keep even the little I can remember. Sometimes I think it will all disappear when I die: thrown out with the trash, like this slow, sick body. But when I'm writing in the middle of the night; when the whole building fills with silence deep and sweet enough to drink, I think of that other scribe, almost a thousand years ago. Setting stories down in darkness, a candle spitting light at the page. And I think that if his stories survived, then these may, too, by chance, or fate, or whatever magic makes you write to me.*

A Chronicle of Bygone Years: famine, terror, war. And the rare, bright miracles: so pitiless in their power to make us hope, to make us go on pushing through our lives. So many stories; woven into hers. But how can I tell you what you need to know? And where does it all begin?

Kiev, November 1941

When everyone else has left the house, she slips out a side door, dodging the glass that hasn't yet been swept away. It makes a small, bright sea in the yard: she thinks of a woman's hair breaking against a pillow, after a night of love or fever. Only yesterday, she might have kept this image, laying it on some table of her mind along with other pieces of the world through which she walks. But already it's too late: she has no time to make poems anymore, no time, and no desire.

It's as much as she can manage to make her way to the Green Library. Where the street used to be, there is only rubble. Two weeks ago, the heart of the city exploded, fires pouring like blood from a thousand mouths. Burning down to this: a vast bruise through which people are slowly, painfully shovelling paths. She walks as quickly as she can, not having eaten since yesterday morning, and hiding, inside her sleeve, a roll of papers like a long, stiff evening glove cut off at the wrist. Turning past buildings that no longer stand: past the ghosts of statues and shop windows, until she reaches the Green Library.

One of this war's jokes, or miracles, that it remains—an island, a refuge that seems no larger than a handle broken from a cup. Now it's the one landmark left, the only one whose roots haven't been ripped from the earth. Welcoming her now, inviting her to wait all afternoon and well into the evening, if need be, for the man to whom she'll give these poems she's carried here in perfect safety. Poems she pulls from their hiding place and holds on her lap. Spreading her hands across them, as if to hide the words staring into the sun.

A leaf loosens from its stem and falls, skimming her face. She puts her hand to her cheek, expecting a scar to have signed its name there. As though she's woken in the middle of the night, as though she's stumbling through the dark rooms of an unfamiliar house, she tries to orient herself, remembering the way the story's turned. That it's the Nazis who own what's left of the city, now that the Bolsheviks have fled. Leaving behind just enough men to blow up the mines they planted months ago in the finest buildings all along the Khreshchatyk. Small packets of explosives stitched to the undersides of floorboards in all the luxury offices, apartment buildings, theatres. So that just when the Germans had finished moving in, they could be blown to pieces. Soldiers and shop girls: street sweepers, news vendors, children.

One of the poems she holds on her lap tries to call back the Circus Building at the moment its huge green dome was kicked away. To slow, even if she cannot stop, what happens. So that, for at least a moment, they stay clean and whole: the acrobats, the dancing horses, all the people laughing in the stalls. So that the dome opens gently, like the lid of a music box, and all those trapped inside it merely vanish. Bones and hair and blood, turned into the trace that a too-hot iron leaves on fine, white cloth.

These papers in her lap: if she can keep them safe until he

comes for them; if he can pass them on to the people waiting for them; if they can manage to find a press that still works; then perhaps her poems will come through this war. Poems that are nothing but the eyes of stories: poems, not the tracts they've ordered her to write. She wants to rouse no one but the dead, all those who have become her dead. They are the ones she speaks with, not these strangers, survivors: ghosts with bad blood, and too much of it. The Organization split, one wing hitting the other while the Germans catch each feather as it falls. Forty shot already. Whether her turn comes this day or the next, there will be the same ending: a gun shoved at the nape of her neck; blood punching into her mouth.

Smoothing the poems crushed in her lap, she tells herself he isn't late; so much of the city is rubble you can't help but lose your way. Even here, the air still tastes of smoke. Looking into the bronze canopy overhead, she's astonished to find leaves, not ashes, fastened to the boughs.

She's tired, so tired. All she wants is to be warm enough, for her stomach to be full enough, so that she can sleep. Sleep the way a stone does: without desire or fear. Without dreams.

The woman in her dreams has the smashed face of that girl she found weeks ago. The girl they chased through an abandoned building all the way up to the roof, from which she jumped to escape being caught. A young Jewish girl, lying just as she'd fallen on the pavement. No one had been allowed to cover the body. When she saw the girl lying there, she rushed home for the one treasure she had left, a woollen shawl. By the time she returned, the body had vanished. So she covered the place where the girl had lain, the mere blood-shape of her. In memory of that girl, she left her shawl and walked away. By the time she looked back, it, too, had disappeared.

So much blood pouring from this city: surely some of it will travel into a distance she can barely imagine, like a star that has never been named. Telling the story of this time, this place. And how, under the ashes and rubble, the earth is no longer black, but red.

Far too late in the year to be sitting alone, all afternoon, in a city park. To warm herself, she sets herself a task, like a child at school: remembering all the different beds she's slept in over her forty-three years.

The cot in the house where she was born. And then, after her parents' deaths, her grandmother's bed: a nest of quilts on the ledge of the clay oven, its fragrance of new bread baked into her dreams. For her four years at the *gymnasium* in town, a pull-out bed in the kitchen of the dressmaker's house. And those first years in Kiev, at the Academy: a cupboard bed in a doll-sized room with a doll-sized heater. Over the French cakeshop on the Khreshchatyk.

The divan in her lover's studio, the jumble of rugs and scarves that screened their joy from all the shadows leaking through the shutters. The army cot on which her son was born, in the dacha at Soloveyko. Weather so cold she'd joked about waking with ice in her mouth. Yet up till the start of her labour she had slept, not on the cot but on an eiderdown before the hearth. Staring into the embers' eyes as snow fell and fell, and she dreamt of summer.

Summers they shared there, she and her lover, in an old-fashioned bed they'd been given. Plain, solid, ugly—but he'd taken his brush to the headboard and footboard, splashing them with pictures. Birches thin as an eyelash; a horse and rider galloping across the sun. How had his heart ever been clear and light enough for such embroidery? Making their sleep an enchantment, a singing round and round of stories. Keeping safe their one desire: to be alone together, all night long.

For a moment, she thinks she hears footsteps: her heart jumps up inside her, beating thick, cramped wings. But it's nothing more than a branch half fallen from a tree, scraping against the trunk.

She tightens her grip on the papers in her lap; permits herself to close her eyes again.

Sleep winding its veil around her: slow, voluptuous. Once she spent a whole autumn afternoon strolling under the chestnut trees on the Khreshchatyk. Holding her baby in her arms, showing him all the shop windows: flowers and cakes, embroidered shawls, puppets, wooden trains.

She might have been walking up and down some street in heaven, holding him safe, warm, small in her arms.

Her head sinking, baring the nape of her neck so it gleams, a new moon, under the knot of her hair. And then her head jerks back. She's heard him now, the man walking down the path, his feet making the noise of a branch, half fallen, scraping the bark of a tree. Slowing his steps, pausing a few feet away from her, stopping altogether.

She keeps her eyes shut, as if the light's so harsh it will scald them. Across from her, so near she could stretch out her arms and touch him, is the man she didn't know she was waiting for, the one she'd given up for lost. Coming to her—rash, helpless, like a lover.

No lover. Not flowers, but a gun, half hidden by the cap he carries in his hands.

II

Toronto, June 1993

Eva stares up at the sky through a maze of branches, thinking it's going to rain, that she ought to round up the kids and head home. Cold rain this early in the summer: the chestnuts are still holding up their stagey candelabras. Remember how Ben, aged two, kept putting the fallen blossoms in his mouth, thinking they were candies, fascinated by the threads of blood sewn through their lips? Ben, just turned eleven, would hate to be reminded of this: Ben, all skinny arms and legs and that fierce look on his face you'd mistake for a frown, if you didn't know him better.

Just the three of them today in this forgotten corner of the park. No flowers, no pond or ducks or apologetic zoo—just a stretch of ragged grass, and enormous trees all linking arms. Eva usually shares this bench with one of the bag ladies who've staked out different pockets of the park. Sharing the bench and whatever food she's brought along with Genevieve, who eats fiercely yet with great discretion, pulling the crusts off her sandwiches; picking out the raisins, which she detests, from the oatmeal cookies Eva offers her. But Genevieve must have found some better company today—perhaps an old schoolmate or a long-lost lover. Eva would like to invent a romance or at least a happy ending for Genevieve. She prefers her own stories to those she finds in books urged on her by friends who are afraid that, given her line of work, she might be regressing. Hence the library book Rache urged her to check out, lying unread in her lap as she peers through the leaves, listening for thunder.

What erupts instead is silence, erasure of all ordinary and expected sounds: birds, traffic, the children's shrieks as they swing upside down from an enormous willow. Silence and a dizziness that rocks between her ears and down her spine, so that if she were ordered to stand up, to save her life she couldn't. How long the silence lasts she can't tell; it's as though she loses consciousness of everything outside herself as vertigo squeezes her, inch by inch. Then suddenly, the world inside her skin comes rushing into her ears and eyes: cells crumpling or bubbling over, the heavy ticking of blood, hairs pricking her skin like small steel pins.

For the past ten years, Eva's worked at a day-care centre: she can tell the difference between shouts of distress and delight from fifty feet away, and with her eyes shut. Taking precautions has become second nature to her—she cannot sit at a table, for example, without pushing to the centre all glasses or cups that seem too close to the edge, a habit that exasperates anyone who asks her over for a meal. She can tell when a small child's started to spike a fever out of the blue, and when he's merely feverish with excitement. But she has no defence at all against what's happening this moment, happening to her, not to Ben or Julie. This is what overwhelms her, so she can't move or speak or shout for help: she's being struck and singled out; shaken to the roots of her hair.

A panic attack, Dan would say. Or maybe something more concrete: the effect of anemia, hypoglycemia—something to be checked out by a doctor, at any rate. But what would she say, how could she possibly explain to anyone what's been happening to her over the last few days? Not the symptoms, but the cause: that she's being watched. That hidden somewhere just outside her range of vision is a stranger, staring and staring at her, till she feels his eyes cutting along the edges of her body, cutting her out from everything and everyone she knows.

The sky is purpling the way it does before an electrical storm, and a strong wind pushes at the leaves, disclosing their rough, white undersides. Ben, hanging upside down from a willow branch, catches sight of someone sagging against the bench where his mother was sitting: a woman with a vacant face. He pokes Julie, who is hanging beside him, dangling her arms. They clamber down from the tree and roll over the grass in Eva's direction, shouting her name. By the time they reach her, she wears her own face again: it was just, Ben decides, the effect of seeing her upside down that made her look so different. But while she's gathering up the apples and cake she'd brought for their snack, her hair and thin shirt slashed by the rain, Eva's heart keeps bouncing, like an acrobat fallen fifty stories into a safety net.

And doesn't stop, even after they've reached her front porch. For as she opens the door, she finds a signal from the person who's been watching her. A sign that she isn't just imagining things. Whether this makes her feel worse or better, she can't yet tell: for the moment it's just lying there in the dust of her hallway floor, a bare white envelope which might as well have her name or "Open Me" engraved upon it. Eva picks up the envelope before it gets trampled, stashing it away in her library book. Then the calm, professional, competent side of her takes over, making sure the kids have changed out of their soaking clothes before she goes to the kitchen phone. Running her hand through her drenched hair as she listens to the message on the answering machine. Assuring her in six languages that her call is important and will be returned as soon as the office reopens tomorrow.

Dan's already two blocks away from Janus Travel when the phone begins to ring. It's rare for him to close the office early, but Alok's desperate to get back to his wife, who's a week overdue with their first child, and Vesna's definitely coming down with 'flu. Besides, after dealing with his last customer, he was ready to hang up a shingle that would read not merely CLOSED, PLEASE CALL AGAIN but GONE FOR GOOD.

He wants to do something to bring himself back to his own, soothing, illusory world, as opposed to the fists of the real one, and so he looks for something he can buy to take home to Eva. Not flowers—she is the one woman Dan knows who will not have cut flowers in the house. She claims she's got an allergy, but he suspects it's the sight of them dying inch by inch that she can't handle. Or, more likely, it's because her mother adores them, lives in a perpetual greenhouse that Eva's sworn off them forever. So he settles for a pound of lichees (most of which, he knows, will be left to shrivel in a corner of the fridge) and a catnip toy for poor, ancient Sugar, which might at least amuse the kids.

Yet he's reluctant, after he's bought his gifts, to take them home. It's only a little past five: he stops at one of the cafés in Bloor West Village, wishing it hadn't rained quite so heavily, so he could sit outside and pretend he's in Prague, if not Paris. Instead, he finds a table tucked inside a bay window; orders a glass of wine. Of course, it's Bulgarian. It would have to be from Bulgaria, he informs the waitress, who smiles as if he's putting a new spin on the oldest joke in the world. When she leaves, he lights one of the cigarettes that he's promised Eva he's sworn off forever, and traces zigzag patterns on the table with his finger.

No one but himself to blame for starting up this business in the first place. His particular business: a travel agency specializing in trips back to the Old Country for what used to be called New Canadians. He named it after the Roman god of thresholds and doorways, convinced that Janus, with his two faces looking in opposite directions, was a far better logo for his multicultural clients than St. Christopher. All of them split like the god's face between the place they'd had to leave and the one they'd gambled everything to find. None of them seems to know or care about the symbolism, however, assuming that Janis is the name of his wife and that he's simply misspelled it on the sign over the door.

His last customer of the day should have known better. Amy Ross, born and bred in Kenora, fresh out of university and head over heels in love with a young man who, in addition to being intelligent, handsome, and resourceful, had defected with the rest of the Bulgarian swim team at Gander some twelve months ago. So resourceful he'd refused to twiddle his thumbs in a Newfoundland motel for the year it would take his refugee claim to be processed. He'd hitchhiked to Toronto, where he'd met Amy, got work teaching swimming at the Y, been accepted into a master's program in physiotherapy, been declared an illegal immigrant and deported back to Bulgaria. And all, as Amy pointed out, tears running down her pale, wide face, tears she'd shoved out of the way with the heels of her hands, all because he wanted to work. They'd planned to get married when she got her teaching certificate, a few years down the road; he'd refused to rush her into a wedding just so he could stay in Canada. So they'd shipped him back to Bulgaria, and neither she nor his family there had heard a word from him since. What, she wanted to know, could the authorities do to a returned defector, and was there any such thing as a cheap flight to Sofia?

He didn't tell her about all the other cases he'd come across in his line of work: the Jamaican nannies who couldn't get permission to bring their own children into the country, even on a tourist visa, and who spent most of their wages on getting back home each year. Or the Chinese students whose requests for asylum were increasingly denied, and who came to him to arrange for their eventual imprisonment or banishment to remote places among suspicious strangers. He simply listened to her story, watching her push the tears from her face, and called up all available fares on the computer screen. Before she left, he gave her the name of an immigrants' aid organization he worked for part-time, people who might be able to help her.

What he's thinking of now, as he drinks a second glass of Bulgarian wine, is not the criminal stupidity and short-sightedness of his country's immigration policy, but the way that woman had sat in his office, weeping without shame, weeping out of rage and love. Recalling, after years and years of forgetting, the way he'd wept when Nella lay dying: tears rolling down his face as he gave Julie her bottle and watched the tubes pumping in whatever nourishment his wife's body could still receive. And it occurs to him that in all the years they've lived together, he has never known Eva to weep, a fact that should astonish him more than it does. Either she feels no grief strong enough to show, or else she weeps, as his mother would say, on the inside. Where no one can see what's going on, not even Eva herself. Or perhaps she's so busy drying everyone else's tears she has none left over for herself.

What had Rache been saying at the party last week— something about Eva being the most sympathetic—no, the most selfless person she knows. Think of how she's carried them, one way or another, Rache had said: all through Nella's illness, and then his own grief and Julie's bewilderment that first year after Nella died. Or the family of that boy at day-care, the one who was killed five years ago in a hit-and-run; Eva still kept in touch with them. Not to mention herself, Rache—the whole grand theatre of her divorce. Mother-Teresa-of-the-Big-and-Little-Sorrows, that's what Rache had called her, cornering him on the stairs outside the bathroom; confessing, with a wicked glint in her eyes, that goodness like Eva's always made her teeth ache. And that, to be perfectly frank, she would find such goodness a little less hard to take if Eva didn't happen to look so much like a punk Botticelli who'd spent her whole life at the beach. Though it was perfectly shitty of her to say so, as he was free, not to say obliged, to point out. And before he could say a word, she'd kissed him, her tongue darting sweet and salty into his mouth, then run back to the kitchen for another glass of wine.

He isn't going to waste time thinking about Rache and her bitter mischief: he ought to be getting home. They are supposed to be going out to a film tonight, or getting in a video, he can't remember which. He doesn't feel like watching anything—he's too caught up in that young woman's tears, the probable outcome of her story. He will tell Eva about it—and Eva will understand. Which is the last thing he happens to need or want right now. She is, he decides, the least political person he knows: that goes hand in hand with the goodness, the selflessness Rache had been jabbing at. Anger, that's what's needed: anger and action, not comfort. What Eva wants to do is turn the whole fucked-up world into a child of two: hold it on her lap, tell it a story. Eva, who never cries, never swears—the best person in the world.

While he's waiting for his change, a plump, red-haired girl in black leggings comes by with a basket of flowers. Something—her brashness, the flicker in her eyes—makes him buy half a dozen roses, meaty-red and prisoned in cellophane. He leaves them along with a tip for the waitress who brought him his wine. And manages to forget the bag of lichees, though the catnip toy makes it safely home.

The kids know, even as they're being sent upstairs to change out of their drenched clothes, that something unusual is happening, that the world they've always taken for granted is starting to shift and tilt. Years later, when they happen to be in the same city and meet up for dinner or a drink at the airport, they will find themselves going back to the year of the Housequake, as Julie will call it. It's something they'll only be able to speak of when they are physically together, side by side, as they were that afternoon, swinging from the branch of a willow tree in an obscure corner of High Park. Julie will talk of how they'd had no warning of what was coming, Ben never having told her of that glimpse he'd had of Eva. How her face had been stolen by a stranger: how, for the first time, he had seen her not as a mother, but as a woman he'd never really know. But so much would happen that year—so many strangers' faces thrusting themselves into his eyes—that this first instance will always seem less important to him than it really was. Or will stay something he needs to keep to himself, no matter how long he's known Julie, how close they were as kids.

On one occasion, when they'll have turned the same age as Eva and Dan were that year of the Housequake, Julie will argue that things worked out for the best—especially for Eva's sake.

Though she'll admit it was difficult—painful, that's the word she uses—for them all. Julie has become a medical engineer; she designs appliances and prostheses for paraplegics, amputees, stroke victims. Pain, Ben will often reflect, is for her far less of an issue than are inconvenience, impossibility. Perhaps it's because of her mother dying when she was still so young—perhaps that inoculated her against the pain of any further loss.

Inoculated, anesthetized. He hasn't been so lucky. There have been so many absences, so many losses in his life that up till now it's been impossible for him to love anyone, even stay in one place with the same person for any length of time. When, for example, was the last time he saw Eva? Though he does send her letters from wherever he's passing through: not letters, but drawings, with some kind of scribble attached, just to reassure her he's still alive, functioning. Unlike Julie, he has no profession to speak of. Instead, he has a rash of stamps and visas in his passport; he does odd jobs until he makes enough money to settle somewhere and paint for six months, and then he's off again.

For the best, Julie will continue, because otherwise Eva would have died inside. Was dying—becoming nothing but a rattle with a pea-sized heart. Everybody thought she was so wonderful, so generous, so loving because of all the noise it made, that heart—but that was only because she'd grown so empty. She had no self—does he see that? No self, no life of her own, till that year when everything fell apart. Does he remember the fights she and Eva had started to have round that time? Over whether she could get her ears pierced, wear make-up, dye her hair blue. "It was so stupid—and I felt so guilty afterwards, I thought it was all my fault that everything happened. And the funny thing is that as soon as I didn't have Eva to fight with anymore, I didn't want any of those things; I went into my scrubbed-skin mode, just so I could give my stepmother a hard time. God, I was awful, wasn't I? And as for Dad—"

Ben will make no answer, only drink his beer and sketch on the menu: a chestnut tree, a warrior in a feathered turban, a church with onion domes. After a little while, Julie will reach out to him; stroke his cheek with the outside of her fingers, trying to smooth out the frown he doesn't know he wears. The way she used to do when they were children, and she wanted both to comfort and to interrupt him. They will look at each other across their empty mugs of beer, across the shouting in German or Dutch or Czech, and smile, just as if they were children, speaking a silent language their parents will never pick up.

Hours after Dan has polished off the macaroni cheese congealing in the casserole dish—his punishment for getting home so late—and the kids have been read to sleep, Eva and Dan make time to talk. About Amy Ross and her deported Bulgarian lover, about the letters Dan will be writing to the minister for immigration and to various journalists who may or may not squeeze a column out of this particular story. Or at least, Dan's talked, and Eva's listened, which she's appeared to do with her customary sympathy. Appearances, however, are not what they seem. For instead of talking in the living room, with its familial chaos of discarded shoes and dog-eared magazines, scattered homework assignments and computer games, they've gone upstairs to the half-finished attic Eva calls her study, the one part of the house which is hers alone.

Though it's all hers, legally, this large, dark house on one of the shabby streets off Parkside Drive. She bought it with her inheritance the year her father died, the inheritance that lets her work for next to nothing at the day-care. The study runs the length of the house, and is austere: apart from dozens of Ben's drawings tacked onto the walls, the only furnishings are an old-fashioned rolltop desk, an equally old-fashioned gooseneck lamp, and two bean bag chairs. They are sitting in them now, these battered remnants of Eva's hippie days in Nova Scotia, that life she's told Dan almost nothing about. Except that they'd tried raising sheep, and then cabbages, and had ended up back in Toronto with the bean bag chairs, a baby, and, shortly after, a divorce.

Dan has finished what he has to say. He looks tired and cross, exactly, Eva notes, the way kids do when they've resisted their morning nap and are trying to make it through till lunch without collapsing. An observation which makes her more, not less, concerned for him: she has always found children to be far more important, far more illuminating in their ways than adults. Yet tonight she has no time for Dan's exhaustion, his anger. Instead of saying something consoling, she holds out her glass for the nightcap of Scotch she's requested. It's a drink she usually reserves for winter, the only medicine she ever resorts to, as Dan reminds her.

"What's up, Eva? Special occasion, or are you coming down with something?"

Are they signs of 'flu or fever, the spell she had at the park today; the summons that sailed into her house? Here she is, pressing the glass against her lips till she nearly bites through, and all because she needs to speak out, to ask for help—a need she's never permitted herself before. How can she begin to talk about what's happening? Hasn't it always been better, safer to be the keeper of other people's secrets, never to give herself away?

"Cheers," Dan says, and Eva shivers, watching him drink, knowing that she has to make up her mind whether to confess. To say anything out loud is to make it real, public: hers, and yet no longer her own. And this is what's shaken her. Suddenly, she's become the centre of someone's attention, she who has spent her whole life trying to pass unnoticed.

Dan is cursed with a perpetually genial face, one that's condemned him to donning the Santa suit at office parties every Christmas. Even when he's feeling most anxious, most shut out, as he is right now by Eva's silence, he sits there beaming at her. Their chairs are so close together he could reach out his hand and touch her if he wanted to. He can't remember how long it's been since they last made love, or even lay in bed, holding each other. Or quarrelled: raging, throwing things, veering crazily between shouts and kisses. They've lived together for nine years, their children are closer than brother and sister, he has turned to her endlessly and she has given him, endlessly, everything but what he most wants, most needs. Not sympathy or tenderness—that erotic equivalent of comfort food. Not goodness, or even absolute fidelity. What he wants is something risky, unpredictable. Rache's tongue, sweet and salty, darting into his mouth, leaving him dumbfounded on the stairs, clutching half a dozen roses.

And now he has to stumble into speech, just to keep himself from falling.

"Earth to Eva. You sleeping with your eyes open again?"

For answer, she gets to her feet and goes over to the rolltop desk that belonged to her father, the one thing of his she'd claimed when the Kingsway house was sold. From a fat library book inside the desk she pulls out an envelope: white, blank, so small he expects it to contain an invitation to a child's birthday party.

Eva crouches down beside him, so close he can smell the warmth of her skin. "This came for me today."

Something about her choice of words disconcerts him. "Came from whom?"

"I don't know. Go on, open it."

Her voice is suddenly thin, jagged. Dan braces himself for what he's about to find: an obscene message, a razor blade, a flattened piece of excrement? But what he pulls from the envelope is nothing more alarming than a photograph. A photograph of a boy, straining in the embrace of a woman who looks to be about Eva's age. A boy who could be Ben, wearing the same puzzled frown on his face, though the woman looks nothing like Eva. Something about her seems familiar; he can't place it, but it bothers him, like an eyelash he's trying to blink away. Eva's watching him as if she expects him to react in some predetermined way; to reassure her about something.

"So?" Dan says. It's the safest kind of response: another question.

"So," Eva answers. "Look again."

He does. It's an old photo, but a good one: quality camera, quality paper. Taken by someone who knew what he was doing. Taken in some foreign place, as well—he can't say where, he just knows it's not Canada, or the States, for that matter. Not because of the backdrop, the landscape, for the photo has none. In fact, the picture is a section of a larger one, gesturing only gradually to what's been cut away. For what first appeared to be bows or roses on the woman's shoulders are really a pair of hands, the hands of a man who's been cut away from the photograph. Dan turns the picture over, but there's nothing stamped or written on the back.

"This is all there was in the envelope?"

"Yes."

"And it came in the morning mail?"

Eva shakes her head. "I found it when we got back from the park this afternoon. It was delivered by hand. By someone who knows where I live. Someone I've never met."

He doesn't know how to say what he's thinking, as he gives the photo back to Eva. That she's exaggerating again—making things up: making stories from what's really only happenstance. Look at her, sinking back into her chair, cradling the photo in her hand as if the figures in it were alive and not mere images. Her voice has lost the rawness of alarm: she speaks now as if she were rocking herself to sleep:

"It has to be from the thirties. Look at the dress she's wearing, and the hair. Long, smoothed over her ears—not a twenties bob. And his sailor top—when did boys stop wearing sailor suits? I wish whoever it was hadn't cut the rest of the picture away. It's summer, of course; do you see how transparent those sleeves are? I like the way she looks. Except for her eyes—do you see how sad her eyes are? He hates being held, you can see that from the way he's pulling away from her. Look how tightly she's holding him, as if she's afraid he's going to run off, do something dangerous like walk across a trestle bridge or play chicken on the railway tracks. She's afraid she's going to lose him, afraid he won't come back to her."

Dan leans across the space between them, needing to touch her, to pull her back. She's flying farther and farther away, like a moon cut loose from its planet. He thinks he's reaching for her face but his hand homes to her breasts instead, the place where her heart should be. She lets it rest there for a moment, as if it were part of some medicinal gesture. Under the tired cotton of her shirt he feels, not the thump of her heart, but an absence, like wire mesh thrown over a hole. He pulls his hand back, rubs his forehead.

"Eva," he says. "Just because someone gives you—hand-delivers—a perfectly innocent photograph—"

"A photograph of my son."

"There's nothing on the envelope, is there? How can you be sure whoever it was didn't get the wrong house, the wrong person? Okay, the boy in the picture looks a bit like Ben."

"Exactly like Ben."

"It's a fluke, a coincidence. It happens all the time. Someone stops you on the street, out of the blue, a total stranger. You know the kind of thing. 'Excuse me, but you look exactly like a friend of mine I haven't seen since high school.' It doesn't mean anything."

She puts the photograph back into its envelope. She can't tell him that it hasn't come out of the blue: that whoever sent it has been watching her, shadowing her. This photograph is proof, black and white. As anonymous, as insistent as any shadow.

"It's not a coincidence. It wasn't dropped on the street, it was sent to me. By someone who needs to ask me something. It's not an accident; it's a message, and I've got to give some kind of answer. But I don't know how to read it, I don't know what to say. I thought you could help me."

Something snaps in him as she says this. The snap of the lid when you open a vacuum-sealed jar. He knows it isn't help she wants, but a witness. She doesn't want his help, and she doesn't want this love he's been carrying around all these years like packages he keeps dropping and picking up and dropping again. She will never weep for him the way that girl in his office wept for her lover. Stupid, stupid to go on like this but he can't help himself, and he can't help her. A phrase from one of Julie's storybooks leaps into his head, the generic description of all heroines: as good as she was beautiful. And she is beautiful, Eva, even though she works so hard to disguise it. Hacking off her hair, dressing in baggy jeans and washed-out sweatshirts that have all the allure of bandages. Doing nothing to disguise the print of forty-three years across her skin, and somehow all the more beautiful for it. Beautiful, and good, and unreachable. It finally came home to him as he put out his hand and felt the hole where her heart should be. And whether it's the shock of admitting the truth to himself, or the need to hit back, he lights on the one thing that has the power to turn that small square of paper into a letter bomb.

"You want to find out about that photograph, that boy who looks so much like Ben? Go ask your mother to help you. Try asking Holly."

When he says her mother's name, there's a twist in his voice Eva can never iron out. He's gone with her to see Holly—has gone for her, when Eva's had 'flu or Ben's been sick and she's had to miss her weekly visit. But that's only made it worse, this rift between them that nothing can mend. The fact that Bluma Yashinsky still scrubs the floors of her poky, third-floor apartment in Ste. Marie de Grâce, while Holly Chown watches her fingernails grow in the most exclusive nursing home in Toronto. That Mrs. Yashinsky's son grew up a working-class Jew and Mrs. Chown's daughter, a WASP princess from rich man's row.

"Listen, Eva, if it isn't coincidence, accident, whatever name any reasonable person would call it—then it has to be what's called family resemblance. Is that what you want to find out? That the kid in that photo looks so much like Ben because he's Ben's—what? Great-uncle? Or let's just play with this one—his grandfather? Which would make Holly's situation—never mind your own—just a little dicey, wouldn't you say?"

"What do you mean, situation? What has this got to do with my mother?" She's looking at him now with such misery, such fear in her eyes that he's suddenly ashamed of this idea he's come up with, a plot no more likely than Eva's account of the photograph.

"It makes no sense, what you're saying, Dan. You don't know my mother. The last thing she would ever—"

"Eva, love, the last thing in the world you can say for sure is what your mother's really like. Think about it for a moment. What does Ben know about you? About the deep-down-inside Eva, the one who folds herself up smaller than a postage stamp, so nobody can find her? What does Ben know of what you dream about at night? What do I know?"

Eva shakes her head, so slowly the movement's almost

imperceptible. She does what a child might, turns her face away; burying it in her hands. *Nobody-can-see-me.* Her hair sticking up in licks of pale flame around her: sharp, delicate as glass.

"Look, Eva, I'm lousy at telling stories, that's your strong suit, right? Forget what I said—why not forget the whole thing? Tear up the photo, flush it down the toilet. Come on, love: drop it for now. Let's go to bed."

Eva says nothing. Now it's Dan's turn to hide his face and disappear.

The attic walls slope, making a tent over her head, a tent inscribed with all the crayon scribbles, fingerpaintings, sketches Ben has done over the years. They've become more and more sophisticated, as to colour and line, but Eva loves the earliest ones best, the lop-sided, big-bellied stick people, the orange grass and green suns that shine like upside-down campfires.

She sits in the bean bag chair, shutting her eyes tight. The way people with vertigo do when forced to the edge of anything higher than ground level. A floor below her, she can hear Dan kicking off his shoes, getting into bed; when that noise shuts off she can hear, if she holds her breath, the children dreaming. She should be asleep with them all; if she wanted to, she could get up, make her way down the stairs, slide into the bed that Dan will have warmed with his thick, sturdy body. But she doesn't know anymore what she wants, or what she should do. Because of what's been given her, thrown her way out of malice or kindness or brute curiosity.

This idea Dan's invented about her mother and some stranger—it just isn't possible. Even if she wanted it to be true, it couldn't be. For what Eva's always known about Holly, even before she had words for it, has been the thin hardness of her mother's body; the way love and desire have always been sealed up in her, or shut out. So that her beauty's all the more incongruous, like a deaf person having an extraordinary singing voice. Opening her eyes, staring into the wild skies made by Ben's drawings, Eva tries to shut out the possibilities hammering at her head. She thinks, instead, of being at work, sitting crosslegged as she is now but holding a three-year-old on her lap and telling six others a story about a fox who runs away to sea.

She's in her element telling stories, making up adventures that have nothing to do with the laws of probability. What she loves are the risky, mazy roots of the unexpected, for she makes up her plots as she goes along, and there's no telling what landscapes her characters will travel through, and whom they'll meet. She knows that uncanny, inexplicable events, night-blooming crises are the very stuff of story-making. And she welcomes the kids' demands for a skateboard, a talking fly, an ice cream van to leap inside the story she's telling; without them, how could she weave that serendipity which is the closest she can come to doing magic?

She's holding that three-year-old snug in her lap, as she'd held Ben before he outgrew the need for laps and storytelling. And she lets herself grieve, just for a moment, for the children she never brought to birth. Each year of her marriage marked by a miscarriage: small, blood x's through the calendar. And just when she'd given up hoping, there was Ben. She hadn't let herself feel anything, right up to the moment when she pushed him out alive into the air. And then it was as if she held her own heart in her arms, red and fierce and astonishing. All the waiting and waiting to see if her son had inherited the illness from which her brother had died, the small brother she'd never found a trace of—no gravestone, not even a photograph, only the vacancy of her mother's eyes and heart. If she could have had another child, if she hadn't been so watchful, so possessive of Ben, who knows? Things might have worked out between her and Jimmy. The way they'd worked out with Dan? Or with her own parents?

She thinks of her mother in a nursing home that might be eight galaxies, not subway stops, away. She thinks of her father, who died in his sleep a dozen years ago, never having been able to make a last trip up north to find that phantom gold mine he'd told her stories about all through her childhood. An image of the three of them insists itself on her eyes: a half-grown Eva struggling to free herself from Holly; Garth holding tight to Holly's shoulders, while a pair of scissors cuts him away. Leaving a space for another man to step in, to take his place. A man who never materializes, who remains an absence, a transparent shadow.

Suddenly, the dizziness she felt in the park that afternoon sets in again, her blood rushing up through her ears. Tinged this time with nausea—as if the floor were tilting, and she can't stop sliding to the edge of the room where the walls should be, but where there's only air. This time she fights it back, pulling herself up, shutting out the light, pushing herself downstairs. There is nobody watching her: she will be her old self again, the self she fashioned so long ago. One by one, she enters the rooms where they lie dreaming: Ben, Julie, Dan. Shuts off the small, angry light of Ben's CD player; moves the cat from Julie's pillow to the foot of the bed; pulls up the covers that Dan's shrugged off. It helps her, it's her only help, to perform small services like these, especially when no one can witness them; when she becomes as good as invisible.

There was a time in Eva's life when she decided that the only way she could survive was by making herself as inconspicuous as possible. Self-less, the way she conceived God to be. When she thought of God, she pictured an enormous, unblinking eye, larger than the earth itself, and able to take in everything, everyone on the planet. At school, a girl she knew, a tall, athletic, Catholic girl, told her of a secret order of nuns who spent their whole lives asking God to forgive the sins committed every second of every hour of every night and day. The nuns would pray and sleep in shifts, for if the praying stopped for even a moment, the world would instantly be drowned in fire.

She's forgotten the time when she believed she'd committed an unpardonable sin. Forgotten the secret order of nuns who kept God's eye from burning up the world. But she's kept on trying to make herself as small, as hidden as she can. Telling stories to children; listening to the story of everyone else's life, while her own falls farther into silence.

To calm herself on the way to the nursing home; to try to hold things in some recognizable perspective, Eva tells herself a story. The story of her mother's life, as far as she's been able to construct it, from scraps of evidence no one had thought to tidy up; from disclosures that came by chance or design from her father, who'd had to explain to her so many times why Holly was the way she was—not odd, not peculiar, but different. And from guesses, hunches, leaps of imagining that sprang not from fantasy but from the need to excuse, forgive.

The story begins with a young woman, just a girl, really, from a family that had once had money, and lost all but the taste for it. And, of course, enough of the trappings to show any young man who came to the house that its daughters knew which fork to use with salad, which with fish. The young man in question was from a family that not only knew which fork to use with any course of the most elaborate meal, but made those forks; or, at least, owned the company that turned out silver forks and photograph frames and teapots by the thousands. True, he was a younger son, but he made up for it by having an unusually auspicious occupation. He was a mining engineer: specifically, gold mines, although his real passion was for substances far more precious than gold. Spessartite, transparent crystals of staurolite, yellow corundum—a whole inanimate menagerie he dreamed of putting in glass cases, in that manor house in the wilderness he would own one day.

But the girl's family only knew about the gold mines, and the girl only thought about the wilderness that went with them. Bush and rocks and rivers: no people to be wooed or snubbed, no high-ceilinged house you could never afford to heat, but a tent on an island in a wide, deep lake. And a husband, of course. A husband off digging somewhere under the ground, leaving you free as the gulls wheeling over the lake.

For her bridegroom was no ogre, no bluebeard, not even a gallant rescuer. He had no clue as to what he was rescuing her from.

He was fond of her family: her parents so lovable, really, in their fecklessness; her pretty older sister, whom he ought to have married instead of the younger one he found so outrageously beautiful, who held her beauty so cheap that she barely knew what a mirror was, and held her dresses together with safety pins. She married her gold miner two weeks after he proposed, and then he went back to the war, leaving her in her old house, with a new name, and a promise to take her away up north, forever.

By the time her son was born, the war had ended. Her husband returned, taking her to a wilderness that was no good to her now, burdened as she was with the baby she loved but could not keep. Her longing to live in a tent, a sail of canvas under the stars, turning into the pain of nursing a baby who was always sick; who'd inherited from his father's side a gene which turned the air he breathed, the clean, bracing northern air, into a thick yellow soup. He lived for two years, and she lived in a pokey bungalow close to the hospital; she lived most of the time in the hospital, and then her son died, and it didn't much matter where she lived. For something had died in her then: joy, the ability to give and enjoy love; she had let them die rather than ever suffer the loss of them again. So that when her daughter was born, she had nothing to give her but the thin, bluish milk from her breasts, on which, perversely, the baby thrived. The child for whose sake they'd moved back to the city, away from all the flags of pain and defeat they'd planted in the bush.

Leaving the jammed subway car, Eva walks the few short blocks to the nursing home, her arms burdened with Holly's favourite flower. She's coming to ask a favour of her mother—if she's in any mood today to grant favours. Eva's request is as impossible as the commands in fairy tales for a mountain of barley and millet to be sorted overnight: for strawberries to be gathered in a field of snow. And yet she has no choice but to make it.

She comes to her mother with her arms full of white and golden bribes. It had been a rule with Holly, almost the only rule, that her house should be full of flowers. In winter, from the most inventive, and thus expensive, florists; in summer, yanked up from the ravine at the back of the house; crammed in crystal vases and jam jars and lavished over every table, mantelpiece, and window sill. They're not something Eva can easily afford, these flowers, but they cost far less than the gifts she used to bring: Ben's drawings. She gave up giving them long ago, when it became impossible to pretend that her mother might somehow notice them. Dead flowers you throw out without a second thought; a child's drawings are another thing.

Holly is crouched by the huge picture window, holding out her hand to a squirrel tensed behind the glass. She doesn't turn to greet her daughter, but hisses, "Go away. You'll frighten him." The squirrel takes no notice of Eva: he stares at Holly's hand, then drops down again to dig up the last of the tulip bulbs.

Eva's learned, over the past few years, never to expect anything like consistency from her mother. Each time she visits, she has to improvise, sometimes resisting, sometimes cajoling or placating. Weeks go by when Holly won't talk to anyone: at other times, she talks unstoppably to herself or to some imaginary companion, no one can tell which. The fact that the doctor's been unable to give more than the vaguest name to Holly's illness is immaterial to Eva: the symptoms from which Holly suffers— memory loss, irrational acts, extreme mood swings—would be no easier to bear for being catalogued. In some ways, Holly's present condition seems nothing more than a freer, purer form of the behaviour Eva's always expected from her. Sometimes Eva thinks it's a game Holly's playing with them all, a sly and stubborn game whose rules she's always changing. She pretends not to know what she's doing: it's the way she used to get through hearts and canasta and all games of strategy rather than luck. Pretending to be flummoxed, without an inkling of which card to play, and causing endless anxiety in her opponents.

Today is a good day: by the time Eva's found a vase for the freesias and shrugged off her knapsack, Holly's ready to leave the window. She holds out her arms to the honey-apricot scent, following Eva to a dressing table with a small cheval glass. When Eva sets the vase on the table, Holly sits down, too, waiting with her eyes closed for her daughter to attend to her.

When she was a child, and her mother was in one of her rare, blithe moods, Eva would be allowed into her dressing room. She would be allowed to finger the necklaces and rings sleeping in their red leather box from Florence, or to twist a cashmere shawl about her shoulders. But what she loved best was to take the silver-backed brush from the dressing table to her mother's long, thick hair. Eva would angle the mirror so that it caught both their reflections: she would brush and brush, while Holly shut her eyes and hummed some tune to herself, and it was as if everything else in the world had vanished, leaving them stranded together on this small, silver island. Sometimes Eva would twist her mother's hair round her head like a halo that would escape if it weren't pinned tight. It was the weight and softness and colour she'd loved—ash blonde, and streaked with gold in summer. All the other mothers Eva knew then had short hair: perky, easy-care. Neither of which Holly was, or ever cared to be.

"There aren't nearly enough supplies. You're going to have to go into town to get another sack of flour. And a can of lard. Don't forget."

"I won't. I'll go as soon as I can." Eva answers softly, without the least hesitation. She has had this conversation with her mother more times than she can remember.

"Flour. Lard. Coffee. Syrup." One word for each stroke of the brush through the hair that's white now, but long and loose, down past her shoulders. It makes Holly look foreign: not from a different country, but from some place where time's all confused. She wears her hair the way a young girl would. And there's something of the arrogance of a young and beautiful girl in the way she sits, with her shoulders held so straight under her silk kimono, and her eyes shut, as if she had no need to check on her appearance in the glass. Eva looks, as she always does now, for the small scar on Holly's forehead, a shiny, fish-shaped scar left by the excision, months ago, of a mole that turned out to be benign.

Eva takes after her mother, so people have always said, though it was never clear whether they meant this as a warning or a compliment. In the old-fashioned books Eva grew up reading, the heroine would be called a beauty, as if it were a profession like lawyer or thief. And with her skin the colour of brown sugar, as if she'd spent her whole life in the mountains; her eyes a blue so light it's almost blind, Holly had been a beauty. She certainly hadn't been a mother, at least not the kind of mother Eva's schoolmates had. It was Garth who'd taken charge of Eva, telling her stories when she was too young to be able to read herself to sleep, taking her to church at Christmas and Easter, arranging for her schooling, the piano and ballet lessons she could never admit that she hated, being all thumbs and forever tripping over her own feet. When she was old enough to fend for herself, her father had abandoned his desk job, and would vanish for weeks at a time to places called Matachewan or Wawa or Pickle Crow, names as seductive to Eva as his rolltop desk, with its dockets and drawers and secret compartments for which she could never find the key. When he'd died, she'd searched for it all through his papers, only to find it at the farthest end of his bedroom closet, inside a pair of cracked, patent leather shoes. Dancing shoes, Holly had called them; Garth had worn them when he was courting her. The key fit perfectly; every one of the drawers was empty.

"Where is your father?" Holly asks, so abruptly and in so sharp a voice that the hairbrush nearly drops from Eva's hand. She puts it down on the table, watching her mother's face in the mirror as she gives the answer she always does:

"He died a long time ago. His heart gave out. We went to his funeral together. You put white roses on his grave, a large bunch of white roses."

Holly nods and leans her head back so that it rests against Eva's heart. Eva holds her hands against her mother's face, pressing their warmth against the coolness, the whiteness of her skin. As if it were written over in invisible ink, bearing a message that only love, the stubbornest love, could make visible. If anyone were to ask her whether she loves her mother, she would say that she has always adored her. Would say this without any affectation. For she has never been able to love her mother the way a child does—selfishly, carelessly—but only as a lover: dazzled and unrequited, never able to take anything for granted, to be sure it would come her way again. A kiss, a smile, five minutes of complete attention.

Holly pulls her head free from her daughter's hands, opens her eyes, and gives Eva a look of fierce reproach. "None of the windows here open. They say it's because of the ventilation system, but that's rubbish. They're afraid that if the windows opened we'd jump out and run—not that we'd get very far. I want you to bring a glazier with you next time you come. I want him to fix the windows so I can open them. You needn't worry that I'll run away. I just want to breathe a little. I want to hold my face against the air."

The room is perfectly silent, as if sharing Eva's surprise at her mother's making such sudden, perfect sense. Eva doesn't remind Holly that she's always refused to be taken for walks in the grounds of the Home; that the nurses have to fight to get her to stay on a bench in the garden for more than five minutes. What fills Eva's eyes now is a memory, sharp and fleeting as lightning. How, on spring mornings, on her way to school, she'd look back and see her mother pushing open the windows, one after the other, the whole house through. Casement windows, leaded, diamond-paned, flung open with a violence it was easy to mistake for joy.

Only now does Eva recall the reason for the freesias, bursting from the vase on the small, dark dressing table. She grabs at her knapsack, fumbling with the straps, pulling out a library book, and from it, a photograph. If she's quick enough, if she puts the picture into her mother's hands, forcing her fingers round the sharp-cut edges, it might trigger something, a name, a word, even just a sound of recognition. Something that will give her a clue, that will come down on one side or the other of the see-saw she's been carrying around in her gut all day: on the one side what she's always known in her bones about her mother; on the other, an impossibility that might turn out to be the truth.

"Look at it, mother. Please look at it. Do you know who they are? Have you seen them before, either of them? You can tell me, it will be all right, nobody else needs to know."

But Holly says nothing: flattens out her hand and tilts it so that the photo falls to the floor. Her mouth is set in the way that says she's tired of intruders, tired of the lights on in her room, the need to make words come out of her mouth. Eva picks up the photograph and slides it back into the safety of her library book; fastens her knapsack and shifts it onto her shoulders. Crouching down by Holly's chair, she presses her head against her mother's breast. Thinking that if she listens hard enough, she'll hear the heartbeat of a mind, a memory that must still be there. Like light trapped in a star so far away it will only reach you long after it's dead.

When Eva gets home, the house is empty: Dan's left a note saying he's taken the kids out to dinner and a film. She plays back the messages from the answering machine, among them a reminder of an appointment she can't remember making at a dermatology clinic downtown—the same place she had taken Holly, only a few months back. There's a far more important call from a friend who's just been sacked—her company is moving to the States. If Eva could give her a ring, she'd really appreciate it; she doesn't know what she's going to do with the kids, and she needs to talk, so could Eva please, please call her back?

Eva has the phone in her hand, is pushing in the numbers, when halfway through she stops and stares at the receiver as if she's forgotten what it's for. What she's hearing now isn't Ellen's voice, her shock at being sacked, but Holly, posing the question she's asked her so many times, her tone imperious or desolate as the mood takes her: *Where's your father?* For a long while Eva stands, staring at the receiver in her hand the same way Holly had stared at the photograph she'd given her. And then something connects, something she should have thought of long before now. She hangs up the phone, grabs her knapsack, and runs up the stairs to the attic.

The albums are just where she put them years ago, when she was clearing out Holly's apartment after moving her to the nursing home. She should have given them to Holly, or at least stored them with the rest of her things in the expensively papered room that Garth's estate is paying for. But no one had bothered with the albums for years: they'd been stored in a locked steamer trunk at the very back of a closet. Looking at her father's straight, stiff printing on the covers, Eva had known that she, too, would leave to their own company whatever ghosts were pressed inside. *Toronto: Wartime. Porcupine Creek, 1946–49. Toronto, 1950–63.* The sight of those last dates had tempted her to put the albums straight into the trash: years she would rather forget existed; when she hadn't wanted herself to exist. She'd kept the albums, sending them into another form of exile in the bottom drawer of the rolltop desk, only out of loyalty to Garth: to that fiction of family he'd tried so hard to hold together.

She takes out only the first two, the ones labelled *Wartime* and *Porcupine Creek*. It's a lie, she thinks, that women are insatiably curious, every one a Bluebeard's wife. Curiosity is a luxury. If you grow up in a house where everyone's keeping secrets, keeping them like unlit matches in air saturated with the emotional equivalent of kerosene, you learn to be cautious. You learn, too, to prefer the stories you make up to the ones that photographs tell. Your own stories you can alter, whereas albums are prisons, each image a cell in which you're confined, unable even to shake your head, though the pages are so brittle they fall apart as you turn them. Black pages, a blizzard of dark instead of snow.

Her father in his naval uniform, on the day he proposed to her mother. The openness, the declaration of joy on his face are so painful that Eva covers the image with her hand. She turns past the photos of the wedding party: the grandparents who'd died when she was still a baby; the spinster aunt who'd gone off after the war to work for the Canadian embassy in Paris; who was said to have married a Frenchman and lived in some sleepy cathedral town ever since. There are no pictures of Holly's brother, blown up with half

his regiment at Dieppe. Or of Garth's older brother, who'd spent
the war years speculating handsomely on a government salary in
London, and stayed on to direct the family business from the City,
spending his holidays with a succession of beautiful young men at a
Tuscan villa no one in the family was ever invited to.

All of them strangers: even her parents—especially them. It's
only when Eva gets to the album of Porcupine Creek that she
starts to recognize Garth and Holly in the images collected here;
that they turn into the people she knows as her mother and father.
Everything she is, everything she's refused to become, rests on this
base which nothing should shake. Eva Chown: daughter of Holly
and Garth Chown. Or Eva X: mother an amnesiac, father
unknown? She thinks of photographs she's seen of bombed or
earthquaked cities: whole houses cracked open, people sitting at
table, in chairs pushed against what used to be a wall. And if they
so much as crumple their napkins or put down their forks, they'll
plunge backwards through emptiness, into the rubble below.

The bottle of Scotch Dan brought upstairs last night is on the
floor beside her. Eva pours herself a glass and gulps it down.
Scotch had been her father's drink: she'd go into his study to kiss
him good night and breathe in the hot, rich smell of it. The best
Scotch, and the best tobacco, bought at a special store downtown.
A man of elegant, disciplined habits, Garth. A family man who
adored his wife and daughter, and had never got over the death of
his infant son, the way some men never get over the deaths of their
sons in wartime. But how does she know this? Maybe she's made
it up because it's what she's needed to believe: the same need that
made her name her son after the brother she never knew. A gift to
her dead father.

Eva forces herself to go through the album to the end: pages and
pages of mining camps, of blurry sunsets over blurry lakes. Human
subjects are far rarer: Holly bundled in what looks like a fur blanket,
standing in front of a bungalow dwarfed by snowdrifts. Garth
standing on a frozen lake with a piece of surveying equipment—Eva
has no idea what—in his hands. Holly again, sitting on a rock, her
eyes wide open in the sun. She's in short shorts, with a scarf draped

round her neck and across her breasts. There's nothing of the starlet in her pose; for all that she cares, the camera could be a rock or tree. And then an utter stranger in this last shot: a young Native woman, her face locked in a frown, her body lumped in men's jeans and a checked flannel shirt. She wears a cap shoved onto her head, one thick, dark braid hanging over her shoulder. There's an entry written in Holly's sloping hand for this one: *Phonsine, on a bad day. Ha ha!*

But no one else. No trace of a story that hasn't been told, a story that might connect them all in a zigzagging line: Ben, herself, Holly, and a man of whom she knows nothing, except that once he was a boy Ben's age, with Ben's face, breaking free of his mother's arms. The man who could have been her mother's lover. She can't bring herself to say "my father"—that title belongs to Garth, will always be his. And yet the man's absence haunts the album, in the same way her dead brother does, his presence nowhere recorded on these crumbling pages.

She shuts off the lamp and sits in the dark, sipping Scotch that turns to a circuit of hot, gold wires inside her. When Dan and Julie and Ben come home, she is still upstairs, sitting in the dark. She doesn't answer Dan's call: if he wants, he will come upstairs and find her here. Or perhaps he'll think she's gone out: he'll listen to Ellen's message on the tape machine and think she's gone over to be with her. It doesn't matter. The only thing that matters now is to put together everything that's caught her up these past few days, to decode whatever plot they make: dizzy spells; a stranger watching her, signalling by means of a scissored photograph. What does he want, who is he really looking for? Holly? Ben? Or, with all his watching, his shadowing, only herself?

She goes over to the large, bare window that looks out over the road. The streetlamp makes a circle like a fallen moon; pressing her hands against the glass, she tries to touch the light, to block it out. And then, as if sending her own signal to someone watching below, she moves her hands towards the window frame, grabs the edges and leans back, her whole body tilting as if she were on a swing. Shutting her eyes, gripping the frame tight, waiting for the swing to reverse its arc; to send her sailing headfirst through the glass.

And now, she's sick with vertigo, so sick she can barely stand. She sinks to the floor, lying with her knees pulled up, her arms shielding her face. She has never felt so helpless, and so exposed. If the house were burning down around her she would not be able to move, even to call out to save herself. She lies on the bare floor, her eyes wide open and her heart like a jar of something soft, dark, that's being spooned out of her.

When the phone starts ringing, Eva runs to it, terrified it will wake the whole house. But all the doors are closed along the corridor: no one else hears anything. Even before she picks up the receiver, she knows something terrible's happened to Holly: a stroke, a seizure. Who would call in the middle of the night except for an emergency?

The voice on the other line is shaky, wheezing: an old man's voice, but she can't make out any of the words. He is speaking in a language she can't understand, has never heard before. Asking her something, again and again, she can feel the urgency in his voice, but all she can do is say she's sorry, can he speak English please, she doesn't understand.

The line goes dead. She puts down the receiver, waiting for the caller to ring back. Wakes and keeps waiting, not knowing whether anyone called at all, whether the whole thing isn't part of the dream she's been having, lying cramped and cold on the attic floor. At last she creeps down the stairs to the room she shares with Dan. He is half-awake as she climbs into bed: when he asks what's the matter, she says, "Nothing. A wrong number. Go to sleep." Something she can't do for a long time. When she shuts her eyes she sees the photographs from Porcupine Creek dealt out across the dark like a fortune teller's cards. Holly sunbathing. Garth surveying. A woman named Phonsine, who must have been Holly's only friend.

Eva falls asleep listening for the phone and wondering what the odds might be of tracing a dreamed voice; of finding Phonsine in

Porcupine Creek. Of her being alive, still, and willing to talk about a stranger she may once have seen in Holly's company, when Garth was away.

An old man, with bad eyes and a heart that ticks as tinnily as a cheap alarm clock. He sits at a desk scarred with messages in blue-black ink, so many that his head swims just to look at them. He places his notebook squarely over the ink-scars, under a lamp whose lightbulb he stole from one of the rooms on the ground floor, rooms which once were used for educational meetings of a kind now frowned upon. He also has a drawer full of candle stubs: he is saving them against the time when there are no more lightbulbs to be pinched from empty or converted classrooms. The light in his apartment is so poor that it's difficult to write without some kind of lamp, even by day.

If you were to ask him what he is writing, he would take off his fishbowl glasses, polish them with a handkerchief he keeps in his breast pocket, and answer "stories." But that isn't the proper word. He thinks of them as a continuation, after an infamous interval, of a chronicle written by another old man with bad eyes and a poor heart. But unlike his predecessor, he has no gods of wind or thunder, no soothsayers or magicians to invoke. And yet the lives he is attempting to set down were full of shock and calamity. And unless he does set them down, it will be as though they never were.

Sometimes he thinks of how much he has seen in his life, though he has never travelled beyond his country's borders. He wonders about the lives of people in other countries, who might as well be on other planets for all they know of his life here. He can see them on television now: they are a different species, their skin and hair and eyes fashioned out of some gleaming, changeless substance, which nothing, not a pen or even a gun, can mark. And yet, he thinks, there must be some kind of connection between us: we are subject to the same laws, if not of history, then of gravity. We all cast shadows.

Overhead, and on all sides, the sounds of his neighbours' lives: quarrels, lovemaking, pots banging, dogs whimpering, toilets flushing. The old man puts his hand to his chest; waits for the pain to get smaller, rounder, till it can fit inside his shirt pocket. And then he picks up his pen, turns to a new page in his notebook, and begins to write.

III
PORCUPINE CREEK, JUNE 1993

Eva's heading north, through endless rock cuts and flooded swamps: spruce skeletons up to their waists in water. She's left behind most of the traffic by now; the towns, the wholesale outlets, the billboards are getting more and more spread out. She'd learned to drive in rural Nova Scotia, on roads so empty that all you had to do was put your car in gear and keep your foot on the gas; this driving, now, reminds her of that. She feels guilty, as if she's playing hooky. And she is: calling in sick to work, explaining that she's having tests done—mentioning the dizzy spells, the ringing in her ears. Sally had been so concerned, so sympathetic that Eva had felt twice the liar she really was. "It's probably just a new kind of 'flu," she'd said. Sally had told her to take as much time as she needed—though the kids would be wild without her. No one could charm them the way Eva could.

By the time she stops at a diner with a Greyhound bus pulled up in front of it, she's having second thoughts. The closer she gets to Porcupine Creek, the shakier she feels. What if she's come all this way to find out nothing at all? Not because there's nothing to uncover, but because there's no one left to tell her. In which case, whatever did or did not happen between her mother and her father, her mother and some total stranger, matters so little she can declare it dead. But what if, by some miracle, she locates Phonsine, the sole proof of whose existence is a forty-year-old snapshot crammed into her knapsack with half a dozen others? What will Phonsine have to tell her—what can she bear to hear? Everything starts roaring and rushing in her head: waiting for a bowl of soup she no longer wants, she has made up her mind to get back into the car and head for home.

And then a slight, pale girl asks if she'd mind sharing her table. The girl's wearing cheap plastic sunglasses and a baseball cap, her body blanketed in the widest-fitting jeans Eva's ever seen, and an outsized flannel shirt. She sits watching Eva eat a bowl of pea soup, and when Eva offers her the packet of cellophane-wrapped crackers at the side of her bowl, the girl nods her thanks, stashing the crackers into a shirt pocket already bulging with a bashed paperback. On her way out of the diner, Eva buys a package of sandwiches and an over-red apple, which she hands to the girl trailing behind her.

"Bo," the girl says. "That's my name. Can you take me to Billy's Bay? I've run out of bus fare. It's nothing urgent, but I'd really like to get there before dark."

Eva's wondering whether she should be calling the nearest OPP station, telling them she's found a missing person. But if she says no, in whose car or truck will she end up, this girl in the gigantic shirt, with her small fuchsia earrings shaped like crayons?

As they pull back onto the highway, Bo thanks her for the sandwich and the ride, but volunteers no information. Instead, she starts grilling Eva.

"What're you doing so far from Toronto?"

"Driving."

"I know that, I mean why are you driving?"

"To get to Porcupine Creek."

"That's not an answer."

"Because. I'm a writer." The lie soft as toffee on her tongue. "I'm researching a book on the mining camps they ran up here after the war. The lives of the women—miners' wives, wives of the company men. That kind of thing."

"You don't look like a writer. What's your name?"

"Eva. What's yours—what's it short for?"

"I see a lot of writers on TV. Those interview shows. You don't have the same kind of—allure, if you know what I mean. No offence."

"No offence. But it's all make-up, you know. For the lights. What's it short for, your name?"

"My grandmother lives near Porcupine Creek. You should interview her. She came here from Poland—at least it used to be Poland. They named me after her. Bogdana. She was in a labour camp during the war. You should talk to her."

Bo picks out the slices of ham from her sandwich, rolling them up in the cellophane. She eats the bread; the apple she stores in her pocket. All the while, Eva's expecting her to tell her story, make confession, ask for help, none of which she does. She knows she should try to draw the girl out, and yet it's so easy, so peaceful riding along in silence. In a few miles, Bo's asleep; Eva guesses she's been up all night. She wishes they could have gone on talking: it would have kept her from rehearsing her own worries. That Dan didn't try to talk her out of this trip, when she expected him to tell her how crazy the whole thing was; that Ben tried to talk her into letting him come along. As if trying to show her how shut out of her life he feels, or how unhappy he is at being left with Dan. How he's never really taken to Dan, keeping his love, his loyalty for Jimmy, whom he only sees for six weeks every summer. Eva sighs. Blood ties, family ties. You're born with family like a chain around your neck: metal rings, each one kissing, biting into the next. And even if you break a link, the chain doesn't dissolve. It just sinks under your skin, you wear it without knowing.

Eva takes the cutoff for Billy's Bay and pulls over at a small plaza on the very edge of town. For a while, she watches Bo sleep, seeing her for the first time without her defences, for the girl's taken off her baseball cap and her sunglasses. Eva's shocked at how much younger the girl is than she'd seemed. Her height had fooled her—she can't really be more than thirteen. In the late afternoon light, her hair has the fineness, the delicacy of a baby's: her face is pale, but with a beautiful light playing under the skin, like sun under white blinds. For a moment, Eva just watches her sleep, as if she could trace the shape of dreams against her eyelids. The girl reminds her of someone, but she can't think whom.

"Bo," she calls, shaking her gently. "We're here."

They drive along the main street into town, to a dilapidated house calling itself an antique shop. Eva waits in the car as Bo knocks at the door. At last a woman in a dressing gown steps out onto the porch. She stares at the girl for a moment, then holds out her hand. It's all right, Eva decides, and slowly pulls away. Trying not to think of Holly, or of Ben; fighting down the desire to stay with the woman and the child receding from her view, but still embracing on the beat-up porch as she drives on up the highway. To the place where she was born, and can no more remember than the birth itself.

Eva gets to Porcupine Creek long after nightfall, and checks into the first place she sees, the Hotel Excelsior. It's not a bad place: dark, old-fashioned, the carpets worn; something like her own house, in fact. She signs the register in block capitals, EVA CHOWN, for anyone who cares to look. Next morning, she'll go round to all the bakeries and bingo halls and coffee shops in town: ask if anyone might know of a Native woman now in her sixties, a woman named Phonsine. Check out the old age homes, the hospitals. The cemetery. More than likely Phonsine will prove to be a dead end, one way or the other.

It's freezing in the huge room, with its old-fashioned grates that let in the noises from the bar below. There's an extra blanket tucked under the Gideon's Bible in the wardrobe; she drapes it over her nightshirt and stumbles into bed. Wondering if the kids are all right; hoping Ben hasn't been snarky with Dan. Inching into sleep, she remembers the hitchhiker she picked up that afternoon, who the girl reminds her of. Herself, thirty years ago. Running away: running and running on the spot.

He runs all the way from the subway station to her apartment block, cradling in his arms the gift he's carrying. In spite of the fact that he's so late, that she will be anxious and exhausted, he feels absurdly happy. As though he were a hero in a fairy tale, bringing the tsar's daughter a treasure made of emeralds and gold. He knows that in some places, not so very long ago, the shops were selling nothing but salt and matches; that in this city they are luckier than most. Even so, he's brought her something she would never dream of having, not in a hundred years.

As she lets him in, she nods towards the room where her mother and her daughter are sleeping. The door is ajar, in case the child should wake and call out for her. "How is she?" he asks, and the woman shrugs. "The same—sick one week, better the next, then sick again. She starts at a new school next week, and I'm afraid for her. You know how cruel children can be."

She has made no move to embrace him: he is still holding his bundle in his arms. Her mouth twitches, as though she's eaten something bitter: the way she folds her arms makes him think of someone shutting the blades of a pocket knife.

"Is it your husband?" he asks. "Did he call again?"

"I don't want to talk about it. Here, give me your coat."

But instead he holds out the gift he's brought her. She doesn't unwrap it but puts it down on the card table she's brought in from the balcony. On the table there's a bottle of vodka, a heel of bread, some cheese and sausage that have curled at the edges. The card table is drawn up beside the sofa bed on which they will lie down

*together later, making quiet, careful love, so that they don't wake
up the child and her grandmother.*

*"I'm sorry I'm so late—the plane was delayed in Frankfurt.
But I've brought you something." He picks up the bundle from the
table, offers it to her again. "Go on, unwrap it."*

*She takes it, suspiciously. "You've turned into a smuggler, too?
Haven't we enough of those round here?" Unwrapping layer after
layer of plastic and paper, until she cries out at last:*

"Dear God. Dear God. Where on earth did you find it?"

*"You can buy them anywhere over there. In any
supermarket." And then, because she is standing with tears
streaming down her face, he takes back his gift, placing it in the
middle of the card table.*

*"I thought you'd be pleased. I'm sorry if I've made a mistake."
His voice is flat, cold; he can barely hold in his anger.*

*"It's just that I'd forgotten. That there were still pineapples in
the world. I'd forgotten they were real, not just something you read
about in storybooks."*

*She goes to the kitchen for a knife, but they do not end up
eating the pineapple. It stands on the window sill for days, its rich,
golden smell filling the small room.*

The next morning, shortly before noon, Eva finds herself in a
bungalow across from the elementary school, a bungalow not
unlike the snow-dredged one in her photo album. But there are
fuchsias in hanging baskets in the glassed-in porch, and the woman
in the La-Z-Boy chair across from her is wearing a floral muumuu.
She is enormous, but not fat: if she wanted to, the woman could
probably open her fist and squeeze Eva into an egg-sized ball, like a
piece of wonderbread. This woman is Phonsine Kingfisher, and for
the last ten minutes she's been sitting with Eva's photos spread
across her lap as though they were bingo chips; as though, if she

played them well enough, they could make up a winning card. Except for the last one, the scissor-edged photo of woman and child that she refused to take, pursing her mouth at its foreignness.

Finally, Eva comes out with it. "You knew my mother?"

"Yeah, I knew her."

Not a word asking how or where she is, what's happened to her in the last forty years. But then, maybe they'd hated one another. Remembering the caption below the photograph, Eva is sure of this. Thank God it hadn't been written across the back: *Phonsine, on a bad day. Ha Ha!*

"Can you tell me anything about her life here in Porcupine Creek? Did you know her well, did she ever . . . "

Phonsine's staring hard at her guest through the small, black-framed glasses on her massive face. She takes in everything: Eva's tramped-out runners, her sagging jeans and sweatshirt. The cropped hair, and the tired skin streaked with a bit of rouge, to make it less anemic-looking. "Here," she says, tossing Eva a box of Kleenex: "Wipe your face. You look like a bad crayon picture. That's better. Jesus Christ, you don't give yourself much of a chance, do you?"

Eva nods her head, as if she were one of the children at her day-care, behaving, so she'll get a story. It's part of the plot, the maze she's stumbled into, ever since that photograph arrived; fluke, coincidence, magic, whatever you want to call it. All of which has led her here to Phonsine, who did not leave town when Holly did, and did not move out to the nearest reserve, and did not die or lose her memory. She's done all right, she wants Eva to know: her son teaches at the school across the road, her granddaughter's studying at university in the States, and she doesn't do so bad herself. She's made a habit of cleaning up at bingo; ask anyone in town and they'll tell you what kind of luck she has. Better than Eva's, that's for sure. Gathering up the photos in her large, soft hands, leaning back the full length of her chair, Phonsine shakes her head at Eva and begins:

"She was so sure you were goin' to be a boy, she was holdin' out for a boy, she wouldn't believe me when I yanked you out and showed you off. Nothin' worked out for her the way she wanted. Not that she didn't get what she was lookin' for—but she couldn't hold onto it. Maybe they weren't the kind of things anybody could hold onto, and that's why she wanted them so bad."

Eva nods her head the way TV talk show hosts do, encouraging, authenticating. Phonsine takes no notice, but smiles at the wicker basket overhead, the rayon fuchsias tumbling from its sides.

"She wasn't one of them butter-wouldn't-melt-in-your-mouth types, the ones who'd never even take a pee without their white gloves on. You know that, you know everything already. But let me tell you how we met, me and your mom. Once upon a time we were next-door neighbours. My uncle's shack, it was right next door to that bungalow Garth bought—this was just after the war; there was a housin' shortage, which means white people livin' next to Indians, and lumpin' it because there wasn't anyplace else to put themselves. Anyways, your mom, she didn't know what to do with the minister's wife, and the bank manager's wife, and the wife of the collectin' officer from the finance company. And they didn't know what to do with her. One time, I remember, they were givin' a party, Garth and your mom, at least Garth was, he knew just how it had to be done, how much rye to get in, and to hire some woman to put together the sandwiches. Anyways, this party's goin' on, we can hear their voices, the women all loud and squealin', except they don't sound like they know how to have a good time, they sound like they need lessons on how to let loose and laugh. And what do you know but there's a knock on our door, and there's your mom, holdin' out a bottle of rye and askin' if she can come in for a while, things are that noisy next door she can't hear herself think."

When Phonsine says "Garth" it sounds perfectly easy, as though she'd known him from childhood. And Holly, too. Eva can see it, yes; her mother had always hated parties, would end up reading a book in her room the few disastrous times Garth invited guests for dinner. This is the truth Phonsine's telling her—so far, at least. Eva takes a sip of the milky, over-sugared tea she's been

THE GREEN LIBRARY

7

given: it's the first thing she's put in her stomach since lunch
yesterday, and she feels queasy. It's one thing to set out looking for
something you haven't a hope of finding: another thing to have
that something plunked down in front of you, have it take on its
own face and mouth and start talking back.

"We poured out the rye and shared it round, and she sat with
us in the kitchen for a while. She and I got to talkin' and it turns
out we're the same age, and we both lost a kid, and well, we didn't
do any kiss-and-hug act, but I guess we knew we could stand each
other. She came over a lot after that, which didn't exactly make her
popular with the Ladies' Auxiliary. But Garth, he never tried to
stop her. I guess he knew he couldn't. That's why he started
buildin' her that house by the lake. No one could understand what
a white woman would do out in the bush all day, but he must've
known, because he kept on buildin' no matter what people said.

"Your mom, she was the only white woman ever seen in these
parts, back then, in a pair of jeans. Damn near gave the town a heart
attack when she walked down Main Street. That summer we spent
on the island, we had a joke, she and me: we'd both dress up in blue
jeans and check shirts, flannel, you know, and we'd put our hair in
one thick braid down our backs—braid thick as your arm. Tryin' to
make out as we were twins, and no one could tell us apart. She liked
that. We took each other's pictures one day, she rubbin' charcoal into
her hair, makin' this big thunder face, and me puttin' on a lady's
pinch-my-nose-and-plug-my-ass look. You've seen the photo for
yourself—you can't damn well tell which one of us is which. No, I
haven't got mine—it went with everythin' else in the fire we had, oh
ten, fifteen years after they left, your mom and her man.

"Which man? That's what you want to know, isn't it? Can't
answer that one, not the way you want me to. Got no name for that
one. Garth Chown, now, he was somethin' different. Nothin' he
wouldn't do for her—like I said, he was even buildin' her a house
by the lake, far away from town as you could get without runnin'
into the lumber camp. Rigged up a tent for her to live in over the
summer while the men were workin' on the house down shore, and
he was off inspectin' some new mine. He wanted her to live in town

with the Macreadys, only she wasn't havin' that. He'd promised her
a tent on an island. That's how he courted her. With stories about
wolves howlin' and the two of them sleepin' under a tent with the
stars scratchin' overhead between the pines. Fairy stories: kid crap.
Me, I couldn't wait till that house was built and she could move in,
and I didn't have to keep an eye on her or anyone.

"That's what he hired me to do—stay by her, on that island.
Balsam Island, she picked it off the map, just for the name—and
he paid me well, Garth did. She paid me just as well, your mom, to
leave her alone once she'd settled in. Suited me just fine. I had
family across the lake, I went and stayed with them, and they
bought an electric stove with the money I made that summer,
watchin' your mom. From a lot of places; there's a whole string of
little islands round Balsam. It was too easy, if you want to know.
But I wasn't spyin': just watchin' out, watchin' over—to protect
her, because that's what he really wanted, Garth. Protect her from
herself more than any bears or intruders. That's the word he used,
intruder. But that one, he was no intruder. She brought him back
with her, didn't she?

"In her canoe—she was always out on the lake, fishin', readin',
keepin' as far from shore as she could get. One day, she was gone
longer than usual, I thought I'd have to go out after her, when just
as it was turnin' dark, up she comes, and there's more than a string
of fish with her in that canoe. She pulls up at the landin' place,
and out steps a man I never seen before. Skin and bones, his
clothes just hangin' on him. No prize, if you ask me. She had to
help him into the tent, and that's the last I ever saw of him. He
must've known somethin' was up—he kept inside that tent
whenever I was watchin'. He was hidin' from me. Maybe from her,
too. Good bleedin' Christ, she was happy then. It scared me, I tell
you—because I knew it wasn't goin' to last, nohow.

"One of the bohunks from the lumber camp, that's who he
was. See, a cousin of mine worked at the camp, bringin' in
supplies for the cook, and I went with him one time. I saw the
whole pack of them, lookin' half-starved, and wolfin' down their
food like it was the last supper. You know, their faces were a little

like ours—they had these wide, wide cheekbones, and black eyes. I asked my cousin who they were and he said Dee-Pees. Brought in all the way from Germany, on boats, just like cattle. They were workin' there to pay off their passage.

"That one she brought back with her—he stayed for near two weeks and then ran off. She was in a bad way for a while, until I made her see sense. Garth, he was comin' back at the end of the summer, whether she liked it or not, and that other one, the bohunk, he wasn't goin' to stay no matter what."

Eva's clutching her mug of tea so hard it's a wonder it doesn't crack. Some huge bird's beating long, cramped wings inside her so she has to fight to keep her balance. She doesn't want Phonsine to talk anymore, she won't believe what she's telling her. It's all of a piece with the décor of the house: the fake fuchsias in the fake wicker baskets hanging from the fake ceiling beams. But it doesn't matter what Eva wants or doesn't want; there's no stopping, no changing this story.

"What happens next? I moved in with your mom for the rest of the summer. No way I was goin' to leave her on her own. She kept waitin' for him to come back; said he'd gone to set himself up somewhere and then he'd be sendin' for her. She got to be a good hand at makin' up her own stories. What else could she do in the state she was in, moonin' around on that slab of rock? Nothin' wrong with tellin' stories—so long as you don't use them the wrong way, fencin' out what you don't want and only keepin' what you do. Stories aren't any good at bein' fences. Too many places they can jump open all by themselves and let all hell run in or out.

"By the time Garth came back, she was near three months gone. Pukin' into the lake every mornin', scared to death somethin' would go wrong, she felt that sick. But sure enough, out you pop six months later, and not a bruise, not a scratch. And I'll tell you somethin' about Garth, the man he was—when he saw she'd be okay, and you were goin' to make it through the spring, there was no happier man in Porcupine Creek or anyplace else. He was no fool, Garth; he knew whatever was taken from him was more than paid back.

"And then, and then. You're a great one for endin's, aren't you? Well, there isn't any endin' to this one, not the kind you want. Garth put in for a job in Toronto. He'd made as much money as he was ever goin' to at that mine he'd been up at all summer. Not that he wanted to live in the city—he only left because of her, left that big new house on the lake. Left because one night she wandered off—took us a whole day to find her. Autumn, that was; lucky for her the black-flies were all dead by then. She nearly froze to death; maybe that's what she was tryin' for.

"We never made promises to write, your mom and me. After she ran off like that, after I helped Garth get her back, there was nothin' she had to say to me. Holly Chown. I never thought I'd hear her name again, till you come sailin' in here. She hit the big time, your mom? She find that bohunk of hers and live happy ever after in the big white city?"

Eva can't say anything for a while, and then she remembers what, a long while ago, she'd been taught to call her manners. She gets up from her chair, saying, "Thanks, Mrs. Kingfisher. You've been very generous with your time. You've been a great help." She should probably say something else; this woman, after all, was once her mother's friend—more than a friend. But acknowledging that intimacy would be out of place. Literally. Because Phonsine isn't here anymore. She's far away, in the country behind her eyes, her mouth screwed up like a proper lady's at a white woman holding a camera. Both of them laughing, as if there really were no differences between them, or none they can't pretend away.

Dan keeps checking his watch, certain she's stood him up, convinced he's been staking out this table in the smoking section of Future Bakery for at least three-quarters of an hour instead of the ten minutes he's actually been here. On the other hand, he almost didn't show up himself, partly because of the very name of the restaurant. Her choice, not his. It makes him feel superstitious, that name, as if he's committing himself to some irreversible act. And he's not set out to be decisive; right now, he isn't certain of anything, except that all of a sudden Eva's been acting in the strangest way, and on the flimsiest of pretexts. A chance photograph, a possibility he offered her precisely because it was so improbable, but which she's taken and run with all the way to Porcupine Creek—if such a place even exists.

He rarely eats here—Eva hates the place. The service borders on hostile, she says, though Dan's never found anything to complain about. He rather enjoys the ethnic chic woven into the décor, finding it an antidote to the kitsch displayed by certain neighbouring establishments: embroidered appliqué on duck-shaped ceramic ashtrays; identical busts of some national hero wearing an astrakhan hat, a walrus moustache and sad, small eyes that make Dan think of West Highland terriers. Unfair, making fun of it like this; merely his own prejudices showing through. But then he'd grown up on cossack-shaped bogeymen; for him, borscht suggests something saltier and far darker than mere beets.

Finally, Rache breezes in, laughing, unapologetic. She's wearing an outrageous outfit made of some knit so slinky that her breasts seem to be doing a shimmy each time she takes a breath. Dan tries to fix his attention on the pendant she's wearing: heavy silver, and shaped like an open window.

"It's so much less obvious than a Star of David," she explains. "Especially for a place like this: Heigh-ho Hetman and away! Off to the next pogrom."

"Rache, please."

"It's okay—they're used to me here. But you do like it, don't you—not my cleavage, the pendant. I got it at the museum in Jerusalem, when I was there for that conference last year. We should go there for our honeymoon. To Israel, of course, not a conference."

"What—?"

"Daniel, Daniel," she laughs, and the pendant, the open window, shimmers. "Are you actually proposing to sleep with me before marriage? Or before our engagement, at the very least? A fine Jewish boy like you?"

He stares at her, his mouth like a jar that's lost its lid. And then he realizes it's a joke. "One of the best," he tells her. "One of the very best."

They order cabbage soup and latkes, and Rache tells him all about the project she's involved with now, something funded partly by government and partly by the charity she works for. In exchange, Dan confides the newest twist in his latest cause, the one having to do with that deported Bulgarian refugee. Rache gives him some pointers on how to approach the Minister, on whose election campaign she'd worked with her customary gusto. It's the perfect word for her, Dan decides. Thinking, more than a little guiltily, that she's the opposite in every way to Eva.

For dessert, they have pastries crammed with poppy seed, and a glass each of Tokay. It must be the wine, he thinks, that makes him feel so raffish, as if he weren't merely out for lunch, but at the very start of some expensive, one-of-a-kind holiday. Impulsively, he reaches across the table for her hand. She looks at him for a long moment, then sticks out her tongue. They both burst out laughing, so recklessly that the two elderly men talking politics at the neighbouring table frown at them, and shift their chairs away.

Walking back to his office, Dan stops in front of a shop advertising packages to Belorussia, Poland, and Ukraine. The lightness of his lunchtime meeting with Rache deserts him: a puzzled look crosses his face. He's remembering the face of the woman behind the cash register at Future Bakery, and understanding for the first time why the woman in Eva's photograph had looked so familiar. She has the same wide cheekbones, the cast of face he calls Slavic. For what that's worth. And he decides, walking on, that it's not worth much: not, at least, worth telling Eva.

A stretch of lake, twenty minutes from the edge of town, along a rough gravel road. The log house her father built—Eva will not stop calling him her father—has proved far harder to locate than Phonsine, but she's managed by tracking down a man the hotel receptionist recommended to her: a retired official of the finance company, Mr. MacLeod by name, who had kept in touch with Garth over the years. He marked the house on her map, telling her it was bought by a young couple who'd grown old trying to run the place as a sportsman's lodge. The husband, who died a few years back, would have remembered Garth better than the wife, who'd met him only once, to sign the papers. Holly would have already been in Toronto by the time the sale was completed, and the couple were new to the area, so they wouldn't have known her even by reputation. Mr MacLeod's voice had been perfectly level when he'd said the word "reputation," for which Eva was grateful.

There's a pained rather than prosperous air about the property: the cabins scattered behind the house badly need repainting. Eva knocks at the front door, and when no one answers, leaves a note explaining that she would like to inquire about renting one of the cabins for a family holiday later in the summer. She slips the note inside the screen door, then heads down the path through a clearing which leads to the lake.

Halfway there, Eva hears footsteps behind her, and wheels round; it's a woman in her early sixties, slightly out of breath with the effort of trying to catch up. The woman's holding Eva's note in her hand: she explains that the lodge hasn't been open for business for several years now, as her health won't allow it. In fact, she's looking to sell the place and move to town. The woman's voice is curiously formal; marked by an accent Eva can't quite place. When Eva asks if it's all right to walk by the lake, the woman seems uncomfortable. "Actually," Eva says, "what I'd really like to do is rent one of the canoes and go out to the island."

"Just take one," the woman says. "As long as you know what you're doing."

Ten minutes later Eva is kneeling in a leaky canoe, heading for a patch of rock she knows already. From a photo in an album, and a story told her by a stranger who has known her from the first breath she ever took. It's almost two o'clock; she'll need at least an hour to get to and from the island, which turns out to be farther from shore than she expected. She concentrates on her paddling, surprised, almost resentful that it comes back to her so effortlessly, this skill she learned at a hated summer camp some thirty years ago. Steering through the clear, cold water, dodging rocks and stumps and the long, lizard necks of deadheads. A flock of geese starts up from the water: she watches the lift of their huge, heavy bums, the black flanges of their wings as they honk their way to a placid stretch a little farther on. Once or twice she rests her paddle, shutting her eyes and letting the canoe rock sweetly under her: what it must feel like in the womb, its blood-warm waters. And then, remembering the task she's set herself, the weight of it like a stone in the bottom of her knapsack, she starts paddling again, till her arms ache.

Reaching the island, Eva finds a flat ledge of rock on which to pull up the canoe, then looks back to shore. Phonsine's voice in her ears, the accent exaggerated, put on to make a fool of her: *"What's the matter? Afraid of ghosts, honey?"* "Yes," she'd like to shout, "of course I am. What are ghosts for, if not to be afraid of?" Shrugging off her knapsack, placing it safely on the seat, the only dry place left in the canoe, she makes her way to the middle of the island, to a small stand of balsam trees.

They make a windbreak, behind which Eva finds the perfect place to pitch a tent. She crouches down and runs her hand over the soft, dry moss cushioning the rock; she can't help seeing a length of white canvas, fishing tackle, pots and pans. And a young woman sunbathing in short shorts and an improvised halter top. This part of the story, at least, rings true. No, doesn't ring true; becomes real. She knows exactly why her mother would have chosen this place; how she'd have loved its bareness, stillness. And hated any house on shore, even a house built of logs and love, as a gift from the husband who never spoke to her in a language she could understand. Because he wouldn't admit her one desire: to live in a wild, free place, as wildly, freely as possible.

The desire Eva can detect so clearly now, in this spare and shut-down paradise. A patterning as intricate, indelible as the veins on agates. That desire she'd never been able to decode as a child, sensing only her mother's endless withdrawals, refusals of love. Thinking they were because of the dead brother, the baby Garth had told her about, trying to make her see why Holly was the way she was; succeeding only in making her feel she could never, ever make up to her mother for the child she'd lost. Poor Garth—he'd tried so hard, he'd known everything and suspected nothing of what Eva's come all this way to learn.

Eva turns her back on the balsam trees, the image of her mother soaking up the now-lethal sun, and returns to the canoe. From her knapsack, she pulls out her pack of photographs. For a moment, she becomes the intent child she used to be, her only company the dead she'd find in the garden stretching down to the ravine: snails, birds, field mice that the neighbour's cat had killed. Burying the dead: a ceremony performed not out of any passion for animals but out of an insistence their deaths be recognized. A recognition she insists on now, preparing to dig a whole world into this ground: a bungalow, a log house, a tent; Garth with his surveying equipment, Phonsine impersonated by Holly, Holly sunbathing. And a boy who could be her own son, with a woman who's a perfect stranger, a woman whose face isn't dead at all, but so alive it would cry out if you tried to tear it.

She finds a sharp stick, bruises her fingers with scraping away the soil, but there isn't enough for digging. She could throw the photos into the lake, but water isn't permanent enough for what she needs. Instead, she turns the photos face down and weights them with a flat, heavy stone, so large you can't tell there's anything buried beneath it. Phonsine's story, and whatever story underlies it, a story that starts in a foreign country, that happens to people she'll never know—all dead, done with. As for herself, she's already made up the outlines of another story, the only one she can accept. If there had to be a stranger on the island, he was no lover but exactly the intruder Garth had feared: *a bohunk from the lumber camp.* Her mother had been raped; the man who'd raped her was no more Eva's father than the rock she's now sitting on, the stick she's scraping against that rock. And any claim the man wants to make on her, on her or her son, has no more power over her than the stick itself, which she breaks over her knee and throws into the lake.

Afraid of ghosts, honey? Not fear alone, but something else, some kind of magic that's brought her to this place where everything began. Watching the small disturbance she's made in the water, Eva moves closer to the very lip of the rock, and holds out her hand. She thought the water would be icy but here, where it just noses the stone, it's warm as her own skin. Water licking her fingers, the fan of bones between knuckle and wrist. She turns her hand so the palm faces upwards; tilts her fingers this way and that so the water touches each ridge, each whorl. The edge of her thumb, its fleshy base in her palm, the little hummocks where her fingers begin. Water moving back and forth, passing each one of her fingers across its lips.

Dizziness shakes her, everything inside her leaping, dancing, like light on the water, countless lights, a dance of small explosions. Becoming that smash of light on the water as it beats against her skin. Until her whole body's burning, her hair and her eyelashes, her breasts and the soles of her feet. Until she has to shut her eyes, the dark behind them crowding with a man and woman, naked, nameless, crying out. Making her see the risk at the heart of it—opening yourself again and again, always wanting more than you can ever have. To keep on wanting; to live always buffeted, knocked off your feet by that wind at your back, pushing you farther and deeper into wanting, longing.

It gouges her deeper and deeper, this sudden knowing of what she's never had; what the two of them had grabbed like master-thieves. Eva huddles on the rock, her head curled into her knees, her arms locked tight round her legs, as if trying to make herself as small, as invisible as something dead or still unborn. Her mother and her lover: the tent around them transparent as lantern-glass. Long after they'd disappeared from that rock, the tent still blazing in the dark, a light fueled by nothing but impossible and thus endless desire.

Slowly, Eva loosens her arms. Lifts the hand she put into the water, touches it for a moment to her mouth. And then she goes back to the grave she made for the photographs. Uncovering them, carrying them to the stand of balsam trees, the flat, mossy rock: the perfect place to pitch a tent. Arranges them in a fan: the bungalow, the lake, the shot of Holly with her eyes wide open in the sun. Till she comes to the last one with its scissored edge: the one that doesn't belong. She takes it back to her knapsack, stores it safely away. From the wind and rain; from the light flaring from her mother and her lover.

Pain like a stitch in her side, as she paddles back to shore. As if she's not canoeing but running, both away from and towards some distant, waving figure. The hand she put into the water burns bright as a new scar; she feels its heat, its roughness travelling the whole map of her body. When she knocks on the lodge door to take her leave, she's half afraid the woman will insist on giving her a salve, a bandage, anything to staunch the light that's pouring from her skin.

But the woman at the lodge doesn't notice anything out of the ordinary, just shakes her head when Eva tries to hand her a twenty dollar bill. Shakes her head and pulls the edges of her sweater closer round her as Eva runs to her car, shoving her knapsack in the back, reversing in a spray of gravel.

The woman watches the car, a black speck getting smaller and smaller, until it vanishes. And then she turns back to the house, readjusting the CLOSED sign on the door, and calling out to the company she's left inside.

"*Tam nema nichoho, Pane Mykola,*" she says. "*Khodit' zi mnoiu, proshu.*"

When he walks into the cathedral, two women bar his way. They are singing in high, strained whispers: parts of the liturgy, all jumbled together. One of them holds out a small metal pail, the kind you might use to harvest berries. He reaches into his pockets, brings out a sheaf of coupons which he stuffs into the pail. The women do not stop their singing; they do not nod or otherwise acknowledge him. Just like the beggar outside, the stumps of his legs wrapped round and round with bandages that have gone the grey of trampled pavement. Only, the beggar had not been singing or praying, and instead of a pail he had a cap with ragged ear flaps.

It is dark inside, and empty: no candles, no smell of incense, but the man thinks he can just detect a whiff of hops, from the time when the cathedral had been used as a brewery. He would like to be able to smile at this, but he can't. He makes his way to the apse, where, in one of the side chapels, a large lump of stone is on display. The carvings that once covered it have been reduced to the marks an animal might leave when gnawing on a bone. It is the closest thing to a relic he can find. He doesn't kneel or cross himself, though he has done this many times in other churches, continents away. He doesn't pray. But he stares at the stone housing the thousand-year-old dust that used to be a man: he says over to himself the names of the people he would pray for, if he could. His daughter. The woman who used to be his wife. His dead father. His mother and sister who may also be dead. He does not say his own name.

The women are still chanting in their strained, whispering way, as if they are frightened some official will catch them and throw them out. They give no sign to the man as he brushes past them, into the morning light.

Eva gets home so late that everyone's fast asleep, and she has to creep up the attic stairs for fear of waking them—creep when she wants to run. She'd driven steadily, stopping only once for coffee and some food she can't remember eating. This time, she'd picked up no hitchhikers and made no detours from her destination: the bottom drawer of her rolltop desk, the third album, labelled *Toronto, 1950–63*.

Eva as a baby, Eva at two, three, all the birthdays up to twelve, with the bakery cake and a banquet of flowers and Holly drifting in or out of the frame, showing half of her face, or just her back. Holly, whose phantom presence reminds her daughter of those kidnap victims in fairy tales: the water nymph, the firebird tricked from her true home by an earthly lover who holds her captive through the child she bears him.

Eva's not looking at Holly now, but at a different kind of stranger, alien, yet intimate with the Chowns' house, or posed to look so. A woman in a smock and slippers standing on a mahogany table, polishing the prisms of a chandelier. A girl: tall, angular, wearing her dark hair braided round her head, just like the woman on the table. The same girl sitting primly in an armchair in Holly's morning room, where Eva's only rarely invited: reading a book from which she refuses to look up.

And finally, the image that's been at the back of Eva's eyes ever since she put her hand into the water of a northern lake.

A boy, bent over a glass display table, his hands gripping the edges. Against his will, he stares into the camera, for he would much rather be studying what's lying under the glass, things still and safe as fossils. The glass case is in her father's study, where Eva is welcome anytime and thus where she seldom goes. Until the boy appears, the boy who, in reaching out for one of the specimens he's been allowed to handle, brushes against her skin, her heart. Her heart that isn't a small gold locket anymore, but something wet and glistening inside her. A star in a sky of muscle and blood.

How can she have forgotten all this? What can she remember? His name and his face; a circle of street light wide and blank as the moon. The game they used to play with one another, on those late afternoons in that vast, dead house. The watching game.

Toronto, 1963

Eva Chown is in love with Alex Moroz, and she can tell no one. Not her mother, who is preoccupied with other matters than the birth of her daughter's heart; not her father, who wants her never to grow older than she is now. And who doesn't know—how could he?—that she's been bleeding every month for half a year now, that the nurse at school has had to show her how to pin a lump of cotton to her underpants and warn her not to wear light-coloured dresses during "that time of the month," in case of accidents. And not Alex's sister, who hates her as much as she, Eva, loves Alex. Hate, love: feelings so formless and unshakable Eva has scoured the dictionary for better words to name them, and has had to settle for "passion."

Eva's passion is for Alex, who has come into her life like an electrical storm: darkness and jags of light; a noise that dins in her ears, drowning out all possibility of speech. So far, she has had to be content with merely watching him. It's as far beyond her power to talk to Alex as it would be to shower him with gifts of gold and rubies, though this is the only form of worship she can imagine. Alex is an unlikely god: the son of the cleaning lady—cleaning woman, her father once corrected her—and the cleaning woman is from a country no one's ever heard of. It's Eva's mother who's asked Mrs. Moroz to have her children come to the house after school on the days she cleans and cooks for them; they can do their homework in the kitchen; they can have something to eat there, too. Of course it's no trouble; after all, who but Mrs. Moroz will cook the food and clean up the crumbs?

It's Eva's father who adopts Alex, just as Eva's mother takes Alex's sister under her wing and into her morning room, where all her books are, the books the girl's as hungry for as she's indifferent to sandwiches and milk. Eva's father has amassed a collection of rocks and minerals that will one day find their way to the Royal Ontario Museum, but now his study is filled with glass-topped oak tables bearing specimens of all shapes and colours. Pale rose, bilious yellow, turquoise not unlike the colour of his wife's and daughter's eyes. Glossy sheets of mica; prime specimens of obsidian and azurite. Alex discovers them one day when his mother is dusting the study. Refuses to leave the room as she asks him to; there is quick, desperate speech in that language Eva can't understand, but which she can't stop herself from hearing as though its voice were in her own head.

She follows the sound down the staircase and along the hallway to her father's study; she holds tight to the door frame, pushing just enough of her face into the openness to let her see him: the boy gripping the edges of the display case his mother has just cleaned, his dark hair falling into his eyes. He stares at the objects beneath the glass, reading aloud the Latin names Eva's father has typed out so carefully on lozenges of paper. While the cleaning woman wrings her dust cloth, bending towards her son but not touching him, pleading with him in a voice he refuses to hear. All he can see, all his senses will admit is the gleam of stone and crystal. And magic names in a private language: a code in which the boy and the collector can communicate from the very start.

For Eva's father comes home early that day; comes upon Eva standing at his study door, watching the scene inside. And what Eva thinks she will never forget is how the cleaning woman turns from

her own language into English, turns with a force great enough to
shatter her words: *"Sorry, meester, dees my son, he no mean bad
ting, he be good styoodent, worrrk harrrd."* And how her father
cuts through the woman's words as though they're the rags she's
polishing with—as though she doesn't exist as anything more than
those rags—and goes straight to the boy as if to turn him out of the
room. But the boy speaks out in a way that astonishes Eva. "What
my mother is trying to say, sir, is that I'm something of a
rockhound. I want to study geology at university."

Something of a rockhound. Where had he learned his English,
the English which fits, tongue and groove, her father's expectations
of how an educated person, a like-minded man should speak? The
words, the voice disarm Mr. Chown: he is silent for a moment,
then asks the boy to describe the properties of the minerals
arranged in the case. When Alex has done so, Eva's father smiles,
not the smile Eva knows, but another one, clean of all emotion and
expectation, a smile that cuts her father and Alex free of the girl
and woman watching them. "Well, then, if you're serious about
this, you ought to spend some time here—uninterrupted." This
aimed at the cleaning woman, who is walking backwards out of
the room, almost as if she's bowing to Eva's father. Later, when
Eva learns the word "abject," she will think of that self-consuming
manner of withdrawal, that way of turning your whole body into
something less than the floor on which everyone else is standing.

There's another girl, watching a woman abase herself before a
boy and a man; a dark-haired girl, watching her brother's defection
to the side of the man who pays her mother a pittance for cleaning
his house. Watching, as well, the fair-haired girl who has stationed
herself at the threshold of this room in which the man who owns
this vast, elaborate house has, without moving so much as his
hand, altered the lives of these people whose language he cannot
understand. Altering them as if they were specimens of crystal or
rock to be displayed to his satisfaction. For Mr. Chown has
arranged that Alex should come, not just when his mother cleans
the house, but as often as he likes to look at the collection; to read
the geology books on Mr. Chown's shelves, and when he is home,

to hear his stories about prospecting sites in the north, which is the landscape of his heart's desire. That Alex works weekends and occasional evenings at Canada Packers with his father, and gives whatever money he makes to his mother, increases Mr. Chown's admiration for what he's prone to call "the lad." Making him an honorary Anglo-Saxon with that word: one-of-us-in-waiting.

Eva nearly always contrives to be there when Alex comes to the house. She pleads extra homework when she should be out for the skating or tennis or piano lessons her father insists she take. Whether her father is home or away, she stays out of the study, stationing herself in the large, open hallway where there's a seat under the oriel window that she will one day be ashamed of, describing it to friends as "pseudor-Tudor." But perfect for theatricals, and there is something unmistakably dramatic in her passion for the cleaning woman's son.

Alex has to walk up a flight of stairs and past the window seat to reach Garth's study. Sometimes, he stands for a long while below the landing, watching her from the stairs. She can hardly bear to breathe as he comes close to her; she never looks up at him; he never says a word to her, though his presence blurs the letters of the book she's reading into a foreign alphabet. It's a game they're playing—he watching her; she receiving his gaze on her skin like a watermark, or the hickeys girls at school make such a show of hiding under the high, white collars of their uniforms.

He never shuts the study door. It's partly pride: he doesn't want anyone to think he feels ill at ease here. Partly shame, too: he doesn't want anyone to think he might be stealing something. It doesn't matter. Once he's inside the study, he might as well be underground for all he knows or cares of anyone, anything but her father's books and the perfect specimens in their carefully dusted cases. Once he's inside, she has lost him, as surely as a princess in a fairy tale; the one who must wear out seven pairs of iron shoes and eat ten stone loaves before she can find at last the lover she's lost.

But on his way to her father's study, he plays a game with her, halfway between a secret and a gala performance. How could you ever get caught in such a huge, empty house, where no one hears you when you cry out, and there are hiding places everywhere? And yet they both know how dangerous it is—how can they not know, being who they are? For all his praise of Alex, Garth would banish him from the house should he discover him eyeing Eva. Those are the rules of the social game; these are the players: not just a boy and a girl but the cleaning woman's son; a gentleman's daughter. Though how there can be anything wrong in the watching game, Eva doesn't know. It has nothing to do with those drawings the girls giggle over at school, or her own anxiety about how, exactly, lovers kiss.

This game she plays with Alex is what she understands enchantment to be: pure anticipation, stretched so fine and so intense she can feel her blood fizzing inside her. So that she has to stop, stock-still, to catch her breath as she's rushing home from school, thinking, "he'll be here today, he'll be standing so close to me I'll feel his breath on my skin. No one knows him the way I do. No one wants him like this."

Wants, and watches. As no one has ever watched her, until Alex. Oh, watched out for her, when she was small, so that she didn't hurt herself, or watched at school to see that she had proper table manners, that she walked with her head up and her shoulders straight. But when Alex is in the house, nodding hello in her direction if his mother's there and he has to show himself to be polite; or better, endlessly better, when he looks at her those few moments on the stairway, stares at her as she keeps her eyes on the book of fairy tales she should have long ago outgrown, then Eva feels as though a thousand matches have been struck inside her, and her whole body crackles with light. Only then is she really Eva; do her name, her face belong to her, at last.

The watching game. She can never say how long it lasted, for there was no time outside those moments of his eyes on her, just endless expectation. Except the last time, the last visit he'll ever pay to the house. It comes like all catastrophes: insidious, extravagant. And then it's over and there's nothing left.

On that day, Eva comes home early from school, too early for Alex to have arrived, though his mother should surely be there. Yet there's no sound of a vacuum cleaner, or of pots being scrubbed. This silence is Eva's first warning, making her tiptoe up the second flight of stairs to her mother's suite of rooms. The morning room, with all her books and treasures; the dressing room and the bedroom, all interconnected, all interrupted by closed doors.

Her mother has always had secrets; for as long as she can remember, this has been Eva's private definition of a mother: someone who keeps the most important things in her life to herself, locked away from you. Keeping secrets like a separate family of children: your rivals, incomparably more beautiful, more gifted than you. Since she could never be one of those phantom children, Eva has always wanted the next best thing: to keep secrets as her mother does. Secrets to stuff into this hole inside her, this space the size of a huge hurt that is her mother not wanting her, not needing or holding her because her arms are always full of something, someone else.

Mrs. Moroz is speaking with her mother, in the bedroom. The door is not quite shut; from her hiding place behind the rack where Holly keeps the dresses she's abandoned in favour of silk pyjamas and kimonos, Eva can hear Mrs. Moroz speaking her broken English, and Holly saying, "But he can't. He can't just go off and abandon you. You're his wife, you have legal rights." Not her mother, but a woman Eva's never heard before: hard, practical, calculating. "How does he expect you to support yourself? Especially if he's taking Alex with him."

Eva crouches down by a heap of shoes, rubbing her forehead against the bareness of her knees, rocking back and forth under the powdery dark of her mother's dresses. And then she stops rocking: lifts her face to where the women's voices are going on and on, though she doesn't hear what they're saying anymore. Suddenly, she understands. It's her mother's doing. Her mother has seen them playing their game—she's found out their secret. No one but Holly can have secrets; keep them. So she's told Alex's father; she's made him take Alex away from her. That's why her voice is so strange now. Because she's lying, pretending to Mrs. Moroz that she wants to help her, when all the time she's been arranging this.

It's the plot of every story she's read in the *Red* and *Green* and *Yellow Fairy Books*: the ploy of stepmothers whose evilness—at first abstract, external as the crowns they wear upon their heads—starts to seep into their skins. Eva gets up from her hiding place and walks over to the dressing table spread with Holly's brushes and combs, the small, expensive pots of lipstick and rouge that have been so beautifully dusted by Mrs. Moroz. The women could come out at any moment; she doesn't care. She doesn't care if they find her sitting here, facing the high, wide wings of the mirror. It makes her all the more fierce, with a fury too precise to be rage. She's remembering her mother as she sometimes appears at the dinner table; wearing her hair loose and long down her back, her face streaked with rouge. Eva stabs her finger into the glistening red: smears it onto her cheekbones and her lips, rubbing the stain deep into her skin till she can see how it makes her lips fuller and larger, and her eyes brighter. She unbuttons the strict white shirt of her uniform so that her neck is bare. And she rakes her hair loose from the ponytail that swings down her back; shakes her head so hard it hurts, and her hair storms round her face, just like her mother's.

Alex is in the study, alone. He's not reading, but standing as she first saw him there, gripping the edge of a display case, staring down at whatever precious stone lies under the glass. He's heard her come in, she knows he has. But he doesn't raise his eyes to meet hers, he won't break the rules of their game, even now, when he knows it's the last time. She walks over to the case he's standing by; places herself on the opposite side, willing him to look up at her, to flash some signal. But her voice is locked or stolen; all she can do is move her hand across the surface of the glass. Putting her hand out flat, the palm upturned, blocking his view.

For a moment, she thinks he wants to slap her hand away. But then he lifts it as though he needs to learn it, all the lines of her palm, the borders and curves, the horizontal bands at her finger joints and the whorls of each fingertip. And her hand becomes something as mysterious, as complicated as a face; something that needs to be interpreted, the print so fine you need more than your eyes to see it. She can feel her body stiffen as he brings her hand to his mouth; each beat of her heart is a small explosion as he takes her hand, and does not kiss it but brushes his lips across it; his lips and the tip of his tongue.

She hasn't known anyone could do this—take a part of her body and turn it into a separate country, a landscape his mouth travels over and over, never touching the same part the same way, twice. His tongue writing a new language, private, secret, along the edge of her thumb, its fleshy base in her palm, the little hummocks where her fingers begin. Moving his lips back and forth across the backs of her fingers, passing each one of her fingertips across his lips, as if the taste of them were something too delicate or too intense to be sucked at, eaten. Her skin is humming, beating, she has never known any pleasure so precise and yet so overpowering. Something is starting here, something so much deeper and more terrible than a kiss that she wants to cry out as he puts his mouth to the place where her wrist joins her arm, the delicate, arching bone and the veins crossing it, the barely visible V of the small, blue veins.

Their hands are still joined when her father walks in, though Alex has time, just, to take his lips from her wrist. So that all Garth sees is the young man he's come to think of as his protégé shaking the hand of his daughter. Shaking it politely, with the old-world courtesy it appears the occasion demands. For, as he lets go of Eva and turns to him, Alex puts out his hand and shakes Garth's. "I wanted to pay my respects, sir. I'm leaving with my father in a few days' time. To go to my own country, sir. Ukraine." For a moment, Eva's father cannot hide the shock unsettling his face, but then he's all right again; he shakes the boy's hand, saying, "Well, well. Thank you for coming to take your leave. Good luck. I admire you."

It is lucky for Eva that her father doesn't speak to her once Alex has left the room. If he had, he would have seen her flushed, smeared face, her shirt open at the neck. But he sits down in one of the deep leather armchairs, with a book in his hands, a thick, dull book whose pages he never turns. He doesn't even see Eva as she runs from the room, hands clenched round something she must keep from spilling, burning the whole house down.

TORONTO, JUNE 1993

The cat's hot breathing over his face; all the noises of a house tossing, stuttering in its sleep. The cupboard closed, every drawer and window shut: magic scrawled across the walls, all the signs he's made with crayon and pen and ink warding off whatever scuttles in the dark. Through the vents, the heat ducts, directly overhead: not the air conditioning but poison gas piped through, the colour it makes: shooting stars, a pale green light, and he can only hold his breath so long. He knows, he has seen on TV what they did to them out of the sky: children screaming and their hair on fire. Or a cloud of poison sifting into their milk, their bones. If it happened to them, it will happen to him, to Julie, here, now: unless he keeps awake, it will travel through all the winds, all the ducts that connect the world, from house to house, wherever people are sleeping. And he can't breathe, and can't sleep, fear tapping its fingers on his throat till he kicks his way out of the covers, stumbling to the door, the hall. A little light thrown down the stairway; he huddles for a moment in that hand's span of light, then crawls up to where his mother sits, his mother come home at last, but so small in the circle of lamplight.

Gooseneck, he recalls the name, the comfort of something out of a story, the goose that laid the golden egg.

For a moment she doesn't recognize him: for a long moment all that she sees is the long, narrow body of that other boy she's been staring at, watching, losing. Until he moves towards her from the doorway where the light has pinned him, and she calls out, "Ben? What's wrong, darling, what's the matter?"

Holding out her arms to him, making a warm circle round him as he burrows against her, the way he used to do when he was so little she could carry him in her arms.

"What is it, love? Do you feel sick?" The tenseness of his body, the hopelessly knotted strings of whatever it is he needs to tell her. Holding him as if he were made of ribbed glass, as if she can shield him the way she did when he was newborn, the whole of him curled in the space between her heart and her throat.

"It's all right, Ben, you're safe, I'm here."

She strokes his face, his hair, as lightly as she can, knowing she mustn't hold him too hard, do anything to smother what he so needs to say and can barely force out. His words like punches muffled by their closeness to her skin.

"I'm afraid. I get so afraid sometimes. Of dying—and stuff. Wars, and poison gas. It's stupid—" He can't tell her, it comes out all wrong.

"Oh Ben, I love you so much, I wouldn't let anything bad happen to you." Whispering, to make him draw closer: her storytelling voice, even though she's telling the truth. She tightens her arms around him, feeling each rib, each strand of blood skeining his heart.

"Everybody dies. You can't make it not happen."

"No. I can't." She remembers something she hasn't thought of in years—how, when she was his age, they'd practised civil defence at school. Learned the sound of air raid sirens, taken home notes saying how, in case of a nuclear attack, they'd be kept at school—under their desks—until the all clear sounded. But what she can't remember is what happened, other than fear sawing her stomach. Delivering the note she wasn't supposed to have read; practising hiding in the open cage beneath her desk—hiding from fallout. Did he try to comfort her, her father? Had he thought it would only frighten her more to talk about it? Or had she hidden her terror at the instructions, so clearly spelled-out; so perfectly useless? She wants to tell him this, gropes for a way of telling him when he interrupts with his own small bomb:

"Why couldn't you live together, you and Dad? Was it because of me?"

"You mustn't ever think that. It had nothing to do with you." Not knowing whether this makes it better or worse for him; holding him tighter as he shifts in her arms.

"Because I think sometimes—if we were all together, I wouldn't feel like this. I wouldn't get so afraid if I thought you and Dad were together here."

"I know."

It's all she can say to him. She's not sure there's anything more to say. Would it be easier for him if Jimmy had beat her or held a gun to her head, like the husbands of some women she knows? If she could say she'd been in fear of her life, and not just that she hadn't been able to pretend anymore? The way she's learned to pretend with Dan. For the kids' sake: to give them a sense of family, security. A serum that hasn't taken, a bogus vaccination mark.

The gooseneck lamp pours down its light, scalding the woman holding her son in her lap. In a few days' time, he will be flying out to what he calls his other family. Every year, she's afraid he'll fly out and never come back; tell her he wants to stay with Jimmy and his wife and daughters. She can already feel the distance in his body as she hugs him; feel him pulling away; refusing the pressure of her love, her fear.

"It's okay now." He breaks free of her, picking up the cat who's wandered in from downstairs.

"Love you," she calls out, watching his thin, sharp body take itself out of the room. Wanting to go after him, sit with him till he falls asleep. But he's pushed away from her; he wants her to let go, now. And so she curls up in the bean bag chair, studying her hands under the glare of the lamp. *Everybody dies.* Some die twice over, by vanishing. Alex. And that other man, for whom she has no name, who vanished from her mother's life. Coming back now into her own through a photograph, and a deliberate, protracted silence. In which her son's voice, telling her his fears, seems even more defenceless, like a single line across a blank page.

Her mother leaves her at the entrance to the schoolyard: children are milling around, waiting for the bell to ring. When they see that the woman has gone, three girls come over to the new girl and stare at her, appraising. The youngest one asks where she's from: asks her, when she's heard the answer, whether it's true that the river that runs through that city glows green at night, and the fish have two heads. The oldest tells her not to be stupid: such things happened only in the dead zone. Still, they've heard that many children have fallen sick in the place the new girl comes from. "Is it true? Are you sick?" the oldest girl asks. The new girl puts her hands to the thick, black braids she wears down her back, tugs them forward as if to prove there is nothing wrong with her, that she is as safe as anyone here. Two boys come up to the circle that's formed round the new girl: they whisper with the oldest girl as the buzzer rings to call them into class.

"Firefly, firefly," they sing. One of the girls who first came up, the one who hasn't yet spoken, puts her arm through the new girl's arm and starts to walk with her into the building. "You better watch out," the boys shout. "It's catching." The two girls walk, arm in arm, into the school, pretending they're alone in the middle of a huge, empty field: that they've no one and nothing to answer to.

"Firefly, firefly!" the boys keep singing.

IV

TORONTO, JUNE 1993

The first thing Eva does after seeing Ben off is spend an afternoon at the reference library. Refusing Julie's invitation to accompany Dan and her to the zoo; ignoring the fact that she hasn't been to see her mother since coming back from Porcupine Creek a week ago. She has, she tells herself, research to do: an affair of extreme urgency, though she can't admit this to Dan, who has chosen not to make any further reference to the possibility he proposed to her over a bottle of Scotch one night in the attic. And who hasn't asked her anything about her trip up north, but has instead avoided her whenever he could, especially when Julie hasn't been there to act as a buffer between them. She knows this should trouble her, but it doesn't. No more than the phone messages piling up for her, each one an accusation of neglect from a friend who has always counted on her open ear, her ready heart.

The books piled in front of her all have to do with Displaced Persons: the people she grew up calling, when she thought of them at all, Dee-Pees. Some of the books contain potted histories of the Second World War; others have pages of statistics on population migrations, or densely footnoted essays on immigration policies in

Canada, Australia, and the United States. But the book she settles on is thinner than any of the others: through interviews, it tells the stories of some of the hundreds of thousands who found themselves homeless at the end of the war. Not just without a roof over their heads, and no family to return to, but without a country. Many of the people who became DPs, she discovers, had fled to Germany when the Soviets marched into the Baltic states, or had been shipped to the Reich from places like Poland and Ukraine. When the war ended, and they refused to be shipped yet again to another kind of Reich, the authorities gathered them into camps. Sometimes these camps were in the mountains; there would be stunningly beautiful views in all directions. But the people packed into the camps were in no condition to enjoy the landscape; after years of forced labour they were sick with impatience. With the desire, concentrated as a block of salt, to start living again after six years of war.

Some of them tell of how they had to stay in the camps for two or three years, or even longer. Some describe how they got out in a hurry, because of an Ottawa civil servant's dream of cheap, imported labour to plug the holes in a war-depleted work force. Canada needed domestics in private homes, cleaners in hospitals, workers in textile mills. Eva reads about a factory in northern Quebec staffed entirely by young Polish women who earned starvation wages working long hours, six days a week. On their one day of rest, the women were shut up in a place not unlike the camp they'd known in Germany. Except that this one was staffed with nuns and priests more concerned to keep them pure than fed.

The men were luckier, in a way. If they passed the medical exams, if they didn't let on that they had more than a grade five education, if they were or pretended to have been labourers in the country of their birth, instead of teachers and writers and doctors, they might find themselves packed off to a port city. From Kiel or Bremerhaven, they would make the crossing over countless miles of ocean, only to land in Halifax and ride trains through endless miles of rock and swamp to mining towns most people in Toronto and Montreal had never heard of. Or if not to those towns, then to lumber camps, miles into the bush.

A few of the interviews deal with the camps. Besides the DPs, there were also regular workers, migrant labourers who'd come to Canada well before the war: a handful of Swedes and Finns, even some Germans for good measure. Some of these regulars were communists who'd been anti-war until 1941 and the invasion of the USSR. To them, the DPs, who'd chosen exile in a Canadian lumber camp over a return to the workers' paradise, were Nazis, pure and simple. As for what the DPs thought of them, Eva doesn't want to think. She can't begin to imagine the tensions in those camps, with all their saws and axes lying so readily to hand.

After they'd paid off their passage, and the terms of their contracts had expired, the men were left to find their own ways south, to whatever jobs they could muster with their broken English. Forty years on, most of them don't complain. At least, they make it clear that compared to what they'd suffered in Europe, this country was a haven. Most of them remained here and made new lives for themselves. That's the phrase the interviewer used, though Eva's suspicious of the way it suggests that making a life is as easy as making a bed. A very few returned home. She flips to the section where the pictures are, trying to find faces that can't possibly be there. Alex's, because he would hardly have been born then: her mother's lover, because she has no idea what he'd look like as a man rather than a boy.

He could have been from anywhere, the bohunk from the lumber camp. In The Dictionary of Canadian Slang, she finds the following definition: "a pejorative term for Ukrainian"—but has Phonsine ever consulted The Dictionary of Canadian Slang? By bohunk, she probably meant anyone from that other Europe: Poland, Hungary, Bulgaria, Romania. Eva slams the dictionary shut. There's no proof, no evidence, and yet she knows her mother's lover was Ukrainian—she's sure of it, as sure as she is of Phonsine's story. Not so much that it's true, but that she has to believe it. Because of Alex, because of the way they've mixed in her head, the man watching her in the park, and that boy with whom she once played the watching game. Because she knows she can't find one without searching for the other.

On the paper she's brought along for making notes, Eva's been drawing: seagulls and pine trees; some of the crystal formations Garth had taught her when she was a child. As she traces the outline of these shapes, a name swims into her head, a name that eluded her the night she stared at a photograph of a dark-haired girl sitting in Holly's morning room. Alex's sister: Oksanna Moroz. One more shadow falling across her path, shadows of people long-dead or lost, or shaken off into that vague, dim ever-after where stories go once they've been told. Except that, for her, the story has barely started. And if the telling's to continue, she will have to keep looking: for the DP who was Holly's lover; for that other DP who might have been her own lover, and for the one person who might be able to tell her something about them both.

Abandoning the books piled in front of her, Eva makes her way to the pay phones, opening the directory to M. It's been close to thirty years since she even thought of Oksanna; at the prospect of hearing her voice now, she feels a tightening in her chest. She can't explain this, except to say that Oksanna had never liked her, had hated being so much smarter yet so much poorer than Eva. The reason turns out to be beside the point: not a single one of the listings in the phone book is Moroz, O. The knot in Eva's chest loosens: far better to speak to Mrs. Moroz than her daughter—if only she could find her, if she knew her first name. What can she do? Phone up each Moroz and make inquiries of any female voice that sounds old enough: "Hello, did you ever clean a house on the Kingsway?"

But Mrs. Moroz could have remarried, could have moved to another city, could have dropped dead anytime in the last thirty years. Oksanna, too—except she knows this hasn't happened, knows she can find her if only she can figure out where to look. Didn't Oksanna graduate at the head of her class, get a scholarship to go to university? Eva opens the directory at a new place and dials a number. Gets the familiar, diamond-on-glass voice of Miss Elspeth Adamson, who doesn't seem in the least surprised at Eva's sudden interest in an old girl from St. Hilda's. Miss Adamson tells her, as though she had her files before her, that Oksanna Moroz went on to study medicine at the University of Toronto. And that is all she knows of her, since Oksanna has been no more loyal an old girl than Eva—despite having been educated more or less for free.

The Yellow Pages are full of doctors ranked by specialty and district; she goes through them one by one, but there's no Moroz. Why should there be? Why should Oksanna have stayed here and not gone off to set up a practice in the States, some place where she could make money, buy herself a house as big as the one her mother used to clean for the Chowns? And why, she asks herself, stunned at her stupidity, why couldn't Oksanna have married, set up a practice under her husband's name?

Because, Eva tells herself, letting the phone book fall back on its chain. Because she can't imagine anyone coming that close to Oksanna. Close enough to be loved, or hurt: it would be the same thing.

TORONTO, 1963

Immediately after Alex's father deserts his wife and daughter, they, in their turn, abandon the Chowns. But Oksanna still goes to Eva's school, the school Eva's mother got her into: she remains the top student, the most conspicuously gifted of them all. Conspicuous in a regrettable way, her teachers agree. There's the way she speaks, for example: her English is fine, she knows all the words, she even has an English accent, but it's too sharp, too clear. And worse than her voice, far worse—there is something so foreign about the way she looks, the way she walks down the hallways, her head high on the long, delicate neck, her braids drawn up in a thick black crown on her head. She is too tall, and too skinny. Unlike her eyebrows: one of the girls leaves a pair of tweezers on her desk, for a joke. Oksanna sits for the whole class with the tweezers in full view, then leaves without so much as glancing at them. This earns her the respect, however grudging, of her classmates. They still call her the Ox behind her back, and make basso profundo mooing sounds as she passes by. Behind her back, but always close enough for her to hear.

Her eyebrows and her braids and her scholarship make her a target, along with her ridiculous, ugly name which only Eva has ever heard pronounced correctly, tenderly by Mrs. Moroz. Not Oxanna, but a soft-sounding k, and then "sahnna," like wind blowing through a field of grass. Since she never speaks, outside of answering her teachers' questions, and since no one can find out a thing about her father, it's impossible for her ever to fit in, as her teachers are always urging her to do. Somehow, the girls have found out that Oksanna's mother is a librarian. A lie-bray-ree-an, they jeer: none of their mothers works, not at a paying job. They are volunteers, fundraisers for the museum, the ballet, the symphony. Their fathers may be no more of a physical presence in the home than Oksanna's has become, but they all have offices big enough for a family of five to live in. Their fathers are CEOs, heads of this and that; they are important.

Oksanna isn't. She is simply, unredeemably different: the other that makes the rest feel interconnected, on side. And Eva can do nothing to help Oksanna or to stop the whispering of the Sarahs and Kates and Jills. For Eva's always known that if the girls stop whispering about Oksanna, they will turn on her instead. Her mother is as different, in her own way, as Oksanna. She hardly ever leaves the house; she reads too much; the few times she does venture out to school functions, her clothes, her make-up are outlandish—so the other girls' mothers say. Eva's father would be all right, the girls think—after all, their own fathers went to school with him—except for the fact that he married Eva's mother. Even the name, Eva, is suspect: Evelyn would be okay, even Eve, though that's stretching it a bit—but Eva? Like Eva Gabor, who may be a movie star, but remains, after all, Hungarian.

True, Eva doesn't stick out the way Oksanna does. Her kilt and cotton blouse and blazer do not come from the second-hand uniform sale. And she doesn't create a visual disturbance walking down the halls, the way Oksanna does. Eva's always hanging her head, looking down at the floor, hiding the startling blue of her eyes. She wears her thick, soft hair tied back, and walks with her shoulders hunched, hugging her books to her, so that the teachers rap her on the shoulders, crying, "Posture, Eva." Oksanna carries her beauty scornfully, outrageously, knowing it's as out of place in these surroundings as a heron in a birdcage. Her rich colouring and olive skin, her black, glossy hair, the breasts which her thinness makes even fuller. She may speak perfect English and smell of Yardley's lavender talc, the girls say, but you only have to take one look at her to know she isn't one of us. After all, what kind of a name is Moroz?

Oksanna moves through it all as though she has enclosed herself in one of those clear, glass domes in which people keep arrangements of sea shells or dried flowers. She hears and sees nothing that could damage the perfect surface of the glass. Oksanna is brilliant, the headmistress has announced this at the prize-giving assembly. They are fortunate to have her at the school, she is destined for great things. But the girls, of course, see Oksanna's brilliance as another liability.

It's Eva who's let it be known that Oksanna's mother is a librarian. It wasn't a lie: she'd worked in a library before the war; she'd been to university. Mrs. Moroz told Eva's mother this shortly after she started working at the Chowns', Holly having insisted Mrs. Moroz put down the mop and have coffee with her on the terrace looking down to the ravine. From the first day she had seen Mrs. Moroz at the house, seen how much she mattered to Holly, Eva had become an eavesdropper, gleaning whatever she could: this story of Mrs. Moroz having been a librarian, for example. It satisfies the girls at school, it confirms their own parents' infinitely higher status as something effortlessly acquired and transmitted, like a gene for fair hair or a knack for giving delightful parties. It is Eva's one gift to Alex's sister: camouflage for the truth. An expensive gift; Eva's perpetually afraid that the girls will see through her story, punish Oksanna in ways that will make their present, careful cruelty seem like tenderness. And it means, too, that none of them must ever come near Eva's house, in case they meet Oksanna's mother on her knees, scrubbing the kitchen floor.

On the first day of the new school year, Eva happens to see Oksanna get off the bus from downtown. It's been over three months since Alex left and his mother and sister stopped coming to the house. Eva's had a whole six weeks of banishment to a camp in Nova Scotia, where she's learned to ride badly, and canoe well, and has written letters to her mother that she knows will never be read. Dull, "today-we-did-beadwork" letters that Garth has urged on her as the best medicine in the world for Holly, who has fallen ill since Mrs. Moroz and her children decamped. Letters that give no sign of Eva's true obsession: lying on her bunk while everyone else is off swimming, opening the atlas she stole from school, finding the place he's been banished to. A dull green splotch on the page marked USSR, the letters so thin she can barely read them. Not Ukraine at all, but Ukrainian SSR. Putting her hand over the page, so her palm touches the whole country, the cities where he might be living—Lvov, Kiev, Dnepropetrovsk.

Eva starts to walk more quickly, as quickly as she can without actually running. She knows she must avoid Oksanna, that it's best that way, safest for everyone, but Oksanna, whose legs are far longer than Eva's, easily catches up with her. She puts an arm round Eva's waist, as girls who are best friends do when they're walking together. And then Oksanna starts to talk, pitching her voice so low that no one coming up behind them could overhear, yet speaking clearly, precisely, so there's no mistaking her.

"I got a letter from Alex today, Eva. He sends his regards. Do you want to know exactly what he said? 'Say hello to the slut for me.' That's what he calls you, Eva—the slut. That's all you are, in spite of your rich father and your expensive house, and your mother who's too fine a lady to know how to slice a loaf of bread. Do you know what a slut is, or are you too stupid? You are stupid, aren't you, Eva? Do you think I don't know what you wanted from my brother? Do you think he didn't tell me about you?" And now Oksanna starts to whisper things to Eva, pulling her closer, brushing her ears with her lips, pouring in words Eva's never heard before, describing things that make her feel as if Oksanna's forcing filth down her mouth. And yet she can't pull herself away, can't shut up these obscene versions of everything Eva's felt about herself and Alex, everything that's kept her alive this whole, desperate summer. It's as if half of her has to hear this, wants to hear anything, so long as it connects her to him.

Oksanna knows exactly what she's thinking; she drops her arm from Eva's waist; shoves her away. "You make me sick. Your mother despises you. Do you think she doesn't know what you're like? She told me. You disgust her. She wishes you'd died when you were born, that she'd strangled you in your cradle."

Oksanna walks on towards the school, holding her books to her breast, keeping her spine straight. Eva stands frozen where Oksanna's pushed her. Only when she hears her classmates' voices in the distance does she start to run. She finds a hiding place behind a thick privet hedge, and vomits her breakfast. She wants to die, she prays she'll die, right here, with her mouth still sore and burning, but she knows prayers don't work. So she wipes her face with her handkerchief, which she then stuffs into the hedge, and runs the rest of the way to school.

No one catches up with her before she gets to the washroom; locks herself inside a cubicle. She takes a notebook from her satchel, tears out a page, and scribbles something which she hides under the top of her knee sock before heading to chapel. By the time they've finished morning prayers and God Save the Queen, everyone in Eva's year knows that Oksanna's mother doesn't stamp books but scrubs toilets for a living. By lunch, the story's made the rounds of the entire upper school; the girls are already whispering it when Oksanna walks past them on her way to the front of the class to recite "Ode on a Grecian Urn" or "The Tantramar Revisited." She makes no sign that anything unexpected has happened: she locks herself into her glass dome and goes from class to class, A plus to A plus. Oksanna even skips a year, whereas it's decided that Eva, because of the effect on her grades of her mother's illness, should repeat.

Eva welcomes the shame of this, the public acknowledgement of her slowness, her stupidity. She knows what she's done, the awful, unforgivable things she must be punished for. When she thinks of Alex, of the touch of his tongue against her palm, she hears all the hateful things Oksanna poured into her ears, and her stomach knots as if she's going to be sick. When she's imagining what it would be like to kiss Alex, for their mouths to press together, lips soft and opening, Alex disappears and it's Oksanna she's kissing. Oksanna's tongue in her mouth, tasting sour, rotten: her own tongue, now, after what she's said about Oksanna's mother.

But, at home, everything sorts itself out. The nurse Garth engaged over the summer has left; Garth himself has taken a desk job at the Ontario Securities Commission, which means that he's never away anymore. Eva is careful not to cause him any worry; she spends much of her time in her room, reading books of fairy tales that she hides under the mattress, the way other girls her age hide pornographic novels. At school, she works as hard as she's able, and on weekends attends parties at the homes of her classmates, girls whose mothers are never odd or ill. With her own mother, Eva is unfailingly considerate. She tries to please her by never asking for anything, by making herself as small and silent a presence as she can.

In her waking life, Alex is dead, though for a time he makes his way into her dreams. It's always the same dream: she's in a park at nightfall, a schoolyard with swings and a stand of tall, bare trees. She's sitting paralysed on one of the swings, struggling to move her arms, her legs when she hears someone coming up behind her. He doesn't say a word, he never moves where she can see his face, he stands so far away that when he holds out his hand he can't even touch the back of her head. And yet she knows it's him, knows it by the shocks leaping from his skin to hers. She feels it in her hands first, the nerves jumping like the sparks she's seen from the streetcars downtown when they swing on the tracks. Her hands and then her legs, sparks crackling the fine hairs over her skin, jolting her free of the stiffness that's kept her prisoned here so long. She leans back, stretches out her legs and starts pumping, making the swing fly higher and higher, just missing his head each time she breaks the arc and comes plunging down. She wants him to jump on the other swing and join her; she wants them both to be free of the ground, sailing somewhere so high that no one can touch them. But all he does is dodge the swing each time she plummets towards him; dodging and shouting at her to jump off, let go. She can't stop, the swing keeps arcing up, up, till it twists and flings her over the bars.

And then the dreams stop, and Alex vanishes for good. Oksanna has already left St. Hilda's for university: Eva squeaks through the grades that remain and gets accepted at a small college in the Maritimes. At a graduation party somewhere in Rosedale, she's introduced to a boy from Upper Canada College, a perfectly nice boy named Colin. When, less than a month later, he deflowers her in the back of his father's BMW, she is pleased to feel nothing.

Toronto, July 1993

Should she wish to, Eva could sit up on the couch where she's lying naked under a large paper sheet, and examine the diploma of Dr. Susan Frost, Dermatologist, MD, FRCP(C), BSP, hanging on the wall beside her. She chooses, instead, to shut her eyes, imagining all the moles and freckles on her body. White sky, dark stars, any one of which may have decided to change its shape and set off an uncontrollable chain of consequences. When she was twelve, Garth had taken her to this same building, where a sweaty young doctor had cut a mole like a brown raspberry from the nape of her neck. Leaving the same fish-shaped scar that flickers on her mother's forehead now, though Holly doesn't seem to know or care.

It's late—she's had to wait forty-five minutes past the time of her appointment, time she needs to spend on research, all the more so as she's making no progress whatsoever. Oksanna Moroz has vanished from the face of the earth, and the odds that this doctor will know her whereabouts aren't worth calculating. Eva wouldn't have come here at all, except for Dan's hounding. Funny, how the less she sees of him, the more attentive he becomes, even taking the trouble to book this appointment for her. She'd been thoughtless enough to tell him what had happened that time she'd come here with Holly. How the doctor—perhaps the very man, grown dry and distinguished, who had cut the mole from her twelve-year-old neck—had advised her to book an examination for herself, her skin type being so much like her mother's. Since they share, among so many other things, a predisposition to the kind of mole that turns cancerous.

When Dr. Frost finally appears, she doesn't speak to her patient but picks up her chart and reads through it, silently. Then she walks over to the examining table, pulls the sheet away, and sends her eyes travelling up and down the body Eva's tried to make invisible by shutting her eyes tight.

"You'll have to turn over so I can check your back."

Eva would know that voice anywhere, through sleep or under water. A girl's arm around her waist; a scrap of paper passed from hand to hand under the distracted eye of Miss Adamson, at chapel. Her stomach cramps; she's afraid she's going to be sick, to throw up all over the immaculate steel and leather of this office, but the doctor doesn't let anything so extravagant happen. It takes her no more than a minute to perform the examination: she is concerned with her patient's skin, not her stomach, and that skin would seem to be as unremarkable as the paper she's now pulling over it, saying, "Everything's fine. You can get dressed now." There's an edge to her voice, as though she has more important things to examine; as though it were Eva who sought her out, and on a fool's errand.

And she is a fool. She has forgotten the one word she ever learned in Ukrainian. And she knows it courtesy of Garth, who'd kept calling the cleaning woman Mrs. Morose, till one day Holly had snapped, "It's Moroz. Moroz means frost." As if any idiot would have known this. Any idiot would have known, could have guessed that Oksanna would change her name as soon as she was able, the names that had given her so much grief at school.

"You have nothing to worry about, not yet," the doctor says, stripping off her gloves, making a note on Eva's chart. "You should protect yourself from exposure to the sun. And keep an eye on those moles on your upper back, between the shoulder blades. You might get someone to help you with that, if you can."

Eva sits up from the table, clutching the paper sheet against her and staring at Oksanna, who is scribbling something on her chart. At last she turns round to Eva; her face is seamless, perfectly professional. But her voice gives her away; there's a stiffness to it that makes Eva think of the rigidity with which Oksanna used to hold herself, walking down the halls at school. "You'll have to get dressed, I've got patients waiting," she says, her eyes never meeting Eva's, but fastening on her throat instead, as if she'd mentally beheaded her. And then:

"If you want a follow-up, you can come round to my house tonight. Anytime after seven."

She walks out, dropping a card—deckle-edged, embossed—on the shabby heap of Eva's clothes. And Eva understands, though it doen't make her any less confused. It wasn't Dan who arranged all this, out of guilt or worry or love. This meeting has nothing to do with Dan at all.

Of course, Oksanna's place isn't anywhere near what Eva calls "the ethnic strip," that cluster of foreign bakeries and butcher shops that some urban redecorator's christened Bloor West Village. Instead, it's right downtown, in the Annex. An old house like her own, but expertly renovated, the brick cleaned, all the stained glass replaced or restored, and none of that feckless, shabby air that gives Eva's place what she calls "character." Three names beside the doorbells, one of them conspicuously different: Pavlenko. Frost. Trinh.

Oksanna appears as soon as Eva rings, as if she's been waiting for her. She owns the whole house, she explains, leading Eva up to the second floor apartment. The top's rented out to a young Vietnamese couple, two medical students. Not because she needs the money, but they're nice enough kids, and the house is enormous, as Eva can see for herself. "They do the housework and gardening in lieu of paying rent," Oksanna volunteers, pouring out two glasses of red wine. She doesn't ask if Eva would rather have white. Perhaps it's because the room itself is so blindingly clear of colour, clutter, anything that could tell a story about its occupant.

"You wanted to talk?"

But Eva won't be rushed. She sits uncomfortably on the white leather sofa, feeling clumsy, contorted. She can't breathe, she can't think; she's with the one person who can help her and she's scared to death of what she might discover. As if the man she'd gone all the way to Porcupine Creek to find might jump out at her from a closet or behind a chair. At a signal from Oksanna, sitting so carelessly on a white leather sofa identical to the one where Eva huddles.

It's already clear, the terms on which they're meeting. There is to be no mention of the house on the Kingsway, or of St. Hilda's school. Oksanna's mother and Holly Chown are also off limits. And as for Alex, Eva can tell without asking that, for his sister, Alex doesn't exist. Has been made not to exist. Oksanna has cut her memory short, like her hair: a deceptively simple, expensive cut. She's still very slender, but that's not what gives her away. It's the globe of sealed glass that nothing can break. Odd that she should have become a specialist in diseases of the skin. A profession involving touch—but then Eva remembers the gloves Oksanna removed after examining her; how they cut off any connection between her hands and Eva's skin, just as there was no connection at all between their eyes.

"Well, Eva? Why don't you begin by telling me—oh, I don't know. Tell me everything that's happened to you since we last met. Let me guess. You're married to a lawyer, and you raise golden labs on a hobby farm somewhere outside the city, not in commuterland, but real country. Am I right?"

"Wrong about everything. No labs, no lawyer, no country life. But I have a son. He's eleven—" Eva stops, abruptly. How much can she tell and how much should she make up? What story does Oksanna want to hear? And Oksanna does want something from her, or why would she have scripted this entire meeting, from the examination that afternoon to this evening's forced chat? More to the point, what has she come here to get from Oksanna? Not just information about an elderly Ukrainian man Oksanna has no reason to know, and not just some word of Alex, an acknowledgement that he's still alive somewhere in the world. Eva needs something far more difficult than this. To make Oksanna help her find the man who was Holly's lover, but to do this without giving Holly away. For once Oksanna learns the story, she'll have it back again, her power to poison, to burn. *Say hello to the slut for me.*

The silence in the room roars in Eva's ears; she has to force herself not to go rushing out the door. Till she finally does the only thing she can: puts her cards on the table. Her single card, which she pulls from her knapsack, shaking it out from the book that's become its home. The photo makes a dark smudge against the sleekness of the glass. A woman, a child, a man's hands, severed at the wrists.

"I'm wondering whether you might know the people in this picture. Maybe not the woman, but the boy—though he must be an old man by now. He came here right after the war; he worked in one of the lumber camps up north, near Porcupine Creek. I'm pretty sure he's Ukrainian—I think he knew my father."

Oksanna picks up the photograph, examining the faces as if she were checking them for scar tissue, or the signs of disease.

"How did you get this?"

"It was put through my mail slot. By the man who was the boy in that picture." Hearing herself say it like this, she's certain; it becomes part of the story.

Oksanna's mouth works as though she's trying to push back a sound of anger or hurt. Eva's astonished; she never dreamed that she held this kind of power over Oksanna. It's unbearable, the pain in this woman's face. At last, Oksanna lets go of the photograph, dropping it at the very edge of the coffee table. When she speaks, her voice is different from the one she's used before: ragged, foreign.

"I don't know the people in this picture. Why should I? I have nothing to do with Ukrainians anymore, boys or old men. I can't help you."

Eva holds her hands out to Oksanna, as if to pull her from the anger, the shame flooding back from thirty years ago. But Oksanna doesn't see, doesn't want her help. She gets up from the sofa, smoothing her clothes, brushing her hands through her hair. And then she gestures to Eva that it's time for her to go.

They move into the hallway, Eva trailing her ancient knapsack with the magic marker stains leaking through the cloth. Oksanna nods when Eva says goodbye, the kind of nod you give to someone you've no intention of knowing. But Eva can't leave it at that. She wants to make it possible for them to talk, to begin to forgive what they did to one another all those years ago. And wants, more than she's ever known it possible to want, for there to be some way of making Alex real again: as concrete as this battered knapsack between them. But all that she can think to say is this:

"You've cut your hair."

Oksanna waits for a moment, as though revising a piece of strategy in some game she's never announced or explained. Then she gives a chill, white smile.

"So have you." And shuts the door.

The same door Eva races back to less than an hour later, having got home, unpacked her knapsack, and discovered that, though her book's inside, the photograph is missing. She rings and rings the bell, but there's no reply. Someone must be in, the photo must still be lying on Oksanna's coffee table. If she hadn't been so upset, so unsure of what was going on, she'd never have let it slip away from her. She has to get it back, even if she ends up ringing all the doorbells together till someone lets her inside.

At last, the ground floor tenant appears, or at least a shadow through the frosted glass. And a voice Eva seems to recognize, yet doesn't know: "Who's there? Who is it?" And then she understands: the accent's changed, become a patterning, no longer a distortion of the words. Eva's so excited that she answers the way a child would. "It's me." And then corrects herself. "Eva Chown. Eva—don't you remember me, Mrs. Moroz?"

Eva's afraid the woman's crept back down the hallway, shut herself into her apartment. But now there's the sound of bolts and chains being undone, and the door swings open.

"*Bozhe miy.*" And a whole flow of words Eva makes no attempt to halt, never mind understand. Mrs. Moroz grabs both Eva's hands, saying, "Come in, come in. You have time for a cup of tea?" as though they'd last met only the week before.

It is painful, in a way Eva could never have expected. Painful to be recognized so instantly, so warmly by this woman who knew her only as a thirteen-year-old; knew her for a year at most. And who, though she has the same striking, strong-boned face, has undergone a metamorphosis in other ways: the tightly braided hair now cut as beautifully as Oksanna's; the cheap, harsh housedresses changed into clothes so simple, so elegant they could only have come from the most expensive shops in town. And yet the quiet kindness Eva remembers so well remains: Mrs. Moroz, making much of her; ushering her to the room's most comfortable chair before she disappears into the kitchen to make tea.

Her apartment is as crowded with objects as her daughter's was starved of them. Eva's disconcerted for a moment: she'd expected the place to be neat as a pin. Then she kicks herself for the arrogance of the expectation: *the house of a cleaning woman, after all.* Everywhere there are paintings, books, newspapers. A kilim hangs on the wall, a kilim much finer than the ones she sees for sale in the expensive shops on Queen Street. Reproductions of nineteenth-century portraits: writers or politicians, she imagines, though several of them are women. Busts of men with huge moustaches. Embroidered cushions on the chairs: pottery that reminds her of things she's seen in the museum.

Mrs. Moroz returns with a tray bearing tea and poppy seed cake, the same cake she used to make in the Chowns' kitchen in the Kingsway house. Eva's desperate to ask about the photograph, but first she must drink tea and eat cake; tell about her mother's illness and her father's death. Tell about herself, as little as possible, though she does mention Ben, and is moved by the joy Mrs. Moroz shows at her having a son. Wanting to reciprocate, she mentions how well Oksanna's doing, how proud of her Mrs. Moroz must be.

As she pours Eva her tea, Mrs. Moroz says only this: "My daughter is a very strong woman. She scares me, sometimes, how strong she is."

Now Eva registers exactly what has changed this woman: language. Not just the shift in accent, but fluency and the simple power that goes with it. Though you'd never mistake her for a native speaker, with her precise enunciation, the formality of her speech, still, her language is Eva's own. *Sorrry, meester, dees my son, he no mean bad ting.* Eva can't drink the tea she's holding to her lips: her mouth is full of words she wants to pour out: apologies, assurances, questions.

Mrs. Moroz smiles at her; she's still a tall woman, her body spare as it's always been. Where did the strength come from, Eva wonders, to heave the vacuum cleaner up and down the stairs; or to keep going, just to keep going after her husband left her? Where does it come from now, that she can say what she has about her daughter, say it with such love and yet such sad recognition? What would she do if Eva were to mention Alex's name? A large graduation photo of Oksanna hangs in pride of place over the mantel, but to Eva's relief there's nothing of Alex in the room. She realizes now what she'd been dreading: a colour photograph of Alex, his wife, and their three beautiful children.

"My photograph." The words jump from Eva's mouth. She explains that she's left something in Oksanna's apartment, that she has to get it back, right now, this very minute. Pleading shamelessly, imagining Oksanna's thrown the photo in the garbage, ripped it to pieces. Mrs. Moroz catches the urgency in Eva's voice; nods her head. Soon the two women are upstairs, Eva frantically running her hands over the empty coffee table, smearing the glass, until she feels a hand on her shoulder.

Quietly, stiffly, Mrs. Moroz gets onto her knees and searches the carpet under the sofa; with the aplomb of a magician, she pulls out the photograph, and still without looking at it, offers it to Eva. There's no way of telling from this woman's face what she knows of Holly's past; no way of telling whether she can help Eva in her searching, anymore than Oksanna has. But still, Eva hands the photograph to Mrs. Moroz, who accepts it as though she's seeing it for the first time. She moves a little closer into the light, putting on the spectacles that hang on a chain round her neck.

Mrs. Moroz says something in Ukrainian, then looks up at Eva. "Come, we had better go back downstairs."

They have finished the pot of tea and Mrs. Moroz has brought out a bottle of plum brandy. Eva has been pouring out to her everything she's kept hidden from Oksanna. How the boy in the photo looks exactly like her son; the trip to Porcupine Creek; the gist of Phonsine's story. Such relief to tell all this to someone she can trust, someone who's both an utter stranger and an old, old friend.

"Do you know who they are?" Eva asks again.

Mrs. Moroz takes another long look at the photograph before she hands it back. "Give me a few days; I will find out what I can."

"Oksanna doesn't know what I've told you," Eva says. "I showed her the photograph, but—" She's suddenly tired, so tired and anxious she can't finish her sentence. Thinking she should tell Mrs. Moroz about Oksanna's distress—warn her, somehow, if a warning is needed. But for once she lets herself ask for something; she needs this woman's help, needs it for herself.

Mrs. Moroz smiles at her, a smile in a minor key. "You must not worry about Oksanna. There is no need for you to see her again. It is better if she does not know you have been here tonight. If you give me your number, I can call you once I have made some inquiries." She smiles at Eva, her voice maternal now, the voice that sings you to sleep and banishes nightmares. "*Ne zhurysia, donyu.* Life has a way of working out."

Eva means to shake Mrs. Moroz's hand, but instead she throws her arms around her. Feeling the strength of the woman's body; something Eva can only call steadfastness, though it's not at all the word she wants. Mrs. Moroz reaches up to stroke Eva's cropped head. She speaks in Ukrainian again, and when Eva shakes her head, she smiles.

"You used to have such lovely hair—that is what I was saying. Such long, lovely hair. Just like your mother."

Nearly the end of her shift, but she shows no eagerness to leave the room, the worn wooden stool on which she sits. Her back against the radiators, though they give out no heat. The building's freezing, even in high summer: all that marble, cold as a corpse's feet. Marble and the ghosts trapped in the paintings: no wonder the place always makes her think of mortuary and museum meaning the same thing.

She pulls the cuffs of her cardigan down over her swollen knuckles. Damp as well as cold here. Under her cardigan she wears a woollen vest, and under that a flannel blouse, with another woollen vest underneath. Like an onion: you could peel her and peel her and find only empty air. What happens to old women who've outlived their children: no heart left, no centre. Her lips purse, a suspicious look skews her face. She hears noises down the corridor: someone is coming to look at her paintings. But the footsteps end abruptly before they reach her room, the corner where she sits, pretending heat from the radiator. Someone curses—a woman who has caught the heel of her shoe in one of the long, wide fissures in the marble floor.

The guard smiles to herself. There's an apple in her pocket, a small, puckered apple that she's saved with a dozen others from her sister's orchard. Kept them wrapped in newspaper on the glassed-in verandah, all through the winter and well past spring. The apple is so soft it will give her no trouble with her teeth. She draws it from her pocket, hiding it in a fold of her skirt until all the noises have died away and she's back in her usual company: the cold, the silence, the damp. As she holds the apple to her mouth, breathing in whatever remains of fragrance in the battered peel, she looks up to the paintings under her charge. Two women on either side of a tree bursting with fruit: thick, red balls, like something you'd hang on a Christmas tree. And the large, still painting she tries not to look at, because it makes her want to cross herself, as she would before an accident on the street. A woman showing only her back. A whole basket of fruit abandoned on a table, and the woman looking into a distance hazy as a cloud. A dark place where she'll have no need to eat or drink, or be comforted with apples.

Three days after her visit to Oksanna's house, Eva's at work, trying to sort out a quarrel between two of the children, when she's called to the phone. "Just take a message," she yells, keeping Ajmer and Will from poking out each other's eyes over a toy tractor they both want to ride. It no longer amazes Eva how sudden and consuming these struggles are; she knows that, contrary to what all the child-care manuals pronounce, such things are never outgrown but only deflected, or disguised. Like the quarrels she's been having with Julie, beautiful, sunny Julie, who's taken to a child's version of civil disobedience: refusing, till the last possible moment, to get ready for day camp, to make her lunch, comb her hair, or put on her shoes. And all because they won't let her get her ears pierced.

Hours after Eva's sorted things out between the children, she gets round to asking about the telephone call. It was from someone named Olya Pavlenko, she's told—Olya Pavlenko being, Eva finally realizes, Mrs. Moroz. Like her daughter, she's changed her name, or in this case simply undone the stitches of another's name sewn over her own. Eva rushes to return the call, terrified that Olya will have given up on her by now. So it's as good as a blessing when she answers the phone, telling Eva she's found something that may interest her.

They meet at the Rare Book Library, Robarts, on the floor where the rare books are housed. They know her here, Olya explains—she's working on a translation project with one of the professors from the Department of Slavic Studies, from which she got a degree several years ago. But there's no need for Olya to explain or excuse herself: this hushed room with its rows and rows of books and all the different worlds they hold—this is her native element, where Eva feels as out of place as if she were one of the sheep she used to tend on that failing farm in Nova Scotia.

Olya disappears into another room, returning with a volume that's been sturdily bound in leather. Yet its pages are so fragile Eva's afraid they'll crack as they're turned. "Poor quality," Olya whispers. "Because of the shortages. All the best paper used to be imported from Paris, but after 1918 there was an end to that."

She translates the title page: *Soviet-Ukrainian Writers Today.* The date Eva can read for herself: 1933.

"These were the best writers in my country," Olya explains. "The ones I went to listen to when I was a student. I heard Olena Teliha many times. A wonderful poet. But look—here is what I want you to see."

She turns to a clump of photographs at the beginning of the volume. Individual portraits of various poets, novelists, playwrights. One is of a very young woman, a schoolgirl, really: black-haired, dressed in a dark cloak and tam.

"Lesia Levkovych. Also a poet—very fine. Most of her books were destroyed, either by the Nazis or the Soviets. As for this book, it's a miracle that it ever appeared. The publishing house that produced it was shut down that same year—1933."

Eva nods politely. It's a poor image: blurry, retouched. Olya turns to the back of the book, to another set of photographs. She points to a group shot. "This was taken at an artists' colony not far from Kiev. Its name was Soloveyko—'Nightingale.'"

Eva bends closer, her heart jumping. Among the people gathered on a sunny terrace is a woman holding back a young boy, the boy straining to break free. The woman in her photograph: the woman who, she can see now, is also the black-haired schoolgirl in her cloak and tam.

Olya pulls a magnifying glass from her pocket. "The man cut out of your picture is Pavlo Bozhyk. One of the leading painters of the Kiev Circle."

Eva takes the glass, examines his face. She should have

guessed he was a painter, just by his hands on the woman's shoulders, the way the long fingers seem to be listening to the blood beneath the skin. He looks older than the woman, in his fifties whereas she can be no more than thirty-five.

"The photograph was taken just before the worst of the purges. Skrypnyk, Bozhyk, Teliha, Levkovych—they all died before their time, during the Terror or in the war that followed it."

Eva isn't listening. There's a sad magic to the way the man is restored to his hands; the woman to her lover—for they can only be lovers, joined as they are. "What happened to them?"

Olya tells her, again. Eva still can't take it in. Eight years after this picture was taken, most of the people in it would be dead. She corrects herself. Killed. She looks again at the woman whose name she knows now: Lesia.

"And the little boy—her son?"

"His name"—Olya runs her finger along the caption under the photograph—"is Ivan." She pronounces it like the French "Yvonne." "No one knows what happened to him. So many people vanished. It makes it sound so easy, that word. As if they just smiled and faded, like your Cheshire cat."

Olya takes out her pen and writes three names on a piece of paper which she gives to Eva. *Lesia Levkovych. Pavlo Bozhyk. Ivan Kotelko.* Eva picks up the book and turns gingerly back to the first section, the photograph of Lesia Levkovych. "I'll write out a translation for you later," Olya says, pointing to the paragraph beneath the picture.

It's all so foreign to Eva, and yet far too close. There's a bloodline, not just ink on paper, but a thin, tough line of blood linking her, now, in this glass and concrete library, with these doomed people sitting on a sun-struck terrace, in a country no more real to her than a kingdom in a fairy tale. Suddenly, the impossible distance between this young, scowling boy in the photograph and her own son has been bridged, and by nothing more than a line of blood.

Eva's turned as pale as the paper she holds in her hand: her very skin begins to feel like this paper: porous, disintegrating. Olya touches Eva's sleeve; asks if she would like a glass of water.

"I'm fine—just hungry, that's all. I haven't eaten since breakfast. Let's go, Olya: why don't I take you out for dinner?"

Eva's choice: The Continental Express, a cavernous restaurant near the Old Mill subway stop. The kind of place neither Dan nor Oksanna would ever patronize. Ersatz-ethnic décor, a mixed-up middle-European menu, with goulash and cabbage rolls and Russian salad. If Olya finds the place offensive, she is far too polite to say, but the more Olya tells her of the past of that place she left so long ago, the more uncomfortable Eva becomes. With the Caravan kitsch of the restaurant, the easy ignorance of the clientele, including her. Everyone, she's convinced, is here for an evening's east-European slumming. Everyone except Olya, who has talked far more than she's eaten. She's been telling Eva about what it was like for that woman, Lesia Levkovych, at the time the photograph was taken. In that artists' colony whose name Eva's had to ask her to repeat, and that she remembers only in its English form: Nightingale.

"Ten years they had, Eva. Teachers and students, painters and writers, actors and musicians—ten years of building something that had never been allowed before. Their own culture, in their own language. Ten years of children going to school in Ukrainian, not Russian—even at the universities, courses taught in our own language, what the Russians used to call 'the peasant tongue.' Publishing houses, newspapers, journals, theatres—everything was allowed, everything that would keep the language alive and open and growing. Khvylovy, Tychyna, Rylsky, Kulish—I was a student, then, I used to go to the lecture halls and the cafés to hear them. All with the same cry: 'Away from Moscow!'

"And everything they worked for, those ten years—wiped out. Stalin sent his man in, Postyshev. He took away our language and gave us Christmas trees, instead. Books were hauled off library shelves, plays banned, theatres closed. Even the museums were ordered to dispose of pottery, embroidery—anything identifiable as Ukrainian. To be Ukrainian was to be anti-Bolshevik; to use our language was to commit counter-revolution. And just when everyone thought things had got as bad as they possibly could, the executions started, with or without benefit of trial. It got so that people would shoot themselves before the state could do it for them. And this was years before the show trials started in Moscow; they used us as—what is the word? Guinea pigs."

Listening to her, Eva feels the way she did in the library—as if everything she'd taken for granted, the very floor she's been standing on, has dropped away. How could people—a whole country—have survived what Olya's just told her? And how could this woman with her talk of artists and lecture halls and executions be the same person who'd cleaned house for a living, whose whole life had seemed to be made of brushes and mops and the sound of rags being wrung out in metal pails?

"Forgive me," Olya says. "I have been talking a blue streak." She likes to use colloquial expressions, the archaic ones Eva's only come across in books.

Eva doesn't know what's expected of her. It's clear Olya's waiting for some response adequate to all this: show trials, executions, shootings. Plots Eva can't begin to imagine, intricate and fatal. And that woman, Lesia Levkovych, caught up in it all.

"Eva." Olya's leaning in towards her, almost whispering. "You have to decide now."

"Decide?"

"What you are going to do."

Eva looks into Olya's strong, clear face, and then drops her eyes.

"But I have decided, Olya; that's why I asked you to help me. To find the man who sent me that photograph. Now that I know his name, I can—"

"Names." It's the first sharp thing Eva's heard Olya say. "Names can be changed, erased, bent to sound English, French, whatever you like. I carried my husband's name for twenty-seven years—did that tell anyone who I really was? It is different for writers, artists—

those are the names that matter, that stand for something. It is a great honour for you, this connection with Lesia Levkovych."

Eva grabs Olya's hands, trying to make her understand. "It's her son I need to find. The only reason I'm sitting here with you right now is because—" She doesn't know how to continue, except by instinct, making the story she wants to believe. "Because he's in trouble, and he needs my help. I have to see him, Olya. I have to talk with him."

Olya shakes her head; gently, she pulls her hands free. "Leave it be, Eva. Do not make trouble for yourself, or for your son. I have told you, no one knows what happened to Ivan Kotelko. He vanished during the war. The only thing you need to know is that the woman in your photograph is Lesia Levkovych. How you came by that photograph, what your connection is with her—this can be your secret. No one else need know. Think of your mother: why should she be shamed? And think of your son, Eva."

Olya signals for the waiter and pays the bill that was supposed to go to Eva. Helplessly, Eva leans her head on her hands. Everything's become so tangled, so confused. Ivan, Lesia: she makes herself give them their names. And everyone else who's come crowding in beside them: Holly, Ben, Oksanna, Olya, Alex. And herself. All joined because of that one ugly word in an old woman's story—bohunk. No papers to prove any of this, no official documents or stamps, just a twisting together of stories. But the man is real and she has to find him; find out what he wants from her, give him whatever it is he asks her for: money, a ticket out of the country, she doesn't know, doesn't care. Five weeks, that's all the time she has before Ben comes back. For one thing she's sure of: none of this must touch Ben—whatever Olya's hinting at, the things it's better not to know about elderly men who should have perished during the war.

Olya takes Eva's hand, pressing it hard, forcing her to look up.

"We are a people who remember, Eva, even when there is nothing to remember but defeat and death. That is the only way we have kept ourselves alive—by remembering."

And now Olya does the most extraordinary thing: as if they were alone in this enormous room, as if it were the most natural thing in the world to do, she opens her mouth and begins to sing the most haunting song Eva's ever heard. Just two words, over and over, climbing and descending in a pattern so simple it can hold all the grief and hope in the world. At the tables around them, people fall silent the way they do when a candled cake appears at the end of a meal, to the tune of happy birthday. And Eva, who could no more sing than strip in public, sits gaping.

When Olya finishes, she lets go Eva's hands. *"Vichnaia pamiat,"* she says. "It means 'in everlasting memory.' You sing it when someone dies; when you want to pay tribute to the dead."

She looks at Eva and smiles, this time without any sadness in her face. "I will make you a translation of one of Levkovych's poems. It will speak to you," she says. "Even in the wrong language, it will tell you what you need to know. So that you can do what you have to now. Go to Kiev, to your grandmother's grave. Give her back her name, her past; honour her."

She's radiant with certainty, as if what she's just suggested is the easiest thing in the world. Eva's about to protest when Olya's next words stop her dead.

"When you are in Kiev, you can do something for me, as well. You can go to see Oleksa. I know how you can get in touch with him."

"Oleksa?"

"Yes," Olya smiles. And then, using the possessive carelessly, generously: "Your Alex."

Water the same unstable blue as a newborn's eyes. Wading through it, she feels her flesh waver on its bones; as she loses the sand, blue enters her eyes and mouth; everything inside her turning to water.

The island is just as she left it. A white tent against the black of the balsam trees, so white she has to shield her eyes. Water spills from her feet, her breasts, her mouth as she walks towards the tent.

On its skin, she sees his shadow. A candle burning, making warm, buttery light, softening the shadow of his sleeping body. She traces the line of his shoulders and hips, the scarred shins, the slant of his cheekbones.

In her blue-grey skin, she makes no more noise than night makes, falling into the sky. She lifts the tent flap, but he isn't there. It isn't a tent at all, just a paper shape, like the teepees she used to draw at school. White paper: it twitches in the sudden wind and sails away. She raises her hands to her mouth, making a cold, blue tunnel, calling and calling his name.

Eva wakes with Dan's arms around her, shaking her gently from the nightmare she's been having. It must have been a nightmare, since she was crying out in her sleep, and her hands are clenched. He holds her, rocking her against him, as if she were the child they never had. After a while, they go back to sleep, facing the same way. Their bodies do not touch, but she is aware of his good, familiar warmth beside her. She feels sad and guilty and confused; bits of her dream come back to her, just for a moment, then dissolve. She knows she was looking for someone, and that he wasn't Dan. And she remembers a woman's voice calling out.

Holly. She will go to see her tomorrow, she can't put it off any longer. She keeps that decision firm in her head, though she retains nothing else of her dream, or of how she woke from it. Dan and she keep their usual distance getting dressed, eating breakfast, making their separate ways out of the house. Their only means of connection now through Julie, who wears one of the crayon earrings Eva has given her, and one of the small gold hoops she's been given by her father. The remaining half of each pair lying side by side in a small blue box filled with cotton batting.

Sometimes, when she shuts her eyes, letting down that thin, skin curtain, they disappear: the nurses carrying soup or syringes on their trays; the doctors with the manner and power of husbands. Soon they will come and go as they like, feed her, feel her, and talk, talk, talk while she's far away in a place she's kept hidden from them all: nurses, doctors, husband, child. The perfect hiding place: an island in the middle of a lake where no one ever goes.

On her island, she can walk right out of her skin: wrinkles, liver spots, the thousand disfigurements of growing old. Out of her skin and into the blood and bones of who she used to be. A young woman, her body light as moss on the rocks where she sits, holding up her face to the sun.

She stays like this until her eyes get accustomed to the harshest light, and she can see farther than she ever could before. She may have been sitting here for a day or an hour or only a moment when she realizes that she's not alone, that someone's walking towards her. Closer and closer, not the one she's been waiting for so long, but someone who could be her own reflection in the wavy glass of a mirror. A woman, her eyes blue like her own, but her hair cropped, as though she's been ill with a high, high fever.

"Tell me what to do. I want to find him, but I'm afraid. Please, mother, help me."

Mother: the word tears the lids off her eyes. This is not her own reflection in the water, it is her daughter: she is not on her island anymore, but back in the house on the Kingsway. That house full of windows that would never stay open; doors that were always shut. Shut, but never locked: how could she run off with a child sewn into her arms? The child who's come back to her now, who will never let her alone, let her be.

"I gave you his name. That was all he left me with: you, and his name. When you were born, I wanted to die. Every time I looked at you, all I could see was how he'd abandoned me."

Two of them she has let inside her. A husband, holding her body in his hands as if it were crystal, turning it this way and that, searching for flaws. A lover, undoing the buttons of her shirt as though they were made of flesh. There's a wind scented with balsam blowing through the room. If she were to close her eyes, she could sail on that wind back to her island, sit with her face lifted straight to the sun. But she can't close her eyes until she makes her go, this woman weeping across from her, tears sliding down her face, the same liquid she floated in so many years ago, inside her.

She takes her daughter's hands in her own, so that their fingers are laced through. Her tongue sharp as glass in her mouth. If only she could use the language of birds—but she will have to spend a long time on her island before she learns that one, perfect tongue. Still, she opens her mouth and speaks, though the words sound like glass breaking, shards rubbed against each other.

"When I lived in the city, I would go looking, everywhere I could think of. Those streets downtown where they spoke his language; I'd stop anyone who looked like him, call out his name. Once I thought I'd found him, but it was a mistake; he left me again, and he never came back. If you'd been a boy, he would never have gone: he wanted a son."

She drops her daughter's hands and puts her own to her face, covering her eyes. If she presses hard enough, long enough, she will go back there, to the island, the one place he knows where to find her. Where she can wait for him quietly as a stone under water. And where no one, not even this child of theirs, can come between them.

Leaving her mother's room, Eva grasps what Holly's given her—in fragments that cut her hands the tighter she holds them. She has all the names at last—even her own. Proof, if she needed it: if she'd been a boy, he would have claimed her. She knows she should feel anger at this, but instead there's only numbness and a curious release. "Olya's right," she thinks. "The man is dead, I owe him nothing." He has made no further signal to her, no gesture or demand. Abandoned her as he'd once abandoned her mother. *I would go looking for him, call out his name.* The phrase plays itself over and over in her head, but this time she isn't thinking of Ivan Kotelko.

She goes to the reception area to speak to the nurses before leaving. They tell her that Holly's been much quieter lately: more tractable. The bad side of this is that she seems to have stopped talking altogether. Did she say anything during Eva's visit? The nurse puts this question with considerable tact, making no allusion to the fact that Eva's face is still swollen from crying.

"Say anything?" Eva repeats. "Nothing you could make any sense of." And then she explains she's going to be away for a few weeks—she'll give them a contact number before she goes, in case anything should happen.

"Going out of the country?"

"Just away. If she should ask for me, tell her I've gone looking."

"Looking? For something in particular—something she's asked you for?"

"Just looking."

Sometimes, when he can't sleep, or when he's stuck, as he is now, in an endless queue waiting for a cup of coffee that will be cold as well as bitter by the time he gets it, he lets himself think of how things might have been if he hadn't come back to this place all those years ago.

He doesn't think of people—that would be far too painful—but of places. How he might have gone up north, to the copper or nickel mines, or found work during the summers on field expeditions out west. Or travelled to places he'd picked at random from the atlas: Coronation Hills, Wager Plateau, Bear Slave Upland.

If he'd been careful, and lucky, and what was the English word for it?—industrious—he might have been able to buy a house, a whole house, on one of those green, quiet streets close to the park where they used to spend their Sundays when the weather was fine. He and his wife would have their own bedroom, and their daughter would sleep in a fine, airy room just down the hall from them, a room big enough for all the toys and books and games they'd be able to buy for her. She would never know a day's sickness beyond the usual childhood complaints: measles, mumps, chicken pox. He tries to remember the English words for these, and can't—it upsets him out of all proportion; if he can't find the words, it makes the whole thing even more impossible, something he can't even fantasize.

Would he have forgotten his own language if he'd stayed behind? What language would he have spoken with his wife, or his daughter? Would it even have mattered? He imagines himself in a supermarket like the ones he sometimes sees on television, on shows beamed in from Germany or California. He sees himself putting a whole pound of coffee beans into his shopping cart, and beside that, aspirin and toothbrushes. Piling his cart full of the most ordinary, necessary things, and thinking no more of it than he does of blinking his eyes.

When he does get to the counter, the coffee's run out. The woman is more exhausted than apologetic; he can't help complaining to her, though it does neither of them any good. There's a café a few doors down he could try, but by now he's lost all desire for coffee, any desire to keep awake at all. He walks out of the shop and continues down the avenue, under the exuberant shade of chestnut trees that try as hard as they can to hide what lies behind them. He wonders, as he walks, what this avenue must have been like before the war, before it was hurled up and torn apart. Before the engineers were commissioned to rebuild it as it is now: row after row of brute blocks, none of them offering the simplest pleasure: a fresh roll, a cup of coffee.

Once you've struggled through one impossible feat, Eva learns, you can rush through a dozen others. Whatever that first act was—the trip to Porcupine Creek, the meeting with Olya in the library, her last visit to Holly—or perhaps, prior and essential to all these, holding out her hand over a glass display case, speaking her first words in the language of desire—she accomplishes this last, scandalous feat with the ease of an acrobat. Flying off to Kiev. The words make her think of a Chagall poster she'd once tacked to her bedroom wall: a woman floating through a window, her body flexible as those wands of Plasticine children play with, bending them into rainbows, tulips. Only, the Chagall woman is floating away from, not towards, the lover who's stretching out his arms to her.

Your Alex. Olya's parting words to her at the Continental Express have haunted Eva, a ghost no one else can see, but a ghost she needs to make excuses for. To Dan, who has stopped complaining about her absences and absent-mindedness, and has shut himself in a cold politeness worse than any shouting could be. To Julie, who spends more and more time at the neighbour's, or with kids from the day camp, sleeping over at their houses. To the friends she avoids when she sees them on the street. And most of all to Ben, who must have noticed the skimpiness of her calls, when all she can trust herself to talk about is the state of their moribund cat: *still eating, still sleeping, still warming the pillows on your bed.*

And yet, what she feels since her dinner with Olya, her visit with Holly is not guilt or trepidation, but an extraordinary buoyancy, that lightness of heart and body that can follow the making of even the rashest decisions. Perhaps this is what allows her to sail through the next ten days: applying for a rapid-fire passport, badgering a visa from the apple-cheeked boy behind the information desk at the Ukrainian consulate, arranging things at work so she can take a long-overdue holiday "to Europe."

Shopping for decent clothes, arranging for the florist to send Holly a huge bouquet of alstroemeria, the one flower that seems to last almost forever.

It's good she has these hoops to jump through, otherwise she might have stopped to ask herself what on earth she'll do once she gets to Kiev. Olya's told her not to worry; everything's become so much easier there now—it's just like travelling to Germany or France. She's writing it all down on paper, what Eva's got to do once she gets there; the information she needs to reach Alex.

The hardest thing Eva has to do is pay a business call on Dan. He shows no surprise at her coming to the office, just an indifference that makes her jump straight into what she has to say:

"I need a cheap ticket to Kiev—the sooner the better."

"There are no cheap tickets to Kiev. Try Budapest. Or Prague, it's beautiful and inexpensive and you can have a decent time there. Nobody goes to Ukraine on a holiday. You'll pay first-class hotel rates for a place where you wouldn't want to leave your dog, you'll get sick of potatoes and cabbage after your first two days, and besides, nothing goes on there in the summer. All the choirs and dance troupes are off on tour in North America, and everyone else is in Yalta or visiting relatives in the village."

"I want the cheapest ticket I can get to Kiev."

"Why?"

"Because."

"Thank you—that explains a lot. It makes it crystal clear why you suddenly want to fly off to one of the most difficult—notice I didn't say exotic—countries in the world. A place where you don't speak the language and you don't know a single goddam soul."

She tries to make a joke of it. "Do you give all your clients this hard a time?"

He doesn't smile; he doesn't look at her, but keeps his eyes on the computer screen. "Look, Eva, I'll make this simple: I don't know what's got into you, but what you want to do is crazy. In this particular situation, you don't know your feet from your hands, to quote a favourite expression of my mother's. You have to say it in Yiddish to get the full flavour."

"I need a ticket, Dan. A week in Kiev—I can't afford anything but rock-bottom."

"Good. Because that's exactly where you'll be when you land in the ex–People's Republic."

She should never have started this, there are dozens of travel agencies she could have used instead. Except that it would have felt dishonest not to come to Dan. Even more dishonest than she's been already.

He erases the information on the screen and bellows to a colleague: "Alok, you'll have to step in here and help this lady. I've got a lunch date." Alok takes down the particulars as Dan stomps out the door: frowns and says he'll do his best, though all the charters are already booked.

The day after the incident at Janus Travel, Dan comes up to Eva where she's labouring at the kitchen table, kneading a batch of playdough for the day-care. She thinks he's come to get Julie, who, in a rare fit of helpfulness, is measuring out enormous amounts of flour and food colouring and salt. But Dan tells Julie to go up and clean her room—a signal he wants to talk to Eva alone. As soon as Julie's gone, Dan slaps down an envelope in the middle of a lake of flour.

"There was a cancellation from a tour group. Don't worry, you can take the flight and hole up in your hotel room for the whole two weeks, if that's what you want. Have a wonderful time."

"Thanks." Eva forces herself to keep on kneading the dough; by now her hands are stained purple.

"Thanks. Well, that's big of you. Do you know how many places I had to phone to get this cancellation? Do you have any idea how much money I've saved you? I suppose that doesn't matter, I suppose our little Eva's so flush, what with her stock options and investment portfolios, that she can afford to fly executive class all the way to the Golden Gates of Kiev."

"I don't have any stock options and you know it. Or portfolios." Eva rubs her forehead with the back of her hand, leaving a mark like a squashed grape over her right eye. "I am grateful. I'd salaam from here to Union Station if my hands were free. Oh God, Dan, I'm sorry. I don't know why I can't just say thank you, and why you can't know that I mean it."

Another time, they'd have embraced, regardless of the food colouring, the flour. But they keep to their separate sides of the table, till Dan breaks the silence:

"I presume you're going to use my name in the *Person to Contact in Case of an Emergency* section of your passport. So don't you think you could tell me even half of what's going on?"

Eva takes a kitchen knife and scrapes the dough from her hands. She asks Dan to get a bottle of wine from the cupboard, and they head out to the back porch, where they're still talking hours later. Or rather, Eva's been talking and Dan has kept perfectly still, hearing about DP camps and artists' colonies in Soviet Ukraine, and lumber camps near Porcupine Creek. About everything and everyone but Alex. When Dan finally does speak, what astonishes Eva is his distress, not at having been kept in the dark all this time, not even at having been lied to, but at the nationality of Holly's lover.

"God, Eva. Of all the things to turn out to be. Ukrainian."

"But I'm not—"

"As far as I can calculate—and I'm passable at fractions—you are exactly half Ukrainian."

Eva gets prickly—she doesn't want this; she hasn't permitted this. "Just because some man from a place I hardly knew about until a month ago happened to inseminate my mother, that makes me Ukrainian?"

"Half Ukrainian."

"Jesus, Dan, I don't see why it matters."

"It's not just Easter eggs and perogies, being Ukrainian. It also happens to be things like pogroms. Your national hero, Khmelnitsky—"

"He's no hero of mine. I don't even know who he is."

"—was one of the great pogrom-makers of all time, and if you don't know that, it's time you learned. Khmelnitsky and his cossacks. They were the bogeymen my grandparents frightened me with, if I didn't behave. It's true, Eva—you have no idea about my grandparents. But let's not get personal. Let's just stick to history. We have the little matter of Babi Yar, and all those jolly Ukrainian guards at the death camps, some of whom are alive and well and living in friendly, all-Canadian towns the length and breadth of this fair land. Just what did he do in the war, this long-lost daddy of yours? Are you sure you want to find out?"

Eva can't answer him, can't say yes or no. She keeps hearing Olya's voice through his: "We are a people who remember, even when there is nothing to remember but defeat and death." There are stories Dan has to tell, stories he'd heard as a child and that she's never had the wit to ask him for. Only they were more than stories for the family who stayed behind when his grandparents left Poland for Canada.

The little matter of Babi Yar, Ukrainian guards at the death camps. If he looked at her now, he would see her shaking her head, a gesture she isn't aware she's making. Saying no to these things Olya has never talked about; no to whatever it was that Ivan Kotelko may have done in that war he was supposed to have vanished in. How can all that be a part of who she is? When she was born here, raised here; when, until a few weeks ago, she didn't even know she had a connection to that man Ivan Kotelko, or his country. Why is everything so densely connected, like a pattern in a Turkish rug? You want to cut a square from the rug, just enough to stand on, but while you cut you're making wounds in other people's lives. The red in this pattern bleeds.

Eva tries to touch Dan's face, that good, genial face as familiar to her as the pattern on the kitchen dishes. He shakes her hand away. "It's not that easy," he says. Eva doesn't know whether he's talking of their peculiar way of living together, or of the journey she's undertaking. Or of his own way of coping with a history both family and public, a world "back there" he never knew, yet where a part of him lives, even now.

He offers no explanations. They sit in silence, watching the moon come up, listening to the dinner party the neighbours are giving in their backyard: easy voices, laughter floating over the fence.

Eva knows that something should be said or done to mend the rift between them, but she can't think what. They'll talk again when she gets back from Kiev. By then, they'll both have had a chance to think, to see things in perspective. A perspective that isn't clouded by ghosts, or history.

She collects the dead bottle, pulls herself to her feet. "It's late—I'll make sure Julie's in bed."

He makes no move to go.

"Thanks again for the ticket. I'll leave you a cheque under the sugar bowl."

"Don't bother. It's a going-away present."

"Don't be an idiot, Dan—I'll write out the cheque right now."

Julie's fast asleep. Eva stands beside her for a while, afraid to stroke her hair in case she wakes. She leaves the room, and stops out of habit beside Ben's door. The emptiness, the silence hit at her heart, and then she hears the cat purring. Blind, deaf Sugar, who should have been put down years ago. Eva goes to Ben's bed, buries her face in the cat's hot fur.

It's the best thing for him, she reminds herself—to have got so far away from this mess of stories and photographs and shadows. Does he think of her at all, when he's away? She pictures him, asleep in a strange bed, his face scarred with that tense, frowning look he'd been born with, though no one could call him an unhappy child. "His vision's fine," the doctor had said. "As for that frown, he's probably copying it from you. Stop worrying, for heaven's sake, and just enjoy him."

Eva leaves the room to the cat, and makes her way to the attic. From an overdue library book she takes a photograph, holding it so tight the edges press into her palms. Did she worry over the frown on her son's face, the woman trying so hard to hold onto him? Did the doctor tell her there was nothing to worry about, in that country where the picture was taken? It's all right, Eva wants to tell her. He made it through the war, your son; he even made it

all the way to Canada. A beautiful woman fell in love with him.
Just like in a fairy tale. The kind with ogres and witches and deep,
dark, all-too-penetrable forests, from which you can never find
your way out again.

The day before Eva leaves for Kiev, she has a last meeting with
Olya, in the park. There is something they haven't discussed yet,
something Eva needs as much as she does the telephone number
Olya's promised to write out for her. She has to know what to say
to Alex about his mother and sister; what message Olya wants to
send through her.

"No message. It is better not to mention us at all."

"Olya, I have to mention you. It's the first thing he'll ask about.
If I can get through to him, that is. You know I don't speak—"

"You will have no trouble there. Oleksa's English is excellent.
Was excellent—and he will not have forgotten it."

Eva has to fight down a sudden panic. "Why should he want
to speak with me? You don't understand. What if he doesn't
remember me—it's been thirty years, you know."

"It is natural for you to get cold hands, Eva. Forgive me, but I
do understand, I understand more than you think. In any case,
Ukrainians are a hospitable people—we treat our guests far better
than we do ourselves."

"Then why don't you go, Olya? Why don't you come with me?"

Olya brushes petals from her skirt; they are sitting under a
catalpa tree, and the breeze is shaking down large, trumpet-shaped
blossoms. Eva has a crown of them in her hair.

For a while, there's silence between them. Olya reaches her
hand up to Eva's head and removes the catalpa blossoms, one by
one. By the time she's finished, she's ready to speak.

She tells Eva how, on just such a lovely summer's night fifty years
ago, she'd gone to see a movie with her girlfriend. At one of the few

cinemas that did not display the sign, *No Ukrainians or Dogs Allowed*. She can remember the story exactly—a romance set in some wedding-cake castle in Bavaria. She'd wanted to leave halfway through, but her girlfriend had persuaded her to stay. So that, when they did leave at the end of the film, they walked straight into a net of German soldiers. She never again saw her family, her friends, the man she was in love with and was going to marry once the war was over. Even her girlfriend was lost to her: they ended up on different transports to Germany. Hers went to a farm in that same Bavaria where the film had taken place, and where she was treated as far less deserving of food or warmth than the dogs or cattle in the barnyard. When the war stopped, she was shunted into a DP camp, where officials she never met decided what to do with her.

The ability of the heart to scar over, if not heal; to survive such continual damage, amazes Eva as she listens. Olya tells of how she nearly went back to Ukraine when they were shipping refugees home, except that one of those refugees fell in love with her, and convinced her to go with him in the opposite direction—France, England, Canada. And such had been her longing to live, instead of endlessly waiting for life to begin, that she'd married him, this good man she did not love, and with whom she had nothing in common but the luck of having survived.

"My husband is dead, my son is as good as dead to me. In the whole world I have no one left but Oksanna. Everything I am now, I owe to her—everything I own: the clothes on my back, the apartment she's given me. A very comfortable coffin. You have seen my books, my kilim and embroidered cushions, Eva. They will all die with me; I have no one to pass them on to. Not just the things, but my love for them. Oksanna has nothing to do with anything Ukrainian now. She has tried so hard to become Canadian: changing her name, refusing to speak the language. When her father and brother went back, she made me promise I would never answer their letters or go to them in any way. She said it was either Oleksa or her, and that I had to choose. If I chose Canada, then I chose her—only her. I am so sick of countries, Eva; of borders. As if people were born with maps where their hearts should be."

She stops, and again, there's silence. Slowly, painfully, Olya gets to her feet. She's an old woman, Eva realizes; she's nowhere near as strong as she once was. Pressing her face against Eva's, Olya holds her for a moment. "Have a safe journey. When you return, we will have a cup of tea together and talk, shall we?"

"Of course," Eva says, holding on to Olya, wanting to keep close to her as long as possible. But Olya pulls away. It's late, she says; surely Eva has packing to do, last-minute arrangements? Suddenly, Eva's thinking of all the things she mustn't forget: passport, ticket, money, phrasebook, hardly noticing what Olya's slipped into her pocket before she walks away.

On her way home, Eva looks up through the maple trees. Streetlamps pour light through the leaves: a thick, green syrup. She digs her hands into her pockets, checking for her housekey, but finds instead two carefully folded squares of paper.

One of them contains the telephone number of Professor Oleksandr Moroz, Academy of Sciences, Kiev, written in an indelibly European script, the ones looking like sevens, the sevens with a horizontal slash through the middle. The other holds a poem, the translation of Levkovych that Olya had promised her. Eva waits to get home before she reads it, sitting on the porch steps with the poem still folded in her hands. Dan is away with Julie for the weekend; she'll have the house to herself. Even so, she stays outside. There's a rustle of leaves all round her: a thick, good smell of rain in the air. She closes her eyes, unable to account for the curious feeling inside her, half delight—as if she really does have wings—half fear, as if she's carrying a huge stone in her belly. Until she realizes it's expectancy—the coming rain, the start of her journey, the poem waiting to be read.

Kindness of Strangers

Out of this maze of streets a stranger walks towards me.
Unpremeditated yet expected, he has perfect manners
and a pair of wings, dwarfed and misshapen,
clotting the place where his heart should be.

Together we walk to a bridge over a great river.
We do not cross but stand looking down
at drifting boats, at streetlamps sunk
like eclipsed eyes.

I open my coat and show him my birthmark,
mud-thick, the colour of dead blood.
He puts his mouth to my breasts;
the stain turns to wine, pours clean away.

His wings break like wishbones
in my hands. Now there is nothing between us.
We stay a long time on the bridge,
the river rising, till it carries us off,

together,
in different directions.
Everything solid has vanished.
The air fills with a smoke like rain.

When the storm breaks midway through the night, Eva's fast
asleep. Wind rushes through the window, sucking at the shawl that
does for a curtain.

Eva has spent her whole adult life looking after delicate,
important things: her growing son and Dan's quicksilver

daughter; the children in her charge, her increasingly fragile and erratic mother. Yet this night she's been unaccountably careless. It's the effect, perhaps, of the poem—she had sat on the porch steps, reading, rereading. Moving backwards and forwards all at once: falling into memory, leaping into a story still to be told. As if, while she'd sat there in the thick, close dark, that other woman, the one who'd written and lived the poem, were walking into her skin.

The green shawl leaps wildly, coming half-unpinned from the window frame. All the papers on the chest of drawers, papers she should have packed away, are shifting, sliding. Waking in the morning, she will panic at not being able to find her plane ticket, only to discover it caught between the sandals she'd kicked off the night before. She will thank the God she otherwise never invokes for having made her copy Alex's telephone number straight into her passport before falling into bed; for having made her put that passport into its leather pouch, which she'd then stuffed under her pillow, the one safe place in the chaos round her. The poem that she'd meant to fold inside the passport, that she'd kept out to read one last time before turning out the light will, however, catch on the wind. Slipping between the bureau and the wall, it will not be found until she moves house, many years from now.

Two other things are safely stowed away. In the leather passport pouch lies the photograph of Lesia Levkovych and her son Ivan, plus a slip of paper Olya gave her shortly after they'd met at the library. It contains an annotated translation of the poet's short biography:

> Lesia Mikhailovna Levkovych, born April 12, 1898, in the town of Zhytomyr. Her parents, both teachers, died in a diphtheria epidemic while she was still a small child, and she was raised in the village of Verkhivnia (home to Honoré de Balzac 1847–1850) by her paternal grandmother. She attended the village school, and later the *gymnasium* (high school) in Zhytomyr. Having won a scholarship to the Academy of Arts, she trained to be

a teacher, but never finished her studies due to the outbreak of civil war in 1918, the same year her first book of poems, *Strangers,* was published. In 1924, she was elected to the Writers' Union and subsequently became involved with the reform movement led by Mykola Skrypnyk, Commissar for Education. She has published two other books of poetry, the experimental *Fallen Angels* and the widely acclaimed *Vigil,* both illustrated by Pavlo Borisovych Bozhyk, founder of the Kiev Circle. In 1922, she married a medical student, Roman Stepanovych Kotelko, who died the following year, a few months after their son was born.

On the other side of the sheet is an extract from a xeroxed article in *The Literary History of Ukraine:*

Among those executed in 1941 for political activities deemed subversive by the Nazi occupiers of Kiev were:

There follows a long list of names following with Lesia Levkovych's highlighted in yellow. There's a note in the margin, Olya's careful handwriting:

"She was taken to Babi Yar and shot, her body thrown in the ravine."

KIEV

All great cities are cut or caressed by water. Cities founded on the shores of seas and lakes, or else with rivers flowing through them, wide, surging rivers tamed by the boats of merchants and travellers. Kiev's great river is the Dnipro. Beginning as a pool of brackish water at the foot of the Valdai Hills, not far from the sources of the Volga, it flows, some thousand miles later, into the warm lap of the Black Sea.

The Greeks named this river *Borysthenes* and the Romans, *Danapris*. To the Turks it was *Uzu* and the Tatars, *Eksi*. But the Russians called it *Dnieper*, and since the Russians have conquered most of the land through which it flows, *Dnieper* it remains in the atlases and history books.

There are songs about the Dnipro, telling how the river has a human voice, a voice knowing far too much of loss and grief. Its waters are said to moan, to gnash over the rocks that once formed gigantic rapids, so that in some places the fall of the river was one hundred and fifty feet. Long before machines were brought to dam its waters, the Dnipro carried rafts of warriors from the amber-strewn beaches of the Baltic, or from the northern wastes. For centuries, the rulers of Kiev exacted tribute from surrounding tribes, sending ships loaded with wax and honey, furs and slaves downriver to the Black Sea. From there, they would sail to the Great City of the Southern Tsar, the city others called Constantinople.

Later, cossacks built fortresses on islands rising from a stretch of rapids navigable only when the river was in flood. Great battles were fought on its shores, and perhaps the Dnipro groans and keens in memory of all the bodies that have floated down its waters. Or perhaps it has to do with the burial mounds past which the river winds, the graves of soldiers, poets, rulers betrayed by the intricacies of fate, or by the simple cunning of their enemies. Some of the graves are of great antiquity, like those of two Varangians who, having sighted a clump of huts at the base of hills on which gold-domed churches were rising, interrupted their journey down the Dnipro to become rulers of Kiev. Good men, or at least no more vicious or corrupt than any others, they were lured one day outside the city gates by the councillor of the boy king of Novgorod. Lured and killed, their crowns seized by the ambitious councillor, who in his turn became a prince of Rus'.

In one of the most beautiful parks in Kiev, there is a monument to these two murdered adventurers, a double circle of purely shaped Ionic columns. At the foot of this monument is another burial mound, for eighteen of the three hundred schoolboys who, some thousand years after Kiev's founding, were formed into a regiment to defend the city against yet another wave of invaders. At Kruty, the schoolboys were slaughtered under the sign of that red star the hero of Bulgakov's *The White Guard* sees rising in the first skies of 1918. Though the river stayed clean of their blood, it must have received their deaths in some other form: in the grief that stunned so many families in that city; in the hard, sharp, unstoppable snow that buried the streets and parks and the very air, that winter.

Not snow but rain on the fine April night when a building, as extraordinary in its way as Kiev's golden-domed cathedrals, burst on fire. A rain of pitch-black graphite; uranium particles lacing the soil, from which all manner of berries and mushrooms continue to bloom, two delicacies anyone who can gather them can still afford. Invisible poison sinking into the wading pools and reservoirs of neighbouring towns; irradiating the Dnipro and all the fish its people catch there summer and winter, hunger clicking louder than any Geiger counter.

Gossamer-fine radionuclides shrouding Chornobyl, the city where, eight hundred years before, Prince Sviatopolk came searching for a bride. Having found her, he set her on his horse and galloped, silken banners streaming, home to the fortress walls of Kiev. Walls that vanished centuries ago, along with their gigantic golden gates. Where those gates once stood, the state has built a replica that fools no one and can protect nothing. Certainly not the children playing in the parks, breathing in contaminated air, drinking irradiated milk, until the authorities advise the children's parents to move them from the city, which for a whole summer is bereft. As singular, as sad as a summer forest stripped of all its leaves.

Less than a hundred years ago, scholars attributed the *Chronicle* or *Tale of Bygone Years* to the monk Nestor, who died sometime in the eleventh century. Recent scholarship disputes his authorship, but what is the scepticism, the science of the last fifty years to the certainty of the previous eight hundred? A story must have a teller; Nestor is as good a name as any to give to that voice, buried long before the body that contained it, in a cell hollowed in a hillside overlooking the Dnipro. The clay in the hills on which Kiev is built made possible the creation of Pecherska Lavra—the Monastery of the Caves—an underground labyrinth of chapels, cells, niches in which repose the mummified remains of monks, draped in brocades that were the gift of Catherine the Great.

In a cell that seems no bigger than a pair of cupped hands, the monk Nestor is writing, fishing stories of murder and piety, heroism and betrayal out of two centuries of darkness. In the way, as his chronicle relates, that a monstrous child was once fished up from the Dnipro. So that princes and merchants, schoolboys and common people sat on the riverbank for the afternoon and evening of that day, marvelling at this thing drawn up from mud and weeds. Neither a monster nor a child but somehow both, and of whose fate, after it had been hauled gasping into the air, the *Chronicle* says nothing.

To the people flying in the plane which took off, three hours before, from the International Airport in Frankfurt—a glass and concrete labyrinth whose endless corridors contain more in the way of treasure (plastic and electronic, silk, gold, and crystal) than do all the coffers of the Princes of Rus'—the honeycomb of caves under the hill remains invisible. As would be the plane to the monk Nestor. Were he to break open the narrow mouth through which his bread and water are pushed each day, grope his way along the corridors, and emerge into the blinding radiance of an ordinary summer morning, he would remark nothing more than a far white scar lodged in the blue overhead. Certainly nothing as superb and horrifying as the monstrous child.

No; from the hilltop where he might stand, roofing his eyes with his hands, he would see no apparition. Nothing but a new moon the sun has yet to push from the sky.

V

KIEV, JULY 1993

Astonishment, pure and simple, jumps Eva as she leaves the plane. Jumps and wrestles her to the ground, so that her point of view, all through the next two weeks, is that of someone at a constant disadvantage, having to look up. The way small children are always looking up at their parents and the world of grown-up people, a world which enchants and infuriates them; a world in which they have limited power and less knowledge. The worlds and worlds of things she doesn't know—this is what assaults her, walking down the steep metal stairs pushed up against the belly of the plane.

She isn't prepared for it: everything around, underneath her becoming unpredictable, so that she'll have to be watching out every moment. If she doesn't observe, carefully, what's in front of her, she won't be able to perform the simplest, most necessary act. Take, for example, the ground. The asphalt at the bottom of the stairway isn't just pitted but gouged; she could put her foot into one of those crevasses, trip and end up in a hospital ward, up to her waist in plaster. By the end of her stay, her eyes will have learned to read the cracks and fissures underneath her feet, whether in marble or asphalt or the hard-packed dust, the saddest colour she has ever seen. But right now she can take in nothing but the bright emptiness of the sky stretching over her, a huge sheet of paper on which she can write anything she likes, tell any story in the world.

On their way to the plane, the cleaners brush past the tour group. Decent, hardworking, prosperous people, who will appear like gods to their relations in the villages that get harder and harder to reach each year, due to the decaying roads, the shortages of gasoline. And in this upright crew of couples, one black sheep: a small, tired-looking woman with fair, cropped hair, and eyes the blue of frozen sky. The cleaners are younger than the crop-haired woman, but with their square bodies in their drab clothes, their rough, scoured faces, they already look like grandmothers.

Two women on their way to remove debris and smudges from a plane which, for them, might as well be a spaceship. Carrying galvanized tin pails, and whisks fashioned out of twigs—the same kind of whisks used to clean those palaces which the monk, walled into his small, dark cell, is chronicling.

Kiev is the mother city of Ancient Rus' which, of course, is not equivalent to Russia, the tour guide reminds them. Her name is Marusia; she's a brisk woman from Toronto and is fluent in Ukrainian and French as well as English, being the daughter of DPs who settled for a while in Lille before making their way to Canada. Had Eva been willing to strike up a conversation on the flight from Toronto to Frankfurt, she might have discovered that the tour guide had sung in the same church choir as Oksanna Moroz, and had gone to folk dance classes with Oksanna's brother, Alex. Marusia and Alex have this in common: a memory of church basements smelling of mushrooms; wheezing record players, the thump of the dancing teacher's foot as he beats out *ras-i-dva-i-ras-i-dva*. She has never contacted Alex on any of her trips to Kiev: she doesn't remember him as a person, someone with an individual existence, but just as one of the pairs of arms that whirled her round a cramped church hall some thirty years ago. A church hall that has since been replaced by a fine, sleek cultural centre, where her daughters learn folk dancing from a graduate of the National Ballet School of Canada.

"We are now entering the city of Kiev," Marusia is saying, her microphone held just the right distance from her mouth, so that her words reach the ears of everyone in the bus with a minimum of hiss or crackle. Eva looks up—she has been dozing. The evergreen forests on either side of the road have given way to large, white, cube-shaped buildings. The expressway takes them past islands of concrete fringed with grass, sometimes relieved by a bank of young poplars. "On your left, you will just be able to see the golden domes of the famous Monastery of the Caves which we'll be visiting tomorrow afternoon. The enormous statue to the right was erected as a memorial to the Great Patriotic War, which we, of course, know as World War II. Ukraine was invaded by German forces in the fall of 1941; casualties, both civilian and material, were catastrophic."

The guide has a great deal more to tell, but Eva can focus on only one thing—getting to the hotel, finding a telephone, and making contact with Dr. Oleksandr Moroz, at the Academy of Sciences. She doesn't notice, and the tour guide does not point out, the large, modern building tucked into a hillside near the memorial to the Great Patriotic War. It is a treatment centre, built largely by foreign donations, for the victims of the Chernobyl disaster.

The Hotel Kiev is one of the better places to stay in this city if you don't have the use of someone's apartment. Its rooms are clean;

the soap, though sliver-thin, can actually be worked into a lather, and the food in the restaurant is plentiful, passable, and cheap. The only problem, Eva discovers, is that the telephones don't seem to work. It's seven in the morning in Toronto and two in the Kievan afternoon; Eva's in that overdrive phase of jet lag in which a few fundamental actions can be carried out. She knows that if she's to get in touch with Alex, it will have to be now, before all the excellent arguments against doing so can derail her. If she's to reach him at his office (though he might have left early, as anyone might choose to do on a Friday afternoon), she will have to take the number written in her passport down to the front desk and have someone dial for her.

Ten minutes later, she is trying to appease a young, but martial-looking receptionist.

"Please. All I'm asking you to do is dial this number."

"This is not a telephone exchange. You have a telephone in your room."

"But it doesn't work—at least, I can't get any sound out of it. Please. All you have to do is dial and say hello and pass the receiver on to me."

"It is possible you do not have the correct number."

"But you checked it for me in the directory. There's only one Academy of Sciences, isn't there?"

At last, the receptionist realizes that this troublemaker—she has no concept of any category called "guest"—will not go away. Pursing her lips, stabbing at the numbers with a long, crimson-coated fingernail that clicks against the keys, the woman succeeds in making the connection. Eva can hear the telephone ringing, and another receptionist picking it up. An irritable exchange, and then a succession of sharp, angry rings. No one there—of course no one's there, it's July, he must be off at the cottage, or in Samarkand for all she knows. How could she have been so stupid as to think he'd be waiting for her, and what in the world is she going to do now?

But then a voice comes onto the line, a man's voice, and the receptionist's saying something Eva can only understand one word of: *Ka-NADA*. The man's voice again, presumably saying he will speak to her. After a small delay, in which the receptionist makes it as physically difficult as possible for Eva to take the telephone receiver and put it to her ear, it happens; there is no going back. She is speaking to him, her voice holding out its hands across a twist of wire.

"Professor Moroz? I'm sure you won't remember me, but we used to know one another a long time ago, in Toronto. Pardon? Of course—Chown. Eva Chown."

She realizes, suddenly, that she has no memory of his voice addressing her directly. The intimacy of the watching game, of their embrace of hands over the display cabinet, had been an intimacy of silence. She can't recall him saying anything to her: she can't tell if his voice is different now: sharper, more British-sounding.

"If you don't remember me, you might recall my father. He was a mining engineer. He collected—"

"I remember your father, Miss Chown. In fact, I remember your whole family, very well."

Silence again, a crater like the ones that sabotage the pavement here. What can Eva do but put her foot in it?

"If it's not too much trouble—I don't want to take up your time, I know you must be very busy—I was wondering—could we meet, just for a short while?"

But he doesn't hear her. Or perhaps his English isn't as good as she thought. Perhaps it's become nothing but a mess of quarters pushed into a parking meter, and he's finally run out of change.

"I'm sorry, Miss Chown. Could you repeat what you just said?"

"I said I wondered if we might meet for an hour or so while I'm in Kiev."

"That would be very nice, but I'm afraid—" A long pause, as if he's holding the receiver to his chest, muffling it. And then he's back on the line. "How long are you staying for?"

"Two weeks."

"You're here on business?"

She hesitates for a moment. "Yes."

Then she hears something shift in his voice. Almost sadly, as if she's taken from him something he's known all along he couldn't keep, he says, "I'm tied up today, but if you're free tomorrow afternoon, say three o'clock, we might meet for an hour. Where are you staying? Then let's say the Ukrainian Art Museum; it's just down the road."

"Whereabouts in the museum—the café?"

"You've never been to Kiev before, have you? Would you prefer that I call for you at your hotel?"

This is awful—the formality, the stiffness. He sounds like a great-uncle doing his duty by a niece visiting from the country. She tells him it will be fine to meet at the museum. He just has to say where.

"Room number seven—the one with the glass paintings."

"That will be perfect. Tomorrow at three."

"You'll be all right till then? I assume someone's looking after you?"

Eva bristles. "I'm perfectly all right on my own."

"I see. Well, then, until tomorrow."

"Wait—shall I wear a rose in my lapel, or whatever you do here? So you'll know me."

"I'll have no trouble finding you, Miss Chown. I'm afraid it's still all too easy to spot the Westerners in any crowd."

The receptionist, whose name is Tamara, watches Eva walk slowly back to the elevator, after wringing from her one more favour: the direct dialling codes to Vermont and Toronto. Tamara wrote them out on a precious piece of hotel stationery, eyeing her as if to ask how, if she couldn't make a call inside Kiev, she expected to manage long distance. She knew the minute she set eyes on Eva that this woman wouldn't leave any tip to speak of. Last month, there'd been an older woman from Montreal who'd pressed a twenty dollar bill—American—into Tamara's hand, saying, "You look so much like my granddaughter." When her shift ended, Tamara had rushed to a hard currency store and bought a Barbie for her daughter, who would be turning six the next day; the doll, as utterly unexpected under the wrapping paper as a cloud or dolphin, would be a treasure to be shown, not played with. Like the toy tea set made of bone china which Tamara's mother had been given as a child, and which had vanished during the war.

No. This woman with her man's haircut and alarming blue eyes won't bring anything good for her or her daughter.

Eva sleeps right through to two in the morning, waking to the smell of sheets washed in unfamiliar soap, and to total silence. The lamp on the bedside table sends out a small, greasy light that merely shows up the darkness in the corners of the room. It barely reasssures her that the talismans she's placed on the dresser are still there: a wallet-sized snap of Ben; a package from Dan that she hasn't yet opened, but which speaks of home in the very lushness of the wrapping paper. And it is lush, compared to the starved-looking sheets, thinner than tissue paper and rough as wood pulp, that do service here for toilet paper, notepads, official forms. She extracts from the passport, where she's put it for safekeeping, the extra customs paper she picked up at the airport: her first, accidental souvenir:

CUSTOMS DECLARATION

Keep for the duration of your stay in Ukraine. Not renewable in case of loss.

Persons giving false information shall render themselves liable under the laws of Ukraine.

With me and my luggage I have:

I. Weapons of all descriptions and ammunition

II. Narcotics and appliances for the use thereof

III. Antiques and objects of art (paintings, drawings, icons, sculptures, etc.)

IV. Ukraine rubles, Ukraine State Loan bonds, Soviet lottery tickets

V. Currency other than Ukraine rubles, payment vouchers, securities in foreign currencies, precious metals in any form or condition, crude and processed natural precious stones, jewellery, and other articles made of precious metals and precious stones, and scrap thereof, as well as property papers.

I am aware that, in addition to the objects listed in the customs declaration, I must submit for inspection: printed matter, manuscript, films, sound recordings, postage stamps, graphics, etc., plants, fruits, seeds, live animals and birds, as well as raw foodstuffs of animal origin and slaughtered fowl.

Slaughtered fowl she has none, but—and here she sits upright, pulling the scratchy blanket closer round her—coming through customs she'd forgotten to declare the ring on her finger, the gold and lapis ring Garth had given her for her twenty-first birthday: the only piece of jewellery she still owns.

She rereads the declaration form, panicking at each new category of the forbidden, imagining the customs officials, in two weeks' time, interrogating her, detaining her for having given false information. She imagines Ben waiting in vain at Toronto airport for her; getting back on the plane and returning to Vermont, where he will live happily with his father, his stepmother, and stepsisters, forgetting everything about her except the fact that she abandoned him.

Ridiculous. If need be, she can go through customs on her way home with her ring hidden in her mouth, like a wad of chewing gum; no one will be any the wiser. But what, Eva wonders, switching out the light and falling back onto her small, hard pillow, what about the other things she's brought into this peculiar country. How, for example, do you classify risk, memory, desire? As raw foodstuff? As crude or processed precious stone?

Panic climbing her skin at the thought of everything entailed by meeting not the black-haired boy she remembers, but the forty-seven-year-old man who'll be waiting for her in the museum tomorrow. He'll be no different from most of the middle-aged men she knows. Balding. Overweight. Discontented. He's an academic, so he will look ten years older than he really is. Or if, by some miracle, none of the above, then he will have a wife, children, maybe a mistress as well—a student or younger colleague. Not *of course I remember you* but *I remember your whole family.* Why and what should he remember? A thirteen-year-old girl, a dim, pale figure in the background of his erotic life. Perhaps he'd only been kind or curious on the phone—or making fun of her?

Disabusing herself of her illusions; it is more like self-abuse, the real meaning of the term. She knows very well what will happen, what can't not happen. Tomorrow afternoon—no, today, in twelve hours time—she will meet the man for whose sake she has come all this way, to this extraordinary, foreign place. And he will be nothing more than this: a perfectly ordinary, middle-aged man, with no trace at all of the seventeen-year-old boy who once made her heart leap up. Like a fish jumping into the air, a fish you catch with nothing but your hands.

In a room the size of a mousetrap; in one of the massively ugly apartment towers on the outskirts of Kiev, a man sits at his desk, turning a piece of lapis lazuli in his hands. He imagines himself as a porcelain plate, or a chip of some friable mineral, under some enormous force. He examines his hands, as if checking the small, fragile pieces of the wrist, the bones fanning out from that wrist to the knuckles. The lapis bruising his palm as he makes fists of his hands, smashing the knuckles against each other, over and over again.

What would be the use? He's remembering a voice on the telephone—not the voice of the woman at the Hotel Kiev, but a voice that haunts him so deeply he can identify it in his sleep, through the stiffest disguises.

What would be the use? There's nothing you can do.

I want to be there.

What you want doesn't matter.

You have no right to keep me away like this.

Rights—what makes you think you have rights? Dear God, haven't you done enough already? If you show your face here, I will shoot you. I will find someone who will take a gun and shoot you dead.

Galina—

For your own sake, leave us alone.

Do you think I care anymore what happens to me?

Then think, just for once, about me.

If I promise not to come, will you let me know the moment you find out?

Yes.

I'll—

She hadn't waited for him to end his sentence. She'd known, just by the heaviness of his voice that he would keep away, at least for the next short while. She'd put down the receiver as if it were the arm of some stranger who'd tried to latch onto her, a beggar, or even a child she could not comfort, having too much trouble of her own.

He can see all this, see and hear it as clearly as if he were standing across from her in the apartment she has never let him visit in Odessa. To smother what he sees and hears, he forces himself to turn to the scraps of paper on which he's writing an article on the discovery, shortly after the war's end, of a deposit of lapis lazuli in a quarry near Kiev. A discovery written up in Soviet scientific journals, finding its way to the West, becoming a matter of great interest to geologists there.

"A wonder of the captive world," the man writes, "and, like all wonders, worthy of our keen attention."

Eva falls asleep again, plummeting through dreams of missed planes and collapsing suitcases straight into the lap of noon. She knows she should get some food into her before setting out for the art museum, but she's hardly able to put a foot on the floor. There's something caught, snagged on her ribs so she can hardly breathe. Here she is, having set out from home like one of those simple girls in a fairy tale, searching for her heart's desire, east of the sun, west of the moon. But meeting Alex is only part of her business in this city. The rest has to do with guns and graves, not magic. How can she begin to tell him that? And what will she do when he asks her, as he must, about Olya, about Oksanna?

To calm herself, Eva goes to the wardrobe and takes out the clothes she's hung there, hoping the creases might fall out overnight. When she'd made up her mind to take this journey, she'd gone to a store she knew only from its windows, windows full of silks in colours so rich you felt glutted just looking at them. She'd come out with her arms full, having spent more on herself in an hour than in the previous five years. Gone the Eva of Goodwill and Bi-Way; newly born, a peacock Eva, dressing to please someone other than a child with grubby hands, or a baby liable to throw up its breakfast over her shirt.

She drapes her silks against her body, drinking in the sheen of them, then turns to the chest of drawers, its veneer scarred, its handles made of some tarnished metal in a shape so ugly you know someone must have given stern thought to its design. Socialist-realist furniture handles. Decadently beautiful, bourgeois clothing. He said he'd be able to pick her out of any crowd—by the clothes she wears, the shoes on her feet? Eva doesn't want to think about their meeting yet; instead, she reaches for the package Dan had slipped into her ticket; the gift she didn't discover till she was at the airport, and that she hasn't had the courage to open until now.

A small, square, flattish package, wrapped in flowery paper, with curled ribbons. Inside, two packs of no-nonsense, guaranteed-reliable condoms. There's a note hidden between them:

> *Beware of the men there—they'll kiss your hand and rob you blind. Just don't let anyone marry you. They're all looking for Western wives. Tickets to ride. I mean it, Eva.*

For a moment, she sits in complete shock, as if she's been hit across the face. Is this what he thinks of her—is this what he thinks she wants; all she wants? She sits holding the package in her hands, listening to the noises in the corridor: chambermaids shouting, a vacuum cleaner loud as a jet plane. At last, she drops Dan's gift into the wastepaper basket and forces herself to get ready for her appointment. But just before leaving she fishes out the package, minus its decorations, and slips it into her shoulder bag. She'll leave it in a more anonymous trash can on her way to the museum.

It's a stone's throw from the Hotel Kiev, and on the same street, yet Eva manages to arrive late. She'd forgotten that she needs to change her American dollars into local currency, a task which the receptionist makes as Byzantine as possible. When Eva asks for directions, just to make sure, the receptionist confounds her by insisting that the art gallery isn't on Hrushevsky street at all but on Tereshchenkivska. Eva's directed to go by tram or subway, since it would take forty minutes at least to walk there. Panic, horror, despair—it would be useless to call Alex; he'll already have left by now. She has ten minutes before they're due to meet; she's about to ask that they call her a cab when an elderly man waiting in the lobby comes up to the desk. He explains, in perfect English, that it's the Russian Art Gallery that's on Tereshchenkivska—she's quite correct, the Ukrainian Art Museum is on Hrushevsky, just turn to her right and walk three blocks—it's right at the end; she can't miss it. He doesn't wait for Eva's breathless thanks, but turns immediately to the receptionist and starts thundering away at her in Ukrainian, or perhaps Russian—to Eva, they both sound the same: intractably foreign.

He'll have arrived hours ago, and not found her—of course he'll have left by now. Why should he stay? For the sake of someone so arrogant, so ignorant of the language that she's at the mercy of sadistic receptionists? She really isn't that late—five minutes at the most, after she rushes up the crumbling steps, spills an enormous amount of the coupons that pass for currency onto the ticket seller's desk, and runs to room number seven. It's more a corridor than a room, and it's empty. She examines her watch, scans the paintings, which she registers only as blurts of colour, and nearly jumps when she hears someone cough behind her. A man with his back to her, inspecting a painting on the opposite wall. A suit jacket, a balding head, stooped shoulders. She waits for a moment, till her breathing's less harsh and her face picks itself up from where it has fallen. "Excuse me," she says, making her way to him. "Alex?" The man turns round as she puts a hand on his sleeve. His eyes aren't black but a watery green. "I'm sorry," she mumbles, forgetting the Ukrainian words she'd tried to memorize on the plane ride over. "I'm so sorry," she repeats, backing up and bumping straight into Alex.

Gold teeth. This is what cracks the image she's kept of him for thirty years. Not a paunch, or baldness, or a habit of twisting his little finger inside his ear, but a rim of gold haunting the enamel of his front teeth.

They are not having coffee in the charming café attached to the museum—there is no café. The Ukrainian Art Museum, despite its six colossal columns, its Roman goddess straddling a pediment crammed with muses and revellers, has a ramshackle interior with nothing but paintings—many of them removed—to tempt the visitor to linger. Instead, Alex is sitting across from her at a small, scarred table, the kind at which other people in the park are playing chess. They are surrounded by enormous trees—Eva can't remember ever having seen so many chestnut trees all in one place before. There's a strong wind pushing at the leaves, so that the equally strong sun spills randomly down on them, and she has to keep shading her eyes as she looks into his face.

He is explaining something about an article he's writing— something about lapis lazuli. She nods every so often, though she cannot follow more than a few words of what he's saying. It's partly the remnants of jet lag, and partly because she can't get used to the sound of his voice. This must be what people felt at the first talkies when actors they knew by image alone suddenly opened their mouths and spoke.

Nothing startling, his words: nothing awkward and nothing in the least erotic. If he remembers anything of their last meeting, he's betraying nothing. She thinks she's grateful for this—it gives her time to catch her breath. So far, he hasn't asked any of the questions she's prepared deceitful answers for—stories, she would like to call them. He sits across from her, speaks to her as though they're intimates and not acquaintances, and can thus take certain things for granted. Such as what has happened over the years to each other and to their families. And what has brought Eva here; why she has sought him out.

He's asking her how much of the city she's seen, and she tells him, artlessly, "Nothing except the museum. And this park. I've been waiting for you."

He takes out a pack of cigarettes, offers her one, which she refuses, and lights one, asking if she minds. She doesn't, though they are the cheap, raw Russian cigarettes she remembers gagging on in her youth—the ones smoked en masse in university classrooms, till even the air would turn green.

"What would you like to see?"

"Everything," she says.

"You're all right on foot? I've no car, I'm afraid."

Their roles are set—native and tourist. He rises from the little table and she joins him, crossing the park and heading down a series of tree-lined boulevards. They keep a comfortable distance between them, as he points out the façade of this building, the history of that. She had expected that his presence, the weight and energy of his body next to hers would shake her, the way, on hot summer days, the pavement ahead of you sways and shimmers; but all she feels now is space, weightlessness. As for Alex, he seems somehow absent, distracted, even while pointing out statues, towers, domes.

The city, he's explained, is divided into three parts: the Hill, or Upper City, where princes and nobles and warriors once had their palaces; the Lower City, called Podol, where tradesmen and craftspeople settled; and finally, Pechersk, where, over the last nine hundred years, a city of churches, monasteries, libraries, museums has emerged. The City of Golden Domes, he says—and she leans in towards him as he does. For he's spoken in the voice of a lover, saying these words. She is starting to learn something about the person he's become: that he loves his city with a passion she can't imagine feeling for hers.

"Then, of course, there's Helltown," he admits. "On the outskirts of Kiev. Concrete cabinets in which millions of us are filed away each night.

He leads her out of the park through a grove of chestnut trees where people of all ages have settled, lost in their books. Back on the main boulevard, Eva finds other things to delight her: over a doorway, a grille fashioned in the shape of a butterfly; a line of laundry strung between two beautifully proportioned columns. Sometimes, she's merely puzzled: by a department store window entirely taken up with a giant-sized Tampax carton; ugly, glass-fronted kiosks, displaying their treasures: tins of Campbell's soup, tubes of Crest toothpaste. Her foot catches in a great crack in the pavement, but Alex makes no move to help, just waits till she's recovered herself, and they walk on. Once, as they're waiting to cross the street, a man comes up to her, speaking quickly under his breath. He's pushed aside by Alex, who points to a currency exchange booth nearby. "One of the vultures," he explains. He leads her past an old woman sitting on a cardboard sheet on the steps of a pedestrian underpass, and they reach a row of pretty buildings painted rose or ochre or cornflower blue: bright, clear colours, with lashings of white trim. One of them, he explains, was built for the son of a sugar baron. "Turkish delight," she says, but he walks on as if he hasn't heard her.

By the time they leave the pretty palaces behind and enter yet another densely wooded park, Eva's exhausted. Could they sit down for a moment, she asks? Now he becomes exaggeratedly polite, settling her on a wrought iron bench and walking over to a nearby kiosk to buy ice cream. She watches him standing in line, pushing a hand across his face, and realizes he must be as tired as she— wonders if he's been walking and talking so steadily all this time to keep himself from asking questions, uttering names he's only been able to say to himself, all these years.

This is the first time she's been able to take a long, open look at him. Jeans and a tee shirt, and a black cotton jacket. No glasses, no furrowed brow, no mark of the professor. The black hair she remembers is still black, but with a steely tone; the eyes are as dark as ever. Now he's turning, walking towards her. And suddenly it's all she can do to take the ice cream from his hands, and not to raise her own to his face, to touch it as if she were blind and soaking up the look of him through her fingers.

I want you. This is what she needs to say. Something as simple, as scandalous as that. They sit side by side on the bench, Eva dazed with desire and hunger, for she's eaten almost nothing since landing in Kiev. The ice cream is rich and sharp, tasting of lemon.

She's not prepared when Alex asks, "Your father?" All she manages is one word: "Dead."

"And your mother?"

She hesitates, but he doesn't seem to mind, or even notice.

"Your mother," he continues, and then stops, taking what's left of his ice cream and throwing it into a garbage can across the path. "Your mother is the most beautiful woman I have ever seen."

"Yes," is all Eva can say. It has never occurred to her that Alex might have been susceptible to the beauty of other things besides her father's collection of crystals. The thought makes her uncomfortable, and she banishes it. And then, because she has asked him nothing about himself, and to shift the conversation away from Holly, she asks about his own father.

"He died last year." As if it were a natural follow-up, he asks, "You're married?"

"No. But I've got a kid. A boy—he's eleven." She crumples the paper from her ice cream into a ball; aims for the garbage can. But her hands are shaking, and she misses. "You?"

"My daughter's thirteen. My wife and I divorced some time ago."

Neither of them says anything more; the silence between them grows spines. Eva can't bear it—it is time for him to mention a dinner engagement and excuse himself; to put her into a taxi and banish her to the hotel.

"Alex," she says, and then freezes. It's the first time she's said his name out loud. She doesn't wait for a reply but rushes straight into it. "It's been so good of you, taking all this time, showing me around. Would you have dinner with me—would you let me take you out to dinner? I have all these coupons, I'm getting a crick in my back from lugging them around. I might as well get rid of them at a restaurant. A good restaurant. Choose an expensive one, will you?"

For the first time that day, he smiles. "They're all expensive, even the ones that serve nothing but head cheese. Expensive for us, that is."

She smiles back at him, relieved that he's sufficiently at ease with her to joke. One of Dan's warnings comes into her head: *ticket to ride.* She shoves it away as they walk off, this time in the direction of dinner.

A former palace, one of the sugar-pretty ones turned into a small, select establishment. The maître d' gives them a table with a view of the river. The menu is in French; on Alex's advice, Eva orders sturgeon, cucumber salad, meringues, and berries in cream. Wine from Georgia and Crimean champagne. Alex lifting his glass to her, again and again. "To women of means."

That is what she'd imagined. What she gets is a decent room, with paintings of cossacks on horseback and imitation portraits of eighteenth-century beauties. There is no menu—Alex simply asks the waitress to bring them whatever's fresh. Or so he explains to Eva, apologizing for the lack of wine or even vodka to drink. He makes conversation, telling her about the city they have just walked through, reciting names she has never heard of, referring to events she makes no pretence to have studied or even encountered in an illustrated magazine.

From a room off the dining hall, accordion music makes its way to their table. Eva looks down at the squares of plain wrapping paper that do for serviettes, and despairs. At her own naïveté, her failure to anticipate. She had imagined, along with the sturgeon and strawberries, a small string orchestra as well, the kind of waltz-schmaltz that makes up her whole idea of Eastern Europe. Alex drawing her out onto the floor, an Eva who has been transformed into a sylph from the ads of her childhood, a sylph in a strapless evening gown, with elbow length gloves and infinite distances in her eyes. She'd been calling up the forties films she loves: *Intermezzo, Casablanca*; waltzing into their tortuous plots on Alex's arm.

He's hardly touching the expensive meal; as the courses come and go, she steals glances at his hands, scarred in the way Garth's were, from fieldwork. She hasn't the courage to look at his face, and so his hands become the focus of her despair and the desire that insists on playing its tune over and over as she pushes a chicken leg across her plate, hiding lumps of gristle under the potatoes. This is more dreadful than she'd ever imagined, harder than if he'd walked straight past her in the museum, refusing to have anything to do with her. The chicken leg begins to blur on the plate, and his hands waver. She'd do anything for a Scotch; she's about to run off to the ladies'—if they have a ladies'. Run off and howl, when finally she registers that he's speaking to her, and that his words demand her full attention.

"We could always go back to my apartment for a drink."

The waitress, leaning out of an upstairs window, sees the couple she has just served making their way through the poorly lit streets. Collects their plates, scraping the uneaten portions into containers to take to her husband and children and father-in-law, all of whom live with her in a one bedroom apartment in what Alex calls Helltown. She will have to take a trolley bus, and then a tram; she will have to walk for twenty minutes across cracked asphalt, under crumbling concrete bridges and through a maze of dumpsters and rubbish bins to get to her building. She is glad the couple has left early, and eaten so little.

The escalator plunges them underground: like sliding down a mountain, Eva decides, the kind of mountain small children draw, an upside-down ice cream cone. She holds tight to the railing, partly to pull herself away from the crowds in front of, behind, and all around her. Silent crowds, for the most part—this is what unnerves her. This and the fact that she has never been with so many people in a subway station before—she can barely breathe. If only Alex were taller; she's panic-stricken that she'll lose him.

But she doesn't—he grabs her arm, in a professional, St. John's Ambulance sort of way, and guides her to the train, giving her a first lesson in crowd control. How to slam your body against a thousand others, carving room to stand and breathe and shove your way to the doors when your stop arrives. Eva fights down the start of classic claustrophobia, reminding herself that she had wanted, above all else, to make contact with Alex. And this she's doing with a vengeance— her body's jammed so tight against his that any sense of touch is cancelled out.

He is still holding her by the arm as they emerge onto the avenue—named after the Red Army, he tells her. It's as though he has charge of a prisoner he's marching off to an interrogation room; he loosens his hold on her arm but doesn't drop it altogether, hoping she won't feel, through the silk of her sleeve, his sheer, unstoppable panic. What does he want from her; what can she possibly desire from him? He should have taken her back to her hotel; they could have had a drink in the dismal bar with its peeling veneer and American rock videos blaring from a TV the size of a soccer ball. But then he'd have had to go home, and tonight he can't bear the thought of being alone.

There are only a few streetlamps lit, and hardly any cars on the road; this is what makes it so unfamiliar. A great city without traffic, as dark as if it were wartime and there were blackouts everywhere. They turn, abruptly, from the long sweep of Red Army Avenue onto a series of small streets that twist at peculiar angles, until they reach a walkway, a set of stairs leading past what looks to Eva like an illustration from a storybook: huts with twisted columns, or just doorways minus any walls, but carved with lappets and fringes. A children's playground, she realizes. She would like to stop for a moment, sit outside in the warm dark, but Alex won't let go of her arm.

The ground floor of the ugly building at the top of the stairs is filled with offices, he explains; it's an old Communist Youth League headquarters. They go through a battered door that appears to have no means of being locked or even fastened, and Alex leads her to the elevator. All this time, she is filled with something between fear and abandon at her utter dependence on this stranger, who has led her into subways sunk so deep they could be bomb shelters; along alleyways bereft of dogs or cats or passers-by, and all the more menacing for their stillness.

The elevator is a snug, black coffin. The door shuts and the blackness stays and they are not moving anywhere. He starts to curse in Ukrainian and fumbles for something—the instrument panel or a book of matches. She can hear him slapping his pockets, can't help but hear him, feel the heat radiating from his body, his arm brushing against her breasts, but he is only trying to light a match. Once the flame spurts, he fiddles with the buttons on the panel, buttons that refuse to connect with whatever wires should be sending them up the eight floors to his apartment. The match fizzles—he lights another and it too blinks out. This is the end, Eva thinks, this is the miserable, ridiculous end of everything.

If she says anything, even one word, he will hit something. Won't be able to stop himself from making a fist and slamming it into the walls of the stupid little box they're sealed in. The blackness starts to smell of her hair, is suffused with the warmth of her skin: soft, sweet as brown sugar. There's only a sliver of space between them, a cup of air to breathe. And because they're trapped, because he's run out of matches, because the very smell of her is so good, he pushes his mouth against hers, hard, while she grabs his shoulders to keep herself from falling.

As the elevator, right on cue, begins to moan its way up.

The steps for each couple are different; the dance is the same, thinks Mykola. Behind the paper-thin wall, his neighbour makes love to the woman he's brought home with him. Even with his earplugs in, Mykola can hear them, or, at least, the crash of the bed against the wall, like someone thrusting a hip against a jammed door, over and over and over again. He sighs, wishing once again that he was going deaf, not blind, in his old age; looking up at the shelves and shelves of books lining the alcove where he writes. Books he's bought at improvised market stalls or rescued from boxes in alleyways; books for which he's traded his mother's amber jewellery and the few treasures left in the apartment after her death: a proper coffee pot, a carved picture frame. The books give the alcove the appearance of a cell or cave; within this shelter, he returns to the notebook on his desk, the page he'd been writing when he heard the couple stumbling from the elevator into the apartment next door.

It's an old notebook, with stiff, black covers. In it, he puts down things he's seen with his own eyes, and stories whispered to him in the dark by ghosts. With his mothy sweater, the cuffs frayed, and the wool worn down to almost nothing where his arm moves back and forth across the page, he could be any scribe or scholar over the past few thousand years. Attempting to pull from the burial mounds a few traces of their occupants—a golden diadem, the bowl of a pipe, a child's toy—before the invaders come and level everything.

This is his one passion now. He records his stories as insistently as the lovers push themselves inside each other's skins. And he is still writing, long after the sounds have stopped, and the peace of exhaustion cancels any need for the small wax plugs he's shoved into his ears.

When Eva was small, there was a special game she learned to play. You found a grassy hill—any size would do, they all looked like Everest from the top—walked up, and lay yourself down with your arms stretched out over your head. You shut your eyes and, waiting till you couldn't bear to begin and couldn't bear to stop yourself, you rolled down the hill, turning over and over so fast your head spun like a top. Everything lurching and whirling inside you, and the sun making hot, gold slashes on the black behind your eyes. Your body a giant stone, its hurtling all the more terrifying since you never left the ground and yet the ground deserted you.

"You'll make yourself sick," someone once said to her, coming up to where she lay, abandoned to the aftershock of stillness. "Sick," the voice repeated, accompanied by a foot prodding Eva's leg. And it was only when she opened her eyes for the best part—the world still whirling round as she lay still, looking up—that she became aware of her stomach, like a flag some hurricane was tearing from its pole. And yet she'd lie there, waiting for the old lady or scornful older child to go away, so that she could climb back up the hill. All the stones that could bruise her, the roots and sticks that could rip her dress, or her skin. The grass itself leaving long green smears on the sleeves of her blouse, smears she would stroke during some incomprehensible class of math or French, to feel the world still shaking like a rattle, deep inside her.

This is how she feels, at four in this world's morning—she has stopped thinking of the time at home, she is beyond that kind of translation now. She leaves the bed carefully, so as not to wake Alex. It's a sofa bed, crammed into an alcove in the living room. Across from the bed is the television, and a desk, and the door to the glassed-in verandah. She opens the door into a narrow space filled with a mop and whisk and pail, plastic cartons and other objects too precious to be thrown away. Pushing her way through them, she reaches the window, slides it open, leaning into the new day.

She has always loved cities in the summer, sleeping with the windows open and hearing footsteps, singing, the slam of a car door. It makes her feel part of everyone else's life, even in her sleep. But here, though the apartment building's in the heart of the city—she can make out a church spire, and an enormous tower bearing a cryptic message, which she later learns is *Sport Hotel*—there's no human sound at all. It's raining outside, small drops slapping the vines on the verandah. Their leaves glisten; she reaches down, picks one and holds it against her; sees her own skin shining, as if she's been running outside in the rain.

A strange city. A strange bed; inside it a man she does not know at all: a lover. Whether for one night or for the rest of her life, it doesn't matter. She feels as though she's only come into her life this very moment. Joy, risk: Siamese twins, their very spines laced tight together. Here she is, standing naked on a verandah that looks out to a hundred others, just like it. Here she is, awake before the sun, wanting to dance, to sing at the top of her lungs, to fling out her arms and watch them burst into leaf and every kind of flower. For once, she is her self; for once, no one and nothing can come between her skin and her heart.

She goes back to the bed, crouching beside it, watching Alex sleep. The sheets are wrenched down to the foot of the bed; he is naked, his hands crossed over his groin as if to protect himself. She puts her head on her arms, sideways; looks at him as if she's spent all her life on a deserted island, and this is the first human being she has ever seen.

Defensive, vulnerable. These are the only words to describe the way his body lies before her now. She puts her hand to her mouth, to keep the words from spilling out. She doesn't want to wake him, she doesn't know what he will say when he wakes and sees her here. He may instantly regret the whole day: the walk, the dinner, the elevator ride to his apartment. He may send her in a taxi back to her hotel and never call again. It doesn't matter. Later, she may be sick with missing him, wanting his body this close to hers, but now it is perfect. She makes a game of it, seeing how near she can come to him without touching.

His skin is the colour of olive wood. She moves so that her nipples almost graze his belly, the hands over his groin, the fine black hairs between the knuckles and the finger joints. She bends down so that her lips are brushing the air nearest his forehead, his chin, the hollow of his throat. And suddenly he's reaching for her, pulling her down so that she covers him like the bedsheet they've kicked off, taking her breasts in his hands as she pulls up and arches over him, gripping him by the shoulders, holding him fast as he comes into her and she rocks, and rocks, their bodies so close there is no gap, not even the breadth of an eyelash between them. She cannot tell, as she collapses against him, whether it is her sweat or his she tastes, just as it is impossible to separate his thick, salt smell from her own rich wetness.

And yet she falls asleep again far sooner than he: with her head nestled into the crook of his arm, he lies watching morning steal into the room, rub its muzzle against all the objects that he's gone for so long without seeing: a shelf of books with badly worn spines, a broken television set, a few specimens in the glass case of a cheap, factory-produced sideboard. Rose quartz, a lump of lapis lazuli, and a particularly fine piece of moss agate, with its dark, fernlike crusts that look, at first glance, so much like fossils.

Toronto, 1963

Each time he gets off the bus and walks down the wide, deserted street leading to the house, he is scared. He likes the sound of the word, *scared,* he prefers it to *frightened* which is like a sieve, dissipating the force of what he feels. His body is a battlefield, that's how he sees it, but the enemies are not divided simply: head and heart. His heart is split in three-times-three pieces, at the very least; between his father and Mr. Chown; between Mr. Chown and his wife; between Mrs. Chown and her daughter. Never mind his mother, his sister, his countries—this one, and the one he knows the way you know something because you've read it in a book. A book you've borrowed, that isn't even yours to keep.

His heart a dull nodule of rock that a hammer's cracked open, showing a glitter of crystals inside. And the most beautiful, the most desirable of these is the woman, the wife of the man he could wish were his father. Guilty wishes, for he loves his own father, whose knowledge of rocks and minerals is all in his hands, what he has chiselled from the earth, breathing in poisonous dust, dodging falling rocks and beams. Guilty, too, because he respects Mr.

Chown, admires him, wants to be exactly like him. To know what he does, to have a house like this, to have so beautiful a wife. Yet for all her beauty, the beauty that stuns him like one of his father's rare blows, she is much, much more than the silk of her skin and hair.

When he sees Holly sitting and reading, or wandering through the house, following his mother from room to room, trying to talk to her of the country she left behind, all the things his mother wants to bury forever; even when he sees her from such a distance that he cannot smell the scent, the sheen of her, he feels his body tighten. Desire making a fist in the small of his back, pulling tight every line of his blood. Till his cock rises like a flag someone's hauled up the pole on a civic holiday. It's as ridiculous as that, cause and effect. He is sure she can see, everyone can see how his body betrays him.

She knows how he watches her. How can she not know, then, how he wants her, wants only to be alone with her for a moment, enough time just to touch her, even her hand. This is why, walking up the drive to what Oksanna calls the castle, he is scared, *scared shitless* as he's learned to say at school. He knows that Mr. Chown— he has never called him anything but Mr. Chown—is away for at least another week. He'd meant to stay clear of the house till Mr. Chown came back, but Holly—and she'd instructed him to call her that; the first time they'd met, she'd stretched out her cool, brown hand to him and said, "You're to call me Holly"—had sent a message through his mother: "Tell Alex the rock collection's dying of loneliness. Tell him to come round tomorrow—Garth insists."

He could never tell Holly that her husband is as important, as necessary to him as she is. That what he values in Mr. Chown is his acceptance of people whose abilities and passions mesh with his own. To Mr. Chown, he's no longer an immigrant with a funny name from a place no one's ever heard of, but a confrère. Perhaps Holly is right, perhaps her husband wouldn't at all mind his being in the house while he's away. Perhaps he wouldn't even mind that Alex has conceived as strong a passion for his wife as he has for moss agates, with their dark, fernlike crusts that the uninitiated take for fossil prints.

She makes him think of moss agates. She is opaque, as they are, and yet with dark places that cannot help but give themselves away, however hidden they may be. When he thinks of her naked body, it's not what he feels flipping through the magazines at the smoke shop, never daring to bring them home. Her body isn't pink and rubbery, but is that soft, dark hiding place he has never been able to find for himself, and that he longs for. In the books he's read, women are always described as having fur or bush, but this is not what he imagines about her. If he were to lift her skirt and slowly reach his hand between her thighs, what he would find would be the shadows on moss agates: ferns moving slowly under water.

He goes round to the back door and calls out hello as he lets himself in. He goes through the kitchen and into the hallway, his voice sounding like a pig's squeal in his ears. It is four in the afternoon, Eva should be home from school, but she makes no answer. And then he feels a huge relief. Perhaps Holly is out as well; perhaps both of them are gone, and he can go straight to the study and not have to think about anything but the book he's going to read, an eighteenth-century treatise on metallurgy, picked up by Mr. Chown in a London flea market, soon after the war. Perhaps the very year he himself was born, in a DP camp in the Bavarian hills.

If Eva were home today, he might finally get up his courage and talk to her. About the weather, or what she's studying at school, though she's no scholar from what his sister says. Oksanna holds Eva in complete contempt. He can't tell her that what attracts him is that Eva's still so young. That though she looks so much like her mother, her hair, her face hold none of the dangers Holly gives out to the very air he breathes. He would like, one day, to meet Eva somewhere outside her parents' house, someplace where she isn't the Chowns' daughter but just Eva, whom he likes to look at when she isn't watching. Not to leer at, but just because it gives him pleasure to see her, the way the sight of a cat soaking up sun on a doorsill gives him pleasure.

No one is home, he has the house to himself. He walks up the wide oak staircase, past the bend where the window seat is, but doesn't head to the left, towards the study. Instead, he waits for a moment, listens, then climbs to that part of the house where he has no right to be. He walks slowly, as if he were under water, the dark, suspended water of a dream. Into the morning room that connects with the place where Holly keeps her clothes and her shoes and her mirrored table. The morning room is empty. There are papers spread across the desk, but they may have been there for days.

He can feel his blood ticking as he moves from one object to another, trying to pick up some sign of her. No trinkets or knickknacks, but small wooden carvings and some soapstone sculptures Mr. Chown must have brought back from his trips to the North. Animals, birds, a hunter; what looks like a sea goddess or mermaid. But Alex can find no trace of Holly's fingers on these carvings, or on the books lying half-opened on the chairs. He leaves the morning room, pausing before turning the handle of the connecting door.

Dresses and dressing gowns. Greens and blues, undulating as he runs his fingers through the silk. He is dizzy with the scent of her that rests in her clothes as intently as a bird on a branch; he gathers up a handful of silk and presses his face against it, trying to keep his eyes open, wanting this intimacy, at least: for the naked skin of his eyes to touch this second skin of hers. He kneels down to where her shoes are scattered under the dresses on their hangers. Into a shoe the colour of cream he puts his hand, as far as it will go. And then drops the shoe as if he's never seen it, as he stumbles to the last door, pushing his way inside.

She isn't there. His face flames, he cannot believe his stupidity, the schoolboy stupidity of imagining she'd be waiting for him on some satin-sheeted bed, her legs parted, her hand both beckoning to and concealing the warm, wet dark. He is about to turn and run from the room, the house, when a pair of hands slips over his eyes: cool hands, with long, accurate fingers, moving from his eyes down to his mouth, tracing his lips and then his chin, and his Adam's apple, which he can't keep from bobbing up and down, like a child's toy on a string.

"Don't say anything," she says. "And don't turn round." But she doesn't release her hands from his throat, his collar bones, his chest, as she traces each rib through his shirt. He is paralysed between bliss and panic, feeling her body press against him, her breasts against the wings of his shoulders. He smells her desire just as he knows she can feel his, as her hands move gently, tenderly down to his sex, her voice as soft as her fingers: *my darling, my love.* Until she says a name, someone else's name, not his. It's as if a glass suddenly breaks in his hand.

He pushes free of her, turns on her, against her; he sees no more than a blur of her face as he rushes out the three connecting rooms, down the stairs, and through the front door. Not caring if anyone sees him pelting down the drive like a lunatic, a thief. Later, he will freeze and burn, remembering that he didn't have to stop to open any of the doors to those connecting rooms. Realizing that she'd left them open, deliberately; that anyone could have walked in and seen the two of them together. She is mad, he will think; mad, or else so unconcerned with hiding and lying, with containing her desire in rooms and moments as small and stoppered as perfume bottles, that it amounts to the same thing.

He never goes to the house again, except for one last time, the day he takes his leave of them all. Holly nods as if she doesn't see him; Mr. Chown wishes him good luck. But Eva is the only one who understands what's happening, Eva, who's no child anymore; who has come to him, smelling the fear and guilt and hopeless desire he feels, a metallic smell, concentrated in the sweat of his hands.

What else can he feel, leaving everything he knows, returning to the locked room of his father's country? Going off with only two gifts, two wounds to remind him of home: a woman's hands binding his eyes; a girl's hand that he puts to his mouth, to keep his fear from spilling.

KIEV, JULY 1993

What do you do when you find yourself transported to another planet? How do you learn to breathe the air and drink the water, to read faces and customs? And what about language? Is there some twist you can give your tongue and ears? So they'll pick up and give out sounds strange as the sight of fish flying through the ordinary air?

Except that nothing here is ordinary, for Eva. Every moment, she is running into things she never knew existed; anything familiar is altered, re-proportioned, as if it has passed through a kaleidoscope. Alex's apartment, for example: it seems almost as small as the playhouse she had as a child, and just as bare, so that you can pretend any furnishings you like, construct views of mountains or forests out the windows, imagine staircases, balconies, enormous fireplaces. And the walls outside are lush with vines. They creep up and over the parched wood, the crumbling cement; they enchant the light stealing into the kitchen, redeeming the chipped arborite, the cracks in the plastic upholstery of the one chair, its padding coming out in dirt-coloured tufts. Each leaf a small, green saucepan, boiling over with sun.

Alex is on his holidays, or else has taken time off work to be with her for the length of her stay. She's kept her room at the hotel, but moved most of her things into the apartment. On their first real day together, they went shopping for groceries at the Bessarabka market, shopping with the coupons Eva stuffed into Alex's pockets. She loved the market building, a huge greenhouse with a painted frieze of everything that's for sale in the stalls below: cheese, fish, flowers, pomegranates. Loved it until he told her that, ordinarily, he never shops here: only rich people, those in government and business, can patronize the Bessarabka.

And then, to console her for this slap in the face of her delight, he told her a story from the war. How the mines that exploded the length of the Khreshchatyk, the fires that raged for months stopped just here, miraculously sparing the market building. And he insisted on buying her a present at one of the stalls outside: a gigantic black shawl, stamped with red cabbage roses, yellow daisies, jade leaves strung from Moorish arches. She has seen old women on Bloor Street wearing smaller versions of this shawl, their pale, slow faces peering out like the heads of tortoises.

It's a risk, this purchase. Because it costs him half a week's salary, and because she refuses, as he suggests, to keep it for home, her own home, but spreads it over the ugliness of his kitchen table. If he sees it as interference, an attempt to stake a claim, he doesn't say. If she's hurt by his need to pay her back for the money she's lavishing on them, she doesn't show it. Perhaps the colours are cheap, garish, after all. It doesn't matter. She can leave the shawl behind her when she goes. She can allow herself the luxury of saying this—referring to leavings, endings—since they're still so close to the start of an enchantment. They are entering a landscape like a huge, black shawl, embroidered with every imaginable colour, every shape and sound. The edges of the shawl draw round them, its rich embroidery becoming roof and walls and floor, a forest so thick with leaves that it's always night. And the animals, the flowers pushing between the trees carry their own light, each one a lantern.

This is their beginning: the shawl's brilliant embrace, keeping everything outside their joined arms from touching them. Slowly, the edges of things will worry the fabric, holes will appear and the light of a world with horizons, borders, will pierce through. At first no larger than pinpricks, no stronger than the light from a star. But magic, however strong, will always run down. Like a music box that can only be wound once, and even then, gently, so as not to break the spring.

Their first few days they spend half in bed and half in the parks which spill all through Kiev. The rain which fell during their first night together has only freshened things: the air is cool, more like September than July. Alex tells her that the housing shortage is so bad, most families live in a one bedroom apartment, sometimes with grandparents as well as children. The only way to survive is to lead as much of your life as you can outdoors, walking in the parks, sewing, reading, talking on benches under a sky of leaves. This will be what she loves most about Kiev, the green which hides so many things: ugliness, corrosion, the stars and hammers and sickles still stamped onto the lintels of buildings or the spans of bridges. But sheltering too: children, courting couples, and the very old, all of them with no other refuge than this splurge of trees.

They are an innocently demonstrative people, the Ukrainians— or at least they are in public. Women walk together arm in arm; Eva watches a father at a tram stop holding his three-year-old son, kissing the child's hair and whispering endearments. But she sees none of those lovers' embraces that happen all the time on the streets of Toronto. Perhaps it's because of the weather, which is unseasonably cool, discouraging eternal moments under the linden trees or in the grass. Certainly she and Alex save their abandon for his fold-out couch, the triple-bolted door of the apartment making them all the crazier in their desire—knocking over the furniture, shouting the roof off, no matter who can hear them through the eggshell walls.

And yet, walking from park to park with Alex, her arm primly tucked in his, or standing so coolly next to him in a museum corridor, she wonders whether this is what ravishes her: not the extravaganza of their private lovemaking, but this public show of secrecy, the theatre they've built between them. How next to a display case, he will find her hand and touch it surreptitiously, his finger stroking the inside of her palm. The press of his arm against hers as he guides her down the street. Astoundingly sweet, addictive, this erotic braille they're perfecting between them.

As for worry, warning: the apartment is so small, their bodies fit so snugly together, there's no place for them here. The photograph hidden in Eva's passport, the biography of a poet killed in the war—they are all shut in the bottom of her suitcase, under the sofa bed. And because they're shut away, she can open: not just her body but her heart, into which so many people had crowded that it had ceased to know its own shape, or the views outside its windows.

She's a newborn baby in this place—as clueless, as helpless as a baby wet from the womb. She can't flip through a newspaper, buy an apple from a sidewalk vendor, ask for directions. Alex is her eyes and ears, her guide, interpreter, bodyguard. For it's not just the language but the customs and survival tactics which mystify her. Alex has to instruct her, their first day together, to take a large cloth handkerchief and a packet of toilet paper with her when they go out for the day, saying you can no more expect to find towels or paper in the washrooms here than dancing bears. It's Alex who carries her public transport pass, so she doesn't have to brave the subway guards. She's always thought it was a joke, the reputation of Soviet women for hostility, until she experiences for herself, in museums and galleries, the jab of dislike towards anyone needing assistance, anyone wanting to linger before a painting or display.

When she mentions this to Alex, he nods his head, but she can glimpse the defensiveness inside him, the barrier between their native worlds. It makes her think of the eyelids on birds, the thinnest membranes that entirely divide, and she vows to say or do nothing that will draw attention to their differences—a vow she is, of course, incapable of keeping.

Alex has refused, point-blank, her suggestion that she could explore a bit of the city on her own to give him some time to himself. In the first place, there are no maps of Kiev to be had. Not just no maps in English; no maps at all. Everything's in flux, avenues and boulevards and subway stations all shedding their Soviet-era names, and new street signs being posted. Second, she can't even read those signs. "I'll take cabs," she says. He tells her that's an excellent way of getting robbed, and a fair bet for being raped or murdered. Never, he warns her, never get into a cab alone. And third, he says, taking her face in his hands, the last thing he wants, right now, is time to himself.

But he knows that she is, if not exactly homesick, then so disoriented she can't help suffering a kind of vertigo. As a cure for this, he asks her, one evening after they've walked through too many parks, down too many streets, to tell him about Toronto, the apartment she's renting, the street she lives on. She's ashamed to admit that she owns a whole house, with twelve rooms in it for only four people. She's happier talking about the park, and the nearest branch of the public library; the day-care where she works downtown, even the No Frills supermarket where she usually shops. Remembering, as she speaks, how food here is guarded under glass in any store that ordinary people can afford.

It's an extraordinary gesture, this asking her about Toronto. She knows how easy it would be to cross from this subject into a room that would turn out to be an exit door. To mention anything that connects with Olya, Oksanna, his past life in what used to be his city—it would be like taking a knife and slashing this cloth binding them so close together. He listens to her talk about High Park, the hanging gardens, the geese in the pond, and then he asks whether she's ever been to the Junction. She shakes her head, and he explains that it's the part of Toronto where he used to live, in a duplex across from the railway tracks. A long way from Roncesvalles, to which all DPs aspired. He says something else, too, about the oddness of calling a part of the city crowded with immigrants desperate for a new world, a new life, after the place where a medieval hero meets his death, by treachery.

"Roland," he says, when Eva doesn't reply.

"I know," she lies, twisting round in his arms and kissing him, before he can say anything else. Kissing him wildly, as if her tongue, as well as her heart, were newborn, free, shameless.

Shameless. It's an expression she remembers from her childhood, only then it was a term of reproach, whereas now she wears it round her like a banner. Shameless in the pleasure she gives him and that he makes for her. She can say anything she wants to him, ask anything, and he understands, just through touch and wanting. Their bodies braided together, taking pleasure as though pleasure were urgent as food and drink. Hearts sliding, tumbling inside them like sleek, red seals in a world that is nothing but ocean.

"Teach me some of the language," she says over dinner one night at a restaurant. He gives her a few, necessary words, writing them out phonetically on a scrap of table napkin. She is utterly defeated. Things that are simple in English turn out to be impossibly polysyllabic. "Pleased to meet you" is *duzhe preiemno zvamy poznaiometesia.* "Excuse me" is *pereproshuyu.* Even "good-bye" is something like *dopobachenia.*

But this single, abortive language lesson is the genesis of their favourite game. They play it riding in the trolley bus or walking through the park or lying in each other's arms in the sofa bed. It's a word game, and it's supposed to be teaching her Ukrainian.

"Tree?"

"Derevo."

"Cloud?"

"Khmara."

"Earlobe?"

"Mochka."

"Salad?"

"Shalata."

"Book?"

"Knyha."

"Sky?"

"Nebo."

"Love?"

He almost doesn't miss a beat: *"Liubov."*

Sometimes he woos her with sounds alone, offering words without translations: *kalyna, kashtan, charivna.* The names of the months are each a poem: *Berezen*, month of birch trees, *Kviten*, month of flowers, *Lystopad*, month of falling leaves.

And then the word game changes into the telling of stories that pass, from mouth to mouth, like long, intricate kisses. Her stories of Nova Scotia, of trying to grow cabbages and carrots and failing at everything but weeds, though it was beautiful, she says—wild blueberries in the fields, whales jumping in the stingingly blue water. He tells her how he would have liked best to be a *chumak*, travelling from the salt flats of the Crimea to villages in the steppes or the mountains. Selling salt from his wagon and telling stories of his life as a young man, a cossack living in an island fortress, riding out across the steppes to fight the Turks or the Russians or the Poles.

He has stories about the rulers of ancient Rus', when Kiev was the city of four hundred churches. About Olha, a ferryman's daughter who married a prince, and became famous as much for her wisdom as for her great beauty. How the Pechenegs murdered her son in an ambush, and how their Khan drank toasts to the prince's courage out of a chalice fashioned from his skull. And the story he loves best, that of another Kievan prince, who was told by a soothsayer that his favourite horse would be his death. With great sorrow, the prince caused the horse, on whose back he'd won so many battles, to be put out to graze in a field far from the city walls.

Returning from a long campaign and learning that the animal had died, he taunted the soothsayer and went to visit the place where the horse's bones lay bleaching. Out of the animal's skull a serpent slid and struck him on the ankle, killing him within the hour.

Everything that makes his country what it is, he says, is in that story. But when she asks him to explain, he takes her hand and kisses, first her ring, then her palm, holding it so that it covers his mouth. And she forgets everything except the image of a skull in a field, a snake pushing through the eyeholes.

They take the terrifying funicular to the Upper Town, to the ethnographic museum, where he shows her an ancient carving of the horse that is the symbol of Kiev. He shows her, too, a pair of serf's shoes woven out of hemp, shoes with chains attached to them. And a *chumak*'s wagon that takes up half an exhibition hall. There are zigzag carvings on the yoke, simple yet full of energy and grace. This is his true, imagined home, she thinks: a saltseller's wagon, a refuge for inveterate travellers and solitaries. But what on these hundreds of glass shelves speaks to her own desire?

She finds it on a Trypillian vase, painted some five thousand years ago: geometric signs for a woman and a man. Each is made of two triangles, vertically arranged, the bottom one pointing up, the top one, down, so that they join at their apexes. Stick arms and legs, hands and feet have been added to each figure, as well as long necks rising from the base of the upper triangles, and circles for heads. There is no difference between the size and shape and importance of the figures, though what Eva takes to be the woman has a fringe hanging from the hem of her skirt, a fringe like a row of icicles. She makes a copy of the figures on a scrap of paper, and hides it away before Alex can see. She doesn't want him to know she's been making a charm to keep the two of them together—not just for these ten days, but for as long as she can imagine. To transform the differences between them—country, language, history itself—into the smallest of particulars, a fringe of icicles.

She will need this charm later that day, as they walk to the top of Volodymyr Hill. Miles down the river at Kaniv, Alex tells her, there's a statue of Ukraine's greatest poet. A serf whose freedom was bought for him by a group of Russian art lovers; a man who painted and wrote poems and joined a secret organization pledged to freeing his country. Banished for ten years to a labour battalion in Siberia, he was forbidden, by a note in the Tsar's own hand, to write or sketch, even to trace lines into the ground with a knife or twig. He survived, returning to St. Petersburg to become fashionable among the gentry and give public readings with Dostoevsky and Turgenev. But not to publish in Ukrainian. Russian, Alex explains, was the language of literature; to the gentry, writing poetry in Ukrainian would have been like putting embroidery on burlap sacks.

"Khrushchev liked to dress up in embroidered shirts—Ukrainian shirts. He made a pilgrimage to Kaniv, to Shevchenko's statue. The newspapers were full of it. Just think, a Russian, the supreme leader of the Supreme Soviet, coming to lay a wreath on the grave of a poet who'd called the Russians cannibals. No one mentioned the offending lines, of course. All that mattered was the visit of a fat, bald man to a Ukrainian shrine, paying homage in Russian. My father was very impressed; he didn't see the irony of it. He couldn't have let himself understand. The funny thing was that no one wanted to understand my father and me after we came back. Because we were speaking Ukrainian, not Russian. And we learned that anyone who insisted on speaking or writing or even singing in Ukrainian would end up in a gulag, or silenced, one way or another.

"Now you can speak and write what you please—except there's no paper to print on, and no money to buy books. It's crazy, Eva; everything here is deeply, seriously crazy. Except for my profession. There's no shortage of rocks—if the universities close down because there's no money to pay the professors, I can always go off and prospect for gold. Disappear into the hills, become a wild man, a finder of stones. Do you know what I'd really like to do, to spend the rest of my life doing? I'd like to take down every courthouse, every prison in this whole rotten empire. Dig the stones back into the earth, where they belong. They don't betray you, stones. They don't make promises, or speeches, or love to you. They don't die on you, either."

They are at the crest of the hill, at the lookout point from which you can see the sweep of the wide, blue river below. Alex is standing behind her; for the first time, he puts his arms around her in a public place. And for the first time, she senses that his passion for her is a need, like the need to cover your eyes with your hands when you can't bear to see what's in front of you. She knows that he's crying, soundlessly, behind her. Suddenly, she's guilt-stricken, thinking how little she knows about him, about the grief he's been keeping from her since they met. As if grief, trouble, were words he couldn't find in English. For the first time in her life, she feels powerless to help—even her hair is too short for him to hide his face in. All she can do is stand with him here, holding his arms around her. Remembering a fragment of the poem she'd been given so long ago: lovers embracing on a bridge, the water below them churning in different directions.

VI

Soloveyko, Summer 1933

Always, she is the first to wake. She and Pavlo have the bedroom; Ivan sleeps on a sofa bed in the porch, at the other side of the dacha. This time there has been little need for such precautions. They are too tired, too worried: at night, they huddle naked under the sheet, their only comfort to lie close together, so close they could be wearing each other's skin.

Always the first to wake. The birds in the garden sing to her alone, and she rises from the bed as though she were immune to gravity and all its lesser laws: weariness, fear, despair. She takes the sponge from its ledge and dips it into the bucket of rainwater; washes the warm softness of her body. For the first time in her life, she's become ashamed of it. Because of stories she's heard of the living skeletons in the countryside, fighting over specks of wheat gleaned from horses' dung. Of the women who are driven to eat their children, or the children, their dead mothers. Obscene, terrifying stories, and yet she must believe everything she hears, everything but the silence of the newspapers. In times like these, the only ones who give even a grain of truth are the storytellers.

Outside, it is already warm: the air feels a little sluggish, a milky haze smudges the hills and trees. Bending to slip on her boots, she is overcome by the desire to run back inside to the bed where her lover sleeps. Slide under the coverlet and wake him with kisses, the way she used to do only the summer before. Remembering how she'd kissed him, once, at the crease of the inner arm. Tenderly at first, and then, without knowing why, only that she wanted to, baring her teeth, nipping him until she tasted his blood on her tongue. Swallowing the blood as if it were some red bead she could lodge inside herself forever.

They have known from the start how it would be: never enough time, never enough dark, safe space around them. Having to turn their cries and shouts of pleasure inwards, so as not to give themselves away to those outside, to the spies and double-dealers. It has only made the pleasure sharper, swallowing those cries and shouts for which there are no words at all. Needing this and only this: his body inside hers, her hands digging into his shoulders, as if hollowing a shelter.

But she does not turn, stealing past her sleeping son, back to the bed where her lover lies. She puts on her boots and walks out into the orchard, through the gate to the meadows sloping up the hill, where the grass grows high as her waist. Even though she keeps to the path, her skirts are soaked with dew. It feels so cool against her skin, cool with the fragrance of clover. Soon it will be too hot to walk outside, even in the shade. Ivan will be cross with headache, he has never been able to stand the heat. As a baby, he was covered all summer long with prickly rashes: only a few years ago, he would lie exhausted on her lap while she fanned him, telling stories about the root cellar at her grandmother's house; how she would spend the hottest summer afternoons looking for treasure in niches carved from deep, yellow clay. How there was no cooler, quieter place than this cellar, like an underground cathedral or catacombs where beets and onions lay exposed instead of saints.

At the crest of the hill she stops, wrings out her skirt. In Soloveyko, there are wildflowers she has seen nowhere else; on the marshy edge of a meadow, she bends down to pink blooms that smell of cream and vanilla. She wishes Pavlo could see them. He will still be asleep by the time she gets back. He is always exhausted these days: after they've talked and talked till the candles burn down, and even the smell of beeswax fades from the air; long after she's fallen asleep, he lies awake. As though the worry were some physical affliction, a cramp seizing on some new part of his body each time he has worked it out of the place it was before.

Nobody forgets: while you are working day and night to bring something new into being, there is always someone marking down your name, biding his time until the wind changes, until it comes shrieking down from the north. Four years that wind has been blowing: trials, denunciations, exile. They thought they'd weathered the worst of it, until now. This is what Pavlo has had news of, even in this summerland so far from loudspeakers and public platforms. This is what has kept him awake long into the night. News of the latest purges, the expulsion from the Party of everyone whose power might have protected them. For all of them here, now, no shelter but paper and canvas, stagelights and the frail wood of musical instruments. No shelter, but the very things that mark them out.

All this they have spelled out to one another, every night for the past two weeks. The crimes they could be accused of, the means by which they could be destroyed. Whether it would be safer for her if he disappeared somehow; whether she should stop writing anything down, commit everything to memory. She thought things would be better away from the city, but it's become all the harder to bear, knowing this may be the last time they will meet here, live together openly. And as the end comes near, the terror they haven't been able to abandon along with their stuffy city rooms rears up at them. Kicks out and stuns them, so there's nothing to do but these simple acts she has by heart, that she can perform without thinking. Rising early on the morning of her son's eleventh birthday: going out into the fields to pick flowers for the breakfast she will lay on a wooden table under the trees.

A poor enough breakfast, given the shortages: black bread; honey in a jar with bees painted onto the sides. And the presents: a book she'd found for Ivan at the Children's World store in Kiev—a book by Karl May about a trapper in the wilds of Canada. And, from Pavlo, the portrait of Ivan he'd been working on all winter, unfinished, but, she thinks, all the better for that. The mere suggestion of the child's face—everything shadowy still: all the possibilities untried. This portrait the one thing that gives her any joy these days: that someone can still see in this way, draw a question mark instead of slashes cancelling the future.

At last, she reaches the field of cornflowers—fringed, blue wings. She stoops to gather an armful, picking them carefully, so as not to pull up the roots, and saying over to herself the poem she has written for her son. A poem, not a tract or declamation urging one of the thousand necessities of the moment. A poem about the day he was born; the way, after he pushed himself into the world, he refused to cry and fill his lungs. As if he were testing the air before he gave up the warm, wet dark he'd nestled in so long. And how she wished, seeing him for the first time, holding him all slippery in her arms, for a cow's rough tongue to lick him. Wanting a stable, not a house: nothing but the heat of her body round him, her tongue washing him, opening him to the air and the sounds of the earth, the way a mouth opens to laugh or sing.

Sweat dribbling down her face, over her lips, but she wants, she needs the taste of it. If ever she is tortured, and sweat or blood runs into her mouth, she will think only of this: picking flowers for her son on his birthday morning. Of the hour of his birth, her whole body contracted, as though she were nothing but a rag to be dipped in blood and wrung out, again and again and again. She will think of the moment of her child's conception; of lying in her lover's arms, turning her face against his chest, breathing in the warm salt of his skin.

If ever she is tortured. The words are something from an opera—sabres and banners and blood. They won't have the patience to torture; there will be far too many of them. She will not be tortured but shot, and she will have time to think of nothing, no one. She wets her lips with her tongue; starts humming a song that her grandmother taught her when she was a child, a song about a birch tree in a meadow.

By the time she's gathered enough flowers, the sun is hot on her back. If she doesn't hurry, they will wake before she returns; will be hungry, cross, already quarrelling. Yet she stops halfway home, hearing a cuckoo cry. They say that if you count how many times a cuckoo calls, you'll know how many years you've left to live. Thank God the bird is feeling lusty, hungry, whatever it is that makes him signal his presence so persistently this morning. She smiles, listening, her arms blue with flowers.

They gather for lunch on the terrace of the White Crane—Pavlo, Lesia, Ivan, Ivan's best friend, and his parents, who run the café. There is also a filmmaker from Kiev, and an artist in ceramics from Odessa, a professor who teaches Ukrainian literature at the Academy in Kharkiv, and Yuri, a sculptor up from Kiev for the day. There is an air of defiant festivity about the meal, because of Ivan's birthday, and because a young actress and her fiancé have just announced their engagement. They plan to be married in September, and they are inviting everyone here to the wedding. Tomorrow, all of them are going home, to the cities where their names are filed on lists kept by the secret police. But today, they open the café's last bottles of wine, to laugh and drink toasts to one another.

The boys break away from the adults and throw stones over the balustrade into the stream below. They have to be coaxed back for the photograph that the professor from Kharkiv insists on taking—a group shot, with one row sitting high up on the balustrade, and the others standing in front of them. Pavlo sits in the centre, with Lesia directly before him. While the photographer is positioning the others, Pavlo puts his hands round Lesia's head, as if her hair were a cup holding the heat of that day's sun. Only when the photographer shouts for their attention does Pavlo drop his hands to her shoulders. Lesia is smiling, though tears cut the corners of her eyes. It is all she can do to hold Ivan close to her,

her arms locked round him, pressing him against her as he strains away, scowling into the sun.

"Why can't I ever do anything right with him? Why isn't loving him enough?" she asks herself, as she will do for the rest of her life. As she has done since he was old enough to know her as a person, not just a mother: as a person to be judged. She knows why he is fighting her now. Because Pavlo has put his hands on her shoulders, as if the three of them really were what they must pretend not to be: father, mother, son. He thinks Pavlo is just her lover—he thinks this because she has told him his father was a medical student, killed by an outbreak of diphtheria a month after she'd given birth.

The photographs are taken, some of the whole group, others close-ups of couples or trios like Lesia, Pavlo, and Ivan. Lesia lets go of her son, and he runs away from her, across the terrace to the hillside. How many years before he will forgive them: before Pavlo can claim him as his son? How to explain to a child the dangers of such acknowledgement? "If they put a bullet through your father's head, they'll put one through yours, for good measure. If they throw him into prison, they'll grab you, too, to keep him company. Or send you to a camp in that beautiful Siberia of theirs, so useful for killing people off. And all for being your father's son."

Lesia reaches up and grasps both Pavlo's hands, pulling them down from her shoulders, over her heart. Someone is sobbing in a corner of the terrace; plates and glasses are being gathered up. When everyone else has left, they are still there, the woman and her lover. Hands locked together, eyes shut against the pressure of the sun.

They are far too thin, thinks the professor from Kharkiv, watching the boys charge down to the river. They are all too thin, this extremely privileged group of people. Because of the rationing that's gone on for over a year now, the bread queues in the city longer than they've ever been, while grain rots in the fields or railway sidings. And the peasant children begging for food at the stations, bones knifing up through their skin, bellies swollen like gigantic blisters. These boys are too thin, but they won't die of it. They are a different species from those other children, the ones whose starved bodies are eating them alive. He wipes his face with his handkerchief: presses the handkerchief to his mouth, as if the image of those dying children were something he were about to vomit up.

Hidden in his apartment in Kharkiv are the few photographs he's managed to take of starving children; of wagons piled with the corpses of peasants who'd dragged themselves to the city. To beg bread from people lining up all night for a single, small loaf. He could have brought the photographs here, passed them round, succeeded in turning the stomachs of his friends, here in this pocket-paradise of Soloveyko. Who know and don't know what's happening, and who can do nothing to help or alter these things, any more than they can stop the machinery waiting for them on their return. Lethal machinery. With luck, some of their children will escape. The very young, who will have nothing to remember, or those old enough to learn the formula for denouncing their parents.

A few of the children. These girls collecting dishes on the terrace; those thin boys running down to the river.

They are playing a game the photographer has no idea of; a game Ivan has made up and whose rules his friend obeys without question. The game is called Secret Army. They are guerilla fighters who must spy on the enemy, arresting traitors, double agents. Freedom for their homeland—this is the cause they must defend.

Ivan pronounces "freedom" with such passion that it makes any place they happen to be—the woods by the river, the cellar under the café—into a hall bright with banners. *Volya Nasha*

Dolya. Freedom Our Fate. The code they write on messages they leave each other in a niche hollowed out in the cellar, secret messages arranging night-time sorties and daytime missions. There's an entrance into the cellar from the hillside; any food stored here was eaten months ago; no one uses the place now but the soldiers of the Secret Army.

They wait just long enough for anyone watching from the terrace to see them skipping stones, playing by the river. And then they make their separate ways to the cellar. It's like theatre, meeting to light candles here while everywhere else is scorched with sun. Like theatre, with Ivan as the director and stage manager and chief actor, though his friend would never tell him so. Because of the intentness of his face, the frown that never leaves his mouth, two lines carved by the words *freedom, fate.*

"Useless." Ivan is speaking into the darkness beyond the candle flames. "All of them up there—useless and stupid and soft. You have to be hard as a knife, you have to be able to slash right through if you want to fight for your country."

His friend says nothing. He is not expected to.

"There was a woman once, a long, long time ago, married to a warrior, a prince of Kiev. Listen, this is important; this isn't just a story. It's history, even if they'll never teach it to you in school. This woman's husband was killed in an ambush, and she revenged him. She worshipped him; he was her whole life because he was her country, too. She wasn't soft, she was cunning and proud and all she wanted was to kill her husband's enemies.

"They wanted to marry her off to their own prince, and to put her son, the boy prince of Kiev, to death. She pretended she was pleased by this; that she was weak and lonely and wanted a husband to guide her. So she invited the men who'd arranged her husband's death to a great feast; she commanded that a bath be made ready to refresh them after their long journey. And when they had all entered the bath house, she locked the doors and set them on fire; burned everyone inside to death."

Ivan has forgotten that he's holed up in the cellar of a country café, telling a story to a boy with fishbowl glasses and a nervous cough. He is the boy prince Sviatoslav, whose grandfather nailed his shield to the gates of Constantinople: he is speaking the ancient language, in which words like killing and burning, treachery and revenge ring out as clear as trumpets, and leave no stain on the tongue.

"Then the enemy's prince demanded to know where his retinue was. The woman said they were accompanying her on a pilgrimage to her husband's grave. And she invited the prince to come to the grave for a funeral feast, after which they'd be married. When he arrived with his soldiers, she gave them mead to drink, and honey to eat, and when they fell asleep she ordered her troops to slaughter them. Not one of them escaped alive. And then she set out for the city of her enemies, and laid siege to it. She had her men burn down every house inside the walls, killing the people who escaped, or giving them as slaves to her followers. And then she returned with her son to their palace in Kiev, and lived with him alone, to the end of her days."

Ivan's friend isn't sure what to say; he doesn't like this tale, he has burned his hand often enough on the stove to be able to imagine what it must be like to be burned alive. But he's held by the passion of Ivan's voice; a sternness he knows he'll never be able to summon, no matter how much he loves his country and his language. Instead of speaking, he coughs, making the candle waver until Ivan blows it out.

"Come on," he says. "They'll be looking for us." His voice is impatient: with the adults, with his friend's weakness, with having to sit in the dark telling stories when he wants to be fighting, like the schoolboys who fell at Kruty.

"Come on," he says again, making his way out of the cellar into the pale blue afternoon, pretending not to hear his friend call out for him to slow down, to please wait up.

Late that afternoon, Pavlo goes off into the fields with a sketchpad and the supper Lesia's packed for him. She takes it for a good sign that he's starting to draw again. Before he leaves, he spends an hour playing chess with Ivan. It's a game neither has much interest in, but it's the one thing they seem able to do together without bitterness or irritation, united in this one thing, their badness at chess.

Pavlo does not kiss her when he leaves, but simply presses his face against her hair. Before she can turn round, he has gone, promising to be back before nightfall. By nine o'clock, she can wait no longer; she leaves Ivan reading at the kitchen table, and starts walking. He might be anywhere—round the next turn in the path, or five miles away, with nothing more than a light summer jacket against the mist that's rolling down from the hills.

A thick, white mist, unpleasantly warm. She walks for what seems a long time, joined by the neighbour's dog. She should take him back, the neighbour doesn't like him running loose, will think she's lured him away. But there's no time to go back, and besides, she's grateful for the company. The dog keeps a few yards ahead of her, the white plume of his tail blurring into the mist that erases everything more than a few feet from her eyes. The mist is oily, opaque; it reminds her of medicines she had to take as a child. How could something so insubstantial be so heavy?

When she stops to catch her breath and looks down at their dacha, she can make out the small lamp at the kitchen window. She calls to the dog and waits for a moment before going farther. It's like being in a dream, this mist, turning the trees ahead of her into shadows unattached to anything. It's like the landscape of a dream she's been waiting all her life to have. At her feet, the dew-soaked grass is intricately clear, she can make out the indentations on each blade. Birds are crying their last calls, the cicadas bleating instead of rattling, as if the mist has cocooned them with wet wool, dragging their thin legs down.

Suddenly, a shape rears in front of her and she screams. It is only a deer, a young buck springing through the grass, the dog blind to it as she holds its collar, ordering it to sit, knowing the dog can feel her panic through her hands. She waits till the deer has bolted halfway across the meadow before she releases the dog. But now he has caught the scent and runs away from her so she must go after him, the tall grass drenching her skirt; each step she takes heavier, harder. Till at last she finds the place where the dog sits, pink tongue panting, as he looks up into the oak tree overhead.

At the man, perfectly still, hanging from the stoutest branch of the tree. This is the most terrifying thing: how silently the body hangs from the branch, how the dog makes no sound, and the birds have stopped singing. How her throat is gagged with white wool, and won't let her call out even his name.

Yuri cuts him down. Yuri, who was waiting at the dacha when she stumbled inside, her dress torn, her hair heavy as stone round her face. Pavlo asked him to stop by that night, Yuri explains; there was something he wanted help with, some favour for Lesia. They follow the dog back to the oak tree, and Yuri carries Pavlo's body over his shoulders, all the way down the hill. She lights the way for him with the lantern; it gives off so little light in the thick, white dark all round them.

VII
KIEV, JULY 1993

His hand slips between her thighs. Like Napoleon's hand under his coat, she thinks, laughing out loud and unable to translate when he asks her, "what is it, what's so funny?" He's starting to pull his hand away when she grabs it and keeps it there, afraid he is angry with her. She falls asleep with his hand held fast between her thighs; dreams she hears him talking on the telephone, his words something she sees rather than hears in the dark. Phosphorescent, like those fish in the blind depths of the sea, the ones that carry lights inside their small, transparent bellies.

Alex waits till she's fallen asleep, disengages himself, and leans over to check the clock on the shelf beside them. Just as he's deciding it would be far too late to phone, the telephone rings in the kitchen, and he runs for it before it wakens Eva.

The voice on the other end of the line belongs to the mother of the woman who used to be his wife. She tells him that the doctors have at last performed the biopsy, but that it will be a week before they know the results. She tells him his daughter is still groggy from the anesthetic; if he calls her at lunchtime tomorrow, she should be able to speak to him. And for the hundredth time she tells him no, it would do no good for him to come; it would only make the child suspicious. Katia thinks she's having a tonsillectomy, something so minor she doesn't need her father rushing five hundred kilometres to her bedside. Galina's there, in any case. She would rather not talk to him, right now. He should arrange to take the train to Odessa in a week's time. If things are all right, he can take Katia on to the mountains for a holiday, just as they'd planned.

Alex asks questions which are impossible to answer, technical questions. But he needs to say something, and his mother-in-law is patient with him, answering each question with "It's too early to tell," or "You will have to ask the doctor when you come." And then there's nothing left to say. The line is poor, and there's no sense holding on, listening to static.

Alex puts the receiver down very gently. He knows it would be useless to try to sleep. He lights a cigarette, and goes to his desk, shading the light so that it won't wake Eva. There's the article on that quarry with the lapis deposits he has to finish; but he can't make himself focus on the words. Crushing his cigarette, he shuts out the light and returns to his bed, to Eva lying fast alseep. He slides in beside her warm body, lies turned towards her, his head against her short, thick hair that reminds him, always, of petals. Petals the colour of ashes.

The girl is lying at the bottom of the sea—she has gills, like a fish, and that's why she can stay here so long, breathing through the water. The air that is really water flows in through slits in the side of her body, a row of flounces, like those on the dress she wore when

she turned ten, and her father came home for her party. She'd
opened the door expecting it to be one of the friends she'd invited,
and it was her father in his leather jacket, his jeans all crusted with
mud because he'd come straight from the site. Bringing her a square
of silk tied up round something that turned out to be treasure, not
pretend but real: a small, pure lump of gold.

When she first discovered the lump in her neck, that's what she'd
thought of: something precious hidden in a square of silk. Water is
like silk. The sheets, her nightdress—they aren't cotton, but water; this
isn't a bed but a soft pillow of sand at the bottom of the sea. And that
crack in the ceiling is really a fishing line that stretches all the way
from Kiev to Odessa.

She follows the line as it drifts back and forth through the
slow, sleepy water. She doesn't understand why her father isn't
here. Her mother looks cross all the time, except when she's
looking worried. When they lived together, they were forever
arguing, her parents; it was supposed to make her mother happy,
leaving Kiev, coming here. But her mother still looks angry, even if
she never shouts these days, hardly speaks a word.

It's too quiet here. She misses her father. She would like to
show him all the treasures she has found: gold, crystal, coral. How
she can lie without speaking, barely breathing, on the still, clear
bottom of the sea.

The weather, which has been brilliant, changes halfway through
her stay. Walking down Volodymyr Hill one night, Eva notices a
thin sheet of cloud, hung like a curtain in amateur theatricals. The
next morning, a white fog has slid over the city—the sky's not
overcast so much as extinguished; all the light's been drowned.

Alex has to go out this afternoon—to the university, to the
bank, to perform errands which, he says, would be of no interest
to her, and would only wear her out. As he leaves, he closes the

heavily padded door behind him, turning the key three times in the lock, telling her she mustn't open it to anyone. Not even the neighbours? Eva asks. She's been introduced, briefly, to the old man next door, who speaks a little English, and once on the stairwell she glimpsed the family on the other side of Alex's apartment: a tired-looking woman with two grown daughters. She would like to talk to the old man, Mr. Savchuk. He's a retired schoolteacher with an interest in history and literature; he'd helped Alex greatly that first year of his return to Ukraine—helped him to get this apartment, too, after his divorce. But Mr. Savchuk has a heart condition, and mustn't be disturbed. He won't be gone long, Alex tells her, and for the first time there's an undertone of reproach in his voice, an undertone she pretends she doesn't hear.

What makes his going so hard is that she's left in a vacuum. The apartment contains no personal effects, no signs of emotional life: photographs, postcards, a drawing by his daughter. Without Alex in them, the rooms appear to her in their true, desolate state. The vestibule, papered in a photograph of autumn leaves, the colours leaking, soured. The bathroom, scarcely larger than the chipped enamel tub; the toilet and its inextinguishable smell of drains. The sitting room with a sofa bed, a wall of bookshelves, and a desk; the kitchen where the stove, the refrigerator are doll-sized, and the shawl-draped table hardly bigger than an ironing board. And last, the verandah, looking out to nothing but the backs of other, equally dismal buildings.

There's nothing she can do but wait out the time that he's gone. She tries to break the vacuum by making a call to Ben. When, by some miracle, she manages to get through to Vermont, Jimmy's wife tells her that Ben's off on a wilderness hike with his father, and won't be back for two weeks. She asks Eva what the weather's like in Paris; Eva answers fine, beautiful, and hangs up as quickly as she can. But just for a moment she keeps her hand on the receiver, the possibility of hearing another English-speaking voice. She knows it would be useless to call Toronto: Dan and Julie are off at a lodge in the Laurentians with Dan's parents. Besides, what would she say? *Am madly in love, hope you're okay.* And would she even recognize her own voice trapped in the answering machine? More and more the voice of a stranger each moment she spends here with Alex.

The mother and her daughters next door are forever quarrelling, so loudly they'd drown out the television if it weren't broken down. Running her hands over the spine of every book on the shelves, searching for a title, even a word in her own language, Eva discovers an enormous textbook published in Toronto, a *History of Ukraine*. She goes out to the verandah, settles herself on the sun-warmed floor, and opens the book to the photographs. Plump, smiling peasant women; corpses on city sidewalks. Bombed-out churches, with only a bell tower standing or a wall from which a few disembodied halos gleam.

She knows nothing about this country. How then can she pretend to know anything about her lover, especially what brought him back, what keeps him here? She has the whole afternoon to fill, and so she skims the book, skipping from Scythians to cossacks to insurgent armies. Learning that, for most of its history, Ukraine has been somebody else's property—a colony of the Austrian or Russian Empires, a fiefdom of Lithuania or Poland. That for three years after the civil war in 1918 it called itself an independent republic. And then the Russians returned, this time as Bolsheviks, turning Ukraine into Little Russia once again. Like Canada, a producer of cheaply priced raw materials, and an importer of expensive manufactured goods. Like Canada, in relation to the United States, and like Quebec in Canada: Quebec before the Quiet Revolution, where you had to speak the language of the conqueror to be heard at all.

But unlike Canada, it's a southern land, its soil extravagantly fertile. A rich land, with no natural defences to speak of—a few mountains in the southwest, but otherwise gentle hills and vast river plains and even vaster, level steppes. Open land, with all kinds of desirable things in it, things so desirable that it attracts wave after wave of invaders, who carry off whatever can be had as booty, even the people themselves. Invaders and conquerors, dividing up the land as if it were a loaf of bread, and leaving the people living on that land with nothing but a crust so thin you could hold it up to the light and see sky through it. And even that crust has been fought over by people who can never agree how to get the whole loaf back. The aristocracy having better things than bread to eat, wanting to keep it in the hands of the imperial bureaucracy; the intellectuals arguing about whether calling the bread by its Russian or Polish or Ukrainian name is more important than dividing it up so that all will get an equal share. And through all of this the peasants, even when invaded and enslaved, keep on bringing in the harvest, and dying early.

There's a mention of Chernobyl—Chornobyl, it's called in Ukrainian. Eva remembers the stories that went round Toronto the year of the explosion, jokes about green snowflakes that burned your tongue. Chernobyl makes her think of chernozem, the black earth she'd learned about in geography class, imagining something rich and dark as devil's food cake. And she remembers, guiltily, one of the things she has come here to do; she sees herself bending down and picking up handfuls of what looks like chocolate cake, at the grave of Lesia Levkovych. There is a mention of her towards the end of the history book, under the heading "Social and Cultural Developments in the Nineteen-Twenties." She reappears as a name in a footnote, in a list of the less prominent victims of the Nazi occupation.

A key turning in the lock, three times. Eva rushes to put the book back on the shelf; she doesn't want Alex to know she's been reading about this country of his; she doesn't want history tearing holes in the magic that's been setting them apart, protecting them. But though she's only skimmed its words, she can't shake off the photographs inside the history book: images of famine, slaughter, ruin. And a name in a footnote, a name annexed to a list of the dead.

Over breakfast the next morning—stale bread dipped into sweet, sticky instant coffee—she tells him there's a place in Kiev she needs to visit. Can he take her to Babi Yar?

For a moment, he keeps silent. And then, as if she hasn't spoken, he says, "We'll go to Pecherska Lavra—you ought to visit the museums there."

"I've had enough museums. I want something real—I want to go to Babi Yar." She knows she sounds like a child saying this: a spoiled and stubborn child. But she's afraid that talking about Lesia and Ivan will involve her in explaining about Olya and Oksanna. She looks up at him, notices the exhaustion in his face, and is about to tell him she's changed her mind when he says that if she wants so badly to go to Babi Yar, then of course he'll take her.

Outside, there is a fine rain falling; neither of them suggests going back for umbrellas. They walk in silence past the children's playground, down the concrete steps on which broken glass is shining, glass no one's bothered to sweep away. They take the subway to the Khreshchatyk, and then walk a few blocks to catch a tram as crowded as the subway car. Jolting, lurching down street after street, Eva can't hide her despair at how pervasive this ugliness is: even the trees can't hide it. The renovations going on here and there, the skips brimming with hunks of rotten plaster don't console her; she sees no workmen, no signs of activity. It's as though all the rubbish has been tipped into the open to be left there forever.

Watching her, Alex taps her lightly on the arm, as if he wanted to point something out, a statue or plaque. But it turns out to be a story he has to tell.

"I met an Englishwoman, once. She was accompanying her husband, who was lecturing at the Academy here. During the reception for him at the Ministry, this Englishwoman, who'd had rather too much champagne, turned to me and started raving about Krakow, where they'd just been. She said she was sure the steppes were something to see, but really, in cultural terms, there wasn't anything here to compare with Poland, was there? And then all that nastiness during the war. The Ukrainians were collaborators, weren't they—welcoming the Nazis with bread and salt, cheering as the Jews went off to Babi Yar. I smiled and poured her more champagne. Her husband came up just then, and she told him how charming Ukrainian men were. I didn't get a chance to explain."

"Explain what?"

Alex lights a cigarette, not asking her, this time, if she minds.

"That the war didn't end for Ukraine till 1951. That civilian casualties in Europe, the whole of Europe, were greatest here. After all, we had both the Nazis and the Soviets murdering our people."

"But in the concentration camps? The Ukrainian guards—"

"Oh yes. They were there." He stops staring at the heads of the people sitting in front of them; turns to meet her eyes. "But Eva, more bloody Dutchmen were recruited by the Waffen-SS than Ukrainians. Three times as many. Did you know that—does anybody know? And yes, five days after the Khreshchatyk was destroyed, the Nazis rounded up all the Jews in Kiev, and yes, everyone watched them walk to their deaths down this very street. Because if they'd done anything to stop the Nazis, they'd have ended up exactly where the Jews were headed. Tell me, what would you have done?"

She stares out the window; imagines herself standing there with her son beside her, watching. Just watching.

"But that doesn't excuse—" she begins. And stops.

"I'm not excusing anything," Alex says.

When they get off the tram, he gestures towards the giant TV antenna, and the cubelike housing units. They're painted the white of dried chicken bones; laundry sags from their rusting balconies.

"*Babyn Yar.* I prefer to say it in Russian: *Babi Yar.* It means the Old Women's Ravine. After the war, they built a dam across the end of it and flooded the place, tried to make a goddam lake. Except that the water was rotten, full of pulp oozing through the pipes. They kept building up the dam, year after year, until one morning the whole thing collapsed and a sea of mud poured into the city. Like Pompeii, only mud, swallowing people as they were stepping onto trams, or sitting down to breakfast, or dialling telephones at booths along the street. They tried again, the glorious engineers—sending in bulldozers, paving over the mud, building this road and those apartment buildings. They had to bulldoze the Jewish cemetery in the process. Those women hanging out their wash—they're standing on bones, millions and millions of human bones.

"Seventy thousand Jews were murdered here. The poor Jews from Podol, the ones who couldn't leave the city when the government cleared out. Men and women; the very old; small children. And after them, some hundred thousand other 'enemies of the people.' Waitresses from the Kiev nightclubs, when the German officers got tired of them. Actors, writers, musicians crazy enough to want to practise their art. The Dynamo soccer team, because they dared to beat the Germans in a match designed to show off Aryan superiority. And the politicals: partisans, insurgents, nationalists. Collaborators and informers, too, once they'd served their purpose."

Alex stops, his breathing harsh in the sudden silence. They are the only ones here, standing unshielded in the rain. He sets off into the park, along a path bordered by young trees. Eva follows, clumsy with the weight of what she's just heard. Things she can't translate into feeling, until she pictures, among those tens of thousands of Jews marched into the ravine, Dan and Julie. And then she is ready to cry out for two imagined victims instead of the countless bodies buried here.

She stops, needing to hide her face. Bending down she picks up a leaf that has detached itself from the drenched branches above her. The leaf is elongated, elegantly shaped; there's a small fleck of crimson on one of its points. The crimson reminds her of cinnamon candy hearts, the kind she loved as a child. She remembers how she'd take the candy from her mouth and paint her lips with it— and feels ashamed to be thinking this here, now. Tucking the leaf inside her pocket, she runs, stumbling, to catch up.

Alex has stopped at a flight of shallow steps, more like a ramp than steps; they climb it slowly, keeping their eyes on the ground and not the monument above them. Eva's seen so many monuments by now, starting with the aluminum warrior-woman on the outskirts of the city. She's afraid this statue will be as inflated and obscene. So she looks instead at the three plaques placed where the ramp finishes: three different languages: Hebrew,

Ukrainian, Russian. People have left flowers and money—the coupons Eva's been so lavish with the past few days. She wishes she'd brought flowers. She can't bring herself to lay money on the plaques. If she had coins, it would be different: coins you can lay on the eyelids of the dead; coins don't tear, or blow away.

Crouching on her heels, Eva runs her fingertips along the roughness of the concrete. Alex waits for her to finish—he says nothing. She feels she ought to make some gesture, not to him, but to the bones piled under her, and the minute fraction of those bones that belong to her. For they do belong. She feels it tugging at her now: that line between herself and the woman she calls at last, with no awkwardness or forcing, her grandmother.

They take the long way back, along the path that circles the monument and the ditch from which the sculpture rises. Green grass, green trees, and black, black crows all round. She waits a moment, then makes herself look up at the sculpture. Struggling forms, gigantic men and women, rain making their black bodies even darker. And at the very top, a mother holding out a baby no one will save.

"There's a tram coming—if we run, we can catch it."

But she can't run, she has to complete the circle round the statue. Thinking that the foundations of these apartment buildings coming into view must shake when the dead turn over in their sleep. Wondering where memory goes when you die—when you are shot in the head and kicked into a ditch. And why the air around her isn't so deeply scarred, so crammed with the memories of the dead that no one can ever breathe here again.

They stand, soaked and shivering, next to a kiosk selling Benson and Hedges and Cinzano until another tram arrives. Alex offers his arm to help her up, but she doesn't see it. Chernozem, she's thinking. What's the name for the kind of soil made of human bones? She keeps her free hand in her pocket, holding the small, red-flecked leaf against her thigh.

Alex has bought tickets for *Swan Lake* at sixty cents each, American, though they cost the earth in coupons. Eva pleads headache: after Babi Yar, she's too shaken up to go anywhere tonight—couldn't they put it off till tomorrow? But Alex insists, and once they arrive at the theatre, she understands why.

Compared to the opera and ballet house in Odessa, it's a modest enough building, he explains: built in the nineteenth century, but with a minimum of gilding and plaster rosettes. The cream-coloured walls, the delicate ornamentation of the dome: he can see that she is taken by it all. Look, she says, pointing out the little girls doing pirouettes in the alcoves during intermission: when one of them loses her balance and topples against her, Eva picks the child up in her arms, kissing her before handing her back to her parents. It makes her absurdly happy, this small gesture of connection; suddenly, she feels so much less of a stranger in this city. The child's parents beam at her, proud to have their child admired by this visitor from abroad: Alex translates a little between them and Eva. Amazed, and a little jealous at how the child's presence has transformed her, so that her face and her eyes, her whole body stream with a gladness, an openness different from anything she's shown to him.

Leaving the theatre, Eva tells him how much she loved the ballet, but then spoils it by saying, "I don't care if they did change the ending—I like it so much better this way." She's thinking of how, in spite of the mournful backdrop, Siegfried is reunited with his swan princess, who does not die but nestles trustingly against his heart. Alex takes this as a devious kind of criticism; he can only just keep the anger from his voice. "It's the only ending I've ever seen them do," he says. Unable to explain that only those who can't believe in happy endings desire them so. Coming to the theatre in all the finery they can muster, showing each other they can last them out, the hard times that have already lasted forever.

There is so much he can't tell her, so much that shoves between them now. It's stupid of him to be angry, stupid and unfair, but he can't help himself. Even her delight in the theatre rubs him the wrong way. He brought her here as an antidote to Babi Yar; to everything she's experienced so far of public culture here: the shoving and pushing on subway cars, the grimness of faces on the street. How can he explain to her the consequences of a culture of suspicion: the expectation that everyone else is out to get you, betray you, and take what is yours? What it's like to live your whole life in a crowded shoebox of an apartment, walk to and from work past buildings brutal in shape and scale, deal continually with objects perfect only in the speed and consistency with which they break down. How it changes something in your psyche, causing helpless sourness, or equally helpless optimism. The kind that gives *Swan Lake* its happy ending.

He keeps his anger to himself as they walk through the dark streets, or wait in the newly renovated subway station, with its imitation-Byzantine chandeliers and grandiose mosaics on the walls. Trappings that ordinarily console him, but that tonight seem to prove everything he thinks Eva's thinking. If only he could get through to her how arrogant she is to presume to judge him, his country, its history. To wince, as he's seen her doing in the crowded shops and subway cars, at the raw smell of so many sweating bodies. Should he confess that one of the things he feasts on when he's in bed with her is the cleanness and goodness of the way she smells? Tell her how his wife used to line them up like trophies on the shelves, the empty containers of whatever she managed to scrounge on the black market—hair conditioner, bubble bath, mouthwash—with their Western labels, their American brand names shining brighter, better than stars?

They will always be playing the swineherd and the princess, he realizes; it makes him laugh as they crush into the subway car, a bitter laughter that puzzles Eva. She thinks of the child she kissed in the foyer, permitting herself, just once, the wish that she and Alex could have a child together. A black-haired daughter they'd take to the ballet, watching her twirl and twirl in the marble alcoves of the theatre. Until she remembers that Alex already has a daughter, whose name she doesn't even know.

He goes out every afternoon now, for longer and longer periods. The first time it was to telephone the hospital without Eva's overhearing him, interpreting the emotion in his voice even if she can't understand the words. He still goes to his office each day to phone, but now it's not just to speak in private with his daughter. He needs practice in abandoning and being abandoned: his true life's work, he tells himself. Loss, absence, these are his daily bread. Loss of his mother, his sister, the country Eva comes from and that he'd once thought of as home. Loss of his wife and daughter, and then his father, and now, in a few days' time, this woman who's materialized so unexpectedly from a past he'd thought was finished.

From these absences, he returns bearing apologies like flowers—showy ones: gladioli or orchids. Not words, he never once talks about the huge crowds on the subways, the endless line-ups at the pharmacies or bakeries, where he might have stopped to get aspirin, rare as hen's teeth here, or a loaf of bread for next morning's breakfast. Not words, but his sheer physical presence, an exhausted body, a face like a lamp that's been smashed. And she goes to him, she can't bear to see him beaten by something far worse than she's felt waiting for him in a small, sealed apartment, reading a history book which tells of nothing but disasters.

She goes to him, suffused with tenderness, and yet their loving is harder, wilder than it's ever been. As if they must make up the time that's been squandered by his absence, fill each new hole as it appears, the holes in his face, and hers now, seeing his pain which she cannot help or even acknowledge, except by touch, in the dark. Yet even when they are most fiercely joined, or when they are simply together, setting out a meal or crossing a street, something presses at them, like a cat butting its head against their legs, demanding to be fed. There are things they simply don't talk about, not just whatever's keeping Alex away from her during the afternoons, but topics of conversation Eva begins to think of as luxuries like champagne or cashmere. To be able to speak of their children or parents; of planning holidays, of work or even politics. Of anything that would take them across the sealed borders of the present.

No horizon and no distance to this passion; no landscape, but only a locked room, a walled city in which she won't admit she's starting to feel more and more a hostage, a prisoner.

Soon after their trip to Babi Yar, Alex leaves her for so long she's terrified he'll never come back. Unfastening the bolt on the door with the spare key he's left her in case of an emergency, she steps into the hallway, leaving the door wide open behind her. She moves cautiously down the corridor, as dizzy in these first few moments of independence as an invalid trying her first steps after a month in bed. Her passport, her money, her plane ticket are all with her, folded into a black leather pouch she hangs round her neck, under her shirt: a talisman, assuring her she can go home again, that she won't be trapped here forever.

She hasn't the courage to take the elevator, and the eight flights down seem suddenly impossible to manage. She hesitates for a moment, then knocks on the neighbour's door: not the one that belongs to the quarrelling women, but that of the sick, elderly man to whom Alex has introduced her: his former teacher, Mr. Savchuk.

His glasses magnify his eyes, making them both vulnerable and conspicuous as they take in the foreign woman who is living with his neighbour. He asks her to come in, asks her in English.

Eva's face floods with relief. "I'm sorry to disturb you, I know you're not well, but I have to talk to someone, I thought I'd go mad if I had to spend another moment alone. It's Alex—something must have happened to him, he's never been this late before."

"Please." He nods towards a chair covered in uncracked vinyl, obviously the place of honour for his guests. Eva sits down gingerly, and he nods again. "Please, madame, I speak very little English, very badly. Will you take a cup of tea? Good. You will wait here, and I will come back with the tea."

His apartment is an exact replica of Alex's, except that there are books everywhere. She glances at her watch, alarmed at how much later it is than she thought; she's about to get up, run down the stairs and go looking for Alex, when Mr. Savchuk returns with a tray and two small cups of tea.

"I have to find Alex. Do you know where he is, can you tell me?"

She's talking far too quickly; he can't understand. But finally he makes out what she wants.

"Ah yes, Professor Moroz. He will be back soon. Please do not worry, madame. Please drink your tea." He has no idea where Alex has gone and when he will be back. But it's better to tell this woman something comforting. Absently, he slaps his pockets, looking for some object to distract her with, and then remembers the photographs of his sister's grandchildren, four of them set in a long metal frame, a birthday gift.

And it does calm Eva down—he has fixed on the one thing in the world that makes her feel competent, in her native element. Three small girls with enormous kerchief-bows in their hair. And a newborn baby. "A boy?" she asks. He nods delightedly, more because she's quieted down than because she's admiring the children. Smiling back at him, Eva says something about how beautiful his grandchildren are. And because he has been so kind to her, she tries to reciprocate. From the black leather pouch round her neck she extracts her favourite photograph of Ben: black and white, and taken at Woolworth's.

"My son," she says, handing it to him, waiting for the admiration he is bound to show. But he's silent: he holds the photograph up to his eyes, so close it nearly skims his glasses. She's about to ask for it back when there's a pounding on the door. Still holding the photograph, Mr. Savchuk rises and undoes the bolts. Alex comes bursting through. He is wild—so wild that he hurls a stream of Ukrainian at her before he remembers and switches into English.

"*Jesus,* Eva, what the hell is going on? I come home and find the door unlocked—Christ, the door's wide open, and you're gone, and I don't know what's happened—"

"It's all right, Alex. I'm sorry. But it was getting so late—I was out of my mind, worrying about you. Mr. Savchuk has been very kind. I was just showing him a picture of Ben, my son Ben. Could you ask him to give it back to me? Then we can go."

Alex speaks to Mr. Savchuk, who is holding the photograph so that it's covered by his hand. He's saying something in Ukrainian.

"What is it?" Eva asks. "What's wrong?"

Alex shakes his head. "He says this can't be a photograph of your son. It can't be, because it's a picture of his friend Ivan, who died in the war."

Nakedness: this is what a respectably clothed Eva feels, sitting at the card table that's been lugged in from the verandah to serve as a dinner table. The kind of nakedness you'd feel if a blast of wind descended on your house, ripping its roof and walls away. Everything has changed; or rather, everything she so carefully shut out for the past two weeks has poured through the door with Alex. He is sitting across from her in Mr. Savchuk's apartment, ignoring a plate of bread and sausage between them.

She knows she should be astonished at having found the one person in this whole city who can tell her what she needs to know about that stranger, her father. But all she feels is bewilderment that the journey that began with a photograph shoved through her mail slot has come to a dead end here.

Alex translates after every few sentences, when Mr. Savchuk stops to take another sip of brandy. The old man's fingers run up and down the glass, as if playing scales; every so often there's a tremor in his voice, the kind of tremor Eva associates not with frailty, but with strong emotion, the kind that can't be faked.

"My friend Ivan. His mother used to bring him to Soloveyko in the summers, when he was a child. She had the use of a dacha nearby, she belonged to a group of artists who used to come for their holidays to the little town where we lived. Most evenings, they'd meet for a meal or a drink at my parents' café. Everyone would sit out on the terrace, drinking, singing, telling stories. They felt free there, you see—or at least, they knew how lucky they were. And they knew how long luck lasts in this country.

"The last summer they all came to Soloveyko was the summer when the Famine ended and the Terror began. The next year, there was no one left to come, or no one who'd dare. By the end of the thirties, the Bolsheviks had got rid of nearly everyone we knew. Painters, filmmakers, writers, professors—vanished. To the camps in Siberia; or, if they were lucky, if they could speak the Russian way, to Moscow. As for our political elite—fifteen thousand of them were eliminated. And that was only 1933. There was 1937 yet to come. The year Khrushchev first came to Ukraine, in order to purge this country 'spotless.'"

He starts to cough, holding his hand over his heart, waving away their concern as he continues the story.

"Ivan's mother was one of the ones who survived, at least for a time. Not that she did anything dishonourable, you understand—she had a child to support; heroics would have been no use to her. But she wasn't a turncoat, either. She was a survivor, one of those who made it through the worst of times, till fate decided otherwise. Laugh at me, if you like. I'm a great believer in fate. There's no other way to make sense of what happens in this country.

"Ivan left with his mother before the end of that last summer. I didn't see Ivan for a long time afterwards, maybe five, six years, and then, out of the blue, I was told he was coming to live with us. His mother was anxious to get him out of the city—she knew how quickly war was coming, whatever pacts or treaties had been signed. And besides, she and Ivan were like the blades on a pair of scissors: they couldn't come together except to cut.

"He was full of grand talk when he arrived—about what was going on in western Ukraine, the part Hitler had taken from the Poles and thrown to his good friend Stalin. Ivan was hell-bent on getting to Lviv, offering himself to the underground. To Stepan Bandera, fresh out of a Polish prison and calling for an army to fight the Russians, the Germans, the Poles—whoever stood in the way of a free Ukraine. A secret army, with all the trappings: ranks and pistols and secret oaths. Bandera was exactly what Ivan dreamed of becoming—a revolutionary who could fire you up with his speeches, make you follow him anywhere. Die for him at the snap of his fingers."

The old man stops to pour another glass of brandy for them all. Eva doesn't let herself look into Alex's face. She knows from his voice how tired he is, but she has to hear what the old man needs to tell. For there's no stopping him: his words pour out as though it's been years and years since he's talked to anyone but himself.

"Ivan died for him, all right, but not in the way he expected. He ran off, just as he said he would—disappeared in the middle of the night. My mother was beside herself, she'd sworn to his mother she would look after him, keep him safe till the war was over. He was barely eighteen, Ivan. But he wanted nothing to do with safety, hiding, lying low. He joined Bandera's people in the west, just as he swore he would.

"What happened then? A thieves' quarrel. When the Bolsheviks saw their allies marching into this country, they saved their own skins and flayed ours. Anything that could be of use to the Germans—anything that could provide our people with some kind of living—they destroyed. The mines and the dams were flooded; factories blown up. They emptied the prisons, too—before they escaped to the Urals, the Bolsheviks shot ten thousand political prisoners in Galicia alone. Galicia, where Ivan had run off to join the great Bandera. For a long time, I heard nothing from him, and then a message arrived from Kiev, where he'd gone on a mission against the enemy. Not the Nazis, not even the Russians, but the moderates in the very underground he was fighting for."

Eva's face is creased with the effort she is making just to grab hold of the place names, the politics: she is still such a stranger here.

"You've heard of Melnyk, Andrii Melnyk? He was the leader of the moderates: like Ivan's mother, he was more at home with books than guns. The organization split in half—Banderites and Melnykites out for each other's blood, and all in the beautiful name of a free Ukraine. Just days after the Germans chased the Bolsheviks from Kiev, Bandera and his group declared Lviv the capital of the new Ukrainian state. The ink on that declaration wasn't dry before the Nazis arrested Bandera and his men. They went for Melnyk and his group a little later. And Ukraine was still no freer than a bird cage.

"Ivan joined the German army on Bandera's urging. They'd set up two units for Ukrainians, units with names a poet might have chosen: *Nachtigall* and *Roland*. Ivan wrote to me just before he left for the front, telling how these units would be the core of a new Ukrainian army, yet another army to rid our country of invaders, once and for all. He tried to recruit me, but by that time I'd had enough of armies, no matter what or who they were fighting for. By then my father had been killed, and my older brother: there was no one else to keep my mother and sister from starving to death.

"So my friend Ivan went off with the nightingales. He was nineteen then. A boy from Soloveyko wound up in his division. That boy—or what was left of him—made it back home. They'd been ordered across a minefield, and the whole front of the division—including Ivan, of course—was blown up. Do you understand me? The men in that division—their eyes and teeth, their bones and the flesh and skin on those bones—

"As for me, I stayed home. I saw women raped and then shot while the bastards were still buttoning their flies. I saw men take a boy—slice off his tongue, gouge out his eyes. And make his mother watch, so she could tell her neighbours what happens to those who help partisans. And everything I've seen has become nothing but stories, an old man bending the ears of his guests. Who are too polite, or else too tired, to ask him to stop."

The bottle is empty; it is almost midnight. Alex asks Mr. Savchuk if he needs help getting up from his chair, but the old man doesn't hear. He gropes for Eva's hand and the photograph she's been holding face down against the table. Gently, he lifts her hand, and turns the photograph so he can look at it again. His eyes behind their thick glass lids are stones thrown to the bottom of the sea. At last, he signals to Alex that yes, he would be glad of an arm to help him up. He walks with them to the door, where he pauses, saying something slow and emphatic in Ukrainian. And then he wishes them good night, sealing the door behind them.

If Mr. Savchuk has been too polite, or too enmeshed in memory to interrogate her, Alex isn't. He wants to know what's going on; will she please explain what business she has with dead men and their history—a history that isn't even hers?

So she tells him, as they sit across from one another, at opposite ends of the sofa bed. About the man who was her mother's lover and, she had thought, her father. Except that, according to Mr. Savchuk, Ivan Kotelko was blown up by a mine, in which case everything she's discovered up to this point, all the stories people have told her, are nothing but fictions.

Alex rubs his face with his hands. "You know what he said when we were leaving the room? He said he'd made a mistake, that his eyes were bad, playing tricks on him. That there's really no resemblance at all between his friend and your son."

Eva twists her ring round and round her finger, refusing to look into her lover's face.

"How do I know you're telling me the truth?"

"For Christ's sake, Eva, what reason have I got to lie to you? And what about you? How can I tell you haven't made this whole thing up yourself, this story about your mother and her DP lover? Though God knows why anyone would want to make themselves part of this country if they didn't have to."

He stops, realizing the same moment she does what's

happened, thanks to the fluke of his neighbour being who he is. Fluke or fate, it adds up to the same thing: Eva's no longer the stranger, the permanently foreign visitor he's taken her to be, but a prodigal, like him. Someone who's had to return to the place where she came from, however little she belongs to it.

Eva pulls the suitcase from underneath the bed, taking out the photograph of Ivan and Lesia at Soloveyko, handing it to Alex.

"Was he lying? Is this whole story, everything I've told you, a lie?"

Alex sighs. "No story tells the whole truth, and no story's nothing but lies. You know that, Eva. All I can tell you is what I think. I think he told us as much of what really happened as he thought was safe for us to know. He thought he saw his friend's face in your son's picture. The same face that's in this photograph, taken, what—sixty years ago? Anything can happen in that long a time."

"But he said Ivan Kotelko died in the war."

"Maybe that's what he needs to believe. Maybe Ivan ran away when he saw which way the war was going; maybe he came across some dead man in a field and changed his uniform for a peasant's rags. Maybe he joined up with people who'd escaped from the labour camps when their factories were being bombed by the Allies. People like my father. He might even have wound up in a DP camp in Bavaria. Changed his name, his history, proved that his lungs were sound, and got shipped to Canada. The people in charge of immigration—they wanted labourers, farmers, industrial workers. Not patriots and intellectuals: certainly no one who'd fought in the Galician division of the German army, like that boy Ivan. Nobody had anything like identity cards, passports, birth certificates at the end of the war. He could have turned into anyone, anything he wanted."

Can she tell how much he wants it to be true, what he's saying—for her to feel some kind of loyalty or just connection to this place? Imagining for a crazy moment Eva staying on here, living with him, never leaving him, as she's bound to do in a few days time. But even as he imagines this, he knows how impossible it is, if only because of the son she's left behind her, and the daughter he can never speak about to her. Because he couldn't bear her pity, and her blame.

He holds her against him, her head on his chest as she taps his heartbeat lightly, evenly upon his arm. They stay like this for a long time, sleep a ghost that refuses to haunt them till well into morning.

At his desk, Mykola takes out the black-bound notebook and leafs through the pages till he comes to what he's looking for. A book crammed with stories, images from something he's supposed to call "the past," but which keeps bleeding into the present and won't be staunched. Time is a river; for Mykola, the river is inside his head. Things get snagged along the river's banks: a pair of scissors cutting into a photograph; a woman's hand touching his face.

Oleksa and this woman with the blue, blue eyes: they are in trouble with one another. He has seen this so many times. Two lovers, like a pair of careless thieves, stealing a few days, even a week to be alone together. Everything, including the air they breathe, the warmth of their skins, becoming part of the astonishment of joy. And then the moment comes when astonishment becomes not joy, but fear. Fear that they could have set themselves up to lose so much, to show themselves so vulnerable. Always, it ends with them walking away from each other, holding the boxes in which they'd stored what they had stolen. Empty boxes, with holes punched through.

Those other lovers, at Soloveyko. The man he hardly remembers, but the woman—she was never careless, or fearful. What he remembers most about her is the calm she carried with her, like a wonderful scent spreading from her forehead, her eyes, even the set of her head when she sat on the terrace, looking out at the sky. That evening, when everyone had gathered for dinner, and they'd started teasing him, a boy of fourteen, about which of the pretty girls he was going to marry. He'd stammered some answer to put them off, keep them from knowing. But she had understood. Of them all, she was the only one who could look at him and read his desire. And the only reason he hadn't been afraid was the extraordinary calmness of her eyes: unstoppable kindness and sadness, too. For she knew already what he would find out so slowly and with so much pain. That her son could never love anyone whose heart and hands were so open.

Long after those evenings on the terrace were over, he met her one last time, when she brought her son back to Soloveyko. Everyone could see how Ivan was refusing to speak to his mother, to do more than shrug in her direction when it came time for her to leave. She made no scene; she simply dropped the arms she'd been holding out and came to him instead, asking if he'd see her down to the station. They walked all the way in silence, but before she boarded the train, she turned to him and touched his face. "Please look out for Ivan. Make sure he doesn't do any damage to himself, or anyone else. Take care of yourself, Mykola." And then she disappeared into the railway carriage.

He had done poorly. Or at least, it was no credit to him that Ivan had come through the war, made it safely to Canada, managed to survive there. She must have known her son was too headstrong, too reckless for anyone to control him. He had argued against Ivan's running away, and then, when he'd seen he couldn't win, he'd given in and helped him go.

Ivan is making a parcel of things from his desk: his school certificates, an adventure book he'd been given for a long-ago birthday, a picture of his dead father, Roman Kotelko. But nothing that has anything to do with his mother. Mykola sits on the bed across from him, watching; at last, he goes to his chest of drawers and takes out the only photograph he has of Lesia. It was taken that last summer the artists came to Soloveyko, a picture of the three of them: Lesia, Ivan, Pavlo. It had been sent to his parents, who had hidden it away when it became impolitic to keep up connections with this kind of past. He had merely transferred it, unasked, from their hiding place to one of his own. Now he hands the photograph to Ivan, who refuses to look at it. But Mykola stands there, holding it out as if to say, if you don't take this, I won't help you with anything else.

At last, Ivan accepts the photograph. He reaches for the scissors in his desk, a long, sharp pair. For a moment, Mykola is terrified the picture will be cut to pieces, but what happens is this: very carefully, Ivan cuts off the upper edge, crumpling it into his pocket. Then he places what remains of the photo into the package, which he seals into an oilskin bag.

They leave the sleeping house, stealing out into the darkness, feeling their way to the root cellar, which is deep and dry, a labyrinth of passages they know as well as they do their multiplication tables. Ivan carries a stub of candle through the maze, leading Mykola to the hiding place they'd made when they were children, playing Secret Army. He slides the carefully tied package into a deep, narrow hole carved into the wall, then plugs the mouth of the hole with fresh clay, making it look as though the wall has never been disturbed at all. It is no worse a hiding place than any other. If Ivan survives the war, he will come back and retrieve his package. If not, Mykola will destroy it. These are the terms on which the two friends part.

They don't even consider whether the cellar, the café itself will outlast the war, the bombing raids, the soldiers shooting at mirrors, smashing empty bottles against the walls. When the war is over, and news comes from the neighbour's son about Ivan's death, Mykola goes down to the cellar, unearths the package, and destroys its contents, all but the photograph, which he locks into a drawer of his desk. Whenever he looks at it, he tries to reconstruct the part Ivan had cut away, and which has been lost. Sometimes he puts his thumb over the face of his friend, the better to look at the woman holding him against her, the sad, beautiful face of a woman, killed, like her son, in the war.

Forty-five years later, a whole world and lifetime later, he receives a letter sent to him at the White Crane Café, an airmail letter that the village postmaster, who'd been a classmate of his, has directed to him in Kiev. That the letter has reached him is a piece of great luck, but not a miracle, since it's no longer considered criminal to have friends or family in the West. The letter is from Ivan, though there is no signature; it sends greetings, but says nothing at all about his life during the war, or in Canada these many years. It asks him to return the package hidden in the root cellar, to mail it to a Toronto address in care of Mykola Savchuk. The absolute assurance that the package is still there, and that he is still alive, takes Mykola's breath away. He recognizes at once, in the very handwriting as well as the wording of the letter, the authority of Ivan's presence. Mykola surrenders the scrap of photograph he's kept so long, enclosing with it a short note, also unsigned, saying that the rest of the package was destroyed long ago, according to instructions, and wishing his namesake the best of health. The photograph and the note he mails off from the central post office in Kiev; there is no reply.

Except this visit, paid him by a woman about whose origins and intentions Mykola refuses to speculate. He has enough to write down in his notebook; he has the whole past to chronicle, and no time to give to the present, which is nothing but the future in disguise. He had thought he was so good at keeping secrets. He was taken off guard tonight by the photograph of the boy, the shock of that resemblance. Well, he has taken it back, blamed it on his eyes. With any luck, they'll think him an old fool in love with the sound of his own voice. It is best for Ivan to be dead in the war. Dead men court no dangers. Besides, it's Lesia's story he's at pains to tell—Lesia's and the story she'd have chosen for her son, in order to protect him. If there's another Mykola Savchuk leading a life in Canada, one with the luck—the fate—he's never possessed, then so much the better.

And he gives the same nervous cough which used to be his substitute for agreement, when he and Ivan had played their secret games before the war.

For the first time, Alex and Eva wake without making love, without even touching one another. Eva's head feels like an eggshell that's been tapped so many times, its surface is a maze of cracks. At first, she tells herself it's the effect of the old man's story, the way it's piled back into her arms all the burdens she's let go of these past two weeks. Then guilt hits her, hard, as she thinks of how she's put all thought of Ben aside; how he could have been waving to her from a desert island and she would have swept right past on the bright sail of her skin. Suddenly she panics, realizing that tomorrow she'll be leaving for home; that the time she's allowed herself here has nearly run out.

This will be her last full day in Kiev; tomorrow, she'll have to get back to the hotel, rejoin the tour group, and board the special bus that, despite shortages of gasoline and engine parts, has promised to deliver them to the airport on time. An overnight stay in Frankfurt, an afternoon flight to Toronto. She goes over all of this in her mind, yet her body refuses to accept it, insisting that its centre of gravity is here and will not be dislodged, any more than the ache that's hammering her head.

She refuses to listen to her body; she washes it in the chipped enamel tub, dresses it in one of the silks she bought for this journey, and sits it across from Alex at the shawl-draped table in the kitchen. The only way she'll get through this day is by thinking, feeling nothing at all. For she doesn't know what she thinks, what she wants, what is possible or impossible anymore. Alex is no help to her: he sits so straight, his hands curled into fists, only his wrists touching the table. When he does speak, it's to say he'll take her shopping for souvenirs, since it's her last day. She keeps her eyes fastened on his hands, so as not to give herself away. He accepts it as over: he will let her leave with the same politeness, the same distance he showed when she called him from the hotel, her first day in Kiev. As if they'd parted ways after that disastrous dinner at the restaurant, or even before, after the tour he'd given her of the city.

He takes her to the rows and rows of ugly shops on the Khreshchatyk; they have nothing she wants to buy, nothing but mass-produced Matrioshka dolls and shoddily manufactured wooden boxes. Next, they try some of the smaller places that sell shawls and Easter eggs, but these shops are dark; they smell of unwashed bodies and bad luck, and she can't bring herself to buy anything from them. There's a bookstore with a coffee table special on Kiev in the window: she tries to dissuade Alex from going in, but he insists. There are no books on the shelves—no shelves except those locked behind a counter, defended by a woman who only grudgingly brings a copy of the book in the window. When Eva opens it, she finds that the paper is ripped through in places; the photographs of places she's seen here, beautiful places, are bleary, the people in them wearing clothes, hairstyles from thirty years ago.

She grabs him by the sleeve, tells him she's had enough. Her head hurts; couldn't they spend the rest of the day in a park, sitting under the trees? He tells her there's one more shop they have to try, and leads her to the street which, curving round the glittery domes of St. Andrew's church, plunges, all cobbles and potholes, into Podol.

There's a craft shop hidden down an alleyway. Among the jewellery and ceramics is a group of small clay figures like the ones she'd seen in the ethnographic museum. A cossack on horseback: a ram with curling horns, and a fox woman with her hand up to her mouth, as if she's just been astonished, or guiltily delighted by something. Eva stands there, open-mouthed. Why didn't he take her here in the first place—why hadn't he known these are the only things she would have wanted, not as souvenirs, but as gifts for them to give each other? While she stands staring at the figures, Alex says something to the shop attendant, who gathers them up, wraps them in newspaper, and takes the sheaf of coupons Eva offers her. They are ridiculously cheap: it's not the price that disturbs her but the way Alex disassociates himself from them, as if he's with her now only to translate and carry out transactions.

So that when they stop for a late lunch at the café across the road, she's prepared, even eager for the quarrel. This man sitting across from her, looking as if he'd rather be anywhere else than with her—she has to call him back to her by whatever means she can. She wants them to stay wrapped up in their desire, and she wants to risk everything by stepping off the edge of this close, dense little world they've made; daring him to follow. And so she asks the question she's left unspoken from the day they met:

"When are you coming back to Canada?"

He doesn't even look at her. "I don't have money to travel. The average salary of a university professor in this country is seventeen dollars a month."

"I mean, to live in Canada. After all, you grew up there."

This time he meets her eyes, a look of contempt or impatience, she can't tell which. "Eva, I was born in Germany and spent a total of five years in Toronto. I've lived in Kiev all my adult life. So how does that make me Canadian? And just what do you think I would do in your country? Start out all over again, work my way up to a job at Canada Packers, the way my father did?"

He takes out a cigarette, lights it despite the angry disapproval of the waitress, whom he pretends not to see. And then he gives his parting shot:

"What about you, Eva? When are you moving to Kiev? Plenty of jobs here, working with children."

Her head hurts too much to shake it. How could he expect her to bring Ben here? And how could she expect him to leave his daughter behind? She pushes her dish of stewed prunes and ersatz cream away from her. It's all wrong, what they're doing; surely there's another language they can use to say what they really mean.

All he sees is the gesture, the pushing away. He takes the dish and slowly, grimly finishes what she's left, pushing the empty bowl back at her.

"Why don't you stay home if you can't live without pizza and Coca-Cola? Why don't all you Westerners, with your big money that you spend like water over here, for Christ's sake just stay home?"

"I wish I had. I'm homesick, if you want to know. I'm homesick for a place where you can buy toothpaste and toilet paper and aspirin at the corner store. I'm sick of feeling guilty just for wanting to be comfortable. I'm sick of the terrible toilets, I'm sick of the slamming and shoving on the subway, I'm sick of all the teenaged soldiers filling up the streets. I'd like to find a café where you don't have to line up for an hour to get a cup of coffee; to sleep on a decent bed and eat a meal on a table that doesn't shake because it's made of such rotten material. I'd like, God, how I'd like to be home. I didn't want to come here, you know."

"So, who made you?" he jeers. "Your mother?"

"No. Yours."

The flimsy table tilts, sending the dishes crashing to the floor. The waitress shouts at Alex's retreating back; gestures in despair at Eva, who helps her pick up the broken china, apologizing in English, as if the damage were all her fault. Eva takes her shoulder bag, shakes out every coupon left onto the table, and rushes out the door.

He's waiting for her; before she can speak, he grabs her arm, holding it so tight she'll wear a bruise above her elbow for the next two weeks. All the way back to the apartment, he never once lets go of her; she never says a word, exulting in the pain, at how it puts him so completely in the wrong. Once he's shoved her through the door and locked it, triple-locked it behind him, they stare at one another, their breath tearing out of them. And then they find a better way to hurt each other.

Not on the bed, but the worn, coarse carpet. Slamming, pushing; eyes open, bodies clenched. Faces cut with this pain that they want more of and more. Till they both arrive wherever it is they've been forcing each other. On a gritty rug, in the slurred light of late afternoon.

Eva gets up as if each one of her bones is broken. She can't remember how she got to the bed—she can't remember Alex getting up from the floor, dressing, leaving the apartment, though he must have, since she's all alone here now.

It's four in the morning—she must have slept for twelve hours or more—but how could she have? She refuses to let herself panic—there's no need to be back at the hotel till noon, she can ask Mr. Savchuk to call her a cab—and then she remembers the door, all the locks and bolts. She runs to the hook where Alex keeps the spare keys—they're still there, he hasn't locked her in. She runs a bath, washes herself twice over, dresses in her last clean clothes. There's nothing to pack—if it weren't so early she could leave right now. She goes back to the bed, absently smoothing the sheets. And then tugs them so they fly up, exposing the dinginess of the upholstery. One by one she folds the sheets, frees the pillows from their cases, piles the whole lot on the kitchen table. There's this at least—he won't be able to say she hasn't cleaned up after herself.

It's cooler on the verandah than she expected. She climbs onto a coffee table that's been wedged between the walls, and sits looking out through the opened windows. At the apartments across the way, imagining another woman sitting just as she is, looking out at her. It's too early for any birds to be singing—whatever birds live in the small, straggling bushes round the apartment blocks.

She doesn't turn round when she hears him fumbling with the locks. When he calls out her name, going from room to room, finally opening the verandah door. She doesn't say a word as he sits down beside her. She doesn't want him to say anything, either. If only they can keep from speaking; part without saying anything ugly. There's been enough of that already. And now she turns, looking him straight in the face, willing him to understand her.

From the circles stamped under his eyes, the whiteness of his face she can tell he's been up all night. He lights a cigarette, and leans back against the wall. There is perhaps a hand's breadth of space between them as they sit watching the darkness lift from the sky. It would be fitting if the day arrived overcast, threatening rain, but they both think, staring up at the sky, that they have never seen a clearer dawn.

A woman with a baby stands on her verandah, looking out into the eyes of the new day. Behind her, a line of diapers hanging like signal flags. The baby's head is pushed up against her shoulder: every so often she brushes her lips across it, inhaling a scent like fresh bread. It's almost time to lay the table for breakfast, but she waits for a moment longer, enjoying the softness of the air that in an hour's time will be dense with noise and smoke.

Just as she's about to go in, she sees two figures walking down the glass-strewn steps below. One of her neighbours, carrying a suitcase; a strange woman she doesn't know. The stranger stops for a moment at the children's playground; walks inside one of the archways carved to resemble a storybook hut, and runs her hands up and down the columns. The man waits for her in perfect patience, without even putting the suitcase down.

"Nadia!"

It's her husband calling, wanting to know why the coffee isn't made.

She turns at once to hush him, explaining that the child's still asleep. It takes only a moment. But when she looks back down, the couple have disappeared. She feels a disappointment that she can't explain—it makes her hug the baby tighter to her breast. When her husband leaves for work, she refuses to kiss him. It's not till noon that she forgets to be cross with him; forgets, too, what made her feel such curiosity, such tenderness, looking out from her verandah, at a dawn like any other.

There's a different receptionist this time, a young woman with a sweet face and butter-blonde hair, who tells Eva that the bus for the airport leaves, not at noon, but at four o'clock—the flight has had to be rescheduled. It is nine in the morning: Eva has no intention of sitting in the lobby all day, with the other members of the tour group. She would like to walk somewhere—just to put one foot in front of the other and to keep on going. But there's only one place in all of Kiev that she knows how to get to on her own.

In the brilliant morning light the museum looks more than ever like a mausoleum. Weeds sprout between the cracks in the steps; the massive columns holding up the pediment are cracked and chipped away. Eva buys an English-language guidebook with the last of her coupons, and proceeds to walk through the building, room by room. She looks at, without seeing, the mahogany-faced madonnas on ancient icons; sixteenth-century hetmans with eyebrows and moustaches like drooping licorice. Genre paintings: village fairs and weddings; wreathed, barefoot children looking milkily, impossibly content.

An attendant comes up to her, an old woman who stands no higher than Eva's shoulders. Her eyes are vague with cataracts; her body thick with layers of mismatched wool. She pours out a stream of Ukrainian, to which Eva can only return a sad shrug, and walk on. There is nothing for her here. All she wants to do is get on the plane and shut her eyes till she gets back to Toronto. Shut her eyes and ears and the pores of her skin, still holding traces of his hands, his tongue. But she makes herself look through this last room, with its paintings from the twenties and thirties. Most of them are the work of a pair of brothers named Boychuk. One of them died young, the other was liquidated, all of his paintings destroyed, except for the ones curators and private owners hid away. His work is starkly formal, like icons, and yet moving, though whether this is because she knows the fate of the painter, or because of the canvases themselves, she can't say.

Eva drops onto a bench in the middle of the room and stares at a painting of two stylized women under an apple tree. They remind her of Olya in the quiet dignity of their bodies. For the first time, it occurs to her that this journey has been an appalling failure, not just for her, but for Olya, too. What will she say to her when she gets back to Toronto? About Alex, or Lesia Levkovych. About this country she neither loves, nor understands. She will have to tell Olya something, make up a story that will give her at least a fragment of what she wants to hear. Even if all she talks about are the paintings in this musem; the work of two dead brothers. And then she remembers that other dead painter—the man cut out of the photograph. Surely there must be something by him in this place. She pores over the guidebook and finds, on the wall behind her, a canvas by one Pavlo Bozhyk, 1880–1933.

A woman with her back turned, looking out over a field stretched far below her. She may be twenty or forty; you can see nothing of her face but the way it curves away from you. Yet you'd know her at once, from any other angle and in any other place, by the calm that surrounds her, a circle of tawny light. On the table behind her, apples are scattered. They look to be carved out of wood, they look as though they could never be eaten. Their leaves are bigger than the fruit, though the fruit is oddly distended.

The field below her, the field you assume the woman is looking at, is perfectly flat, with ponds and rivers and hedgerows spreading as far as you can see, under a sky threatening rain. There is something terrible about the way the woman is positioned, so that she can't avert her gaze but must look straight into the clouds pushing towards her, moving in across the fields. And now Eva sees something just as frightening in the utter flatness, the defencelessness of the land. Anyone could sweep down and take it. Roll across it with tanks or drop bombs from planes hidden in those dense, white clouds.

It's a portrait of Lesia Levkovych; Eva knows this though the guidebook makes no mention of the name. It's a painting of the woman Eva has seen in a photograph, over whose bones she walked at Babi Yar, but who has only now become a physical presence. Right now, she can hear Lesia breathing; she is waiting for her to turn round and speak to her. Because of the poor light, or her own despair; perhaps because this portrait was so clearly painted in love and fear, Eva feels as though the frame has vanished, the very paint turning to a topaz-coloured haze. A terrible acceptance pours from this woman, a nimbus of shadow, not light. And Eva has never felt so frightened, so desolate in her whole life as she does standing here.

The guard comes up behind her as if to scold her for standing too close to the painting, breathing too loudly. But the old woman merely slips her arm through hers in the simple, affectionate way Eva has seen women walking or standing together in the streets, the parks of Kiev. It moves Eva beyond measure, this gesture by an utter stranger, this speech in the one language they have in common.

They stand as close together as mother and daughter. And the fact that there's no tie between them, that the woman had no need, no duty to comfort Eva makes her gesture more consoling. After the ugliness with Alex, the way they'd harrowed each other—this woman's arm through hers, holding her up, helping her hold herself together so she can get through this last day and make it home again.

Gently, Eva pulls her arm away, knowing it's late, that she has to get back to the hotel before they leave without her. If only she could say this to the woman beside her, make some sign. All she can do is hold the woman's hand in hers; look into her face. The seamed skin framed by a headscarf, burst veins under filmed, brown eyes. A face she finds beautiful, because it moves her, moves her out of herself. And only now does a word come back to her from her lessons with Alex those first days in Kiev.

"*Diakuyu.*" Thank you.

"*Nema za scho,*" the woman says, pressing Eva's hand, and returning to her seat by the radiator. Eva leaves without looking back, holding what she's been given. A woman with her back turned to her; a woman standing beside her, arm in arm. Absence, presence, like a body and its shadow.

She almost walks right past him, into the lobby where the tour group is complaining about the flight being delayed. She doesn't want to see him or speak with him. They've said everything they could, there is no kick or caress left to give. But he says he needs to talk with her, and she can't refuse without making a scene. They go into the restaurant, which is nearly empty, and order strong, bitter coffee. Sitting across from one another like this, not touching, not speaking, they might be an old married couple, Eva thinks. If Alex had stayed in Canada, who knows? They might have been celebrating their silver wedding anniversary with a trip to Ukraine.

From his briefcase, he takes a brown paper package and hands it to her. It's the shawl she deliberately left behind—on the kitchen table, under the folded bedsheets. She's about to give it back to him when he pushes something else across the table: a group of photographs.

"My daughter," he says. "Katia."

Eva reaches for the photos as if they were the child herself. Alex's daughter has wide brown eyes and a full mouth. Her whole face is open. And she's already being held: in one of the pictures, she nestles in a woman's lap, and the woman has long, thick, blue-black hair, just like her daughter's.

"We had only the one child, and everything fell apart after she was born. We began to quarrel over what language she'd speak. I thought it was simple—Galina would use Russian with her, and I would use Ukrainian. She'd grow up with the two languages, and learn English at school, later on. English, German, Finnish for all I cared. But my wife wanted us to move away, to Moscow or any other Russian-speaking place. So Katia would feel no split in her tongue, no tug of war as to who she was, what she belonged to. I told her we were fine right where we were. And so we fought in whispers, in an apartment where we could never have a moment or a room to ourselves; we fought for six years over what language she should speak."

Eva tries to signal to Alex that he mustn't explain. She wants neither apology nor confession now. But she can't catch his eye; he is staring down at his coffee cup, and she can't trust herself to touch him.

"That spring, I sent Katia to spend her holidays with some cousins of mine in a village north of Kiev. She knew them—knew their children, the names of their dog and cat; I'd taken her there half a dozen times already. You can't survive in this country without knowing someone in a village—to get fresh food; to keep up the language. That's where Ukrainian's spoken, Eva; where it's kept alive. I thought it would do her good to be out in the country, away from all our fighting. At first, Galina refused to let her leave, but Katia wanted to go so badly. I took her up on the train, with the new bicycle we'd bought her for her birthday, and came back to Kiev the next day. It was still term time, Galina and I had classes to teach; it was only for a week.

"A nuclear power plant explodes, and no one tells us anything. To keep our children indoors, to keep them from drinking milk, to give them potassium iodide to stop their bodies from absorbing radiation. You can't imagine what it was like—not just in the towns and villages by the plant, but right here in Kiev. Chaos, rumours—people packing the trains as if it were wartime, fleeing the city for anywhere except the dead zone. Where Katia was waiting for me, not knowing what had happened, only that everyone was whispering, and that all of a sudden they wouldn't let her out to ride her bicycle. But she was all right, Eva: there was no sign of anything wrong with her.

"After I brought her back to Kiev, she was evacuated with all the other children—she spent the summer at a Young Pioneer camp, and then we took her to the mountains. I was away so much that year, in places where it was impossible to telephone. When I did see Katia, I didn't notice anything different about her: she'd always been delicate, getting every kind of cold and fever. But now she was tired all the time, Galina said. The doctors told us not to worry; everyone told us Kiev was safe, even though Chornobyl was operating again. But my wife knew—and I wouldn't let myself see what was happening. We stopped fighting over language that year and started in on Katia's health. It got so we couldn't spend half an hour in the same room.

"Galina applied for all kinds of posts in the south, where the weather's so much milder, and you're near the sea. But everyone else wanted to move south, too. By the time a job came up for her in Odessa, we'd been divorced for a couple of years. Galina's mother moved in with them, she took care of them both, and for a while Katia seemed to be getting better. But now they've found a lump in her neck. Most of the cancer they've developed, children in Belorussia and Ukraine, is cancer of the thyroid, something only adults are supposed to get. Do you know what they call children sick with radiation from Chornobyl? Fireflies: the kids who haven't fallen sick yet call them fireflies."

"Alex, oh Alex."

He doesn't hear her. She sees the heaviness of what he's told her, a weight he shifts from shoulder to shoulder.

"I have to ring the hospital today, to find out the results of the tests. I know already what the doctor's going to tell me. But what in God's name will I tell her? What do I say to my daughter when I go to her?"

She reaches for Alex's hand, but he draws it away.

"You mentioned my mother yesterday."

She'd thought she wasn't going to have to pay for that spiteful remark in the café. Then it comes to her that this is a chance she's been given—a parting gift she can make to him, like the shawl he's given back to her.

"I saw your mother before I came to Kiev, Alex. Your mother's the reason I came here. She'd found out about you from people she knows at the university, professors who've got contacts here. She knew where you worked, how I could reach you. She asked me to find you—you must have known that, Alex, you must have guessed."

He says nothing. He stares stubbornly over her head at the poppies flaring on the wallpaper.

"She's an old woman, Alex, and she loves you. Let me take

her something from you, even a few words. Let me take her a photograph of Katia."

He grabs her hand, pinning it down with his own.

"Listen to me, Eva. You have to promise not to tell my mother anything about Katia. Don't even tell her you've seen me. Say I was out of town at a conference, or on a field trip. That it was impossible to contact me. There's nothing she can do for us. I don't want her pity, or her love. You mustn't tell her anything, I forbid you."

Eva tugs her hand free. At last she understands what he's been trying to tell her in this roundabout way: bringing the shawl back, showing her the photographs of Katia. He's not just explaining about his daughter, or warning her about his mother. He's making sure she understands just how and why he's let her into his life the past two weeks. Using her like a bottle of the aspirin so hard to find here; refusing to tell her this story till it's too late. Forbidding her— giving her orders, expecting her to stay quiet and guilty and good.

"For God's sake, Alex, what kind of a threat can your mother be to you now? Maybe she could help Katia—have you ever thought of that? Maybe Katia isn't going to die, maybe she's going to come through this just fine. You don't know yet, you're punishing yourself by thinking the worst. Go ahead and punish yourself, but it's not going to do your daughter any good. You think you're being noble, giving up any help, any happiness that comes your way. When really it makes you feel so damn good. Makes you feel you're standing straight as a soldier, when all you're doing is running away."

A small crowd has gathered in the restaurant, people from the tour group, staring openly, relishing the drama. Alex looks as furious as Eva does. He waits for a moment, hoping their audience will disperse, and then he doesn't care who hears him, what pours out of his mouth.

"Just where can I run? And tell me this—what choice do I have? I don't have your freedom, Eva. I don't have your carelessness. You come to this country for two weeks, and you spend more money than most of us see in a year. You find out everything you need to know about the man who fucked your mother, and you think you know everything there is to know about the man you've been fucking like there's no tomorrow."

Eva gathers up the shawl, her hands shaking. Only when she's halfway across the room is she able to turn and face him.

"There are two things you never taught me how to say in Ukrainian, Alex. 'I love you.' And 'Fuck you.'"

She's forgotten all about her ring, the lapis and gold ring she neglected to declare, coming into the country, but the customs official doesn't even glance at her hands. Still, her stomach's churning as she waits for the passport booth to open, standing for an hour in the narrow, crowded hallway where no one's thought to place even a wooden bench. The rest of the tour group leaves her to herself; she's grateful for this, because if someone were to speak to her, even ask her the time, she might slap him, or burst into tears, or both. She's better by the time they finally board; she's given an aisle seat, and a headset, and a small package of what proclaims itself to be *The World's Most Sophisticated and Exclusive Nut*. She remembers how difficult it was in Kiev to buy even staples—flour, butter. She remembers the large sack of onions under the bench in Alex's kitchen. Emergency provisions.

Next to her, two older women are talking in hushed tones about the water in Kiev—they've been told you need to drink at least ten glasses a day when you're there. It's the radioactivity, they say; there's enough of it around, still, to make you always thirsty.

Eva turns her head away. She can't bear to look at the city vanishing behind them, the golden domes, the broad, glinting river.

Only a few people notice the plane overhead. One of them is a child in the gardens of the Mariinsky Palace. He is riding a tricycle along the paths between the sycamore trees; he is going faster and faster, his grandfather shouting behind him to stop, but the delight of recklessness is so strong that he lifts his feet from the pedals and throws his head back. To see, high above him, higher even than the treetops, a shape he recognizes as a jet. And then his tricycle goes crashing into a park bench; he is not hurt, but furious that something so stupid, so rooted and solid could have struck him down like this. He starts to cry; his grandfather tries to comfort him, and he wriggles out of his arms and back onto the tricycle, forgetting the jet, knowing and caring nothing about its passengers or destination.

The girl on the bench, to whom the old man is apologizing for his grandson's carelessness, has been watching the plane as well, thinking about the people lucky enough to be travelling on it to places she's seen only on her television screen: New York, Berlin, Paris. Thinking, too, of the woman who'd run up to the reception desk before boarding the van to the airport; run up looking like she was about to shout at her. But instead she'd pressed an envelope across the counter, then rushed off. In the envelope were fifty American dollars. She has them with her here, in a shoulder bag looped round her neck, to be safe. The girl lifts the mass of her butter-blonde hair; winds it into a coil at the top of her head, wondering what it would be like to chop it all off, to wear it as short as a boy's, like that woman's hair.

And then she starts thinking of how long it might take her to save enough money to travel abroad. She wouldn't want to stay away forever; of course she'd come home. It's just that once in her life she would like to put her foot over the border into the West, that place she thinks of as a gigantic California swimming pool. She knows that it will take forever to save enough even for a ticket to Prague or Budapest; feels it the same way she does the cramp she gets in her legs from standing all day at the reception desk, helping tourists who complain endlessly about the lack of this and the shortage of that. And yet the fifty American dollars tucked into her purse hum to her like a music box that plays on and on without ever needing to be wound. She smiles with her whole heart at the old man who has come to apologize to her, such a warm, hopeful smile that he forgets to scold his grandson as the boy rides off again under the chestnut trees.

VIII

TORONTO, AUGUST 1993

The day after her return, Eva phones Olya. She'd thought she'd do anything to avoid the woman who's become her lover's mother. Ex-lover; ex-mother. But when she wakes in her empty house, wakes up at what would be dawn in Kiev, but which is still the middle of the night here, she's consumed by the need to speak to her. She makes herself wait till what could be called a decent hour, filling the time by writing to Ben, who's still off hiking with his father. Making up a story about her trip to Europe, a story authenticated by the souvenirs she's picked up at Frankfurt airport: miniature replicas of the Eiffel Tower, Swiss cowbells, a Bavarian beer stein. She doesn't want him to know where she's been; there's no need to say anything about Alex—no point now. Or to tell him of that other person she went to Kiev to see. She can spare him that: they don't sell replicas of Babi Yar at the airport in Frankfurt.

She wakes Olya when she calls, inviting her over to the house for tea, explaining that they'll be quite private here, since Dan and Julie are still in the Laurentians. She thinks that if she speaks to Olya on her home ground, she may just keep control of things. But even as Olya walks into the house, Eva doesn't know what she is going to tell her, or how. Though she's accepted the fact of losing Alex, she's made herself a little cache of possibility, thinking she needn't do the one thing he'd never forgive her for: telling his mother about her granddaughter.

She kisses Olya hello, takes her into the kitchen to put on the kettle. While she's getting out cups and milk and sugar, thinking out a story that will tell this woman what she wants to hear without giving Alex away, Olya interrupts:

"Please, Eva—where is your watering can? All your plants are dying."

Eva has no watering can. She always uses the teapot. Olya fills it and starts with the coleus plant over the sink, watering expertly, without spilling a drop. When she finishes she hands the teapot back.

"He is well?"

Looking out of Olya's face are Alex's eyes; how has she never made that connection before, that he has his mother's eyes? And why is it that this undoes any story she could make up, the fact of him watching her like this?

"He has a daughter, Olya. She's Ben's age, or a bit older—her name is Katia. She's in hospital—it may be cancer."

The kettle starts screeching. Both of them stand watching it, unable to stop the noise. And then Olya moves to take it off the burner, to go through the motions of making tea.

She doesn't speak until the two of them are sitting at the table. "It is important," she says, filling Eva's cup, "very important to keep busy, keep doing something. Otherwise, you go under. If your hands are not busy, your head takes over, and your thoughts—they can drown you sometimes."

"Yes," Eva says. But she sits with her hands round the cup, unable to drink.

"Did he ask you not to tell me?"

"How did you know?"

"I know my son." She puts down her cup, covers her face with her hands.

"Don't Olya, please don't. I'm sorry I told you. Alex was right, I shouldn't have, I don't know anything anymore."

Olya reaches for Eva's hand; squeezes it hard. "It is all right—I am thinking. Not grieving, just thinking. Drink up your tea, Eva. There is nothing to worry about—nothing is solved by worrying. I told you, what you have to do is act, be always doing."

She picks up her bag and pulls from it a large parcel.

"I almost forgot—I have brought you some books to look at. I thought you might want to learn more about Ukraine, now that you've been there. So that when you go back you will know what you want to see in other places, not just Kiev. It is such a beautiful country, and so rich in the things that matter."

Olya puts her hand out to stroke Eva's hair. "Don't worry," she says. "He knew you'd tell me. Even as he asked you not to, he knew." And then she moves towards the door. Eva follows her, trying to think of something to say that will keep her from leaving.

"What are you going to do? What can you do?"

Olya doesn't answer. The women walk out onto the porch, shading their eyes against the sun. Next door, a boy is getting onto his bicycle: he spins down the drive and onto the street, lifting both hands from the bars, flicking them in, out; making the whole gesture as cocky and splendid as he can. They watch him as he wheels down the street and out of their sight. Olya shoulders her bag and starts down the porch steps, but before she gets to the bottom, she turns to Eva.

"I would like to learn how to ride a bicycle," she says. "I would like to be able to do that." And then she walks down the street, in the same direction that the boy has gone.

Eva sits on the porch steps, hugging her knees. She thinks of all the things she could have told Olya—about the portrait she'd found of Lesia Levkovych, about going to Babi Yar, about meeting Mr. Savchuk. She remembers the clay figures from the craft shop in Podol: she'd meant to give one to Olya.

She doesn't believe what Olya's said about Alex. It was spoken out of kindness. Olya's kindness: Eva realizes how much she's been counting on this to make up for losing Alex. She holds her head in her hands, her palms pressing into her eyes. What if Alex wanted to keep his mother from knowing about Katia because he was afraid she'd blame him, as his wife did? Afraid, too, that she'd love the idea of this grandchild she's never seen far more than the memory of the son she'd lost so long ago. He must be so alone now: every connection he's had with the women in his life—mother, sister, wife, lover—broken. And what she's just told Olya may break things even more. She looks up, as if Olya might still be walking down the street and she could call her back.

But Olya's gone, and Eva sits on the empty porch of an empty house, an endless summer day to get through before she can fall back into bed. The only act, right now, she feels capable of.

Her last day in Kiev, she wanted more than anything to come home. She remembers the scene in the café in Podol, all the terrible things she said to Alex about his country, all the things she told him she was homesick for. And it's true, she never felt more Canadian in her life than walking through the streets of Kiev, riding the subway, applauding *Swan Lake* at the Opera and Ballet Theatre. But now she feels like a tourist in her own city, unable to take the commonest things for granted, telling herself how people in Kiev would never believe this—"this" being the endless supplies of gasoline at service stations, the pyramids of oranges and pineapples in grocery stores, the fleets of perfectly innocent taxis. A week after her return and she's still keeping a careful eye on the pavement, looking out for fissures into which she could stumble, cracking an ankle.

She's been spectacularly alone since coming back. Julie has sent a postcard to Ben, but there's been nothing at all from Dan. She hasn't heard a word from Olya since her visit. The friends who used to crowd her answering machine with their requests for time and attention have gone elsewhere for help, or else managed to sort things out for themselves. And when she goes past her favourite corner of the park on her evening walk, she sees no one she knows: even the bag lady seems to have disappeared for good. It saddens Eva that she'll never know for sure what's happened to her. Saddens her the way everything does, these days, so that she catches herself staring at nothing for hours on end, or fighting to put one foot in front of the other to get home from work at all.

It's not that she's been suffering from want of human contact; the day-care is bursting, no one's been able to take holidays this year because of the recession. No one but Eva. She wonders whether her fall into another country, in and out of Alex's life, has left scars on her. But no one remarks anything out of the ordinary, and as each day passes, she can feel the Eva who was Alex's lover becoming more distant, almost invisible.

She spends hours drawing with the children, teaching them the Trypillian figures she'd seen in the ethnographic museum in Kiev. They are delighted with them; they are so much more satisfying than the stick figures they usually make. And she tells them some of the stories Alex had given her: about the snake hidden in the horse's skull, the ferryman's daughter turned ruler of Rus'. Sometimes, she goes to the museum after work; not to the dinosaur rooms that she's seen too many times, or to the insects and armour which are Ben's current favourites. She's wanted to stay on the ground floor, in the high, light corridors where the rocks and minerals are arranged. Spending her time going back and forth between the display cases, reading the names of the different specimens on exhibit.

Rhodonite, and malachite, and chalcedony. They are soothing in their strangeness and formality, these names. And the stones themselves, colours and formations that make her think of a kaleidoscope, except that these shapes stay fixed, which makes their beauty all the more frightening. She remembers Garth explaining to her the extraordinary beauty and complexity of crystals, the mathematical relationships that govern their formation, relationships she used to think of as a dance of numbers. She wonders if any relationship between people can approach the durability, the beauty of crystal formations. Though Garth had explained to her, as well, how rare it is to find a perfect crystal; had tried to teach her to locate the distortions, interruptions of their development.

When the museum shuts, Eva takes the subway home. Skirting through the park, putting off the moment when she'll have to turn down the street and confront her house: dark, hot, silent except for the radio she never turns off. She's given up on meals, just grabs whatever's still edible in the fridge, and sits on the back porch, looking out at the weed-wild garden. Once, when she's sitting with a plate of cold pasta on her knees, the radio starts playing a tune she last heard in a foreign restaurant. Fritz Kreisler, a voice announces: *Liebeslied*. Months later, raking the garden after the first frost, she'll find a plate and fork tumbled into the remains of the goldenrod, and will remember dancing with Alex that first day they met in Kiev. She'll have forgotten by then that they never danced together at all.

Late one afternoon, Eva hears the phone ringing, just as she's climbing the porch steps. She fumbles for her key, convinced that it's Alex; that if only she can get to the phone before he hangs up, everything will come right for them. But it's not Alex, nor is it Dan, who should have been home yesterday, with Julie. Instead, Olya's voice pours into her ear, a voice no longer calm, wise, but jumpy with what Eva recognizes as expectancy.

She's calling from the airport, she explains. She's on her way to Kiev, from which she'll travel to Odessa, with Alex. Katia's as well as can be expected: she's started intensive treatments, which will continue through the summer. Olya doesn't tell her what Alex said when she first called him: she doesn't mention Oksanna. Eva doesn't ask. It's almost as though Olya's talking to herself, as if she's phoned only because she can't contain her excitement.

She tells Eva that she doesn't know how long she'll be gone

for; she can't thank her enough for having made this contact with Alex, making it possible for her to go to her granddaughter now. And then they're calling her plane, and she has to run. She gives Eva her love and is gone before she can promise to phone her from Ukraine, or even to write.

Eva puts down the telephone and goes upstairs to Ben's room, where the cat's asleep, as usual, on the unnaturally tidy bed. She tries not to recognize what it is she's feeling. Envy, that Olya's going off to be with Alex, that she'll meet his daughter, claim the privilege of family. Envy, and stranger still, something she can only call homesickness. Not that the country Olya's rushing to is home for Eva now. But neither is this huge, empty house, or this city with its well-lit, cared-for streets. Home is somewhere in between, a borderline, not a country—or so she thinks, holding Ben's pillow against her; remembering Alex's sofa bed. *Home is where your dead are buried.* It's something she's sure she's heard Olya say, though she can't remember when. But it makes her get up at last and go to the attic; find the library book that now holds not just the photograph of Lesia and Ivan, but the red-flecked leaf she'd brought home from Babi Yar. She holds it to her lips for a moment, and then returns it to the book. She will have to take the novel back to the library, she tells herself; pay the fine. Lie to Rache about having read it—or not: Rache won't have expected her to.

Ben's flight has been delayed for another half hour; Eva gets herself a coffee and finds a chair in the No Smoking section of the waiting lounge. But the picture of the cigarette with a red line slanting through it makes her think of Alex, the occasional cigarettes he would light after making love. She puts her hand to her head; it hurts. It hurts to remember, and it hurts to go through the days in a stupor, changing diapers, telling stories, forcing herself to put on the lights when she comes home, take a walk around the block, read a book when she can't sleep at night, which is every night. It will be better now that Ben is coming home. It will have to be better.

The newspaper she's reading has an article about the Children of Chernobyl, photographs of children with bald heads and various skin diseases, being welcomed in Canada by the groups that are sponsoring their visits. One of the books she has read during the long, sticky nights when she could not sleep is about Chernobyl. She has learned how the dead zone, the land around the plant itself, the fertile land contaminated by radiation, is far vaster than anyone had originally assumed. She has read how whole villages were evacuated on special buses, and of the grief caused to children when their pets, especially their dogs, had to be left behind. The image sticks with her: children watching out the wide back window as their dogs run alongside and then after them, yelping and straining to catch up. The bus racing faster and faster, until the dogs, exhausted, finally limp home. Turning into packs of wild scavengers, destroyed by men in anti-contamination uniforms who visit the villages with rifles, and shoot, one by one, the animals the children had loved so much.

She'd read the book through, till she was so tired she could barely turn the pages. Afterwards, she couldn't sleep. Everything round her became treacherous; even her pillow she imagined to be lined with razor blades, like doctored apples at Hallowe'en. To calm herself, she picked up one of the books Olya gave her and found pictures of whitewashed houses, like the café Alex had taken her to in Podol. In each of them, a clay oven built into the wall. People used to heat stones until they were boiling hot, put them in the oven, and then set bread inside to bake. On the wide, flat ledge over the oven, children would sleep, children and old people together. Eva finally fell asleep imagining the warmth of nestled bodies, the scent of baking bread.

People are starting to rush to the sliding glass doors by the Arrivals section. Catching sight of Ben coming down the escalator, she makes a dash through the doors and holds out her arms to him. Wanting to embrace the child who is not dying of radiation exposure; who has come home to her again. He is embarrassed by her excess of emotion; he wriggles out of her arms.

"Don't, Mom, everyone's watching. I'm okay. Let's go. Everything's fine."

But it's not. That evening, she finally hears from Dan. He's not calling from Montreal, where she supposed he was delayed. He's here, downtown, in the house he's found to rent. Close to Harbord Bakery, he says, as if the bagels he goes to buy there every week are the main reason he's moved out. He'll come by next week—when Eva's at work—to get the rest of their things. Not much, it turns out: he's bought Julie brand-new furniture, a lace canopy for her bed, a whole wardrobe for the school he's decided to send her to, a private school, for girls only. They'd like Ben to come over and spend a weekend, soon. She could bring him, stay for dinner. Rache would like to talk with her.

"Rache," she says to him. Just the one word. Not an accusation—she hardly has the right to that. An acknowledgement, of both her shock and the fact she knows it's finished, that long process of unravelling between them. Of course it would be Rache. She remembers the way they'd talked on the back porch, the eve of her departure for Ukraine. Thinks of the cossack figure she bought at the craft shop in Podol: remembers what Dan had said about the bogeyman of his childhood.

"Eva?" Dan asks. "Are you okay?"

She tells him she's fine—she'll let him know about Ben, about dinner, as soon as she can.

When he learns that Julie and Dan aren't coming back, Ben shrugs his shoulders and keeps on playing with the kitten they got at the Humane Society last week, after Sugar finally died in his sleep. Ben's changed over the time he's been away; either he doesn't mind Julie being gone, or else he doesn't want to show it, not to Eva, that is. He's announced that he's old enough to go down to the park on his own now; he's had street-proofing up to here at school, he can manage fine. He's not going to talk to strangers, she doesn't have to worry. She does, but she lets him go, if he promises to leave her a note saying where he's gone, and when he'll be back. He's always with a pack of kids, so she figures—she has to figure—that he'll be all right.

For the disruptions that started at the beginning of the summer have completely stopped. No one is following her, watching her, doubling her shadow. No summons, no signal, unless she counts the postcard from Olya, bearing the words *Greetings from Kiev*, and an address where she can be reached: Alex's apartment building. There is no message from Alex. Eva crumples the postcard—a bleary sixties photograph of some monument or other—and throws it in the garbage. Only to burrow, a moment later, through coffee grinds and grapefruit peels, rescuing four inked lines: not an address so much as a memorial.

This is the way her search has ended: a path petering out into a waste place. The stories she's been told have littered her life like unexploded bombs, and the thing to do now is dispose of them. As she must dispose of her longing for Alex. She's gone so far as to call a man she met through Ben's school. She asks him to come to dinner and develops a fierce migraine that makes her cancel the invitation at the last moment. The man is interested enough to call her the next day and ask how she is. She listens to his message on the answering machine, and never calls him back. How can she explain she panicked at the thought of going to bed with anyone other than Alex? How all that night she lay with her hands crossed over her breasts, holding her breasts as if she could take from them the impress of Alex's hands.

Tonight, when she cannot sleep, she takes out the photograph of a woman holding a young boy in some long-ago time, in a far-away place. She wonders about the man cut out of the picture, inventing a body for him, a face from a pair of lopped hands. Who cut him away? His lover? Her son? And what happened to him after that summer they spent at Soloveyko? Dead before his time,

Olya said. All of them dead—except for the boy, unless Mr. Savchuk's story is true. Mr. Savchuk, with his cough and his bad heart, who seems to know so much—she could have asked all kinds of things, if only she hadn't been so blind, so caught up in herself, in Alex. Things about the woman who was her grandmother, the woman caught in this photograph. She touches Lesia's image, but it's not enough, she needs more than her face.

Eva lets the photo fall from her hand. She wants something impossible, and because it's impossible, wants it all the more. She wants this woman she's connected to through coincidence, stories, a resemblance that can't be explained away. Connected to not just by blood, which means so little now, but by the choices other people made, the desires that pushed them. She wants to force Lesia out of the black and white photograph; grab her, question her, this woman who must have learned how to give and to take whatever joy she could, and when that joy was taken from her, learned to survive. Who must have been constantly changing shape to keep her pain from cutting and twisting her, turning her words into the howl of an animal in a trap, an animal with its leg cut off.

I can hear you laugh at every word I say, Lesia. The way you hold your head, the set of your shoulders, accusing me: "What do you know of animals with their legs caught in traps? How can you so easily dismiss the howl of an animal? Have you ever achieved that absolute of expression?"

You stand here laughing at me through all the holes, the ragged parts of this story I've been given. I know what happened between my mother and your son, I can understand that. But how did you go on with your life, each day, how did you go to your death? That's what I need to know.

You were the same age I am now when you died. I want to undo that death, to make a happy ending for us both. I want the villains killed off, the lovers reunited, everyone given a chance for happiness, now, if not forever after. My son's pulling away from me; my lover's only a shadow, a shadow cut off from my body. Tell me how to live with this, with longing for what I'll never have again but can't stop wanting. How do I survive, Lesia, how do I get by? Show me.

But Lesia's face is turned away from her, her eyes focussed so intently that she vanishes into whatever it is she sees. Eva stares into the empty space in front of her: keeps staring and wanting and waiting.

At last she picks up the photograph from where it's fallen; puts it back inside the rolltop desk, beside the cache of clay figures she brought back from Kiev. One of them is a woman shaped like a fox; for the first time, she notices there's a small hole cut into the base. The fox woman is really a whistle, a child's toy. She puts the figure to her mouth and blows, a high, hollow sound. No one, she thinks, is listening.

The day after her conjuring of Lesia Levkovych, Eva pays a visit to her mother—her first visit since her return from Kiev. This time she hasn't brought Holly any flowers; the alstroemeria she'd sent before she left for Ukraine were thrown out long ago. The room looks strange without flowers; stranger still because Holly isn't sitting in her usual place by the window. "Your mother's being difficult again," the attendant tells her. "She didn't want us to dress her—just wouldn't co-operate. We got her out of bed and into that lovely chair by the window, and then we left to do the other girls. By the time we brought the lunch trays she was back in bed. She's stubborn, I'll give her that."

Eva sits by her mother's bed, waiting until the room is free of everyone but Holly and herself. Waiting, as she's always done, for some sign of recognition, acknowledgement. But Holly's farther away than ever, she can tell that just by looking at her. She will no more open her mouth to speak to her than she'll fly out of the room, fly right through the glass and out of the city, back to her island, her lover, the moment she first found him. Found herself carrying his child. This is what's hardest for Eva: that from her time with Alex she has brought back nothing, kept nothing, made nothing.

She reaches for her knapsack, takes out a package wrapped in brown paper, which she places in Holly's lap. When Holly makes no move to open it, Eva takes the package and shakes out a huge, black, garishly printed shawl, which she drapes over her mother. The thinness of Holly's body shocks her: nothing but a fan of bones under the skin. Eva lets go of her mother's shoulders. Suddenly, she can't bear to play this game any longer; play with the shell of what used to be her mother. Suddenly, it strikes her as obscene that she should be trying to force love, language—they are the same thing— from this woman who has won, if nothing else, the right to refuse such demands. All this time she's been trying to hold Holly to her, like a dress covering her, enclosing her. And all she has to show for it are pins in her flesh, and nakedness.

No, Eva decides. This woman is not her mother; needn't be that mother, anymore. She is something infinitely more important: a woman like herself, a woman damaged by loss and grief. A woman whose mind and memory aren't absent but turned in another direction. Her face, that Eva wanted to be a mirror, returning only her image, holds Holly's own longing, instead. And it's only now that Eva truly resembles her, beyond any coincidence of hair or skin or eyes. They both wear the shock of loss, the openness of longing on their faces.

Eva turns out the light and sits beside the bed, listening to Holly's breathing, to a darkness rich as the shawl with its extravagance of flowers. As she goes, she offers one last gift:

"Alex says you're the most beautiful woman he has ever seen."

One afternoon, soon after school starts up again, Eva catches sight of Julie. She calls out to her, and Julie detaches herself from a group of identically kilted girls. Runs across the street without looking and stops just inches away from Eva, who is holding out her arms. But Julie takes her hand instead and shakes it, the way she's learned at school. Eva remembers the etiquette of greeting adults from her years at St. Hilda's: show respect and keep your distance. She hugs Julie anyway, then holds her at arm's length, looking at this child she doesn't know anymore. The scrubbed face, the carefully brushed hair, the closed-over pinpricks in her earlobes. Remembers the earrings she'd bought her at Frankfurt airport, earrings shaped like gondolas.

"We aren't allowed to have pierced ears," Julie tells her. "Rache says it's crazy." And then she grins at Eva. "But I like it."

Eva's holding Julie by the shoulders, trying to keep herself from holding on. "Do you have time to come back with me, to see Ben? We can get in a pizza, I can phone your dad, it'll be all right."

Julie shakes her head. "I've got too much homework. Besides—" She looks back to where her friends are waiting. "I've got to go now. Say hi to Ben for me."

Before she crosses the road, she turns to Eva and yells out, "Did you know they're getting married? *Married*. Rache is having a baby." And then she's dodging the cars and has disappeared down the street before Eva can call out to her to be careful, can call her back to ask if it's really true, if she's sure. Stupid questions. She's just as glad, now, that she never got up the courage to call Dan, to have that long talk with Rache.

Eva stops trying to make connections with other men; gives up checking the mail as soon as it arrives for something other than bills and flyers. She sets her house in order, finally paying the library for that book she's lost, the book that sits in the desk in her study, holding a slice of a photograph, and a small leaf with a crimson point. She gets through her days at work thanks to the children, and she gets through her evenings thanks to Ben: his schoolwork, his drawing, even their arguments about how late he can stay up. It's only the nights and the weekends that push her against the wall: during both she dreams, sometimes of Alex, more often of his city: the pastel palaces, the chestnut trees, the darkened streets. To exorcize this city she pushes herself out of the house one afternoon, when Ben's off at the park with his friends. Sets off, one Saturday in late September, for the Junction.

Growing up where and as she did, she's never been to this part of Toronto, or at least never really seen it. There was an old train station, he'd said, a beautiful building, but she finds no trace of it. The duplexes across from the railway tracks are still there, though: he'd lived in one of them, four people jammed into the second floor of a dingy brick container rented out by yet another immigrant family trying to make their way up in the world. She decides on one of the halves of houses: chooses it because it is so tired-looking, sagging under the very colour of its bricks, the shit-brown of hardship. He'd told her about the torn sheet pinned up in the window overlooking the street; how the first thing his mother did, once there'd been money left over from paying rent and buying groceries, was to buy a remnant of brocade to make a proper curtain for that window. For the world and themselves to see, each time they came up the walk, that if their luck was low, their hopes were high. That they deserved better, and would make good. It might be that same scrap of brocade hanging in the window now—faded, cracked, a museum piece in its own way.

She doesn't want the people who live there to think she's snooping; she walks to Venus Variety a few doors down; pretends to look round, then comes back again to the place she's made into Alex's house. An old woman has come out to sit in a rocking chair and catch the sun. The porch is hardly big enough for the chair; the view over the railway tracks, desolate.

He used to climb up the iron bridge spanning these railway tracks; she remembers him telling how he'd climb up and look out as far as he could. He never described what he saw, and she hasn't the heart to go up now and take the view. He saw the future, probably: the one he was imagining for himself out of what he'd read in Garth's books, and what he'd heard from him about the mines up north. When what he was really facing was the past, that place his parents had been torn from. DP, displaced person: how calm, how quiet those words make it sound. When your life and everything you've ever wanted have been ripped across like cheap satin.

Eva starts walking: past The Money Angel and Bolkonsky Graphics to Dundas and Keele, where she notes the sign hanging above the paved-over trolley tracks. Neither trees nor grass; not even a weed interrupting the asphalt. She hops onto a bus heading west, noting how the attempts at gentrification dwindle away, the stores still clinging to false fronts that get sadder and sadder the more violent their neon signs. Where did they move, Olya and Oksanna, once they were on their own, once Oksanna had taken charge of that new life they were trying to begin? One of these side streets, one of these shoebox-houses with a patch of grass and plastic awning?

He is with her in all of this; a shadow on the pavement, a figure on the bus or glimpsed through a shop window on the part of Bloor to which she's made her way. Bloor West Village: what she used to call the ethnic strip. As if they were all one and the same, Poles and Hungarians, Lithuanians, Ukrainians. All foreigners: what Garth used to call New Canadians—"new" suggesting the rawness of a blister, something needing treatment, cure. But they're still here, the old-world bakeries, shoe stores, meat markets. Everything she's always avoided, thinking ethnic synonymous with sham-exotic.

She sees things differently now. These markers of other worlds, the impossible-to-pronounce names in the office windows of lawyers and dentists and doctors connect to something real, something that won't go away just because it's had to be abandoned. She wonders how many of the people passing her on the sidewalk, speaking languages that sound both foreign and familiar, have left behind families in Kiev, Warsaw, Vilnius. Families and cities and landscapes they've fled, or torn themselves from; all the decal embroidery and Easter eggs and folk dancing they find here a source of pain, not nostalgia. Pain because they got out, and the others didn't. And because what they've left behind, however threatening or threatened, is no longer theirs, but is changing, even as they are.

When she's too hungry, too tired to walk any farther, she stops for coffee at Future Bakery. All around her, posters of buildings she's visited in Kiev; people talking in the language she's got used to not understanding. These two old men at the table beside her, arguing over the ruins of a walnut torte: politics, it must be, for there are occasional words in English: G-7, welfare, recession. The old woman with a spotless white kerchief drawn over hair like a raft of steel pins; a younger woman, dark, dramatic-looking, sweeping in, a huge shawl over her shoulders: black, with Moorish arches and hot-pink cabbage roses.

She fixes her eyes on the Pet Shop sign across the road, the painted parakeet that rain and sun are slowly driving from its perch. She has come here to prove to herself that she's in Canada, not Ukraine; that her life is here, not there. But instead of banishing Alex, the café brings him home to her; she's fantasizing about how they'd come here for a drink after work; how he'd spend whole Saturday afternoons reading Ukrainian newspapers or exchanging news with the other emigrés. Fantasizing, the way Holly must have done all those years ago, haunting the neighbourhoods where she thought she'd find her long-lost lover.

Eva pushes away her coffee and gets up from the table. The Filipino man reading a computer manual, the two Jamaican women discussing the art exhibit they've just seen downtown—they seem as comfortable in this place as anyone else. Because to them it's just décor, it connects with no place other than here, now. Even the flyer on the window, advertising a fashion show in aid of the Children of Chernobyl: something she would have dismissed, before, as moral kitsch, to go with the cross stitch on the ashtrays. Now all she can think of, reading the flyer, is Alex's daughter, her body shaken to the roots by chemicals; by a disease that's eating her alive.

That night, after an argument with Ben, who stayed far longer at the park than he promised to, Eva goes to her study and sits down at the desk, pulling out paper, pen, stamps, an airmail envelope, and a badly crumpled postcard. It takes her a long time to write anything after the date and salutation: she is much more at home with speech, and hopeless at making requests, especially to people she hardly knows, like Mykola. But at last she does fill one side of a sheet of paper, into which she folds a photograph. She addresses the envelope using the card Olya sent her, opens the letter one last time, and takes out the photo. Touches the faces of the woman, the boy; runs her fingers along the scissored edge. Then seals both letter and photograph inside.

On her way to work the next morning, she stops at the post office, reminding herself how easily her letter could go astray; how likely it is that the recipient may never answer. And then she walks on, along the line that's been drawn for her between two countries, two planets. Her heart beating too loud: short rips of cheap satin, the kind you find on chocolate boxes at Venus Variety.

As Eva's dragging herself from work one afternoon after a hell-week, with too many kids screaming and not enough time to comfort them, someone calls to her from a car parked outside the day-care. When she walks over to see who it is, the passenger door swings open. The woman at the wheel is wearing dark glasses and a scarf hooding her head; Eva can't tell who she is. And then a voice pipes up from the back seat: "Get in Mom, we're late."

"It's okay, there's plenty of time," the woman says. Easily, as if she's used to speaking with him; as if he's used to taking her word for things. Eva's so startled by this improbable equation—Oksanna and Ben—that she hesitates instead of simply grabbing her son from the car. "Come on," Oksanna says, her hands moving over the gears. Eva's terrified the car will speed off without her; the next thing she knows, she's slid into the seat beside Oksanna and is turning, helplessly, to her son.

"What are you doing here? You know you're not supposed to—"

"Take rides from strangers?" Oksanna heads the car in the wrong direction; wherever they're going, it isn't Eva's house. "Don't worry about that. Ben and I have been friends for some time now."

Eva's dumbfounded. Why is Oksanna doing this, what does she want from her—and from Ben? It appalls her that she has no control over what's happening, no way of knowing what Oksanna knows and how much she's told Ben. She doesn't even know what it's safe for Ben to hear, and what she means by "safe." She pitches her voice low and hisses at Oksanna, "Stop the car and let us out right now. Before I call the police."

Oksanna hands her the cell phone. "Go ahead. Although I'm not in the habit of kidnapping people, Eva. We're going on a drive, that's all. A little holiday to celebrate Thanksgiving. Right, Ben? Don't worry about clothes or a toothbrush—I've packed for you. Nothing fancy; we won't need that where we're going."

Before Eva can open her mouth, Ben leans forward, his voice happier, more excited than she's heard it in a long time.

"We're going up north, Mom. Oksanna's taking us to see my grandfather." And he holds the kitten he's brought with him up to Eva's ear, so she can hear how fiercely it purrs.

Ben is watching TV in the motel room; Oksanna and Eva are in the bar of The Happy Traveller Motor Inn, somewhere near Billy's Bay. Eva hasn't said a word to anyone since they left Toronto; Oksanna has concentrated on the driving. But now she pushes a glass of rye and ginger over to Eva and salutes her with her own.

"To happy families."

Eva doesn't touch her drink, only looks at Oksanna and shakes her head. "I don't want to know why you're doing this, but I suppose you're going to tell me. I suppose I have to know, whether I want to or not, now that you've roped Ben into it."

"The same way you roped my mother?" Oksanna takes a long swig of her drink; her neck looks slender as a blade of grass. It makes Eva think of the princess and the pea, but that's ridiculous, it doesn't make sense. Nothing makes sense anymore, least of all her being here with Oksanna.

Who is leaning over to her, as if to whisper something delicate, confidential in her ear.

"So, you finally screwed my brother. Congratulations."

Eva's about to get up from the table; walk away. But in the end she sits back in her chair, tapping her glass, till she can trust herself to speak.

"Who told you—Olya or Alex? Because it had to be one or the other, and I would really like to know. Unless, of course, you've all been playing games with me, your whole happy family."

"It wasn't my mother, Eva. And certainly not my brother. As far as I'm concerned, I don't have a brother. My mother hasn't said a word about you, though she's a terrible liar. And I'm a very good one."

Oksanna's voice is like her eyes: dark, and clear and cold. Eva wants to shake her hard enough to make her stutter, but settles for another question instead. "Why did you arrange that appointment at the clinic? Why couldn't you just have called me at home?"

Oksanna plays with her beer mat, tracing out the letters on it. "You could say the whole thing—what's the expression? Fell into my lap, that's it. How could I have passed it up, Eva—the chance to pull just a few of the strings, just this one time? I knew your mother was a patient at the clinic; I'd seen her name in the appointment book the day you brought her in. And seeing she was such an old friend— almost family, you could say—I looked up her chart, and found what my colleague had advised about you. It was all done with your best interests in mind, Eva. I got the nurse to book you in for an appointment; you showed up—and then it seemed only decent to ask you over. That was one of your father's—of Mr. Chown's expressions wasn't it? *Have the decency to behave yourself in my house.* I wanted you in my house for a change, Eva. On my home ground. Surely you understand by now?"

Oksanna signals for another round of drinks, though Eva's barely touched hers. And before Eva can say a word, Oksanna turns on her.

"I think it's time I got a chance to ask some questions. About this little matter of my mother, for example. I hadn't known you'd got in touch with her until I found your name and number on a slip of paper by her phone. I wasn't snooping, or at least, not in the way you think. And do remember—it was you who showed me that photograph. If you hadn't come round, my mother would never have got mixed up in any of this."

"You're the one who asked me over."

Oksanna drops her eyes, goes back to fiddling with the beer mat. "That was my turn to be stupid.

"When I called the number on that piece of paper, I found out that you weren't at work, but on holiday. In Europe, of all places. And then, just after you get back, my mother tells me some amazing news. The prodigal son has finally got in touch; his daughter's ill, she needs help, urgently—our help. It wasn't hard to put things together, Eva; to figure out what you'd been up to with my brother."

Eva grabs Oksanna by the wrist. "I want to know what you've told Ben about this grandfather of his. I don't want to make this conversation any longer than it has to be. And I want you to know I'm taking Ben home with me on the bus first thing tomorrow. You can do whatever you like—as far as I'm concerned, you're crazy, certifiably crazy."

Oksanna pulls free from Eva's hand. "I'm afraid I'm not crazy, Eva. I'm simply doing a favour, an important favour for an old friend who's turned out to be someone you really ought to know."

"Why? Why should I know him? It isn't me he wants to see, anyway; it's Ben. That's why he sent me the photograph—to let me know, right from the start, what his intentions were. That they had nothing to do with me, though I was too stupid to understand."

Eva puts her drink down so abruptly that it sloshes over the sides and onto her hands. Oksanna leans back in her chair, watching Eva's face, her own softening so that Eva hardly recognizes her anymore.

"I'm going to tell you a story, Eva. It's not going to make things any easier, but it might help you understand what's going on.

"A while back—not too long ago, but a while before you wound up on my examining table, I heard from an old friend of my mother's. Someone I hadn't been in contact with for years and years. He asked me to come and see him; he said it was urgent. So I went. He was in a rooming house not far from where you live. Maybe the twentieth rooming house he'd stayed at in as many years. A room with a bed, a chair, a desk. Hooks on the walls for what few clothes he had.

"He was in bad shape, Eva, I could see that at once. His lips were blue, as if he'd been swimming for a long time in cold water. He told me he was in trouble and asked if I could help. He was terrified the immigration officials would be after him, because of irregularities in his record. It's too complicated to explain—let's just say that these irregularities could affect his legal right to stay in Canada. You see, he's one of those DPs who were shipped here after the war, to a lumber camp up north. When they shut down the camp, he made his way to Toronto and got work here and there. Nothing grand, nothing he needed perfect English for. There was usually something in the Ukrainian community for him, and if there wasn't—well, he'd been hungry before. He got his citizenship under a false name. It didn't matter to him then; he was always planning to go back home one day, back to Ukraine.

"It wasn't just a fantasy, Eva. That's why there could be trouble now. After he left the lumber camp, he got involved in all kinds of—let's just call them political activities. They had to do with changing things so he'd actually have a homeland to return to. He was in contact with people he'd known in the DP camps. People who got their money from some pretty shady sources, and put it to uses that were just as shady. It's a whole other story; I can't go into it now. In fact, I'm sick of it; it's one of the reasons I wanted to get away from anything to do with Ukraine, from all those Ukrainians who were so busy trying to get back home they had no time for their own country, this country. So let's just forget that part of the story, okay? The important thing right now is a sick old man: not a war criminal, not a thief or extortioner. He was obsessed with the idea they were going to deport him, he was so frightened he couldn't eat anymore, couldn't sleep, and he had no one to help him. All he needed was a safe place to stay and a bit of money. Just enough to keep him alive a little while longer. And the safest place he could think of was the first place he'd come to in Canada. A place no one would expect him to return to.

"As soon as I could book a few days off work, I drove him where he wanted to go. I found a place for him to stay, a fishing lodge where the business hasn't been the best for the last few years. The owner's been very glad to have him; he's no trouble at all, she says. I left her some nitroglycerine tablets to give him every day, and my number to call in an emergency. She and I understand each other very well—she's from Poland, by the way, another DP, like her husband. He died five years ago and left her the lodge. Luckily for us, she stayed on.

"Shelter was only part of what my mother's friend asked me for. There was something else, something as important to him as being able to disappear from Toronto. He told me that since he'd moved into the area, he'd taken to going to High Park in the afternoons. He liked to sit and look up through the branches of the trees; he said he liked to hear children's voices. There was a woman who often came to the park, a woman he seemed to recognize from somewhere he'd been a long time ago. He followed this woman home one day; read her name on the doorplate; discovered it was the same as that of a woman he'd once known up north. He didn't know how to approach her, he said. Even if he'd spoken perfect English, he wouldn't have been able to find the words. He needed someone to plead his case: someone like me. To explain that, however extraordinary it might seem, he'd once known her mother; wanted to know if she were still alive, if there were any chance he might see her, speak to her.

"When I found out that the woman in the park was you, and that Holly was the woman he'd known up north—I have to confess, Eva, it felt good. To have my old schoolmate come and call; to be sitting across from her, knowing that her mother, though she'd never stooped to cleaning up other people's dirt had, let's say, let down the flag in other ways. And then you pulled out that photograph and I realized that what he wanted wasn't you or your mother, after all. When you told me you had a son, and when I saw that photo—all I could think of was how he'd lied to me."

Eva doesn't understand anything anymore. It's too complicated: Oksanna's telling her far too much, and yet not nearly enough. All of it makes her want to keep Ben as far away as possible from the whole tangled mess: politics, history, the shadiness Oksanna's mentioned.

"You're right, Eva—he doesn't want to see you, none of this has anything to do with you, except that you happen to be the mother of his only grandson. In our culture, being female doesn't count for much, except for bearing sons to carry on the name. When my father had had enough of Canada, of being made to feel like dirt because he couldn't learn the language well enough, the proper attitude of respect towards the Smiths and the Macphersons, he never dreamed of asking me to go back with him. And the crazy thing is that I would have cut off my right arm to return to the place where I should have been born. Oleksa had to go instead—Oleksa, who would have given his right arm to stay. But we weren't even asked, and so we got to keep our right arms, my brother and I. That's another story, too, Eva.

"I took to going to High Park, a certain corner of the park, at a time of day when the kids are out. On one of my visits, I saw Ben— it was easy enough to recognize him from the photograph. The resemblance is almost frightening, isn't it? That physical echo I've seen again and again in my practice. I'll treat the mother and then, years later, the daughter for the same sun spots, melanomas. Though maybe it won't last, this resemblance between your son and your father. Maybe it's something that can be seen for a year before it vanishes. I've seen that happen, too."

Eva isn't interested in theories of resemblance. She twists her ring round and round her finger, seeing Ben and Oksanna in the park together, that slight frown on Ben's face relaxing, disappearing. "Tell me exactly what you said to him. How you got him to come with you."

Oksanna shrugs. "It wasn't so hard to make friends with your son. I made up some story about having lost my cat—he said he'd look out for it, that he had a new kitten and was scared to let it outside. We talked about cats for a while, and then I went home, but I showed up the next afternoon and the next, and he remembered me, and we talked about a lot of things. He misses not having a family—I mean brothers and sisters and grandparents. He explained that your mother was ill, that her memory was sick, that's how he put it, and that all his other grandparents were dead. And I said, 'What if one of your grandfathers were still alive? What if your grandmother had a secret she was keeping from your mother, but that she wanted you to know?'

"You've every right to be furious with me, but fury isn't much use against history, is it, Eva? Family history, public history, things you can't hide or change, however much you'd like to. What else did I tell him? That his grandfather had been a soldier, a seventeen-year-old soldier in the underground, going on secret missions. How he'd fought with the partisans against the Nazis, how he'd been captured and sent to a German prison camp, and how, when the war was over, he'd made his way to Canada, where he'd met a beautiful young woman. I told him that they'd fallen in love and had a baby, and that the baby was you. And that the man had had to go away, because his enemies from Europe, from the war there, were after him. How, when it was finally safe for him to come back for the woman and their baby, they'd disappeared without a trace. And how he'd searched far and wide for them for many, many years until at long last he found them.

"A love story—and a war story. The war part of it is true enough. The point is, I didn't have to force Ben to listen, Eva. He wanted to hear all this, he was hungry for it. And he wants to meet his grandfather. There's no need to be ashamed of the old man, you know. He's an extraordinary person."

Eva finished her drink long ago. She sits perfectly still, divided between rage and confusion. She could tell Oksanna what she's found out about Ivan from Mr. Savchuk, destroy this gleaming hero, soldier, resistance fighter. But what would be the point—and anyway, what does she know for sure? How much of what Oksanna's said does she actually believe? And what else is Oksanna hiding? It doesn't make sense. If this old man was a friend of Olya's, why did he get in touch with Oksanna? What kind of a friend has he been to Olya? And why hasn't Olya ever mentioned this to Eva? Who's telling lies, and who's telling stories, and what difference is there between them?

Oksanna gets up from the table, waiting for Eva to return with her to the motel room where Ben fell asleep hours ago, the kitten curled on his bed. Eva has no choice but to join her. For in all of this ragged cloth, there is one unbreakable thread: Ben's need for this grandfather he's been so miraculously given. He'll never forgive her if she takes him home without this meeting Oksanna's so carefully prepared.

It's dark outside and the air's as cold as if there were snow, not leaves on the ground. Leaves the colour of blood and rust.

IX

PORCUPINE CREEK, 1949

He lies in his bunk while the others clump about, sorting through their things, getting ready to leave this place they've hated as much as they've hated any of the camps forced on them. He lies on his back, his head on his arms, remembering their first day here. After the starvation of the war and the minimal rations at the refugee camp; after endless retching on the tub that shipped them from Bremerhaven to Halifax, after the few stale sandwiches they'd been given on the train, to arrive here and find the tables crammed with sausage and salami, bread, pickles, cheese, cakes with nuts and raisins. As though the cooks had prepared a feast for every last DP in Europe, a feast to raise them from the dead, when, as they discovered the next day, it was everyday fare, no more, no less. And then to walk out of the canteen and find food enough for ten families heaped in the garbage bins at the back, flies swarming over the greasy, oozing mess. It had made him throw up the meal he'd just stuffed down his throat. Thinking of her bones scraping at her skin, how you could almost see through her hands when she lifted them against the light.

She would still be in the camp in Bavaria: they had wanted only unmarried men, able-bodied and undereducated. He had lied, almost all of them had had to lie to make it sound as though they could barely read and write. That all they wanted to do with their lives, once they'd crawled off the ship into Canada, was cut down endless stands of trees, or scratch in the earth for nickel. Move up to a factory job one day, somewhere further south, near a city with taverns and amusement parks and sidewalks instead of bush. It had been easy enough to lie. The hard part had been riding out of the camp, catching sight of her with the man she'd married, the one who was the real worker, who didn't have to spend a month roughening his hands to pass the examination. He didn't even know whether she'd seen him leave in that convoy; whether she'd have cared if she had. Her white, white face, with the deep hollows of her eyes. Black eyes and black hair, and bones like knives under her skin.

He reaches towards the log wall beside the bed: there's a space large enough for him to put his fingers through. In winter he'd blocked it with moss and a little lime, and whatever rags he could scavenge. Snow would still whirl through the gaps, even the tightest-packed. They would fight to get a place closer to the stove: a gasoline barrel with a pipe in its side, connecting to the roof. Not too close to the stove, or you'd wake with a blistered face, but somewhere near the middle of the room, where it might be possible to sleep without dreaming. Dreams of being caught by the teeth of your own hunger, stuffing a bleeding mouth with grass, devouring dirt and roots and blades all crushed together.

He had gone to her thinking she could make everything start over for him, that everything he'd had to do or had done to him in the last six years could be exploded by the touch of her hand. If you can bomb a city out of existence, why not memory? But she told him she was a dead woman. She was nothing, she said, but a hole dug out of the ground for men to throw their garbage in. How was she supposed to heal him, comfort him? *With what? And what would you do with a wife?*

She was right, of course. To get to Canada, you had to be solitary as each tree you cut down: you have to mate with the wilderness, that's the joke in the camp. The men clowning, disguising a need so desperate you couldn't call it lust anymore; bringing bouquets of wild flowers to the trees, kissing the bark so hard their lips start to bleed. Sometimes, they'd be allowed into the nearest town—a walk of ten miles, each way—but never with money enough to buy more than a couple of beers. No whore is going to give you ten minutes of her time for a bottle of beer; no decent woman will have anything to do with a bohunk from a lumber camp.

This is one of the things no one ever told the journalists who came up from Toronto. Other things got reported: the sit-down strike, when they discovered that in another camp, owned by the same company, the loggers, all Canadian-born, made a dollar more a day than they did and for far less work. Or the threats from the camp bosses, threats to deport the trouble-makers who complained about rotting cabins, gasoline stoves. Deport them, the bosses said; ship them back to Germany, and from Germany to their homelands, and from these homelands on to gulags. All this got told, some of it was even printed in newspapers picked up on city streets by women with gloved hands; businessmen in fedoras. But as for how each night the cabins were filled with bodies caught in the crossfire of desire and despair, despair having its own smell, like a damp cellar, a cellar used for storing bodies, not bottles—no one ever said a word.

He's an indifferent chopper of wood; he has made next to no money here. And he's refused to go onto the less bruising, worse-paid jobs—clearing the slops in the kitchen, making kindling for the cookstove and the baths. It isn't the hardness of the work, but the way he is treated, the way they are all treated by the Canadians in the camp: as second-class, second-rate: a less murderous contempt than that shown to *Ausländer* and *Ostarbeiter,* but contempt all the same. Bohunk, the first English word he learns in Canada.

And now, just when he thinks he cannot stand it anymore, when he still has three months of his contract to honour, they let him go, they empty out the whole camp, except for a few guys who are the boss's friends. There is no more work for the DPs—they can get their asses out, right now. They have very little money, less English, and no easy way of getting to Toronto. Even if they walk the whole way, once they arrive there will be no jobs for them. The communist says it's the game plan of the bosses. Bring dumb bohunks over, work them till they drop, then kick them out and let the blackflies eat them for breakfast. Only now—after all he's made himself get through, after all the times he's told himself, if you can just get through one more day, one more hour, and then another after that—only now does he give up. It is so simple and so sweet; it gives him the most peace he's known since he was a child and his nightmares could be banished by the sound of his mother's voice.

Instead of walking out with the others, he'll lie back in his bunk till the camp is empty, then take a path into the woods, one that he knows will lead to the shore of the lake. There he can build himself a shelter; catch fish, gather berries. A crazy scheme, but what else could he have hatched, shut up in this cabin with fifty other men; unable to talk about anything that matters in case he says something that will get him deported? Crazy but possible, at least in the short term, because he knows how to survive in the woods. When he was a boy, he'd read nothing but adventure books that told him all these things: how to build shelters, how to trap and hunt, live off the land. There is nothing anymore but the short term. The worst he can do is come crawling back to camp in a week's time, saying he took the wrong turn into town, got lost in the bush.

The worst is different from anything he ever imagined. Real madness, not just a touch of sunstroke. Lying starved, exhausted, his face in the earth to protect him from the blackflies, double blackness against his eyes. No desire anymore to find his way out, to make it through, once more, by the skin of his teeth. Desire only for her: something that grabs him at the base of his spine, pulling tight, tight. This hopeless desire to touch her face, just to run his fingers slowly over her lips, her brows, the lids hooding her eyes.

So that when the woman touches the back of his head; when she presses her fingers so lightly against his bloodied, bitten face, wiping away the dirt with a handkerchief dipped into the lake, he thinks it is she, and the first word he's able to speak is her name, over and over. This woman doesn't understand, takes the words for mere sounds, a plea for help, for comfort, in a foreign tongue. And perhaps they are. The only certain thing is that she answers what she thinks he's saying, answers with her arms that help him into the boat she's pulled into the water; help him onto the island where she's living, knowing everything he thought he'd learned by reading a children's book fifteen years ago.

Answers him with her body, into which he folds himself, at first like a child burned in a fire, who needs to sleep in ointment-soaked bandages. And then, when he is better, when he is able to open his eyes and see that he's still an ocean, a continent away from the one person in the world he can love, her body is his only help. If you can wipe out six years of killing and hiding and running with blind, pure lust, without any other language than cries and moans, then he does this with the woman who has rescued him.

The woman he'll turn from when she has healed him, and fed him, and opened to him again and again without fear or shame. The woman he'll abandon, because she's not the woman he's been searching for. Because the wildness, the strength of her cries will have begun to shake him far more than the sound of wolves howling across the lake.

X

Porcupine Creek, October 1993

They reach the lodge by early afternoon. It's a fine day, pines black against a sky so clear and hard you could carve shavings from it. They left the motel at sunrise, stopping only for an hour at lunch. Neither Oksanna nor Eva has slept much—you can see it in their shadowed eyes, the shortness of their tempers, which they're trying hard to keep in check. But Ben is ready to leap out of the car and clear across the lake in his eagerness to arrive.

Mr. Marchenko is not in his cabin, says the woman who runs the lodge; who, if she recognizes Eva, makes no sign. He has gone down to the lake, she explains. If they take the trail to the left, between those rows of birch, they will find him. She'll have dinner ready whenever they want.

Eva has to call out sharply to Ben to stop him from running on ahead. He waits for them to catch up with him, holding the kitten in arms ridged with scratch marks. Perhaps it's for the animal's sake he waits; or perhaps it's out of shyness, even fear: trusting the mother whose love he can take for granted rather than the grandfather he has never met.

The women walk carefully along the trail, mindful of the

branches that have been blown down, and pulling their jackets
tighter round them. When they reach the end of the path, the view
opens up; they see the shoreline, a canoe rack, and a boathouse
near which a figure's sitting, looking out over the water. He must
have heard them for he turns in his chair and waves. It's more than
a wave, it's a summons. This time when Ben starts to run, Eva
doesn't call out to stop him. She waits with Oksanna a little
distance from the boathouse, watching Ben hesitate for a moment,
then hold the kitten out to the old man in front of him. Watching
as the man takes the animal, holds it tight against his chest and
strokes it, looking all the time into the boy's face. And then she
doesn't want to see anymore; she retraces her steps along the path,
turning her back on the boathouse, the lake, the distant rocky
island with its fringe of balsam trees.

Eva and Oksanna help Mrs. Rakowski with the dishes, though she
insists there's no need. Ben is asleep already—he played a game of
checkers with his grandfather, and only agreed to go to bed on
condition that he be allowed to spend the whole day tomorrow
with the man he's already calling *dyido*. He is charmed, that's clear:
by the sheer presence of this gaunt old man; by the stories he's been
hearing, stories about the princes of Kiev and their campaigns
against the Pechenegs and Khazars, stories his mother's also heard,
but from a different teller. Eva has said very little all evening. She
has sat and watched her son listen to an old man's stories, as if
merely by looking on she can make sure nothing gets said that will
damage the terms she's agreed to, regarding the old man.

What does she feel towards him, this stranger with the manner
of a grand duke in exile, the cool civility superiors bestow upon
their underlings? It's clear that's all she is to him: not a daughter
but the woman who has given him his grandson. And her response
to this is—nothing. No pain of rejection, no dislike or even

jealousy. Nothing. This is fine, she tells herself; right now, she has enough on her plate without the burden of calling this man "father," of jockeying for acknowledgement. She doesn't even know how to address him. As Mr. Marchenko, which is the name he goes by now? As Mykola, the way Oksanna does? Ivan? Nothing seems right. But it doesn't seem to matter to the old man, who nods to her when necessary, and who otherwise ignores her. It's clear that whatever she could learn from him about his mother or her own will remain untold. Although he speaks English well enough with Ben, she is reluctant to approach him except through Oksanna. And there's something about Oksanna's manner when she speaks to him, a mix of relief and distress, that puzzles Eva.

After they've finished the dishes, and the old man has gone to bed, Mrs. Rakowski offers the women a glass of the vodka her nephew brought from Warsaw last year. "Things are very bad there," she confides. "We are lucky we all got out." She says this in an encompassing way, meaning Oksanna and Eva as well as Mr. Marchenko, her unofficial paying guest.

Eva excuses herself, pleading tiredness—she can barely keep awake, she says. But that's not what drives her away. She can't help thinking of the ones who can't get out, or who have refused to do so. Alex, Katia, the young receptionist at the Hotel Kiev, the old woman in the art gallery who'd stood with her, trying to comfort her. Staring up at the cold, clear sky, the shelterless stars, Eva thinks of her house in Toronto—a mansion, a palace compared to the apartments in Kiev. She imagines all of them living there together: Ben and Julie and Katia, Olya and Holly; Oksanna, and even Ivan-Mykola, for whatever time is left to him. And because this is a vision bound by no logic, only possibility, she adds on rooms, lavishly: for Daniel and Rache and their baby, Jimmy and his wife and daughters.

And Alex.

Wanting only this—that the people she loves and needs most in the world, whose lives are unstoppably connected with hers, should all be gathered under her roof for as long as they might wish to stay; that she might shelter them all. She can hear Dan's voice, rebuking her as he always did for wanting to kiss everything better, hold everyone in the world in her arms. *Happy families*. Why are the joyful, the simple solutions the ones that can happen only by miracles, by moving heaven and earth?

However bright the stars are this night, it's far too cold to stay outside any longer. She makes her way to the cabin, where Ben is fast asleep. Covers him up against the chill of the night; lays her hand lightly on his forehead, as if to smooth away any anxiousness or fear. While he goes on dreaming of a chalice fashioned from a prince's skull; a snake crawling from a horse's bones to kill a warrior king.

An old man who cannot sleep, who lies on the narrow bed with its clean sheets and rough woollen blanket, breathing in the smells of pine and cedar. The lumber camp, whatever's left of it, can't be more than a few miles from this place. He can't walk there to find out, and it's something he will not ask about. Better to let the past soften and rot, like the logs left on the last woodpile, the abandoned huts, the dining hall with its empty tables.

He puts his hand to the cabin wall, testing the mortar, searching for gaps. There's the boy to think about; what he needs to know, and what he's capable of hearing. A story. He will have to tell him a story, one with a great deal of weaving and folding and hiding in its lines. Hoping that the child, remembering the story as a grown man, will undo the folds and see what he's meant to find.

There's bitterness in this: that he should be telling stories the way his mother always had: to console him when he'd been lying ill in the darkened rooms of his childhood; to win him back when he'd run away from her, the smell of her lover on her skin, in her hair, so that he couldn't bear to have her hold him. That flooding happiness of hers, that joy he always wanted to contain—what her lover gave her, and what she took from him. What that other woman had as well, the woman whose body he'd wrapped round himself like a dressing on a wound: the woman who'd given him the belated, marvellous luck of this child.

Now he finds himself a storyteller, the telling of this one story the most important, dangerous thing he's ever had to do. Yet look how the making of it has fallen so easily into his hands: the miracles and coincidences, the illusions and deceptions on which any story with a shape, a meaning depends.

Seeing the boy for the first time, he'd felt his weak, useless body vanish, leaving nothing but the skin of his eyes. As if he were eleven years old, not again, but for the first time; as if there were a whole life yet to happen to him. And he'd thought of all he could undo, having his life over again in a time and place where death wasn't always fingering your neck. He isn't sure whether they understand this—Oksanna or the boy's mother. That what he wants from meeting the boy here is just to put his hands on his head, give him a blessing and receive one in return. A chance for a life to unfold in exchange for a life cut off.

The boy's mother will not stop him from talking to her son. The boy's mother: he cannot call her by her name, it is too like his own. The one claim she'd made on him, the woman on the island, so many years ago: telling him her name; demanding his in return for the life she'd given back to him. So that she's the one person on this whole continent who has ever called him by his name, his own, true name.

The old man turns in his bed: he has never liked sleeping with his back to a door. He makes himself shut his eyes, listening to the silence of the enormous sky overhead. Everyone, everything he's ever fought for is dead or lost. Only this one possibility, kept for him until the very last, the one thing he'd never hoped for. Tomorrow he will tell his story, tell it to the boy alone, and make him promise to keep it secret, even from his mother. Tell it in such a way that the boy will not judge, will not pull back from him, but will come to know the truth when he becomes a man. Know and forgive him as she had done, all those years ago.

Eva sleeps badly, tangled in long, grey dreams, waking to the sun as it arrows through the spot where the curtains don't meet. She gets up and covers Ben with the blanket he's flung off in his sleep; pulls on last night's jeans and sweater and goes out to the porch.

She would like it to be in her power to change the conditions under which she's here. To make this into a holiday she happens to be spending with her son, the holiday they should have gone on years ago, but never have and never will, since summer's the time he spends with his father. And now he'll connect this place, the island she'll show him this afternoon, if the weather stays fine, with this man he's come so quickly to love.

And it is love, she can't pretend anything else. When he wakes, his first thought will be of going to the old man in the next cabin; hearing his stories and giving the kind of promises the very young make to the very old, even if they stay unspoken. What choice does she have but to let him go? And if this love becomes something she can't control; if his horizon suddenly fills with the flag of a strange country, and the old man's stories become the line of his desire, tugging him away from her, what then?

Stretching out her arms, she tries to shake the sleep from them, sleep and the longing that things could be other than they are. Making her way down the path to the shore, she tries to take pleasure in the amazing mildness of the morning; in being the first one up, having the whole place to herself. But when she gets to the lake, she finds herself cheated even of this: there's a bundle of clothes near the boathouse, and a towel. She can make out a swimmer in the water, a swimmer who must be mad to go into the lake at this time of year.

Before Eva can turn away, Oksanna's started wading into shore. It seems so invasive to be here, intruding on the privacy of someone else's nakedness. But then, remembering Oksanna's eyes on her own body, reading the open text of her skin on an examining table, Eva grabs the towel from the sand, and walks towards the lake.

She is beautiful, Oksanna, her body tall, slender, unmarred by childbirth or the years she carries on her bones. She walks with the same arrogant stride of the fifteen-year-old Eva knew at school. Taking the towel held out to her, as if Eva were simply an attendant she expected to keep waiting, Oksanna rubs her hair dry, then her breasts and belly and thighs. It's impossible to imagine that body untouched by a lover, and yet Olya's said there's never been anyone in her daughter's life, anything but her work. How does she manage, Eva wonders, turning away as Oksanna steps into her clothes; embarrassed by the strength of her need to know.

"I'm going for a walk along the shore," Oksanna says. "You might as well come with me."

There's sand enough at the water's edge, though sometimes they have to dodge driftwood logs washed up on the beach. The sun is gaining possession of the sky; Eva stops for a moment and raises her face to it.

"You shouldn't do that. You should be slathered in sun block, even in October," Oksanna warns.

"Are you?"

"No." She starts to laugh, and sits down on a piece of driftwood too high to climb over. Eva joins her and the two of them rest in silence for a while, drinking in the warmth of the sun.

"What are you going to do with him?" Eva asks. "Keep him here all winter?"

"Keep him here as long as he lives. He won't see the spring, not without a miracle." She waits for a moment, then asks, "What do you think of him?"

What kind of answer she's supposed to give, Eva doesn't know. "He's not what I expected," she says at last. "Ben adores him, that's clear."

Oksanna doesn't respond, but stares as if she's seen a sail on the horizon. And then she speaks, to the lake, not the woman beside her.

"He started coming round after my father walked out on us."

Eva starts to shiver, in spite of the sun. She, too, has seen a possibility, and before she can stop herself she's spoken it. "He was your mother's lover."

"No. He was mine."

Oksanna keeps staring out at the lake; Eva has to strain to hear her. "Oh, he would have been my mother's lover, if she'd let him. He'd fallen in love with her at the camp where they'd both been herded after the war. She married my father instead. Not out of love, either, though she's been faithful to his memory, if that's the way to put it. Shall we head back?"

They return the way they came, Eva wondering if she's heard Oksanna right. But then she starts to speak again, and there's no doubt left at all.

"My parents left the camp a while after Mykola did, but it was years before they settled in Toronto. Mykola went out west after the work ran out in the lumber camp, and he lived in a lot of places when he came back to Ontario. He'd been in Toronto for months before he heard we were here, and that my mother was alone. He came to see her, which was brave of him. We weren't too popular in the community then, because of my father leaving us. Not the act itself, but the politics that went with it. There were about thirty families that went back to Ukraine—you had to belong to the Labour Temple, you had to be a good communist, or pretend to be, for them to let you back in. Whether my father pretended or really believed, I don't know. It doesn't matter anymore.

"Mykola came to visit us when no one else would. My mother—I think she was afraid of him. She was younger then than I am now, Eva, and she told him she wanted nothing more to do with 'that business'—that's what she called it. She said she had a child to support and something to make of her life. She had no room for him; he would have to go.

"She didn't have room, but I did. He carried himself like a soldier, and there was always an aloofness about him, so that however he earned his living you thought of him as distinguished, important. He was working as a janitor at the Ukrainian Cultural Home, and had a room set aside for him in the basement, next to the furnace room. That's where we'd meet. When I told my mother I was doing research at the library downtown, I would go to him there.

"He was old enough to be my father. Maybe that's why I was in love with him. And I suppose I must have reminded him enough of my mother, when he'd first met her, that he let me keep coming to him, night after night. I didn't care if we got caught, I didn't care what would happen to him or to me. I just wanted him. It was the only thing that kept me sane after my father left us. I would have done anything to keep him. Except the one thing he ever asked of me, till now.

"I had made plans for my life, I was going to make a place for myself that no one could ever take away from me. When I told him I was pregnant, he ordered me to keep the baby—he was almost out of his mind about it. He said he'd marry me if only I would have his son. Not his child: his son. It was my father, all over again, my father choosing my brother over me. I began to hate him then, and to hate what was growing inside me.

"A woman I knew, a DP who'd been a doctor before the war, helped me. She didn't want to, she didn't have the right equipment, she said there might be complications, and there were. Scarring, so that I could never conceive again. That's all right, I've come to terms with that. I could never, never have had that child. My mother knew nothing about it, and she never will. She's still after me to get married, raise a family. It's not too late, she says; she knows women who've had perfectly healthy babies, even at the age of forty-five. My poor mother—I owe her something, don't I? For letting her go on hoping like that.

"And now he's come to me, all these years later, asking for help. How can I refuse him? He's an old, ruined man, who won't live out the winter. And I'm tired, Eva. I'm so tired of hating when I want to love."

Oksanna rubs her hands up and down her arms, trying to warm herself. Eva reads her differently now, the perfect skin something parched, starved of anyone's touch.

"I'm tired of hating my father, and hating Oleksa for being the one my father chose over me. My mother wants to be with Oleksa,

Oleksa's child, and I've paid for her ticket, I'll even bring the child back here, if that's what they want. You have a choice when you're young: you either surrender to whatever's stronger than you are or you make yourself so hard, so sharp that nothing can hurt you. But I'm not young anymore. My bones are a bundle of knives, they're always cutting me and anyone who comes too close. Do you understand, Eva, do you hear what I'm saying?"

Eva puts her arms round Oksanna; tries to hold her. It's like putting your arms round an iron pole, there's nothing that hugs you back, nothing to hold onto. After a while, Oksanna breaks free and walks away. Up the path, back to the porch of the main house where they're waiting: Ben, and the old, dying man who used to be her lover.

Eva leaves Ben in his grandfather's company for the rest of the day; he is making drawings for the old man and listening to his stories. Oksanna is talking to Mrs. Rakowski about financial arrangements; no one notices when Eva slips down to the lake, taking a battered, leaky canoe out to the island.

She is glad to have come here alone. She wouldn't have been able to manage one person more, not even a child, like Ben. For this island is crowded with ghosts—not just those of the lovers, and of Garth and Phonsine. But of her own self, coming here at the start of all these stories, letting the desire she'd buried all those years ago struggle to the surface of her skin.

Eva sits cross-legged on the rock where, just after the end of the war, a tent was raised. That tent has vanished, like the photographs she left behind to mark its place. Staring into the black space inside her shut eyes, she has a sudden sensation of sliding through a chute, a blood-warm, blood-dark chute that is her mother's body, the flesh shiny and fast like the walls of a playground slide. Tipping from uterus down birth canal and through those wide, astonished lips that push her into air and light. Yet the womb which tipped her out is linked to that other womb, the one that harboured the man who is her father. A series of connecting rings: her mother, her grandmother, herself. Women with their own histories, moving in and against a time and place that are as much a part of who they are as their names and faces.

Fatality, randomness, choice: the jaggedness of it shakes her till she thinks she'll never be still again. Holly, Lesia: their lives, their stories—she carries them in her bones, in whatever she makes of herself. A self with a face she'll never get to see, knowing only the direction in which it's turned, the direction in which desire, all the pain and joy and risk that make desire, keeps pushing her.

When Eva opens her eyes again, the sun's exactly where it was; the wind keeps blowing through the balsam trees, neither harder nor softer than before. She runs her fingers over the surface of the rock, feeling its fissures and irregularities. Something Alex had once said comes back to her—something about loving rocks because they don't change, they don't disappear or die on you. And she realizes now what marks her off from Alex: that she would rather, a thousand times rather, live with wind or water or the warm, perishable touch of skin.

There is the canoe ride back to shore, and then the rest of the afternoon, the evening meal, and another night to get through before they can head home again. She thinks how wrong she's been to worry about the old man stealing Ben away from her—to think she could hold on to him, keep him for herself. As if there were only one Ben, the one she's fashioned for herself. She lets the canoe drift for a moment in the silent lake; looks at the cold fire of the trees along the shore. Till she can tell herself she's glad she's come back; glad it's ended here, this story. As far as it can end, for any of them.

Eva promises to bring Ben back to see his grandfather over the Christmas holidays. This seems to satisfy all concerned except Ben, who doesn't see why they can't stay longer, even if there's school tomorrow. When it comes time for them to get into the car, Ben goes back one last time to where his grandfather sits on the porch. He hands him the kitten, putting it into the old man's arms with a graveness, a tenderness that signals it is his to keep.

They get home just after nightfall. There's a small avalanche of mail which Eva collects from the floor, dumping it onto the kitchen table. It will be nothing but bills—it can wait till she's got Ben to bed, taken a shower, poured herself a drink.

She tries not to feel how empty the house is with Dan and Julie gone; how dismal it is coming back to it like this. She toys with the idea of calling someone—Ellen, whom she never called back all those months ago. She should phone, apologize, ask her to come over. And she will, but not tonight. Instead, she sorts through the mail blanketing the table: supermarket specials, a plumber's bill, charitable organizations, and an envelope that stands out from all the rest. The quality of the paper is poor; her name and address have been typed on a badly faded ribbon. A machine postmark, a return address in a foreign alphabet.

Kiev, 13 September, 1993

Eva,
"Fuck you" has no literal equivalent in Ukrainian. We'd say "schob ty zdokh," which means something like "go to hell." Most of our oaths have to do with disease, not sex: "kholiera," which means cholera, for example. And if you really wanted to insult someone, you might say "ty kurvyn syn"—"you're the son of a whore." Which hardly seems appropriate in this case.
"I love you" is simple: "Ya tebe liubliu."

It can never work, isn't that what I'm supposed to be saying? We don't speak the same language, the same history. Sometimes I think this country has no history, just a chain of disasters that people have turned into songs and stories. That's how I came here, Eva, sailing down the river of my father's stories. The worst thing that can happen to a Ukrainian, he would say, is to die in a foreign country. God reserves his worst punishment for those who forget their homeland.

Let me tell you something, Eva. What I couldn't say when you were with me here.

I came back so he wouldn't have to know himself as someone who'd failed at what mattered most to him, the one thing you didn't need luck or money for: love of your homeland, your language. He brought me to what he thought was my native soil, mine and his, and it turned out I had to cram my head full of yet another foreign language, all the more foreign because it was so close to my own. My father bit his tongue, and I sold mine for a degree in geology, and a position at the Academy of Sciences.

The year after we came back, it all started up again, not that it had ever stopped, but it became especially harsh, the persecution of dissidents. People I knew at the Academy: professors and students. Writers, musicians, painters. From one day to another, they would disappear, either to psychiatric hospitals or some hole where they'd tend sheep all day or shovel shit from barns. Or be found naked and strangled in cellars. All because they wanted to live and work in their own language. Everything follows from language here, Eva. You are what you speak, and I chose to speak the language of the coward and collaborator. Oh, I never informed on anyone, I just stuck to my rocks, my field trips, my research, and never said a word, when I could have. Just a word, in my own language, would have been enough.

For a long while, I told myself it was because of my father. The only pride he had, the only success he could point to in his whole life was that he'd given me the chance to be someone, to do something for his country. I was the antidote to his every bout of grief over my mother, my sister. And I hated every minute of that lie I was giving him. I didn't realize how much I hated it until I married Galina. You were right about my knack for suffering, Eva. To punish my father, I fell in love with a Russian woman; to punish myself for hating my father, I fought to the death with my wife; to the death of our marriage.

All of this is why I can't leave, and why I could never have asked you to stay. They say it will be fifty years before things get better here. Not even better, just back to the way they were before, so that we can afford to eat, and light up our streets at night, and fix up the little boxes they give us to live in. Fifty years if, by some miracle, there isn't a Russian invasion, or civil war, or another Chornobyl. It's got into my blood by now, being locked into what my neighbour Mykola calls fate, if you don't mind so extravagant a term. So that the sum total of what I am is just this: where I am, where I have to stay. A place that turns out to be as far away from you as if I lived on a star.

I have finished that article I was working on, the one about the lapis lazuli. Did I ever tell you that story? Not long after the war, there were reports of a vein of lapis found in a quarry just outside Kiev. It was written up in the top scientific journals of our glorious Union, this miraculous show of lapis in a place where it should never have been. Even in the West, geologists started speculating about the possible causes of this freak of nature. Until we got glasnost, and the mystery unravelled. When Western geologists came out to see the quarry for themselves, they discovered the whole thing was a hoax. It would be hilarious if it weren't so pathetic—a handful of sub-standard geologists needing to make themselves look important, never thinking people would want to see this marvel for themselves, to test the story.

Things are going from worse to even worse here. Now we've had an official state of economic emergency declared. Business as usual: disaster. But we're all optimists, or else philosophers. Oh yes, and mafiosi, too—there are more than enough of them among *us. But somehow we're still here; there's still a "here" of our own. This is what we call a happy ending now: being able to postpone disaster for at least another day.*

Here is my own happy ending: Katia is having chemotherapy every month now, which is better than every week. She's practising her English with my mother. I haven't seen much of my mother: she stayed with me for a few days, and then I took her down to Odessa. I can't get back as often as I'd like, distances and the fuel shortage being what they are.

I miss you. Did I tell you words weren't my strong suit? I miss you, Eva.

You may have heard that it's impossible to carry on a correspondence with anyone living in Ukraine. Your letters never reach us—ours get rerouted in the oddest directions. Even if you bribe the postal clerk. So it would be better to phone—if you care to phone and tell me how you are. Though the lines are terrible, and it's horribly expensive, of course.

This affair between us is impossible, Eva—that's why it makes me feel so much at home.

He has written his name in Ukrainian, and she has just enough of the alphabet to make out the sound of the letters: *Oleksa.*

They are too different in their allegiances. Crystal and skin—how can the one avoid cutting or dulling the other? And the sheer physical distance between them, even if she could afford to fly to Kiev every summer, or bring him here—if he would let her buy his ticket. For all but two or three weeks a year: living through words, not touch; folding desire into shapes compact enough to fit inside an envelope, or through a telephone wire. And what if things in Ukraine don't lurch on from one emergency to another? What if they blow up, instead, into a war or another Chernobyl? And yet that rich, beautiful country Olya believes in must be there, too, for all those who, like Alex, won't or can't abandon it. For her as well, if she so chooses.

Eva sits at the kitchen table, her hands in her hair, reading and rereading the letter from Alex—Oleksa. Remembering how shocked she'd been at their first meeting by the sight of the gold in his mouth. Now it seems to her something he was born with, something put there by history itself. The gold in his mouth is one with the gold of the monastery domes, all the cupolas and icon screens he'd shown her in his compulsion to prove that his city was more than fissured asphalt, vacant streetlamps. That it possessed a splendour all the more astounding for its lack of ordinary things. She thinks of fairy tales in which the heroes end up with gold coins pouring from their lips whenever they speak. And how, if he were kissing her now, she'd be searching for the gold in his mouth, feeling it glow against her tongue, a slow, soft burning.

There is six hours difference between Toronto and Kiev. If she calls now she will wake him up, and she knows he needs his sleep. No one wants to be woken at four-thirty in the morning. When she dials, there's nothing but silence at the other end: no busy signal, no ringing, just a blank. She tries again, dialling each number slowly, carefully, like a child printing out the alphabet. Again, nothing. She calls the operator, forcing herself to keep her voice calm as she gives the number and the operator tries, once, twice, three times to connect her. "Would you like to try again later?" the operator asks, and Eva shakes her head. Then, remembering no one can see her, she stammers, "No, yes—I mean please keep trying. As long as it takes."

She is drawing as she waits: the two Trypillian figures, made from a near identical assortment of lines and circles, and yet different, separate, their arms kept to themselves, one on the hip, the other held up against the face, as if to obscure whatever expression of hurt or delight may be hiding there. Nothing is happening; it is getting later and later and there seems no possibility of ever getting through.

Until by some miracle she hears a phone ringing at the other end of the line. A dozen rings before he picks it up and she makes out his voice. The connection is poor, but still, she can hear his voice, and at last he understands who's calling him.

He says her name. For the moment, this is enough. This is all that matters.

XI

KIEV, NOVEMBER 1941

In a pathway of the Green Library, on a bench under a bronze-leaved chestnut tree, a woman sits waiting, as if for a lover. Even with her eyes closed she can tell the lateness of the hour, feel how cool the light is, how the shade has deepened. By now, she knows the man she's waiting for will not arrive to meet her. There can only be one reason he isn't here—they've caught him at last, while he was making his way to her. Caught him on a street corner, or at the Bessarabka market where you can buy, at extortionate prices, the bitter horse chestnuts that have become a delicacy these days.

She knows that if he has been caught, then so has she. It is only a matter of time, a difference of settings. Will she be arrested in her room, so bare now that she's lost all her books and paintings and photographs? Or will they come for her here, turning the very leaves against her?

It is easier not to panic if you have your eyes closed. She holds the papers in her lap even tighter, wondering if there's time to dig a hole and bury them. She would have to have a waterproof tin, or at least a rubber sheet to wrap them in, and she would have to dig very deep. If they blew up the city library, why not this place: if they have burned books, why not complete the act and burn down the trees in this park where people have come for so many years to read in the green or golden shade?

She can hear footsteps in the distance. It is hard to sit and read when you're dizzy with hunger; when you have no coat on your back, just a sweater someone passed on to you, a sweater looted from the shops the day the Germans rolled into Kiev, their faces shiny as their tanks. The footsteps come closer. She tries to make a game of it, to guess who it will be before he speaks and gives the game away. Another poet, who'll be glad of one less rival. A neighbour, who is cold enough to turn her in for an armful of firewood. Her landlord, who's been declared *Volksdeutsch* by the occupiers of his city; who's entitled to eat white bread now, while the rest of them are lucky to get sawdust. Or worse than any of these, and far more likely: someone within the Organization, someone who'll betray her to the Germans, and then be betrayed, in turn.

If you could go like this, with your eyes shut, without having to look at the face of your betrayer; if you could go blind as some people say you can go grey with terror. The only reason to open her eyes would be to look on the face of someone she loves. If she is lucky, whoever it is who comes for her will not march her off to the Gestapo; will not shove her into a van packed with others just as exhausted and emptied as she. He will, instead, interpret her refusal to get up as an aggressive act; will put his gun to her head and leave her here.

The footsteps slow down as they approach, as if whoever has come to arrest her is reluctant to do so. She holds on, as hard as she can, to the idea of where she is, to the arms of the trees in the Green Library. The one place left in the world where the heart of each poem or drawing or story survives. A place you can go even as you're forced off the roof of a burning building, into the net of your death. The Green Library, the Green Library she says to herself, over and over. And suddenly, because the wind has changed, or the man in front of her has shifted his position, so that the light falls differently across her tight-closed eyes, she knows, even before he speaks, who it is that's come for her.

"Please get up. You'll have to go with me, mother."

On the arm of her son, the woman leaves the park where she's sat all afternoon, and heads back into the ruined city. As she walks away, the poems she's left behind her start to rustle in the evening wind. One by one they take to the air, some to fall into the grass, others to sail towards the great river that flows through the city as it always has, in spite of mines and bombs and ceaseless rifle fire in the Old Women's Ravine.

He holds her arm in his. No matter that he's making sure she doesn't run away: in the only way left to her, she is holding her son again after so many years; telling them both the one story that can help them now. And as they walk up the path cleared between heaps of rubble, the path that used to be the Khreshchatyk, her eyes become like trick mirrors at a country fair. Through them she sees the toppled buildings restore themelves. The twisted dome of the Circus Building flies back, enclosing clowns and acrobats and bareback riders who are still performing to the people in the stalls. The bricks of the Children's World Shop come back together, and its shelves brim with bright, unshattered toys. Here is the Continental Hotel, where, still a schoolgirl, she had danced till morning with her lover; here the café where she first read her poems aloud, so nervous her lips began to bleed. And here is the registry office where she let a good man she never loved put a ring on her finger and a name to her lover's child.

She knows her son's been made to think that she's his enemy. It helps her to know that if she has to die, her death will keep him safe a moment longer, perhaps even long enough. If he does survive this war, he'll have a bitter life. There will be little happiness in it, and less love. And yet her arms are full of both, she can scarcely walk from the weight of love she carries.

Here she is, at the end of a fine November afternoon, going down the Khreshchatyk with the son she never thought to see again. He has taken her arm in his, for all the world to see. Behind them, their shadows dance in the fierce evening light, all the fiercer because it knows that cold and darkness follow at its heels. But as she makes her way down the avenue with its brilliant lamps, its fine windows full of rare, beautiful, perishable things, the radiance of her face makes you avert your eyes. For she has never in her life known such extremity of joy as this moment, walking down the Khreshchatyk, holding her son in her arms.

Some of the information in this book has been taken from the following sources: *The Encyclopedia Britannica*, eleventh edition. Robert Conquest's *Harvest of Sorrow: Soviet Collectivization and the Terror-Famine*. Milda Danys' *DP: Lithuanian Immigration to Canada After the Second World War*. "The Misunderstood War," a review by Norman Davies of Gerhard L. Weinberg's *A World at Arms: A Global History of World War II*. Anatoli Kuznetsov's *Babi Yar*. Grigori Medvedev's *The Truth About Chernobyl*. Solomeya Pavlychko's *Letters from Kiev*. Orest Subtelny's *Ukraine: A History*. Joan Walker's *Pardon My Parka*. Alan Weisman's "Journey Through a Doomed Land: Exploring Chernobyl's Still Deadly Ruins."

I am grateful to the historian John-Paul Himka for reading selected passages of this novel and thus saving me from many a blunder. Any errors that remain are my responsibility.